feel-good stories'
Sunday Express

'Heartwarming and positive . . . **will leave you with a lovely cosy glow**'
My Weekly

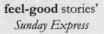

'A **fun**, feel-good read.'
Good Housekeeping

'A **gorgeous** story to lose yourself in'
Bookish Bits

'As **comforting** as hot tea and toast made on the Aga!'
Veronica Henry

'Thoroughly **enjoyable**'
U Magazine

'Such a **charming**, feel-good story'
Carole's Books

'This book **ticks all the boxes**'
Heat

'Reading a Cathy Bramley book for me is like coming home from a day out, closing the curtains, putting on your PJs and settling down with a huge sigh of relief! Her books are **full of warmth, love and compassion** and they are completely adorable'
Kim the Bookworm

'Cathy Bramley has quickly catapulted herself into my list of favourite authors . . . *Wickham Hall* is a **heartflutteringly lovely and laugh-out-loud** story wrapped up in a stunning package'
Page to Stage Reviews

Do you know that feeling that you love a story and its characters and setting so much, **you just never want the book to end**? That's exactly what *Wickham Hall* did to me'
A S

'... our day, ... it ge... ... ay to my list of fav... ...te reads of the year'
Alba in Bookland

'Between the irresistible characters and the desirable setting, *Wickham Hall* is **impossible to resist**'
Daily Express

'Cathy delivers a **wonderful, warm**, lovely story'
On My Bookshelf

'A **fabulously heart-warming** and fun read that will make you just want to snuggle up on the sofa and turn off from the outside world'
By the Letter

'Another absolute corker from Cathy Bramley. **She just gets better and better** – creating beautiful locations, gripping and lovely storylines and fantastic characters that stick with you a long time after reading'
Little Northern Soul

'A **delightful** cast of characters in a setting where I felt right at home instantly'
Rachel's Random Reads

'**Truly delectable**'
Sparkly Word

'**Warm, funny and believable** . . . grab a copy of the book and a mug of tea then curl up on the sofa and enjoy!'
Eliza J Scott

Cathy would love to hear from you! Find her on:

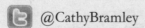 Facebook.com/CathyBramleyAuthor

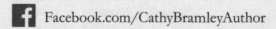 @CathyBramley

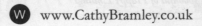 www.CathyBramley.co.uk

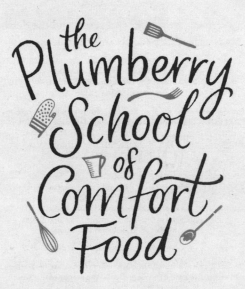

the Plumberry School of Comfort Food

Cathy Bramley

CORGI BOOKS

TRANSWORLD PUBLISHERS
61–63 Uxbridge Road, London W5 5SA
www.penguin.co.uk

Transworld is part of the Penguin Random House group of companies whose
addresses can be found at global.penguinrandomhouse.com

Penguin
Random House
UK

First published in Great Britain as four separate ebooks
in 2016 by Transworld Digital
an imprint of Transworld Publishers
First published as one edition in 2016 by Corgi Books
an imprint of Transworld Publishers

A CIP catalogue record for this book
is available from the British Library.

ISBN
9780552172080

Typeset in 11½/13pt Garamond by Kestrel Data, Exeter, Devon.
Printed and bound by Clays Ltd, Bungay, Suffolk.

Penguin Random House is committed to a sustainable future for our business, our readers
and our planet. This book is made from Forest Stewardship Council® certified paper.

MIX
Paper from
responsible sources
FSC® C018179

1 3 5 7 9 10 8 6 4 2

To my best friends, Lisa and Alison xx

Food, Glorious Food

Chapter 1

My stomach rumbled as I pulled the pan out from under the grill. I'd been slaving over my laptop at the kitchen table since first thing and now it was four o'clock. I'd only had two chocolate Pop Tarts to keep me going all day.

Even by my standards, that was a bit meagre.

There was more to making the ultimate fish finger sandwich than met the eye, I mused, prodding the fish to make sure it was cooked. To be proper comfort food, it had to meet my very stringent criteria. The bread had to be soft and white. I'd bought a new loaf from the corner shop this morning specially. The fish fingers must be good ones; life is simply too short for anything less. I keep a box of Captain Birds Eye's best in the freezer at all times, alongside my stash of cottage pie, lasagne and tikka masala ready-meals.

I spaced the four golden strips of breadcrumbed cod evenly across the bottom slice of bread, taking care to leave a gap in the centre for easy slicing. Next the ketchup – Heinz, of course. I gave the bottle a firm shake and added a neat stripe to each of the fish fingers.

Rosie, my part-time housemate, steamed into the kitchen wearing a sports bra and shorts and turned the tap on full blast before fetching a glass.

'Just in time to witness my pièce de résistance,' I announced, sliding the plate away from the spray of water.

'Please tell me that's not your Sunday lunch?' She waggled her eyebrows sternly. 'Wait till I tell Nonna.'

Rosie's Italian grandmother believes lunch on the Lord's Day should consist of at least four courses, take the entire morning to prepare and the entire afternoon to clear up.

I sliced through the sandwich and sat down at the table.

'Yep. Protein, carbs, vegetables . . . a perfectly balanced meal,' I said. OK, *vegetables* was stretching it a bit, but the bottle did claim to be full of sun-ripened tomatoes . . . 'And more importantly, it only took me twelve minutes. Sorry, Nonna.'

'You should treat your body as if it belongs to someone you love,' she said with a tut. She twisted the cap off a tub of seaweed extract and shook two tablets into her hand.

I watched her knock them straight back with a gulp of water. 'Who do you love – Nemo?'

Rosie choked mid-swallow and spluttered with laughter. 'Touché, Princess Prick and Ping, touché.'

I pretended to give her a dirty look.

She referred to me as that because of my over-reliance on the microwave, although she didn't spend much time in the kitchen either. Nor anywhere else. Rosie was too busy to spend long doing anything. I don't think I've ever seen her relax. Not completely. Even when she watched TV she had her phone in her hand, her iPad balanced on her knee and her laptop on the coffee table in front of her, each device tracking different social media campaigns for her clients. She was totally dedicated to her job and she'd been promoted twice since I'd known her.

She moved in when I realized that I needed a lodger to help pay the mortgage after splitting up with my fiancé. Not that she didn't have a property of her own; she'd had several over the years. In her spare time she bought and renovated run-down houses, selling them on for a profit, which she squirrelled away. Her plan was to buy a big house for herself and be mortgage-free by the age of forty. I had no doubt that she'd do it.

'I'm detoxing,' she explained, rattling the bottle of vitamins under my nose, 'because I love myself.'

'And I,' I said with my mouth full of sandwich, 'love fish fingers.'

Actually, I agreed with her: food is about love. To cook for someone is to show them how much you care. My problem was that I'd lost that loving feeling. Or, more accurately, that loving *someone*.

'How's the project going?' She sat down and read the document open on my laptop. 'Need any help?'

Spending all day working might not be everyone's ideal Sunday but it had provided the perfect distraction from the sadness of today's date, which I wasn't ready to tackle yet. Besides, tomorrow's meeting was unusually important.

'I think I'm there,' I said proudly, removing the elastic band from my wavy brown hair. I ruffled my fingers through it, wishing for the umpteenth time it was as dark and glossy as hers. 'I've got an amazing idea for improving customer loyalty: the *One, Two, Three Plan*. Instead of incentivizing purely new customers, this is about giving existing customers reasons to stay with us for a minimum of three years. I've come up with loads of benefits.'

'Sounds great,' Rosie said, stretching her face, a gesture I recognized as stifling a yawn.

'It is, honestly,' I protested. 'Even Liam thought it was good. Better than his will be, he reckons.'

'You've shown Liam?' Her mouth gaped. 'Have I taught you nothing about office tactics?'

I gave her my oh-ye-of-little-faith look. 'Of course I have; I wanted his opinion.'

My boyfriend of six months, Liam, was also my colleague in the marketing department of Solomon Insurance in Nottingham. We shared an office, which had worked out just fine so far: not only did we manage to indulge in the occasional illicit snog at the far end of the office, but we helped each other out with problems and pooled our best ideas for the good of the company. Admittedly most of the ideas came from me, but he was good at other things like persuasion and flattery. And if you'd ever tried getting extra printer paper from our office manager you'd know just how important those skills are.

Rosie lowered her head to the table and groaned. 'Oh, Verity.'

'Look, I know you want me to fight tooth and nail for this job, but that's just not me,' I said with a laugh, laying my hand over hers.

A few weeks ago Solomon's had been bought out by an American company which had sent in a man with a hatchet to trim the fat from our friendly little firm. His name was Rod Newman. He didn't talk, he yelled. He didn't listen, he yelled. And he had the attention span of a goldfish. So far three people from accounts, five from sales and two from personnel had been deemed to be 'fat' and had disappeared the very same day.

Tomorrow it was marketing's turn to display our leanness. Liam and I had each been asked to present a plan to improve profits and we'd been warned that Ruthless Rod would give one of us the heave-ho based on our performance. And the other would be promoted.

I'd questioned Liam about his plan, but he'd scratched his head and said he was still working on it. He always did fly by the seat of his pants. I didn't dare tell Rosie I'd offered to help him pull his pitch together. If I got the job, fine; if he got it, also fine. These days I just couldn't get worked up about things; *que sera, sera*, as Doris Day would say.

She lifted her head and gazed at me fiercely. 'You are the better candidate, Verity Bloom. Make it happen. Make that job yours.'

'Yeah, yeah.'

She sighed and strode into the living room and seconds later I heard her boinging about to her celebrity fitness DVD. I cleared away my plate and closed the laptop.

It was time for the bluebell walk with Gabe and Noah.

Five minutes later, I'd twisted my hair into a messy bun, added a smudge of eyeliner to my green eyes and shoved gifts of a bottle of real ale and a chocolate dinosaur in my bag. I said goodbye to a puffing and sweaty Rosie and was about to slam the front door when I remembered something I'd almost certainly need . . .

'Tissues, tissues, tissues,' I muttered under my breath as I bent down to rummage through my half of the bathroom cupboard, pushing aside bottles of conditioner and body lotion. 'Oh gosh!'

I dropped to my knees and stared at a new, untouched box of tampons on the bottom shelf. I did a quick calculation and my mouth went dry. No doubt about it: my monthly visitor was well overdue.

My heart thumped and a hand flew to my stomach automatically.

I couldn't believe it hadn't occurred to me before now; it was so unlike me not to be on top of this sort of thing. I gave myself a shake and told myself not to jump to conclusions; sure, the time of the month had been and gone, but more than likely it was just a bit late. Perhaps deep down, I was more bothered about the threat of redundancy than I realized? That would be it – stress. Very common. A baby, though . . . A thrill shivered through me and my mind whirled with the implications.

I focused on taking deep breaths as I let myself out of my little townhouse and into the golden sunshine. I jumped into my car, started the engine and set off in the direction of the Trent Canal.

The thirty-minute journey was the perfect length to examine my potential pregnancy from every angle. My

13

conclusion was this: practically speaking, I probably wasn't having a baby, but if I was, I'd cope. Like always. This wasn't the first time something unexpectedly life-changing had happened to me and I doubted it would be the last. As to how I actually felt about becoming a mother of my own baby . . . I wasn't ready to let those thoughts in quite yet.

As I parked in the lane by the canal I made a deal with myself. I'd buy a pregnancy test on the way home so that I could stop all this speculation. But in the meantime, I was putting this new development on hold and concentrating on what really counted, today, this minute, which was being here on this special day with the Green men. (That's Gabe and Noah's surname, by the way, not their skin tone.)

I crossed the grassy bank and started along the towpath. It was bliss to be outside in the warm early-evening air and I felt the tension in my shoulders melting away with every step. A row of pretty barges decorated with hand-painted signs and cheerful flowerpots stretched along the water's edge and as I got closer, I spotted *The Neptune*.

'Daddy, she's here, she's here!' I heard Noah squeal.

My three-year-old godson, dwarfed by a bright yellow life-jacket, was bouncing up and down on the deck of their blue and silver boat. Gabe scooped him up into his arms and the two of them waved like mad.

I felt my heart swell with love for them both. Gabe with his tousled curls, baggy jumper and shorts and Noah, a miniature replica of his father. And all I could think was how incredibly sad it was that Mimi was missing from the picture. Suddenly, the feelings of grief that I'd been holding back all day rushed to the surface and my eyes began to burn.

Today was the anniversary of the death of my best friend, Mimi.

Two years ago Gabe had found his wife dead on the bathroom floor. Sudden Death Syndrome at only thirty years old. Gabe lost his childhood sweetheart, Baby Noah would never remember his mum and the sunshine had disappeared from my life in a flash. No warning, no explanation and no time for goodbyes . . .

I blinked furiously, plastered on a smile and raised my hand high.

'Hello!' I sped up to meet them.

Gabe lowered Noah to the deck and held out a hand to help me climb on to the boat and I sent a mental message to my lovely girl.

Oh Mimi, I miss you so much. I'm here with your family and you're gone and that makes me feel terribly guilty. The irony is that you'd love this: all of us getting together for a walk in the woods . . .

'Welcome aboard *The Neptune*, landlubber,' Gabe said with a lopsided smile. He stooped to wrap his arms round me.

'Thank you, Captain.' I hugged him, feeling the rough wool of his jumper against my cheek.

'How're you doing?' I murmured, looking into his soft grey eyes.

He shrugged and laughed softly. 'Noah gets me through. As ever.'

Noah tugged on my jacket. 'Auntie Vetty, did you know chocolate is in your bag?'

'Noah Green,' I said, holding his hands and standing back to examine him, 'I think you've grown even taller since I last saw you. And yes, I do know that.'

His eyes grew wide when I gave him his chocolate dinosaur.

'You're not too big for a cuddle, are you?'

He launched himself at me and I picked him up, squeezed him as tightly as I dared and buried my face in his baby curls. He was such a precious boy.

'I do love you, little man. You know that, don't you?' I laughed as he wriggled free.

Tears threatened again as I remembered how much Mimi had longed for a baby, and how devastated she'd been when

15

she'd discovered she was infertile. I'd been there every step of the way with her, determined to help her get her wish, whatever the cost. Gabe, too, of course. Team Baby Green we'd called ourselves. We'd stuck together through the disappointments and the tests and the drugs. Our collective joy knew no bounds when Noah was born and Mimi had so loved being a mum to the tiny bundle of boyhood. Only to have her life wrenched away from her a year later. Tragic didn't begin to cover it . . .

And now I had to love her son especially hard to make up for the loss that he didn't yet fully understand.

I met Gabe's gaze and we shared a sad smile. Life could be very cruel sometimes.

'I hadn't even had the chance to say I loved her that day,' Gabe murmured, rubbing a hand across his face.

'But she knew,' I whispered, squeezing his hand. 'We all knew that.'

'Next time I'm in a relationship, I'll tell her I love her every day.'

My ears pricked up; this was new.

'So there'll be a next time, then?' I asked.

He shrugged casually enough but I noticed a flush to his face. 'One day, yeah. I hope so.'

'Well . . . good,' I said brightly, looking down at my shoes.

Gabe had never been able to contemplate another woman in his life. It looked like he might be ready to move on and, truthfully, I wasn't sure how I felt about that.

Chapter 2

A few minutes later, I'd kissed Noah's entire collection of soft toys, marvelled at the no-sew curtains Gabe had made for the living area of the houseboat and the three of us had gone back on dry land to begin our expedition to the woods.

Gabe and I each held one of Noah's hands as we ambled along the towpath, both of us content to listen to his cheerful chatter.

The sun's rays sparkled across the surface of the water and the boats strained gently against their moorings. Birds tweeted merrily in the cluster of hawthorn trees that lined the path as they settled themselves in for the evening. Many of the boating people were out on deck, some sipping beers, a few cooking food on barbecues and calling to one another from boat to boat. There was almost a holiday atmosphere along the canal and I felt my happiness gradually returning.

This is heavenly, I thought, which was apt considering the spiritual nature of our excursion.

A month after Mimi died, Gabe and I had trodden this path with Gloria, Mimi's mum. Noah had been too little to walk. Our solemn little group had scattered Mimi's ashes in her favourite place – a clearing in the woodland where the bluebells bloomed – and we'd each spent a few moments alone with our thoughts.

Shortly after that, Gabe had sold up the family home,

abandoned his law career and moved himself and his baby son on to the canal and into a narrowboat just a stone's throw from Mimi's woods. He'd retrained as a French polisher and now he restored furniture for a living. He also made extra money taking stressed-out city-types for weekends on the waterways, leaving Noah in the capable hands of his paternal grandparents, which was a treat for all concerned.

Our bluebell walk had become an annual thing and a lovely way for us all to gather and remember happy times.

'Shame Gloria couldn't be here,' I said, during a lull in Noah's running commentary.

'Hmm.' Gabe frowned. 'I've hardly heard from her since her plans to open a cookery school took off.'

At the age of sixty-five, Mimi's mum, a former food stylist, had decided to open a cookery school in the Yorkshire village of Plumberry, half an hour outside York, where she was originally from. It was from her mum that Mimi inherited her love of cooking and I guess it had rubbed off on me too. Not that I cooked any more. Not since Mimi died.

'You don't approve?' I looked at him sharply.

He wrinkled his nose. 'I think she's taking on too much at her age.'

'I hope you haven't told Gloria that?' I grinned.

Mimi's mum was one of the most independent women I knew; I couldn't see her taking kindly to that sort of comment.

He lifted a shoulder. 'No. But she's too busy to see us these days, too busy even to make it here this evening because the fitters are late putting the ovens in or something. And the building she's taken on . . . it's an old mill; well, half one. That's some responsibility.'

I nodded sympathetically but I could see both sides. Gloria had felt so bereft after losing her only daughter that she couldn't bear not to be busy. She'd been involved with food her whole career and when I'd spoken to her at Christmas, she said opening a cookery school would be a new way to use her skills and spread her passion for cooking.

Funny how grief affects us all differently. Mimi and I used to post videos on YouTube of ourselves making stuff in the kitchen. It was just a bit of fun – neither of us was professionally trained – but we had a laugh doing it. But as soon as she died, I closed the channel down and deleted the videos. *My* passion for cooking died with Mimi; there was simply no pleasure in it without her.

We turned off the towpath, crossed the wibbly-wobbly bridge where Noah insisted we threw sticks into the water and then waded through long grass to the edge of Mimi's woods.

Spring has definitely sprung, I thought, as we delved under the canopy of the woodland. The trees were covered in a froth of pink and white blossom and now and then petals floated down through the shafts of sunlight, giving a magical illusion of snowflakes in springtime. The path was lined with tall stems of frilly white cow parsley and zingy lime ferns and I let my fingers brush gently against their feathery fronds as I walked.

Noah raced around, zigzagging in front of us, pretending to be a racing car, and Gabe fell into step beside me, resting his arm casually on my shoulder. The ground was dry thanks to several days of unbroken sunshine and the air was filled with the pungent smell of wild garlic and an earthiness which, in that random way that one thought can lead to another, somehow made me think of fertility, which in turn sent a shiver of something along my spine.

Hope.

It was *hope*, I acknowledged. My internal debate during my drive over here had centred around the practicalities of being pregnant and what Liam was going to think about it and what to do about work. But deep down, I knew that if I was expecting a baby, it would make me happier than I had been for years; probably since I'd heard that Mimi's IVF had worked and that one of the eggs we'd all got our hopes pinned on had been fertilized.

'Toad!' yelled Noah with glee.

'Where?' I stopped in my tracks.

Gabe squatted down for a closer inspection but courtesy of a poke with a stick from Noah, the creature crawled off into the undergrowth.

'How do you know it's a toad and not a frog?' I asked, impressed.

Three-year-old Noah gave me a look layered with sympathy and triumph.

'Aunty Vetty,' he sighed, dropping his stick and sliding his pudgy little hand into mine. I felt my throat tighten; I hoped he'd never grow out of doing that. 'His back was all lumpy. Frogs are smooth. Everyone knows that.'

'Silly me,' I said with a giggle, and lifted his hand to my lips for a kiss. 'It's a good job I've got you to teach me these things.'

'Look, Verity.' Gabe pointed through the trees to where a ray of golden sun picked out the nodding heads of bluebells in the clearing. 'Thousands of them; I'm sure there are even more than last year.'

He was right and the beautiful sight took my breath away.

'Mummy's favourite flowers were bluebells,' I said to Noah, swallowing the lump in my throat.

He nodded, retrieved a torch from his pocket and wriggled away from me to shine its beam under logs, looking for more toads. 'Cos they are blue like her eyes.'

'That's right, dude.' Gabe ruffled his son's hair. 'And Mummy had the prettiest, bluest eyes in the world.'

Noah stuck the torch back in his pocket and crouched down to examine the underside of a fallen log.

'Turn the torch off, Noah, or the batteries will run out,' I reminded him.

The little boy straightened up immediately and switched it off. 'Like Mummy's.'

'What do you mean?' I asked.

'My mummy's batteries ran out,' he explained, blinking up at me with those green eyes that tugged at my very soul.

Oh my God. That boy.

My heart might explode. I heard Gabe clear his throat and I couldn't bring myself to look at him.

'Come on,' I said gruffly, giving my godson's hand a squeeze. 'Why don't we pick some flowers to take back to the boat?'

Noah and I busied ourselves collecting bluebells while Gabe lowered himself on to a tree stump and disappeared into the memories of his happy marriage for a few minutes.

I reached for a tissue and dabbed my eyes.

Gabe's doing a great job, Mimi. He is the best dad ever and I know I'm biased, but seriously, Noah is a child genius! I didn't know the difference between frogs and toads and I'm thirty-two.

The novelty of flower-picking wore off as soon as Noah had a plump handful. I looked at Gabe; he had a bunch in his hands too.

'We'd better get those in water,' I said softly, touching his shoulder.

Gabe stood and nodded and the three of us headed back towards the bridge.

'Are you coming to ours for tea?' Noah asked. 'Beef stew will be there. And sweetcorn,' he added, hopefully.

'Yes, please come, Bloomers,' Gabe added.

I gave him a hard stare for using my teenage nickname.

'Sorry, couldn't resist,' he said with a grin. 'Seriously, some conversation *not* about the comparative size of dinosaurs would be hugely appreciated. And I'll share that bottle of beer with you?'

'I'd love to,' I shook my head apologetically, 'but I've got to get home, I'm afraid, boys.'

'Oh,' Noah whined.

Gabe's face fell too and my heart twisted with guilt.

'Wise move,' he said stoically, gesturing for me to go across the bridge in front of him. 'My cooking's not a patch on Mimi's.'

The guilt deepened then; poor Gabe, he was getting better in the kitchen, but before Mimi died he barely knew how to turn the oven on.

'Sorry, but I've got a big day tomorrow, I need an early night.' And I'm not drinking beer before doing a pregnancy test, I added to myself. 'But I'll come back soon. Promise.'

'Good, because I need lessons with a needle.' He grinned. 'Noah asked me to sew up a hole in his pyjamas the other day. I sat down on his bed and ended up sewing them on to his duvet by accident.'

As we walked back along the towpath towards *The Neptune*, I wrapped an arm around Gabe's waist.

'I'm so proud of you, Gabe; Noah is a credit to you.'

'Thanks.' His step faltered and he took a deep breath. 'Verity?'

I turned to face him. 'Yes?'

He swallowed before murmuring, 'He needs his mum.'

My heart heaved in my chest and I was the first to look away.

I could so easily climb into Mimi's life like a pair of jeans that fit perfectly. I loved Gabe dearly and between us we'd do a fantastic, if slightly unconventional, job of bringing up that little boy who meant so much to us both. But deep down, I knew it wasn't the right thing to do; Noah might need a mum, but Gabe and I could never be more than just friends.

I tightened my arm around him. 'I'll be the best god-mother I can be, Gabe, I promise. But I can never replace Mimi.'

I hugged and kissed them both warmly before they climbed back on board their boat and I made my way back to the car, wishing there was more I could do to help out that darling, lonely man.

'What's in the bag? Chocolate?' Rosie grabbed the plastic carrier bag from me as soon as I came in the door.

So much for the detox.

'Er . . .' I looked at her shiftily as she pulled my ninety-nine per cent accurate pregnancy test from the bag.

'Holy cannelloni!' Her dark eyes stared, saucer-like, in the gloom of the hallway.

'Probably a false alarm, but yeah, I might be having a bambino,' I said, going pink. 'And seeing Noah tonight has made me realize that I hope I am.'

Rosie gave me a huge hug. 'If that's what you want, then I hope so too.'

I hugged her back. That's what I loved about Rosie; she was completely non-judgemental. She knew my job was precarious and I had a sneaking suspicion that she wasn't that keen on Liam, but despite that I knew she'd always be my cheerleader.

'Thanks, Rosie. Liam said he might come over after the party tonight, so we can do the test together.'

One of the remaining women in personnel at Solomon's was having a fortieth birthday party in town. Everyone from work was going, even Ruthless Rod, but I'd promised to see Gabe and Noah so I'd declined the invitation. I'd stay awake until he arrived and then tell him the news. We were in this together, after all.

'No, no, no. Listen to me.' Rosie took a step back and prodded my shoulder in time with her words. 'You. Say. Nothing.'

I began to protest. 'But Liam has a right—'

'Agreed,' she said, folding her arms. 'Tell him after the presentations tomorrow. I know you. If you're pregnant, he'll persuade you to let him get the job, on the basis that you'll be leaving soon anyway. You're too generous for your own good. And if you are expecting a baby, it will be a damn sight more difficult to get another job before it arrives than to keep the one you're in.'

'OK, OK,' I agreed.

Anything for a quiet life. But I didn't mean it. I absolutely could not wait to pee on that stick . . .

Chapter 3

I woke the next morning to the cheerful sound of birds chirping outside my window and bright sunlight seeping through the curtains. Not a bad start to a Monday. I lay still for a few moments, with the duvet pulled up to my chin, aware of my steady heartbeat. I was all alone: Liam hadn't arrived after all. I must have fallen asleep around eleven without taking the pregnancy test. Perhaps Rosie was right, I decided, flinging back the covers and going to make tea; if he had come over on the way back from the party, slightly worse for wear, watching his girlfriend pee on a stick might not have been the ideal end to his evening.

I laid my hand gently on my stomach while I waited for the kettle to boil. Weird really: until yesterday afternoon, becoming a mother wasn't on my agenda at all. Now it was all I could think about. The timing wasn't perfect. Liam and I hadn't even discussed moving in together, let alone starting a family. And if I was being completely honest with myself, did I truly love him with all my heart? Enough to make a go of it with him? We'd been together such a short time, I supposed it was impossible to tell. Anyway, one thing was certain: I'd be keeping this baby, whether Liam wanted it or not.

Rosie was always out of the house for seven – she called in to check on the builders before work – so I had the house to myself. I took my tea to the bathroom and turned the shower on full blast.

Perhaps I should send Liam a quick text now, or Face-Time him? I could do the test and we could share it.

I caught a glimpse of my morning face in the mirror. Maybe not. Besides, he was probably rushing to get ready for the big pow-wow with Rod. Talking of which, I should be doing the same.

Within forty-five minutes, I was ready for anything in a smart black dress and heels. My laptop was packed and I'd even managed to eat some toast. I bent down in the hall to tuck the pregnancy test into the side pocket of my laptop bag – I would find a quiet moment to do it at work – when the landline rang.

'Morning, Verity. Oh excuse me.' Mum yawned down the phone at me. 'I'm so tired.'

'Goodness! I'm not surprised; it must be three in the morning in Canada!'

'Wanted to wish you good luck for today. So I set my alarm.'

My hand tightened around the rectangular box. *How did she know? How?*

'You'll be lost without the job,' she continued.

Oh, she meant the meeting with Rod. I smiled at myself in the hall mirror. Of course she did.

'Thanks, Mum, good of you to remember.' I felt my face soften. It was good to know that even though we lived miles apart she hadn't forgotten me.

'Although, I suppose it's worse for men to be made redundant, isn't it? Thinking about it, perhaps you should let Liam get the job and drop hints about settling down together. Perhaps find a little part-time job instead.'

'I think I should give it my all and let the best man or woman win, Mum,' I replied, through slightly gritted teeth.

'That's what your father said.'

My heart squeezed; good old Dad.

'But I can't help hearing that old tick-tock, love,' she went on with a sigh.

Mum worried about me, she thought that at thirty-two I was leaving family life too late. Dad was laissez-faire in his parenting style and kept his opinions to himself. Mum was much more vocal, even though she didn't need to be; I was painfully aware of the fickle nature of women's fertility, having been through it all with Mimi.

She means well, I reminded myself, as I thanked her, promised to keep her posted and rang off. I bet she wouldn't dare say anything like that to my sister-in-law.

Mum was in awe of my brother Matt's wife. Matt went to Canada for a temporary engineering contract five years ago, lost a filling eating almond biscotti and ended up falling in love with his dentist, Celia. He got married, had two kids and never came back to the UK. Mum and Dad wasted no time in moving to Canada to help out. And where I'm concerned, Mum can't help dropping boulder-sized hints about my failure to swell the family numbers. I normally bat them off and laugh, but today I felt my insides go all tingly. Maybe today she'd get her wish.

I arrived at Solomon Insurance at eight forty-five. Just over two hours until my meeting with Rod. There was still no sign of Liam and he hadn't answered any of my texts. I hoped he was OK; he was probably up all night working on his presentation. I turned on my laptop, opened up my *One, Two, Three Plan* and tried to rehearse my pitch.

I lasted two minutes; it was no good. I couldn't concentrate on anything until I'd taken that test. I grabbed my bag and headed for the ladies' loos. I locked myself into one of the cubicles, sat down and flicked through the instructions.

I remembered doing something like this with Mimi once. She was a whole day late for her period and deliriously excited. We'd gone to Sainsbury's to buy a test and raced straight to the customer toilets. The test had been negative and we'd stayed in that cubicle, mopping up her tears, until someone banged on the door and threatened to call security.

Anyway, I blinked away the memory. Back to me . . .

Wee on stick, wait three minutes, look for a blue line. Easy peasy. I peed on the stick. Checked my watch and waited. A wave of nausea rippled through me. Morning sickness or simply nerves?

Before I had a chance to decide, the door banged open and stiletto heels tippety-tapped across the tiled floor.

'Coo-ee? Verity, are you in here?'

'Hi, Melanie,' I said with a grin.

Melanie was our most glamorous member of staff, permanently tanned and perfectly coiffured. She had been the previous managing director's secretary and now worked for Rod. She was twenty-five and had worked here since she left school at sixteen; she knew all the gossip and had super-long nails, which clattered on the keyboard as she typed.

'Oh, Vee-Vee!' she squealed.

I grimaced. I'd lost count of the times I asked her not to call me that. I'm sure she didn't mean it to, but it sounded like a pet name for lady-bits to me.

'Oh God, that was loud,' she groaned. 'Can a person be too loud for their own head?'

'Good night, was it?' I smirked. Melanie had gone out with the rest of them last night. It sounded like she had had a good time.

'You going to be long? Only . . .' Was that a pregnant pause? I allowed myself a second smirk. Melanie cleared her throat. 'I need to talk to you. This is a bit . . . you know?'

No, I didn't know. And right this moment, I wasn't sure I wanted to know either. I was in the middle of something rather important.

I glanced at my watch.

Two minutes to go.

Seriously? This must be the longest three minutes in history. I looked at the stick but the little window on the end wasn't giving its verdict yet.

'No, not long. Two minutes? I'll come to your desk, shall I?'

'Listen,' Melanie said breathily. It sounded as if she was pressed right up to the other side of the door. I wriggled on the loo seat uneasily. I'd hoped for a little privacy, but Melanie wasn't one for picking up on hints. 'Liam said you'd be cool about it, but I just wanted to check. I mean, you guys were together for, like, months!'

Cool about what? What was she talking about?

'Vee-Vee?'

Her voice jolted me back to the present. 'Six months, actually,' I replied, still unsure where this was heading. Had she overheard something about redundancies in the marketing department? And how did Liam know? He hadn't even arrived yet.

'Yeah. I've had a crush on him ever since he started at Solomon's, but you got in there first.'

I knew that. Melanie and I had even had a bit of friendly banter about it when Liam first asked me out. I'd told Liam, who'd professed to being flattered but said he preferred women who were his intellectual equal. I remembered feeling hurt on Melanie's behalf at the time.

I went really hot all of a sudden. This wasn't a work-related conversation at all, was it?

I couldn't drag my eyes away from the stick.

Ninety seconds left.

'I'd never dip my chips in another girl's gravy. But now that Liam's not your gravy,' she said with a giggle, 'let's just say that last night I double-dipped. Do you know what I mean?'

'I think I do, yes.' I swallowed hard. Unfortunately, the image was only too clear.

One minute.

'I must say, you kept very quiet about splitting up. I mean, are you OK?'

So Liam and I had split up? My heart thundered against my ribs. Nice of him to let me know. I will not let on how much this hurts, I vowed, pressing a finger to the tears welling in my eyes.

'Er, yes, fine.'

'Only I'd hate us to fall out, now that me and Liam are an item,' Melanie continued.

So forty-five seconds before I learn if Liam is going to be the father of my child, I discover I'm dumped. Great.

I thought back to last night, when I lay in bed waiting for him, my eyes darting from my phone to the pregnancy test on my bedside table . . . What an idiot. All those texts I sent him about keeping the bed warm for him and what I was (or wasn't) wearing . . . Oh, the embarrassment. How could he have gone behind my back like this? I thought our relationship meant as much to him as it did to me. OK, we might never have won romantic couple of the year, but even so. I checked my watch.

Thirty seconds to go.

Whatever the result, it looked like it was too late to be sharing the news with Liam. That gravy boat had sailed . . .

'Vee-Vee?'

I dropped my head into my hands and groaned, 'No.'

'Whew!' she sighed. 'Muchos reliefos! By the way, Rod wants to see you at nine . . . oops, sorry, it's already ten past. You'd better get your skates on.'

'Nine?' I gulped. 'Our meeting's not until eleven.'

I heard Melanie's heels scrape towards the door. 'Uh-huh, he deffo said nine. To get it over with, he said. I'd better go. Good luck!'

The door banged shut and I looked at my watch. The three minutes were up. I scrutinized the little white stick. No matter how hard I stared and how many times I twisted it to check it at different angles for a clear blue line, the little plastic window remained clear. It was definitely negative.

I dropped it into the waste bin and bit back my disappointment as I splashed cold water on my face.

I wasn't pregnant and my boyfriend was someone else's gravy. I might be being over-sensitive, but perhaps today was really not my lucky day?

Dashing back to the marketing office to collect my presentation, I spotted Liam's laptop case on his desk. The man himself was nowhere to be seen. I was glad about that; the mood I was in, I might have punched him. Or burst into tears. He was probably pressing himself against Melanie at the fire escape doors or something. There was a knot of tension in my stomach and I could feel a pulse beating at the side of my temple as I jogged along the corridor to Rod's office. I paused and forced myself to take a few calming breaths before knocking.

Rosie's words suddenly came back to me: *You are the better candidate, Verity Bloom. Make it happen. Make that job yours.*

I bloody well intend to, I thought, straightening my spine. Rod was standing at the window staring down at the street, jingling coins in his trouser pockets.

'Sit,' he bellowed, throwing himself down into a huge black leather chair. He folded one leg over the other and proceeded to jiggle his ankle.

I'd barely warmed the visitor's chair in Rod's office when he delivered his news.

'Verity,' he announced, with a slap to the desk, 'this gives me no pleasure, no pleasure at all.'

One sentence.

It told me all I needed to know. But I had to listen to him for a further ten minutes while he blathered on about difficult choices, lean times and creating a business fit for the future. A future that I was clearly not to be a part of. And to add insult to injury, Liam was, Rod informed me.

I glanced at the two copies of the *One, Two, Three Plan* still squarely on the desk in front of me. He hadn't even asked to see my profit-improving proposal.

As he lectured on, I felt myself getting more and more annoyed. I'd spent hours working on this; it wasn't fair of him not to even let me fight for my job. Finally, when he stopped to draw breath, I jumped in.

'Rod, I've been at Solomon Insurance for five years, I know the business inside out and—'

'Exactly!' Rod stuck his hands out. 'You've let the bad times drag you down. I get that. It's understandable. You need to get out there, Verity.' He flung an arm towards the window. 'Find something new to excite you. Get the old juices flowing.'

'But, Rod,' I countered, pushing my presentation towards him, 'I assure you my juices are in full flow.'

I regretted that particular turn of phrase but ploughed on, ignoring the heat that had risen to my face. 'Look at this. I believe my *One, Two, Three Plan* will deliver long-term profits.'

Rod's eyes flew to the front page of my document. 'Ah, Verity.'

I wriggled forward in my seat. Fantastic, I had his attention.

'It will incentivize our existing customers and—'

'Whoa.' Rod held up a hand. I closed my mouth.

'This is awkward.' He fixed me with a steely stare, looking anything but awkward. 'The word on the street is that you and Liam were, er, close . . . ?' He raised a leery eyebrow. 'But I have to draw the line at presenting his idea as your own.'

Liam's idea? Rod must have got confused. I shook my head firmly. 'No, this idea was mine, I assure you.'

'OK, OK. This one's yours,' he drawled. This time the eyebrow was more bemused. 'Just very, very similar to the *Three, Two, One Plan* that Liam told me about last night. Great party, by the way. We had fun; shame you couldn't be there.'

'Liam told you last night?' I gasped.

Not content with sleeping with someone else, last night my ex-boyfriend had also stolen my ideas, thus stealing my job.

The absolute git.

I didn't believe it; how could Liam do that to me? I felt sick suddenly and there was an ache deep in the pit of my stomach. Actually, that might be the late arrival of my period. Great.

'Uh-huh.' Rod nodded.

I blinked at him. I wanted to defend myself, to deny that I'd stolen anyone's ideas, but my throat had closed up and I was completely speechless.

'Go and see personnel, they've got all the paperwork and details of your redundancy package.'

With that, he tossed the document back to me and stood up, extending a hand to signal the end of our meeting.

'Try to see this as a positive move, Verity. As the saying goes, "When life gives you lemons . . ."'

'Rub them in your cheating, thieving boyfriend's eyeballs?' I said, squeezing his hand as hard as I could.

And on that fleeting note of triumph, I flounced out of his office and slammed the door behind me.

After spending a few minutes with personnel, who told me I was on immediate gardening leave and that I'd receive a redundancy payment in the post, I was back at my desk, shoving my personal belongings into a plastic bag. I couldn't get out of there quickly enough. I'd spotted Liam in Rod's office looking all smiley and relaxed and I wanted to make my exit before he returned to our office. I planned to have it out with the slimeball at some point, but not here; I didn't trust myself not to make a scene. I shoved the last item, an unopened box of Cup-a-Soup, in my bag and shut my desk drawer.

'Verity?'

Too late.

Liam was standing in the doorway, arms outstretched, his brow furrowed with penitence. He was tall and wide-shouldered with coppery hair, hazel eyes and a permanent look of dishevelled schoolboy about him that I'd always found cute. Until now. Now I found it annoying.

'I don't know what to say.' He blinked at me forlornly.

'How about, "I am a dishonest, deceitful, unfaithful knob"?' I said, folding my arms and glaring at him. His eyes were set too close together, I realized. A sure sign of dodginess. Why had I never noticed this before?

'Rod backed me into a corner last night, Verity. Literally. You know how forceful he can be. He asked me what my big idea was for today's meeting. I panicked.'

There was a photo frame on Liam's desk that I'd bought him. He'd put a picture of Katy Perry in it instead of me and I'd pretended not to be hurt at the time. I should have known then. The git. I swiped it off the desk and dropped it into my bag.

I exhaled with frustration. 'Why not just tell him your idea?'

He shrugged and took a step towards me. 'I couldn't help myself.'

'Are we still talking about the intellectual theft of my *One, Two, Three Plan* or you acquainting yourself with Melanie's white bits while I was at home waiting to take a pregnancy test?'

'What? Er . . .' The colour drained from his face and he tugged at his shirt collar to loosen it.

I couldn't deny a glimmer of satisfaction at his display of panic. I hefted my bag over my shoulder and caught a whiff of the aftershave I'd bought him for Valentine's Day as I scooted past him to the door. A wave of sadness hit me then as I remembered the good times we'd had.

'Don't worry, I'm not pregnant.' I sighed.

Liam slapped a hand to his chest. 'Oh, thank God . . .'

His voice trailed off when he caught sight of my sharp stare. 'Well, it is probably for the best,' he added sheepishly.

And to think this morning I was contemplating starting a family with this man; I could have been pregnant with his child right now. I deserved better. My future children deserved better. And now I had an answer to my own question: did I truly love him with all my heart?

No.

'Agreed,' I said, mustering a defiant smile. 'I think I've had a very lucky escape. And good luck with the job; you'll need it.'

And with that I marched out of Solomon Insurance for the last time.

Verity Bloom had left the building.

Chapter 4

A couple of hours later I was consoling myself with lunch in front of some blissfully unchallenging TV when my mobile rang from the depths of my handbag. I sighed and set down my Bounty bar. I was at a critical stage: I'd nibbled all the chocolate from the sides and base and I was about to attempt the removal of the thick bit on the top without snapping it.

But the interruption was worth it: it was Mimi's mum Gloria on the phone.

'Darling, have you got a mo? I'm not disturbing you in a meeting, am I?'

I sank back on to the sofa and refused to look at the chocolate. 'Not at all. I'm only having lunch. At home.'

'But that's terrible!' exclaimed Gloria after I'd outlined the events of the morning. 'Never mind; his – *their* – loss is someone else's gain, I'm sure.'

Gloria was very well-spoken, with a voice like double cream: all rich and luxurious. She had elegant looks to match, too. A dainty elfin face dominated by startling blue eyes like Mimi's had been and chunky golden highlights in her cropped hair. I could hear her signature armful of bangles jingling down the phone.

'Thanks, Gloria,' I said quietly. 'I hope you're right.'

At the moment it felt like solely my loss. My life had fallen apart when Mimi died. I'd been cast adrift without her after all we'd been through together and it had taken me two years to get back on my feet. Now I felt like I was back at square one.

'Have you any idea what you're going to do?' she asked.

I'd been asking myself the same question all morning. I had enough money to tide me over for a few months and I was sure Rosie would stay on as my lodger if I needed her to, but what was I actually going to do?

'Not yet.' I sighed. 'I knew redundancy was a possibility, but I didn't expect to lose Liam at the same time. I just feel . . . totally rejected.'

'Oh, darling girl, you've had a rough day but try to think of it as *redirected*, rather than rejected.'

'OK.' I sniffed, unconvinced. 'Anyway, I'm sure you didn't call me to hear all my woes?'

'No.' Gloria paused.

I glanced up at the TV screen to catch the tail end of a nappy commercial and fumbled for the remote to turn off the TV. I'd passed approximately three thousand pregnant women and pram-pushing mums on the way home and I'd had enough reminders about my unpregnant status for one day.

'I feel wretched for not coming down for Mimi's bluebell walk. I thought about her all day and you and Gabe, of course, and mostly little Noah. But I just couldn't get away. The cookery school – or bomb site, as I ought to call it – was in chaos and I didn't dare leave the workmen to it, especially as they'd come into work on a Sunday at my behest. Did it go well? I mean, you know . . .'

The breath caught in my throat as I thought back to yesterday and our pilgrimage through the woods, the three of us bound together by the person who'd loved us the most.

'It was . . . calming, Gloria. I think of her all the time, too. But somehow being there amongst the bluebells makes me feel closer to her. We all missed you, though,' I admitted.

'Noah's growing up; he even talks about his mum now and he's such a clever little chap.'

I recounted the comment he'd made about Mimi's batteries running out.

'Oh, the darling little mite,' cried Gloria, her voice suddenly wobbly. 'I'll call Gabe and invite them up to stay. Although, perhaps not at the moment, I can't cope . . . Oh heavens, what a poor excuse for a grandmother I am.'

I heard a sob in her voice and felt a sudden wave of anxiety for her; she was normally so unflappable, so in control, just like Mimi had been. 'Gloria, what's wrong?'

'I'm a fool, that's what's wrong. Whatever possessed me? I'm a food stylist – a *retired* food stylist. I cook, I make things look beautiful, but I'm not a project manager or a businesswoman. I'm not even a teacher, for goodness' sake. What was I thinking?'

Gabe had said that his mother-in-law had bitten off more than she could chew; perhaps he was right.

'Then maybe you need to have a rethink. Perhaps starting this venture isn't right for you?' *At your age*, I added mentally. I kept that to myself; Gloria might be sixty-five but she probably thought she'd outlive us all. She'd certainly outlived her only daughter . . .

'I'm committed now.' She sighed. 'I've signed a five-year lease, sorted out a business loan, which I've spent. But I'm completely out of my depth, wading through problem after problem and in too deep to back out. And I'm so close to it that I can't see the wood for the trees.'

My heart squeezed for her.

It was at times like this that I missed Mimi's presence the most. She had been so good at talking people out of their gloom. She could point out the silver lining in any situation and had always been the light to my shade. I had a sudden flashback to the time I'd refused to come out of my bedroom after a disastrous fringe incident at the hairdresser's, aged fourteen. She had been the one to convince me that I could pass for eighteen with my new look and had chopped off her own fringe in solidarity.

I didn't know what I could say to make things any better for Gloria, so I just listened while she explained about the half-finished website and the full-page advert she'd booked to publicize the open day that she now suspected wouldn't happen and the health and safety inspector who kept phoning for an appointment and the granite worktops that had cracked . . . The list was endless.

No wonder she was stressed; I was exhausted just listening to her.

'I'm sorry,' she said, finally stopping to draw breath, 'you've got enough on your plate without listening to the mess I've got myself into. I'd better let you get back to your lunch.'

I looked at my nibbled chocolate bar; she'd be appalled if she knew how badly I was eating these days. She sighed so deeply down the phone that my heart ached for her.

'Gloria, don't apologize. I'm happy to be your sounding board any time. And if you need ideas for your opening day, let me know. I've spent the last ten years working in marketing and I'm sure I could come up with something. It's not like I'll be busy with work for the next few weeks.'

'Thank you, darling, I will. I don't suppose . . . ?' She hesitated. 'No . . . I couldn't ask.'

'Ask!' I admonished her with a laugh. 'The worst that can happen is that I can't help.'

'OK.' She drew in a deep breath. 'Would you come to Plumberry and work for me? A month, say, just to get the cookery school up and running?'

My heart plummeted to somewhere close to my knees. Me and my big mouth.

'You look like death,' declared Rosie, getting to the point as usual when she arrived home around seven.

'Thanks.'

I was in my bedroom, arranging my clothes in piles on my bed. She launched herself on to the mattress, dispersing my carefully folded selection of cardigans, and tipped out the contents of her plastic bag on my bed.

'Mocha, oatmeal or toast?' she said, lining up three miniature pots of paint for me to see. 'For the hall, stairs and landing in the new house.'

Toast. My stomach rumbled. Left to go cold. With real butter. That sounded comforting. It had been a long time since my chocolate bar. Sometimes when I couldn't be bothered to cook (i.e. a lot) Rosie and I would make a toast mountain and plough our way through it while the soaps were on. I could feel one coming on tonight.

'That one,' I said, pointing at the pot of oatmeal. I dumped two pairs of jeans on the floor and joined her on the bed. 'I've done a rash thing.'

Rosie's eyes lit up and she rolled on to her side to face me.

'Please tell me you've slashed Liam's tyres?'

I couldn't help but laugh as I shook my head.

I'd already filled her in on the Liam-Melanie-redundancy affair. I'd phoned her on the way home to let off steam with a good rant. She'd exploded with fury and had suggested every sort of retribution, from suing the backside off Liam to taking Rod to an industrial tribunal to plastering naked photos of Melanie all over Facebook (not sure where Rosie would have obtained these from or whether Melanie would actually have been bothered but I appreciated her rage).

'Do you know what? He's welcome to the job and Melanie's welcome to him,' I said with conviction. 'I thought we might have had a future together and I thought I cared about the job, but the thing I was most upset about today was not being pregnant. And now I realize that even that is probably a blessing in disguise.'

There'd be plenty of time in the future for babies. Preferably with a man who'd stick around long enough to at least do the pregnancy test with me . . .

'That's the spirit, but if you change your mind and want revenge,' she leaned forward and whispered menacingly, 'I know people, if you catch my drift.'

'I'll bear it in mind,' I said, pressing my lips together to hide my chuckle.

Rosie made the most of her Italian heritage and liked people to think she had connections. The truth was that her mum and grandmother ran a village café in the north of the county and her dad was a university lecturer. Not one of them has displayed even the teensiest Mafia-like tendencies in all the time I've known them.

'So what's the rash thing, then?' she said, stretching back on the bed, hands behind her glossy dark head of hair.

I grimaced. 'I've agreed to move to Yorkshire for a month to help Gloria open her cookery school. I said I'll leave in the morning.'

'Wow! That's brilliant! Come here.' Rosie sprang up and pulled me in for a bone-crushing hug. 'I thought you'd be moping round here for months. But in barely,' she flicked a glance at my alarm clock, 'six hours, you've got your life back on track. I am bursting with admiration. So what's holding you back?'

I chewed my lip. 'I'd do anything to help Gloria, but—'

'You'll do anything to help anyone. That's half your problem,' said Rosie wryly. 'Go on.'

'The cookery school, being with Gloria twenty-four-seven . . . It's all the things I've been trying to avoid since Mimi died wrapped up in one neat parcel.'

'Oh, Verity,' she murmured, squeezing me even tighter.

After Mimi died I lost my appetite. I couldn't face eating and before long I couldn't face cooking either. Every time I opened a cookery book or looked up a recipe online, I'd hear her voice in my head doing a commentary like a TV chef: 'Add fresh herbs right at the end so they keep their colour and flavour.' Or, 'You can prepare this dish up to two days ahead.' And things like: 'Cool hands; that's the key to successful pastry.'

It was torture.

I pulled away from Rosie's hug and gave her a wobbly smile. 'You know what I'm like in the kitchen these days. Imagine that on a larger scale in a cookery school . . . day in, day out. I don't know if I can do it.'

Not only that, the guilt I felt at going to Plumberry in Mimi's place – at living the life that she should be leading – lodged deep in the pit of my stomach like a stone and I wasn't sure I could bear it.

I refused to let the tears out and tried to put my feelings into words. 'If Mimi was alive it would be her going to Gloria's rescue tomorrow. Not me. I feel as if I'm stealing her life. I get to hug her husband, I get to kiss her baby boy and now I'm going to live with her mother. It's so not fair.'

'No, it's not.' She gripped my shoulders and gazed at me fiercely. 'But you are alive and it's time to make your own heart sing. It's as if you're waiting for permission for that to happen. What would really make you happy, Verity?'

'Well . . .' I blinked at her.

I couldn't think of anything.

And then a memory of Mimi and I making meringues the month before she died popped into my head. Noah was having a nap in his pushchair in the hallway after a walk and we'd decided to use the rare moment of free time to bake. But we must have done something wrong because the egg white wouldn't go stiff no matter how much we whisked it. We'd had fits of giggles but carried on regardless and ended up making pancake-flat meringues that had all run into each other in the oven to make one giant meringue. We then tried to cover it up by pretending we were making pavlova anyway but the whole thing crumbled when we tried to peel it off the baking parchment. We'd been videoing ourselves for YouTube and had been helpless with laughter, and when

42

we played it back our words were unintelligible and all that could be heard was squeals and squeaks.

That was over two years ago.

Gloria had moved on and was starting a new project. Gabe had completely altered his life to suit his and Noah's new circumstances. But somehow I'd got stuck. I was living in limbo, too afraid to move forward. I was like those meringues: without Mimi I'd crumbled and couldn't find my way back to happiness.

I blinked the tears from my eyes. Rosie was still waiting for an answer.

'I'm not sure any more,' I said finally.

'Then I'll tell you.' She reached across and wiped a stray tear from my cheek. 'You are the best marketing person I've ever met, with the best ideas, and if you can make insurance sound interesting, just think what you could do for Gloria's cookery school. That will make you happy.'

I opened my mouth to argue, but she closed my jaw with her fingertip.

'Don't cook, don't even go near the kitchens if you don't want to, but go! I'll look after the house. In fact the builders have found a well in the kitchen of the house I'm doing up, so they've had to stop work while they wait for a building inspector to come out. It's bound to cause some delays. I'll be living here a bit longer than planned, if that's OK with you? And I've just had another bright idea: we've got a new intern starting at work next week who's looking for somewhere to stay. Joe or John or something, can't remember now, he could move in here.'

She sat back and folded her arms, looking pleased with herself.

Oh. She seemed to have everything covered.

'So, any more excuses why you shouldn't go?' Rosie cocked an eyebrow at me.

I shook my head. 'You make the toast, while I finish packing.'

Chapter 5

The next morning, I waited until the commuters were safely at work, programmed my phone's satnav to take me to Plumberry and made my way leisurely up the motorway to Yorkshire under a golden spring sun.

I was quite curious to see the village that had enticed Gloria away from city life. When Mimi and I had been growing up, she and her mum had lived in a small suburban house close to the centre of Nottingham where Gloria had an easy journey to work. She was a food stylist at the big TV studios, creating all manner of beautiful dishes that were used on screen, from soap operas to police dramas. She had worked on the set of chat shows, too, prepping food for celebrity chefs to use in their cookery slots. When the studios closed down, she moved back to York where she'd grown up and worked on the food pages of the Sunday newspaper until she retired five years ago.

And then a year ago, she traded her modern apartment overlooking the River Ouse for the delights of a stone cottage in Plumberry and two rescue dogs, Comfrey and Sage, a pair of miniature dachshunds, who she'd brought with her the last time she came to Nottingham. I hadn't visited her so far in her new abode and as I turned off the main road at a sign saying three miles to Plumberry, I felt my stomach flutter with joy. After the emotional events of the last couple of days, what I was really looking forward to more than anything was one of Gloria's special hugs.

The road was winding and narrow on the approach to the village, but gradually the undulating countryside opened out and I passed farms and large country houses and eventually smaller, more modest homes just outside the village. I turned into the high street and felt a smile tweak at my lips; I could see the appeal for Gloria straight away. Plumberry was chocolate-box picturesque: its little shops had old-fashioned striped awnings, large wooden planters brimming with tulips and primroses lined the main street and the buildings themselves were all made from chunky yellow stone.

My satnav was giving me more orders, so I dragged my attention away from the view and concentrated.

'Turn left into Hillside Lane.'

I obeyed.

'You have reached your destination.'

'Thank you,' I replied, reversing my little Fiat smartly into a space outside number eight.

I climbed out of the car, circled my shoulders and stretched. Hillside Lane was – unsurprisingly – a hilly sort of a road with a row of tall three-storey cottages on both sides. Gloria's cottage sat at the top and my eye followed the slope down and beyond the edge of the village to the bright yellow fields full of rapeseed flowers and a silvery streak of water running between them.

My new home for a month was rather lovely.

I raised my hand to knock on number eight but before my knuckles had made contact with wood, the door of the next house flew open.

A woman with cherry-red lipstick and dazzling blonde hair flung her arms out. She was short with generous hips and a large chest and was dressed in a long colourful kaftan. As she lifted her arms, the hem rose up to reveal fluffy kitten-heeled slippers and red toenails to match her lipstick.

'Verity? It is, isn't it, I recognize you from Gloria's description,' she said in a broad Liverpudlian accent.

'Yes,' I said, nodding. 'I'm Verity Bloom.'

'A *waif*,' she said, with a pretty face and in need of a good meal. We'll soon sort that out, don't you worry.'

'Oh, thanks,' I replied, going pink. *I think*.

A waif? I was thin, I supposed, at least thinner than I had been. Two years of not bothering to eat properly, without baking cakes and puddings, had had an effect on my waistline.

She grabbed hold of my shoulders and kissed my cheek noisily. 'I'm Mags, and am I *glad* to see you.'

'Lovely to meet you too,' I said, glancing through the front windows of Gloria's house. No sign of life.

'She's not in. I'm the welcome party,' Mags said with a grin. 'Come in, chuck, you must be *exhausted*!'

With that she turned away and scurried into her own house and so I followed, hoping there'd be an offer of tea. A long corridor led past the staircase and to the rear of the house. The walls were lined with faded photographs of celebrity chefs from the eighties and nineties and there was an old-fashioned telephone on a table in the hall with a velvet stool tucked under it.

'You've got a lovely house, Mags,' I said, peering through an open door to see a cosy sitting room with two armchairs facing a pretty, tiled fireplace. 'Who else lives here?'

'Just me.' She turned and fluttered heavily mascaraed lashes. 'But if George Clooney ever gets fed up of married life, I'm sure I could squeeze him in.'

'Join the queue,' I laughed as she gestured for me to go through the kitchen door ahead of her.

The kitchen was long and narrow with French doors at the far end overlooking the garden. A small round table with two chairs sat in front of it and on the floor, in a patch of sunlight, were Comfrey and Sage, Gloria's dogs, curled up around each other.

'Go and say hello to the boys,' she said, bustling to put the kettle on. 'Cup of tea?'

'Perfect,' I said, bending down to stroke Comfrey. Sage scrambled to his tiny paws and pushed his damp nose into my palm.

'Hello, you two gorgeous things,' I laughed. They were easy to tell apart; Comfrey was the colour of brandy snaps with a pinky brown nose and a white muzzle, while Sage had a dark chocolatey coat with an almost black nose. They both had irresistibly silky ears.

'Well, this is nice.' Mags beamed as she poured tea from a pretty floral teapot and pushed a matching cup towards me. 'Milk, sugar? Take a biscuit.' She nudged a plate piled high with an assortment of homemade shortbread and something oaty-looking.

'It is,' I agreed. 'But you needn't have gone to so much trouble. I'd have been happy with a mug and a packet of Rich Tea.'

'Well, I don't get many visitors.' The tiniest hint of sadness flittered across her face before she winked at me. 'Besides, Gloria made all these.'

The dogs, I noticed, were now sitting to attention beneath the table and I reached down to pet them.

'Pair of gannets,' Mags tutted. 'I dropped a toast crust earlier; Sage had digested it before it hit the floor.'

'And where is Gloria?' I said, biting into a delicious flaky biscuit. Yum. I wouldn't be waif-like for long, with these treats on offer.

'Interviewing at the cookery school. She apologizes for not being here but an opportunity to employ a Michelin-starred chef cropped up at the last minute. She wants someone to share the teaching with her for the first month.'

I raised my eyebrows as I sipped my tea. 'I thought Gloria was going to run all the courses herself.'

'So did Gloria.' Mags chuckled. 'But reality has bitten, big time. "You'll work yourself into an early grave," I said to her yesterday when I was trying to sort out front of house. Then, as luck would have it, word got to her late last night about some top chef from Manchester being at an unexpected loose end.'

'Oh,' I said, wondering why Mags was sorting the front of her house. 'That sounds like me; I'm at an unexpected loose end too.'

'Not any more you're not, chuck.' Mags drained the tea from her cup and passed me a set of house keys. 'I'm to hand you these. Go and get settled into the guest room on the top floor and then Gloria says to wander down to the cookery school any time after one.'

I stowed the keys in my pocket, placed my cup back on the saucer and fed the last crumbs of my biscuit to the ever-watchful sausage dogs.

'Thank you for a lovely welcome, Mags. I'll stick my bags in the house and then take the dogs out for a little walk before I go and see Gloria. They can show me round Plumberry.'

It felt odd letting myself into someone else's home, especially as it was my first visit, and I was glad that I had Comfrey and Sage for company. I decided not to hang around, preferring to wait for Gloria to give me a proper tour later, so I simply left my bags in the hallway, stuffed the keys and my phone into my denim jacket pocket and set off to explore the village.

The three of us made slow progress. I was happy to take a closer look at the shops I'd seen as I'd driven along Plumberry high street and the dogs, who seemed to know everyone we passed, stopped to be petted and to investigate every lamp-post and leaf we encountered.

Plumberry, I quickly realized, was foodie heaven.

I hadn't been able to see what sort of shops those pretty green and white striped awnings were hiding as I drove in but now I peered into every window. The lady behind the counter in the cheesemonger's waved at me as I stared at the myriad varieties of cheese piled up in the window. Next door was an organic bakery; the smells wafting out of there made my mouth water. The dogs tried to tug me into the butcher's shop, but I was more interested in the sign advertising tastings at the wine merchant. I passed a deli with lovely wooden bowls displaying olives and stuffed vine leaves and tiny red peppers filled with cream cheese. And finally, I came to a greengrocer's with a spectacular rainbow display of fresh fruit and vegetables on wooden tables outside. There were one or two other shops, too – a gift shop, newsagent's and florist – but food, I noted, was definitely important to the folk of Plumberry. I bet none of the villagers would bung a readymade lasagne in the microwave and call it dinner. It seemed like the perfect spot for a cookery school.

On the other side of the road was a clothes shop – much more up my street – set between a small supermarket and a pub that looked closed for business. I led Comfrey and Sage to the edge of the pavement and was about to cross over when my phone beeped with a text message.

'Sit! There's good boys,' I said, reaching into my pocket whilst keeping a firm grip on their leads. 'This might be Gloria.'

My heart bounced as I saw the name flash up on the phone: Liam.

This had better be another apology, I thought, opening the message.

Could I just explain the details of my *One, Two, Three Plan* to him because he realized he hadn't really understood it . . . ?

What? Un-bloody-believable! I prodded the delete button angrily as heat flooded my cheeks.

The absolute nerve of the man. He steals my idea, takes my job and then expects me to help him out? Not a chance, buster.

I attempted to stuff the phone back into my pocket but

I was all flustered and it got caught on the denim flap and clattered to the ground. I bent down to retrieve it but as I did so I somehow managed to drop the leads.

'Wait! Heel!' I yelled as the little dogs took full advantage of their freedom and ran as fast as their dinky legs could carry them back along the high street.

Arrghhh!

I scooped up the phone and ran after them, my heart thundering against my ribs. 'Comfrey! Sage! Come back.'

What if they ran across the road and into the path of a car? Oh God, I'd only been here five minutes . . .

The dogs darted between the legs of several shoppers and bypassed others. A little girl lunged at the leads as the dogs flew past but to no avail.

I wove round them all, shouting out random enticements in between my apologies. 'Excuse me! Here, Comfrey, biscuits! Oops, sorry! Sage, look – sausages!'

A man stepped out of the cheesemonger's as the tearaways scampered towards him. He jumped out of their way just as I was aiming to squeeze behind him. We collided and he sent me crashing into the shop window.

'Oof!' I grabbed my shoulder, panting with exertion, but he ignored me and dropped to a squat. He stuck his forefinger and thumb in his mouth and gave a shrill whistle.

Comfrey and Sage stopped immediately and stared at him. Thank goodness.

The man delved into the brown paper bag he was carrying and held out a hand to them. 'Cheese? Come on, fellas. Here's some cheese,' he called in a strong Irish accent.

The two errant canines trotted up to the man's outstretched fingers, tails wagging, and took the cheese from him greedily.

'Thank you so much,' I gasped, completely out of breath. I scooped up the leads and clasped a hand to my chest. 'Comfrey and Sage, you pair of monkeys, you frightened me half to death. If I'd lost you . . .'

'The dogs have good taste,' the man chuckled, producing more cheese. 'And great names.'

'Thanks.' I allowed myself a small smile, Gloria would be so proud. 'Their owner has good taste too.'

'I'm sure she does,' he said, grinning up at me, and I got my first proper look at him.

The word 'rakish' sprang to mind.

His thick dark hair was a bit wild on top and looked like it had to be tamed on a daily basis. He was my sort of age, with dark eyebrows to go with the black hair and eyes as brown as espresso. His face was pale and he had that trendy unshaven thing going on: a bit more than stubble but not quite a beard. He looked nothing like Liam. Which had to be a good thing.

'Oh that's not me, I'm not their owner and I've got no taste at all,' I laughed.

'No?' The man raised an eyebrow.

I shook my head. 'Give me one of those round baby cheeses wrapped in red wax and I'm anyone's. Well, not quite anyone's, obviously,' I added hastily.

Top marks for first impressions, Verity, now he'll think you're a nympho with a cheap cheese habit.

'Right.' He nodded, rubbing his chin thoughtfully. Or possibly hiding a smirk. 'Well, the dogs certainly appreciate a bit of handcrafted, local cheese.'

Oh gosh. That sounded expensive.

'I'm so sorry; let me buy you some more.' I cringed, reaching for my purse. The one I'd left at Gloria's house. 'Oh. Embarrassing. I appear to be cashless. Like the Queen.'

My face began to heat up.

'Forget it,' he said, rubbing Comfrey behind his ear. 'It was my pleasure. Sorry about knocking you into the window, by the way.'

He stood up and gave me an apologetic smile.

'Oh, any time,' I said, trying to ignore the throbbing in my shoulder.

'I'm Tom,' he said, holding out a hand.

I scanned his outfit: a navy jacket, his collarless shirt was untucked and he wore suede desert boots. I approved.

'Verity Bloom,' I said, shaking his hand.

He had slender warm fingers and there was a blue plaster on one of his knuckles and a woven leather bracelet on his wrist.

'Pleased to meet you, Verity Bloom.'

'I'm very grateful that you came along when you did, Tom, and I'll tell Gloria what a hero you are.'

Small village, everyone seemed to know everyone, even the dogs. He was bound to know Gloria.

'Gloria?' He looked at me quizzically.

OK, maybe not.

'Yes. My friend's mum . . .' Why say that? Why mention Mimi? I shook my head and corrected myself. 'She's a friend.'

'Your friend's mum's friend?' His mouth twitched.

The dogs, sensing that I could be here some time, flopped on to my feet and I glanced down, glad of the distraction.

'I'm not normally so incomprehensible, I think the prospect of seeing Gloria's dogs being squished under a car after being in Plumberry less than an hour has made me all blabbery.' I gave an awkward laugh.

'So you're not local?' He peered into his bag, laughed softly and folded the top over.

I shook my head. 'Just visiting.'

'I've not been here much longer than an hour myself.' He grinned, shifting his brown bags from one arm to the other. 'Listen, I've just bought some olives, a sourdough loaf and I now have a very small piece of Yorkshire Blue. I was going to get some red wine from the wine merchants over there and have a picnic on the church bench. Will you join me?'

A picnic lunch: my favourite. With a tallish, dark and very handsome stranger. What's not to like?

'No, thank you, I can't because . . .' I paused. Why couldn't I? Because I only split up with Liam yesterday and so far during this conversation everything that had come out of my mouth had been drivel?

He raised his eyebrows. He really did have lovely eyes. 'Because you only eat Babybel?'

'No, because Gloria's expecting me.'

What am I, twelve?

Tom shrugged. 'Shame. Well, I'm sure I'll see you again, Verity.'

'Sure,' I said, 'bye for now.'

I tipped the dogs off my feet, watching Tom surreptitiously as he set off towards the wine merchants, only to return immediately.

'More cheese, I think,' he said with a wink.

'Sorry.' I pulled my lip between my teeth. 'Again.'

'Good decision, coming to Plumberry today, boys,' I announced to the dogs as I headed back to Gloria's cottage to drop them off. 'So far everyone has made me feel very welcome indeed.'

Especially the dark-haired Irishman with a penchant for blue cheese . . .

Chapter 6

At one o'clock, the dogs were back in their basket in Gloria's kitchen and I was pulling my little car into the cookery school car park between two tradesmen's vans.

Oh my goodness, the place was amazing. I climbed out of the car and turned around slowly. Even though it was just a stone's throw from the village centre, the setting was unbelievably picturesque. I'd known that the cookery school was housed in half of an old mill, sharing the space with a micro-brewery, and I'd imagined something industrial and dark. But the building in front of me was made from beautiful warm stone, had acres of glass and was set alongside the tumbling waters of a river. The old waterwheel was still there too, giving an olde-worlde charm to the place.

There were other little businesses dotted around the edge of the car park in smaller converted buildings: a candle-maker's, a handmade furniture shop and some sort of art studio. It was all very bohemian. Behind the mill, on the other side of the water, there was a spectacular view across steep green hills and rocky outcrops. It was wild and rugged and my nostrils tingled with the sheer vitality of the landscape.

A petite figure with short golden hair dressed in a stylish off-the-shoulder jumper and jeans appeared through huge glass doors.

'Verity, you came! Welcome to Plumberry!'

Gloria waved and scurried towards me.

'Thank you for inviting me!' I cried.

I ran to meet her and five seconds later she had her arms round me, rocking me from side to side.

Whenever I saw her we hugged like this: silently and tightly, just for a moment. I reminded Gloria of Mimi and vice versa. For me it was Gloria's vivid blue eyes, her tiny feet and the oval shape of her fingernails that instantly plunged me straight back to doing makeovers in Mimi's bedroom when we were fifteen. And for Gloria I guess it was the fact that I had been her daughter's best friend and holding me was the closest she could get to holding Mimi again.

I felt a momentary pang for my own mum, wishing I could do this with her more than just once a year, which was all we usually managed. We may not always have seen eye to eye – she liked to give me advice that I was too stubborn to take – but I did miss her.

'It does my heart good just to look at you, darling girl,' Gloria declared, stroking my cheek.

Her blue eyes sparkled but beneath them, dark shadows hinted at too much stress and not enough sleep. She stood back to inspect me. 'Although I still think you're too thin.'

'Er, pot and kettle,' I chided gently, taking in the hollows under her cheekbones. 'Mags – who I love, by the way – has told me you're working too hard and now that I'm here I shall be making sure you take care of yourself.'

Gloria tilted her head to one side and twizzled her bangles round on her arm. 'There's nothing to worry about, I assure you. Once the cookery school is open and we've got through these teething troubles, life will be as smooth as hollandaise sauce.'

I grinned. 'Not *my* hollandaise sauce, I hope. I've only made it once and it had lumps of scrambled egg in it.'

Gloria smiled. 'I'm sure we can sort that out, just as soon

as you've sorted out my website and brochures and—'

'OK, OK,' I chuckled, tucking my hand through her arm. 'Aren't you going to show me round first? This place is to die for, by the way; look at those hills and the old mill and the river! Totally gorgeous.'

Arm in arm, the two of us strolled into a large reception area. Two men were plastering the walls, while another was wiring modern light fittings to the ceiling. The air was dusty and smelled damp from the wet plaster and it was hard to imagine that Gloria would be ready to open her doors to paying customers in two and a half weeks' time.

'There's still plenty to do,' Gloria said, reading my mind. She swept her fringe from one side of her forehead to the other. 'But the builder assures me that we'll be ready on time. Lovely building, don't you think? If you can see past the mess.'

I nodded, taking in the high ceilings and deep windows. Several doors led off the reception area as well as a staircase with lovely wrought-iron balusters. 'Fabulous!'

And it was fabulous. But deep down I was concerned; this place was huge. When Gloria first said she was opening a cookery school I'd naïvely thought she'd just have a few students over to her kitchen at home. But this was a major undertaking.

'Reception will be Mags's domain with a desk over here,' said Gloria, indicating one area of the space. 'She'll be our official welcome party when our students arrive. She's given herself the title of front of house manager.'

'She's going to work here too?' Mags's earlier comment finally made sense and I was relieved that Gloria had her on the team. 'I approve. She does a great welcome; your guests will love her.'

'She's certainly larger than life,' she said with a smile.

We carried on through, Gloria opening doors to show me the cloakroom, food preparation areas and storage cupboards.

'And this is my favourite room,' she said, pushing open a pair of double doors.

'Wow,' I breathed. My eyes must have been as big as dinner plates. 'It's lovely!'

The big space was empty except for a huge cream Aga and black granite worktops at one end with a row of half-finished kitchen cupboards behind it. A man was laying large floor tiles at the opposite end. One wall of the room was made entirely of glass with a view out on to a wooden deck overlooking the river. Through an open door, I spotted a kitchen prep area with a sink, fridge and shelves, mostly empty except for a kettle and a tray of mugs and tea-making things.

'The tutor will work here,' said Gloria, walking behind the cooker. 'There'll be a big mirror above the hob so students can see what's going on, and the tables and chairs – when they arrive – will be set up either lecture style or as a dining room. I see this room as more relaxed; the students will be watching and tasting rather than cooking.'

I shot Gloria a look of confusion. 'They won't be cooking?'

She laughed softly. 'Come on, the tour continues upstairs.'

We walked back through reception and up the stairs. The first floor was just one large open space except for an office partitioned off in the far corner. On the far side was another door, but it was closed and I couldn't see where it led. A team of four joiners was hard at work fitting the kitchens. Men were hammering and banging and power tools thrummed, drilled and whirred. A radio blared out, adding an extra noise to the cacophony and a thick layer of sawdust had settled over everything. I coughed as Gloria led me to the back of the room.

'There'll be a teaching workstation at the front,' she shouted above the noise. 'And twenty student kitchens, sharing an oven between two.'

Twenty? I blinked at her. 'Gloria, it's all wonderful, in fact I'm blown away, but—'

My voice was drowned out by the piercing whine of a drill and the two of us smiled. I linked arms with her and drew her back downstairs to the tranquillity of the wooden deck overhanging the river.

'This is much more restful,' she said, perching herself on a plastic chair at the edge of the deck.

The river was quite narrow here and the water flowed gently over the rocks. The bank on the other side rose steeply and was shaded by trees.

'Very peaceful,' I agreed, leaning on the wooden balustrade and breathing in the fresh moist air. I turned to gaze into her eyes. 'And much more conducive to talking. This is a big venture. Much bigger than I'd imagined.'

She looked down and began to turn one of her bangles round and round on her arm. 'I couldn't do nothing, Verity. Retirement and I were dangerous bedfellows. Sixty-five probably seems ancient to you, but I could live for another twenty-five years. Being active makes me feel alive. And I've got forty years' worth of recipes in my head and on scraps of paper in my recipe bible; I can't wait to pass them on to other people. I've missed working as a food stylist and this will give me a chance to be creative again.'

I stared up at the old mill and my heart twisted. Mimi would have been so excited to be part of this. Once again it was me who got to play a part in her dreams.

'Mimi would be very proud of you, Gloria. She always said you were unstoppable.' We smiled at each other. 'But this is more than being creative with food,' I added. 'The management of a business this size will take over your whole life.'

Her eyes lit up mischievously. 'Who's to say I need to run it myself? I could install a manager, someone young and clever.' She nudged me with her elbow. 'Like you.'

My mouth gaped. That wasn't on the agenda. 'Er—'

'Who knows?' she continued breezily. 'But right now, I need this. I need to be busy.'

The look that she gave me was so loaded with determination and confidence that my heart melted.

'Do you know what?' I said, leaning down to press a kiss into her honey-gold hair. 'Right now, so do I.'

One of the workmen appeared, leaning on the door frame. He pulled his dust mask down to his chin and a cloud of dust puffed out of it.

'Sorry to interrupt, Gloria,' he said, rubbing an arm across his forehead, 'but which side do you want the hinges on these cupboard doors?'

'I'll be right with you, Neil. I'd better press on,' she said, turning to me with a little sigh. 'Why don't you go home and unpack? I'll see you later.'

I frowned. 'Don't you want me to start straight away?'

She stood up and shook her head. 'I'll tell you everything that needs doing tonight. I've invited my new chef to join us for dinner and Mags has offered to cook so the four of us can have a pow-wow. Although as Mags is a bit of a party girl, goodness knows how much we'll get done.'

'I can't wait,' I laughed as Gloria trotted off behind Neil.

By the time Gloria arrived home I'd completely unpacked, taken Comfrey and Sage for a second walk and listened to the story of how Mags met Gloria while she chopped vegetables for dinner. It seemed they were far more than simply neighbours: they'd met years ago when Mags was working for a publisher specializing in cookery books. She accompanied one of her celebrity chefs to the TV studios to promote a new cookery book, bumped into Gloria behind the scenes and the two women hit it off instantly.

Mags packed her off upstairs with a glass of wine for a bath and I was despatched to lay the table in the dining room. I set out glasses and cutlery for four and was just looking at the many framed pictures of Mimi and Gabe's wedding and Noah's christening when the doorbell rang.

'That'll be Tom,' Gloria called over the banister. She was enveloped in a fluffy white robe. 'Let him in, please, I'll only be five minutes.'

The dogs scrabbled past me, yapping madly as I made my way along the hall.

'We met a Tom today, didn't we, chaps? The dog whisperer with posh cheese.'

I opened the door and there he was, the same Tom. 'Oh! It's you!'

'Verity Bloom.' He smiled and his eyes crinkled at the corners. 'I had a feeling I might be seeing you again.'

'Oh?' I blinked. 'Did you?'

Comfrey and Sage threw themselves at his legs with gay abandon. I was more restrained but my stomach fizzed nervously. Oh God, all that stuff I'd blabbed about having no taste and eating plastic cheese and this must be the chef with the Michelin star.

He nodded. 'I figured there couldn't be too many Glorias in a village this size.' He held out a bunch of orange tulips. 'For you.'

'Thank you,' I said, genuinely touched by the gesture. The last time someone bought me flowers was ... I couldn't even remember. A long time, anyway. 'So you're the cookery school's new tutor?'

'Yep, on a temporary basis. I'll be sharing the teaching with Gloria, running the kitchen, planning courses, ordering supplies – that sort of thing.' He bent down to fuss the dogs. 'And dog whisperer with posh cheese. But no cheese this evening, I'm afraid, guys.'

I stood aside to let him in. 'You heard that?'

He winked. 'Yes. But don't worry, your secret's safe with me.'

'Phew, thanks.'

At least Gloria wouldn't find out about the dog lead incident.

He leaned in close and I felt his warm breath in my ear. 'I won't tell a soul you're anybody's after a mouthful of Babybel.'

I opened my mouth to protest but both Gloria and Mags appeared in the hall.

'Tom! Come in, let's get you a drink.' Gloria clasped his arms and kissed both his cheeks.

'I've brought red and white,' he said, producing two bottles of wine from a bag. 'I didn't know what we'd be eating.'

'You look so delicious I might eat you, chuck,' Mags declared, plucking the bottles out of his hand. 'Five minutes, ladies and gentlemen, take your seats please.'

Tom's eyes widened as he watched her sashay back to the kitchen.

'So the main teaching kitchen will be ready only a few days before we open,' said Gloria, taking a large gulp of the wine Tom had poured her.

'Which is when?' I asked.

Surely she wasn't still hoping to be ready in a fortnight? The place had potential, but Gloria had been spot on yesterday on the phone when she'd referred to it as a bomb site.

'May fifteenth,' said Gloria with impressive confidence.

'Two weeks on Friday?' I said, doing a rapid calculation.

Eek. I looked across at Tom; his eyebrows flickered but he didn't give anything away.

'I think we should aim to run a test course before then,' he said evenly, leaning forward to take a piece of crusty bread from the basket. 'I need to know all the ovens are calibrated correctly, that the demo kitchen really works properly and that everyone can see.'

Gloria tapped a finger on her lips pensively. 'I'll do my best, Tom. The downstairs Aga kitchen is already working, so if you want to test recipes out, and so on . . . ?'

'Ta-dah!' Mags swept into the room bearing a large casserole dish. She lowered it down to the centre of the table, removed the lid and flipped the oven gloves over her shoulder. 'Wait till you taste this, Tom. You'll be begging me for more.'

He grinned and rubbed his neck awkwardly as Mags began ladling stew into bowls. She set a huge bowl in front of me.

'This'll put hairs on your chest, Verity.'

'What is it?' I asked, fanning the steam from my face.

'A pan of scouse. My mother's old recipe.' Mags beamed. 'Don't be shy with the red wine, Tom, top me up, there's a good lad.'

'Mags grew up in Liverpool, didn't you, Mags?' Gloria took a spoonful and blew on it.

'The posh end, mind.' Mags sat down and immediately got up again and left the room. 'I forgot the pickles.'

I caught Tom's eye and we shared the tiniest of bemused smiles.

'Everyone had a pan of scouse on the go when I was growing up.' Mags plonked a jar of pickled onions and one of red cabbage on the table, scooped up some of the stew on her bread and closed her eyes. 'Mmmm. Takes me straight back. Nothing but good, honest ingredients; you can't beat the taste of home.'

'I agree, my mum's stew and dumplings does it for me,' said Tom.

'Me too. You can forget your fiddly foams and poncy purees.' I shuddered. 'I like to see food served plainly, not in fancy dress. What's your signature dish, Tom?'

'Er.' He didn't meet my eye and helped himself to more bread. 'That would probably be pan-fried scallops with a lime foam and minted pea purée.'

Bugger.

I swallowed. 'Well, no wonder you won a Michelin star,' I said, focusing on my bowl.

'Tom was the head chef at Salinger's in Manchester.' Gloria raised her eyebrows as high as they could go to indicate how impressive that was.

He cleared his throat. 'But my partner and I have gone our separate ways. New horizons beckon.'

'I'll drink to that.' Mags chuckled, taking a gulp of her wine.

'Thanks.' Tom gave her a tight smile. 'What about you, Verity? What sort of cook are you?'

I waved my fork in the air dismissively. 'My housemate Rosie calls me Princess Prick and Ping.'

'Good grief,' Gloria murmured.

Mags snorted and elbowed Tom in the ribs. 'Sounds like a Thai stripper.'

Tom choked on his wine and banged his chest. A few drops of wine escaped from his glass and splattered on to his shirt. 'Sorry, wasn't expecting that.'

He looked down at his white shirt in dismay. 'Damn.'

'Whip it off, love, and I'll wash it for you.' Mags tipped him a lascivious wink. 'You're amongst friends.'

'Really?' He grinned. 'Will you whip yours off in front of me?'

She leaned forward until her ample bosom was almost in his dinner. 'Are you asking?' she drawled in a low voice, fluttering her eyelashes.

'Heavens, Mags, put them away,' chuckled Gloria, 'and stop harassing my staff.'

'You spoil all my fun,' Mags tutted.

Poor Tom was still holding his shirt away from him with his fingertips. I popped into the kitchen and returned with a damp cloth.

'Here, dab it with this.' I held it out and he took it with a grateful smile. 'And no, not a stripper. Let's just say I'm a convenience-food junkie. Pop it in the microwave and ping – done in no time.'

Tom looked at me with disdain. 'Like ready-meals?'

'What's wrong with that?' I felt uncomfortable all of a sudden.

He shrugged. 'I don't understand why people make excuses not to cook and put up with eating bad food.'

'Not everyone has the time,' I retorted.

'You can still take advantage of the freshest, seasonal produce without taking an age to cook it,' he argued. 'Where's the respect for quality and taste?'

'It's about priorities, I guess,' I snapped back.

Gloria laid a hand across mine as a gentle warning. I pressed my lips together and took a deep breath. As much as it pained me to admit it, Tom had touched a nerve.

'Mind you, you did admit earlier that you had no taste,' he continued blithely. 'This is very tasty, Mags, although the pickles aren't for me.'

I felt like I'd been smacked in the face; I wish I hadn't fetched him a cloth now. Even Mags looked taken aback.

'For your information, Tom, I can cook,' I said. 'I just choose not to. But when I do, my food is comforting and cooked with love and—' My words caught in my throat as a sudden rush of emotion sprang up from nowhere.

For Mimi and me, our cooking sessions had always been mostly about having fun and much less about how the food ended up. Nothing like Tom's school of thought at all. He could stuff his pea purée up his—

'I'm sorry, that was rude. I've got no right to criticize.' He rubbed a hand through his hair.

Mags patted his arm. 'You're passionate and who can complain about a man with passion, eh, ladies?'

He gave me a tight-lipped smile. 'Forgiven?'

I nodded. 'Sure.' *Not really.*

Mags picked up the ladle and scooped up more scouse. 'Now, who's for more?'

She dolloped some in Tom's bowl without waiting for a response.

'Anyway,' Gloria said, looking anxiously from Tom to

me, 'Verity's role will be to promote the cookery school, to come up with lots of ideas to make sure we get people through the doors. Especially on our open day.'

'Gloria,' I piped up, clearing my throat and feeling very glad we'd changed the subject, 'what is the name of the cookery school?'

Gloria squirmed in her seat. 'I've just been calling it The Cookery School.'

'No, that's too generic. You should have *your* name in it,' said Tom blackly, 'then no one can take it from you.'

'How about Food, Gloria's Food?' suggested Mags.

'Oh, I like that.' Gloria squeezed her friend's hand across the table. 'What fun!'

Personally, I thought that sounded too much like a café and not at all like a cookery school.

Tom shook his head. 'I meant your last name. What is it again?'

'Ramsbottom!' we all chorused.

Tom's lips twitched. 'OK, then, maybe not. You need it to sound professional.'

'And not like a sheep's bum,' Mags added.

Gloria exhaled thoughtfully. 'I take your point about professional, Tom. But I want my cookery school to deliver food that's like a hug on a plate. A love of food is more important to me than being cheffy.'

'What about the Plumberry School of Food?' I said suddenly. 'The village is a food lover's paradise, that would make sense.'

The other two nodded their approval until Gloria's face lit up.

'The Plumberry School of *Comfort* Food,' she cried.

'That, Gloria Ramsbottom, is perfect,' I declared, raising my glass. 'A toast. To the Plumberry School of Comfort Food.'

Chapter 7

For the next few days I threw myself into my new life in Plumberry. In Gloria's cottage I had the dearest little room at the top of the house with views across the Yorkshire Dales and my own en suite shower room. Comfrey and Sage, in spite of only having the shortest of legs, had taken it upon themselves to wake me every morning by scampering up the stairs and barking at my door until I let them in and up on to the bed for a cuddle. It was a lovely way to greet the day.

Mags and Gloria were inseparable and watching them together reminded me so much of the pleasure Mimi and I used to derive from each other's company. I didn't really know why they kept separate houses as they took it in turns to cook each night, and they didn't mind a bit that so far I hadn't returned the favour.

However, I did help Gloria make beef wellington on my first Friday night. In true Gloria style, it was not only delicious, but it was a feast for the eyes and I'd been quite emotional as the three of us sat down to eat. The fact that the first proper dinner I'd cooked in two years was a team effort with Mimi's mum made the meal all the more delicious. I'd missed cooking, I realized, and eating proper food. Spending time with Gloria in her kitchen did make me remember Mimi, and the two of us had shed a tear together after the others had gone on that first night after

Mags's scouse, but it also made me feel as if I was regaining a part of me that had been missing since she died.

My old job at Solomon Insurance, Ruthless Rod and even my relationship with Liam seemed like memories best forgotten, although I did miss my little house in Nottingham. I'd spoken to Rosie a few times and apparently Liam had turned up on our doorstep after I'd ignored all his messages. Rosie had taken great delight in telling him I wasn't there.

'Told him if he showed his two-faced face again, he'd be swimming with the fishes,' she'd informed me briskly.

In fact, the only person who was sad about my break-up with Liam was Mum.

'Oh love,' she'd groaned down the phone when I'd rung to update her on my whereabouts. 'I just want to see you settled.'

'I know, Mum,' I'd replied, 'but I don't think I should settle for anything less than I deserve, do you?'

And right now a month in the delightful village of Plumberry with no man troubles was exactly what I deserved.

I started work on Wednesday and spent two days with a web designer building a website and a day at the printers, where a very nice man drew us a logo for the cookery school. Between us we concocted a leaflet for the open day, some advertising for the newspaper that Gloria had booked and had the beginnings of a brochure worked up. All we needed to add to it were some glossy photographs and a calendar showing the courses. The former would have to wait until I had something other than a building site to photograph and the latter depended on Gloria and Tom coming to an agreement on which courses the school should run.

The following Monday was a bank holiday. The builders, true to their word, were on track for Gloria's planned opening day and as paint started to appear on walls and kitchen equipment began to arrive by the pallet load, I noticed the worry lines disappearing from her face. The pacing I'd heard in the middle of the night when I'd first arrived had lessened too.

Today, however, with no workmen on site, the cookery school was mercifully quiet, so Tom had suggested that we gather to hammer out the finer details of the calendar. Mags, Gloria, Tom and I, plus our newly recruited kitchen assistant Pixie, sat out in the sunshine on the deck on the new wooden picnic tables. Pixie had a uniform that consisted of burgundy Doc Martens boots, leggings and T-shirts, which she continuously tugged over her hips. She wore her black hair in a pony tail with a long fringe that covered her sturdy eyebrows and had black glasses that reminded me of Velma, the clever one from *Scooby-Doo*.

Mags made tea and Tom brought out a plate of delicate petits-fours, which he'd made in the Aga. And with the dogs stretched out across Gloria's feet in the May sunshine, it almost felt like a little family get-together.

'We need to open the cookery school with a bang,' said Gloria. 'Exciting courses at enticing prices. Perhaps some introductory offers?'

'I've had a brilliant idea: BOGOF,' I threw in, taking one of Tom's tiny cakes from the plate. It was covered in thick dark chocolate and topped with a piece of walnut and a coffee bean and smelled heavenly. 'Buy one get one free. It'll boost numbers and it's always nicer to cook with a friend, isn't it?'

In my book, cooking with a friend was the only way to do it.

Gloria met my eye and smiled. 'It is.'

'But tacky,' Tom said with a frown. 'No offence, Verity, but that sort of promotion cheapens the offering more than any other marketing strategy. We need to be seen as experts. Gimmicks aren't the way forward, believe me.'

'None taken,' I said, quashing the urge to pick the coffee bean off my petit-four and lob it at him. I sank my teeth into the cake instead. It was the most exquisitely intense hit of chocolate I'd ever tasted and it took all of my willpower not to groan with pleasure. 'Although I completely disagree.'

There was nothing wrong with being passionate. Nothing at all. But he took everything to do with food so seriously. I much preferred him when he was rescuing the dogs from certain death or giving me flowers.

We locked eyes and his mouth twitched with the merest hint of a smile. I looked away; he was so annoying.

'Let's talk about the schedule,' Gloria intervened smoothly. 'The courses we'll run in the first week should give a true flavour of what the Plumberry School of Comfort Food is about.'

'Comfort food, then,' I said, wiping the chocolate from my mouth with a napkin.

Tom sat up tall. 'Something spectacular that you wouldn't cook at home. A five-bird roast, boned, stuffed and—'

'Hugely expensive,' said Gloria, raising an eyebrow.

'And posh,' said Pixie, wrinkling up her nose.

'And probably takes all day to cook,' added Mags.

'What about Sumptuous Stews?' Gloria said. 'Comforting, achievable and—'

'A bit boring?' said Tom, rubbing a hand through his hair. 'People come to a cookery school to learn, to be inspired. We need to show them how to do the things they shy away from at home, like boning fish or, I don't know . . . making confit of duck.'

'Confit? What's that when it's at home?' Pixie rolled her eyes.

I suppressed a giggle as a look of irritation flashed across Tom's face.

Pixie had turned up last week looking for a job. She was twenty-five and had a Yorkshire accent so strong that Mags sometimes had to translate for Tom. She already worked at the weekends in the Plumberry cheesemonger's and evenings in the pub in Pudston but was saving up for her own place so she could leave the home she shared with her big family.

'I need more hours and the cheese shop hasn't got any to give me. I'll do anything,' she'd pleaded to Gloria. 'Wash up, chop onions, even empty the bins.'

And as Gloria wasn't a fan of doing any of those things, she'd given Pixie a job. 'She's a mucker-inner,' she'd told me. 'And not afraid to get her hands dirty.'

She was also not afraid to voice her opinion, even if it rubbed Tom up the wrong way. I liked her a lot.

'How about taking cheaper stuff that a family can actually afford and doing something special with it? You know, making the most of their budget?' Pixie continued. She picked up a teaspoon and began to push her cuticles back with it.

'Everyone's right,' I said diplomatically. 'We need courses that teach people skills they can use, with ingredients they can afford or perhaps at least splash out on now and again. But no one comes to a cookery school to make cottage pie, we need to inspire people. I agree with Tom.'

'You do?' He raised a cynical eyebrow and I willed my cheeks not to redden.

We all stared at the large sheet of paper on which Tom had written 'May Calendar'. It was still blank apart from the heading.

'Why don't we do a bit of market research?' Mags suggested. 'I can go out into Plumberry tomorrow and ask.'

'Good plan,' said Gloria. 'I'd come too but we're having a health and safety inspection.'

'And not me and Pixie either,' Tom said. 'We'll be busy unpacking twenty sets of kitchen equipment for upstairs.'

'I'll come with you, Mags; marketing's my job, after all,' I offered. 'Tom, do you think you could rustle us up some little tasters to hand out to people?'

'Sure.' He grinned, fixing me with his dark eyes. 'I usually find blue cheese has them eating out of my hand.'

'Ooh, yes.' Gloria beamed as the blush I'd been holding back burst forth. 'And make sure you invite people to our open day too.'

'I will,' I said, looking Tom in the eye. 'I'll invite everyone who looks like they have good taste.'

The next morning, Gloria dropped us off on Plumberry high street armed with clipboards, questionnaires and plenty of freebies. Tom had used the Aga to make blue cheese soufflé croutons and miniature lavender shortbread bites and we planned to entice people to answer our questionnaire with them. He was never going to let me forget the blue cheese thing, I could tell. It was delicious, though, as was the shortbread, so I wasn't complaining.

'We should have matching aprons,' said Mags, taking a tray of food from me.

'We will have next week.' I stuck the clipboard under my arm and tucked a couple of spare pens in my pocket. 'I've ordered some black ones with the logo on. All students will get one to keep and we can sell them in reception too.'

'Gloria was right, you're full of bright ideas.' Mags eyed me appraisingly. 'I'm so glad you came to Plumberry.'

We positioned ourselves near the war memorial in front of the church and put on our most welcoming smiles.

'Thanks. Mimi isn't here to help her mum, so I thought I should be,' I said, aware of the familiar pull of sadness tugging at my heart.

Mags gave me a sideways glance. 'But you are enjoying yourself, aren't you?'

I nodded. I'd been going through the motions back at home, just doing enough to get through life, not daring to enjoy myself too much. I'd held back from giving things my all. Perhaps all that stuff with my job and Liam and the pregnancy scare had to happen to jolt me out of my apathy?

'I feel a bit guilty that my life goes on whereas my friend will be forever stuck at thirty. But yes, I'm enjoying myself,' I confirmed.

'Good, because life's for living, Verity,' Mags said brightly. 'Never forget that. And take pleasure where you can.'

'That sounds like a good policy,' I said, heartened by the advice.

'Works for me. I call it my principle of pleasure.' She popped a crouton in her mouth. 'Mmm, now that is pleasure.'

'Ooh, look, some public,' I whispered as an elderly couple approached. 'They can be our first customers.'

'This reminds me of standing in bookshops with my authors, praying someone would come over and talk to us, or even, God forbid, buy a blooming book,' said Mags out of the side of her mouth. 'Good morning, lovelies, have you heard about Plumberry's new cookery school?'

After seeing off a good few of our samples the couple moved on. They didn't want to come to the cookery school but might pop down on opening day if we'd be handing out more free food. The husband pointed out that his wife's cooking couldn't be improved upon, which made us both forgive him for snaffling so much shortbread.

For the next fifteen minutes, we were bombarded with people content to eat our samples in exchange for giving us lots of ideas for cookery courses. Bread-making seemed to be popular, as did learning to make your favourite take-aways. I could imagine how well that last one would go down with Tom . . .

'Do you miss publishing, Mags?' I asked, during a lull in the proceedings.

'Not any more. I did at first, but when I met my partner, Otto, his career was just taking off as a food writer. He was never what you'd call a celebrity, but he was quite in demand at the time. I moved into his flat and it made sense for me to give up work to be his unofficial, unpaid manager. We never married; he'd been married before and still bore the scars, so he joked. We had a good life, but I did miss the hustle and bustle of the publishers. Then one day he died from a heart attack. His kids swooped in like vultures to claim their inheritance and I suddenly found myself homeless.'

'Even though you'd helped him build up his career?' I said, outraged on her behalf.

She shrugged. 'Since then I've mostly done freelance editing, but I think I was born for the job at the cookery school. I was made up when Gloria told me about it. We should have brought stools,' she grumbled, 'my back is killing me.'

We sat down on the base of the war memorial. Mags set her tray down next to us and I stretched out my legs.

'Mags,' I began tentatively, 'I think Gloria's new venture is great, but Gabe feels a bit neglected. As if she's too busy for him and Noah these days.'

She picked up a square of shortbread, broke it in half and handed a piece to me. 'I think she felt that he wouldn't want his mother-in-law under his feet. That's why she keeps her distance. After all, he'll move on one day, won't he, find another girl. That would be hard for Gloria, to stand aside and see her daughter's child being brought up by another woman.'

'I guess,' I mumbled.

It would be hard for all of us.

'She prefers them to come for a week at a time, for a little holiday, and hopefully as Noah grows up he can start to do that on his own. Just him and his granny.'

I sighed. 'As long as she does invite them.'

I'd make sure they came up to the open day, I decided. Get them all together. At least then Gabe would see that Gloria had time for him and Noah. And perhaps it would reassure him that she hadn't bitten off more than she could chew by opening the cookery school.

'Verity, get up, get up!' Mags scrambled to her feet and I did the same. 'See that man over there?'

I looked across the street to see a slim tall man in his fifties. He wore sandals, had his hands in his loose linen trousers, and his whole demeanour seemed to radiate serenity.

'Yes.' I nodded.

I watched in amusement as Mags delved into her pocket, retrieved a red lipstick and reapplied it perfectly without a mirror.

'That's Gloria's accountant, Dave. He is the sexiest man in this village.' She giggled and nudged me. 'Cooee! Dave!'

Dave looked over and raised a hand. He crossed the road to join us and Mags bent down to pick up her tray.

He gave her a shy smile. 'Greetings, Mags. They look delectable.'

'Dave!' She pushed his arm playfully and made a show of pulling the front of her blouse up. 'Naughty.'

Poor Dave didn't know where to look. 'I meant the . . .' he stammered.

I took pity on him. 'I'm Verity Bloom, a friend of Gloria's.' I stuck my hand out. 'Here to handle the marketing for a few weeks.'

Dave looked relieved at the change of subject and shook my hand. 'Good to make your acquaintance. Although marketing sounds expensive.'

I smiled; he'd have fitted in nicely at my last company. 'Not as expensive as having a cookery school with no customers.'

'Fair enough,' he conceded, inclining his head. 'Anything to ameliorate business gets my approval. What are you up to here? Gloria won't make a profit if she gives everything away for free.'

'You have to speculate to accumulate,' I said smoothly. 'Isn't that right, Mags?'

'Oh, it's only a few titbits, try before you buy,' said Mags, pushing the tray closer to him. 'Go on.'

He held his hand up. 'Looks delicious, Mags, but I'm fasting today.'

'You look fit, Dave,' said Mags, squeezing his bicep. 'Have you been working out?'

He turned a gentle shade of pink. 'Ashtanga.'

'Bless you!' Mags replied.

'It's a type of yoga,' he said solemnly. 'I practise every morning.'

'Practice makes perfect, Dave,' Mags said with a wink. 'You'll have to show me your moves.'

Dave shuffled from foot to foot and glanced over his shoulder as if looking for an excuse to make his escape. His rescue came in the form of a group of teenage girls who'd just left the little supermarket armed with cans of fizzy drinks and packets of sweets.

'Free food!' one of them shouted, pointing at our trays.

'An onslaught of rapacious customers,' Dave said with palpable relief. 'I'll see you next week at the opening.'

I watched as he shoved his hands back in his pockets and strode away.

'He's very earnest,' I murmured, trying to associate him with Mags's description of the sexiest man in the village.

'Nah, he just hasn't learned my principle of pleasure yet, I'll show him. Now gird your loins, chuck.' Mags eyed up the approaching girls. 'This lot look hungry.'

An hour later, we had empty trays and a clipboard full of suggestions. Gloria was going to be delighted; most customers fell distinctly into the comfort food market, wanting to learn things their parents or grandparents had made. There were also a few mentions of things like cooking on a budget and entertaining for special occasions to appease Tom and Pixie too.

'Come on, Mags, let's head back,' I said, packing everything away in bags. 'That was a good morning's work.'

'Agreed.' Mags chuckled. 'And knowing how quickly news spreads in this village, I doubt there'll be anyone left who hasn't heard of the cookery school by this evening.'

'Then my work here is done.' I grinned as she dialled Gloria's number to arrange a lift back.

The people of Plumberry had spoken. There was a definite buzz about the imminent arrival of a cookery school in their village and people were excited. And so, I realized, for the first time in a very long time, was I.

Chapter 8

It happened the following Monday with only four sleeps to go. Just like that, seemingly overnight, the lovely old building transformed itself from a dust-encrusted bomb site into an almost-ready-to-open cookery school.

The breath caught in my throat as I wandered from room to room, marvelling at all that Gloria and her team of workmen had achieved in the last couple of weeks since that teary phone call that had had me racing up the motorway.

The mill still held echoes of its two-hundred-year-old past: the wooden beams upstairs, the rows of deep windows, the brickwork, now painted pristine white, and of course the waterwheel outside. But now there was a bright, modern and welcoming feel to the interior: Mags's large curved wooden desk complete with computer, telephone switchboard and spacious drawers hugged one entire wall of the reception space ('Beam me up, Scotty,' she'd said with a whistle when she saw it). The rows of spotlights in the ceiling lit up even the darkest corner and the huge terracotta tiles, thanks to the builders, would be warm underfoot in winter. Gloria's homely touches were evident throughout, from the wicker umbrella stand by the doors to the fluffy plum-coloured towels in the cloakroom. There was even a wicker basket for Comfrey and Sage in prime position near the front windows.

On the ground floor, the Aga kitchen had taken delivery of a number of chunky oak dining tables with matching benches and I could already imagine the room full of eager students introducing themselves to each other over coffee and homemade biscuits as they oohed and ahhed over the view of the river.

There were storerooms on both floors as well as prep rooms. They'd been swept and scrubbed and the shelves were now bursting with sugar and spice and all things nice, including umpteen types of flour, pasta in every conceivable shape and size and more varieties of rice than I even knew existed. There was every gadget imaginable, from blenders to brulée blowtorches, mandolins to Moroccan tagines, alongside an assortment of complicated-looking chocolate-making kits. There was nothing, it seemed, that the Plumberry School of Comfort Food lacked in the way of kitchen paraphernalia.

Mimi would have loved it here. I could hear her in my head, gasping over all the lovely new equipment. What I wouldn't give to spend an afternoon cooking with her at that fabulous new Aga . . .

I carried on upstairs to peep at the teaching kitchen and stopped at the top of the steps to take in the transformation. The large room seemed to fizz with sparkly newness. Twenty immaculately clean workstations set around ten gleaming new ovens were kitted out and ready for action. Inside every cupboard was an identical set of pans and baking trays and on the granite worktops sat pots of cooking utensils in shades of red, green, blue and pink, adding a splash of colour to an otherwise calming palette. It all looked so inviting that I was almost tempted back into the kitchen myself.

But not quite. Tom had made it perfectly clear that the kitchens were well beyond my remit. Even Gloria had barely had a look-in so far.

I spotted Gloria in the office at the far corner of the

kitchen and went to join her. She was the picture of casual elegance as usual, dressed in a voluminous cream jumper that complemented her honey-blonde hair. She looked up as I entered the little room and her eyes searched mine with a mix of nerves and pride.

'Gloria,' I grinned, 'you've built a cookery school.'

I wrapped my arms round her and the two of us gazed across the teaching kitchen.

'I have, haven't I?' she murmured. 'What do you think of it?'

'It makes me want to stick a pinny on and roll up my sleeves,' I admitted, kissing her soft cheek.

'Then it's already a success.' She smiled back at me and I felt my heart lift with affection for her. 'Today marks a turning point for us,' she continued. 'We'll be cooking for the first time. Tom and Pixie are baking bread later, getting the ovens on to check they're all accurate. And I'm testing out the recipes in the Aga downstairs for my One Pot Wonders course on Monday.'

'So it will smell as well as look wonderful.'

I released Gloria and wandered over to the desk I'd appropriated for my own use. I kept it relatively neat and tidy in contrast with Gloria who I could barely see sometimes behind piles of paperwork. I flicked on the computer and a flurry of emails appeared. I'd sent the first month's cookery course calendar off to the printer and updated the website with it and the first batch of brochures were due in any minute. It had been a manic time, but I was calmly confident that all was on track.

Gloria remained in the doorway and I heard her sigh softly.

'The open day will be a triumph, Gloria; half of the village has said they're coming.'

She turned to face me and sagged against the doorframe.

'Do you think so? Have we done enough?'

'Yes!' I chuckled. 'I've sent press releases out to every

newspaper, magazine, radio show and even the local TV news programme. And have you heard the phone in reception?'

Her eyes shone as she nodded. Since the telephone company connected the line for us, it hadn't stopped ringing. Mags had been glued to her desk answering enquiries for the last two days.

Gloria flicked the kettle on and peered inside two mugs before adding teabags.

'And the courses?' she mused. 'Do you think we're being a bit optimistic running so many next week? We need at least five people to come to each to cover our costs.'

Hmm, numbers were still low. My priority had been promoting the open day and so far we'd had lots of interest in the courses but precious few actual bookings.

I crossed my fingers behind my back. 'It's early days and I'm sure we'll get people signing up on the spot at the open party.'

The office phone rang just as my mobile beeped with a text message.

Gloria answered the call and I glanced at my phone, hoping it wouldn't be Liam again. I had to give him ten out of ten for perseverance; he'd been phoning or texting me almost daily since I'd arrived in Plumberry. It was a shame he didn't score so highly in fidelity or honesty. But it wasn't Liam, it was my mum wondering if I'd be going over to Canada in the summer to visit (I probably wouldn't be; I couldn't afford it for a start), asking if there were any suitable men at the cookery school and wishing us luck for a successful launch from both her and Dad.

'That was Mags practising her switchboard skills,' said Gloria. 'Your boxes have arrived from the printer.'

'Great. And that was my mum – my parents say good luck for Friday and send their regards.'

'I'm glad you keep in touch with your mum. Such a shame when she moved abroad, you must have missed her,

80

especially just when you and that chappie split up. What was his name?'

'Chris,' I said, focusing on keeping my voice neutral.

'You know, I got the impression Mimi felt very guilty when he called off your engagement and moved out, as if she was somehow to blame.'

'She wasn't,' I said. 'Chris and I had irreconcilable differences. He gave me an ultimatum that I wasn't prepared to give in to. At least it happened while we were only engaged. Better than six months into a marriage.'

She set a mug of tea on my desk and carried one for herself back to her own desk. 'You were such a godsend to Mimi when she was going through all that fertility treatment. What did you call yourselves?'

'Team Baby Green,' I said softly.

Me, Mimi and Gabe. The three of us against the world; at least that was how it had felt at the time.

'I don't think she'd have managed half as well without you.' Gloria sighed.

And now I don't manage half as well without her.

I swallowed the lump in my throat, pushing the unwanted memories down, deep down where they couldn't do any damage. 'Anyone would have done the same and I'd do it again in a heartbeat.'

'Still—' Gloria looked determined to discuss it, but I jumped in quickly to nip her in the bud.

'Mum says why not do a course for men? She's been married thirty-five years and Dad's repertoire still only runs to something on toast.'

'Actually, that's not a bad idea.' Gloria tapped her lip with her fingertip thoughtfully.

I thought about Gabe, attempting to cook tasty meals for him and Noah in that little galley kitchen on board *The Neptune.* I'd spoken to him the other night and he said he'd do his best to come to our open day on Friday. As had Rosie, who sounded like she was having a very stressful time at work. I hoped she'd come; I missed her energetic presence in my life.

I turned back to Gloria, who was mulling over possible course names. 'Meals for Men? It's a Man Thing? Meat and Two Veg?'

We both giggled at the last one.

I opened the course calendar on my computer screen and cast my eyes over it for inspiration. There were lots of lovely things on it, but most of them looked a bit daunting.

'How about Cooking for the Complete Beginner instead?' I suggested. 'That way it needn't just apply to men. I had tons of friends at uni who couldn't even boil an egg. You could also do Cooking for One, but that might sound a bit lonely, although it could turn into a sort of speed-dating course with the added benefit of learning new skills, I suppose.'

'Possibly. Let me look in my recipe bible.' She retrieved a large folder from her top drawer, popped on a pair of reading glasses and began flicking through it. 'There must be lots of people who suddenly find themselves partnerless or a single parent and struggle to adjust to cooking for one. But you're right; it does sound a bit grim.'

A summery memory of Mimi, Gloria and I playing a mammoth game of Monopoly and munching our way through bucketfuls of popcorn suddenly sprang to mind. Gloria had been partnerless as long as I'd known her but it had been anything but grim. I knew next to nothing about Mimi's father, I realized.

'Ah, here we go. Easy Entertaining, Simple Solo Suppers . . . I've got recipes for every occasion.'

'You were a one-parent family,' I began tentatively, watching as she separated out some sheets of paper and set them on her desk.

'Yes, although it was by choice. So no struggling involved.'

'Really?' I grinned at her.

She was such a feisty, independent character. Mind you, two weeks ago I was facing the prospect of being pregnant and had instinctively known I'd go it alone if necessary. Maybe I had more in common with her than I realized.

'I hit thirty and decided the time was right to have a baby. I was single at the time, but that didn't put me off. I persuaded a friend of mine to, you know, do the honours.' She mouthed the last part and I bit back a chuckle. 'Mimi saw him a few times when she was little. He was a cameraman at the studios when I met him; he runs a diving school in Thailand now. It wasn't a turkey-baster job but not far off.'

I choked on my tea and wondered whether she'd ever had this conversation with Mimi; it was certainly news to me. 'People really do that?'

'Oh yes.' Gloria nodded airily, twisting her bangles round on her wrist. 'We got there in the end with help from a couple of mucky mags. Fortunately, I turned out to be pretty fertile so it didn't take us many attempts. First and only time I've bought porn.'

My jaw dropped.

'Porn?' Tom appeared at the door to the office and startled us both. I hadn't seen him in his chef whites before. His sleeves were rolled up and his arms looked sinewy and strong and primed to debone a whole cow or something. He raised an amused eyebrow at me. 'Did I just hear that Gloria's been buying porn?'

'Er . . .' But before I had a chance to formulate an answer, Gloria flapped a hand at him.

'*Prawns*,' she said with a tinkly laugh. 'I was telling Verity about a monstrous seafood centrepiece I did for the Beeb set on a bed of ice. It took me three years to face a winkle after that.' She gave me a sideways glance and winked.

I bit back a snort.

Tom looked a bit confused but thankfully didn't ask any more questions.

'Right.' He stroked his stubbly jawline and nodded. 'Talking of fish, I've been invited to a taster evening on Wednesday with Fresh from the Sea, a new seafood supplier in York. The invitation was sent to me when I was still at my . . . the . . . you know, the old place, but I thought I'd still go; they might be useful contacts for the cookery school. Would you like to come with me, Gloria?'

Her shoulders sagged. 'I'd love to, but I can't spare the time this week. Verity could go, perhaps?'

'Would you?' He turned to me. 'According to the invitation, their seafood sounds amazing. They've got lobster, langoustines, oysters and there'll be a sashimi chef there too. Tempted?'

I hesitated. I still hadn't made up my mind about Tom. He was very attractive and my first impressions of him when he'd caught the dogs for me had been good. But he took his food so seriously that I wasn't sure an evening spent gargling oysters would be much fun at all.

'I'll pass if you don't mind,' I said. 'I'm more of a fish-finger girl myself. Having to coax something out of its shell before you can engage with it is not for me.'

'Really?' He tilted his chin. 'Personally, I like that sort of challenge. Never mind. I'll, er, go on my own.'

On his own? Now I felt bad. And hot. Why was I going red? We were only talking about crustaceans.

'Is it me,' I got to my feet and opened a window, 'or is it getting warm in here?'

'It'll be even warmer soon: I'm turning the ovens up to full temperature any minute.' He grinned.

Tom and Gloria began to discuss their schedule of last-minute jobs for the day and I retrieved my own to-do list. There wasn't much more I could do in the office. The website was ready, all the advertising was done and I'd booked an official photographer to take lots of shots of smiling people. I had some phone calls to make at some point but with Mags still answering the reception phone and Gloria and Tom debating the merits of flaky over puff pastry I couldn't concentrate in here.

'I'm popping out,' I announced. It was a warm sunny day – I could collect the leaflets from Mags and go and drop them off at shops, hair salons and local offices, starting at the little businesses nearby. 'I'm going to drum up business. Bye, Gloria. Enjoy the seafood tasting, I'll see you both later.'

'Bye.' Tom raised a hand and then clicked his fingers. 'Oh, while I remember! Just a date for your diary: we're having a run-through on Wednesday afternoon, trying out some of the canapés for the open day and testing a few dishes.'

'Will we get to taste the famous lime foam?' I teased.

'My food,' he said earnestly, 'will blow your mind.'

On Wednesday afternoon, Gloria, Mags, Pixie and I gathered in the Aga kitchen for our (certainly mine and Pixie's) first taste of Michelin-standard food. The aroma alone was making my mouth water. And after two days of solid promotion, either with the phone stuck to my ear or pacing the streets of Plumberry, I was really looking forward to this. The dogs had sneaked under the table, but Tom shot me a warning look as I began to lift Sage on to my knee.

'Sorry, doggy,' I whispered, pushing his little paws down to the floor.

Tom set a selection of platters on the table in front of us wordlessly. His forehead was creased with concentration and when I smiled to give him some encouragement, he didn't smile back. He certainly took this tasting business very seriously. I'd been anticipating a fun afternoon.

'This is all very grand,' exclaimed Mags, reaching for a pastry boat containing something fishy-looking. 'Don't mind if I do.'

'Not until I've talked you through the food,' said Tom briskly, whipping the platter away.

Mags tutted. 'Spoilsport.'

'So we have pear and gorgonzola crostini, venison meatballs with a plum sauce, asparagus mousse and crayfish pastry boats with lemon mayo,' said Tom, introducing each dish in turn. He leaned back against the front of the Aga. 'I've used local ingredients as much as possible.'

'Can we dig in *now*?' Mags asked.

Tom nodded and she launched herself at the crostini.

'Now,' she paused to pat the crumbs from her mouth, 'that is up there with my scouse recipe.'

His nostrils flared slightly. 'Thanks.'

'I'm not really into posh food.' Pixie took her glasses off and polished them on the bottom of her T-shirt. 'What's the point as long as it's tasty?'

'We eat with our eyes, Pixie,' Gloria explained.

The dogs were clamouring to climb on her knee and she pushed them away. 'When I worked in television, I learned to make the most of that. Presentation is very important. All right, all right, boys, I'll find something for you.'

She rummaged in her handbag for dog food.

'Hmm.' Pixie looked unconvinced as she picked up a meatball and wrinkled her nose. She shrugged. 'It all looks the same when it comes out the other end, as my granddad would say. God love him.'

Mags, who had been reaching for a tiny china spoon filled with asparagus mousse, pulled a face and took a sip of water instead. As if Pixie's image wasn't vivid enough Gloria chose that moment to tear the top off a sachet of meaty chunks in gravy and tip it into the dogs' bowl.

I swallowed hard and even Tom looked pale.

'It all looks amazing, Tom, well done,' exclaimed Gloria, turning her attention back to the canapés. After washing her hands she lifted a pastry boat to her mouth and then hesitated. 'Although . . .'

Tom raked a hand through his hair and exhaled impatiently. 'Although . . . ?'

She squirmed under his stare. 'I'm just wondering whether it might be too . . . cheffy. Does it really say comfort food?'

Tom threw up his hands. 'Fine, let's serve everyone cheese straws, shall we? That will certainly impress them. Come to The Plumberry School of Comfort Food and learn how to open packets. Brilliant. Absolutely brilliant.'

He marched over to the Aga, muttering to himself, and the rest of us exchanged awkward glances. He opened the oven door and slammed another tray of food on to the cooling rack. I caught the words 'why do I bother' and my heart squeezed for him.

'I think this is exactly what we should be serving, and that's coming from Princess Prick and Ping,' I said softly, hoping to thaw the atmosphere. 'Tom, I've never tasted anything like it. It's edible art. And whether people who come to our open day ever cook like this at home or not, the food that they taste when they're here will probably stay with them for ever.'

'That's true, Verity,' said Gloria humbly. 'I'm overthinking it. Forgive me, Tom.'

'Nothing to forgive,' he assured her, placing a new plate in front of her. He sprinkled chopped parsley over it from a height. The way really cheffy types do. 'Goose and chestnut chipolatas. Enjoy.'

'Well, it gets my vote.' Mags speared a piece and ate it. 'Posh. In a nice way,' she added hastily.

'I'm inspired,' I continued, dipping a venison meatball into the fruity sauce. 'You make me want to be a better cook, Tom.'

My stomach flipped as I was speaking. I'd started off with the aim of mollifying our highly strung chef, but now I realized that there was a kernel of truth in my words.

His dark eyes softened and he nodded.

'Me too,' said Pixie in a small voice.

'Tom's performed his magic on these ingredients,

transforming them into something incredible, just like you've done with this old mill, Gloria.' I looked at her and then at Tom. 'I think your dishes are the perfect way to welcome visitors into the cookery school on Friday.'

'Hear, hear,' cried Mags, giving him a round of applause.

'Just as well,' he said gruffly, but I could see he was pleased, 'because there are enough supplies to make two hundred of each canapé in the larder. And Pixie, I'm expecting you to help me.'

'Two hundred!' Pixie gasped. 'Well, that ought to sharpen my knife skills.'

Tom's eyes met mine. *Thank you*, he mouthed across the table when no one was looking. He looked at his watch and winced. 'Right, final call for the seafood tasting in York. Any takers?'

We all shook our heads so Tom left alone.

'Don't eat anything dodgy,' I called after him. 'We need you in tip-top condition for the rest of the week!'

Chapter 9

At eight o'clock the following morning, the landline at the cottage rang. Gloria was out walking the dogs, so I picked up the phone.

'Uhuhuf,' said a muffled voice, followed by a long moan.

'Pervert,' I replied briskly and replaced the receiver with a tut. I had enough to do today without listening to heavy breathers.

It rang again almost immediately. Right, this time I was ready for him. I picked it up and inhaled ready to emit a piercing squeal when the person on the other end spoke.

'Verity, don't hang up,' croaked a man, sounding less pervy this time.

'Who is this?' I frowned.

'I must have eaten something dodgy at the Fresh from the Sea party.'

This time I recognized the Irish accent, even if it was barely above a whisper. It was Tom. And he brought me bad news.

Half an hour later I pulled into the car park. *Stay calm*, I reminded myself. We had over twenty-four hours until the start of the open day. Surely Tom would have recovered by then? Of course he would; it probably wasn't food poisoning at all, maybe he'd just overdone it with the free drinks last night.

My phone beeped as I climbed out of the car and I glanced at the text.

I've called the doc because I've just coughed up blood.

Poor Tom. OK, maybe it wasn't the booze.

All but one of the tradesmen's vans had gone from the car park and only Neil was still here, hanging a beautiful plum and cream sign bearing the cookery school's name above the doors. We exchanged our hellos and I ducked underneath the ladders and went inside. Mags was already sitting in reception going through emails and Pixie was practising her barista skills on the new coffee machine.

'I prefer instant really,' she admitted, placing a tray of frothy lattes on Mags's desk. 'But don't tell Tom. I had to listen to a lecture about the world's best coffee beans yesterday. Panama, in case you're interested.'

'Have you got plenty to be getting on with, Pixie?' I asked, blowing the top of my steaming latte.

'Loads.' She nodded. 'Gloria wants the cheese-making equipment set up upstairs to do demos tomorrow and Tom left me a list as long as his face yesterday and I'm only half-way through it. Why?'

'Because Tom's going to be late in.'

I explained that he could barely crawl away from the bathroom, he was vomiting so much. Which must have been rather unpleasant for the friend whose flat Tom was staying at. I left out the bit about the blood.

'Hell's teeth,' Mags grumbled, tipping an Everest-sized mountain of brown sugar crystals into her latte. 'Whatever you do, don't tell Gloria, she's a bag of nerves. She's already asked me twice this morning how many are booked on to the One Pot Wonders course on Monday. Only four so far and she's panicking that someone will drop out. She's also convinced that everything has been

90

going too well and something was bound to go wrong at the last minute.'

We stared at each other ominously. The last thing she needed to hear was that her chef was indisposed for the foreseeable future.

'What if he doesn't come back in time to make all those canopies?' Pixie frowned so hard that her drawn-on eyebrows joined up.

'*Canapés*. He'll be back.' *Hopefully*. I gulped. 'Where's Gloria now?'

'Practising her garnishes.' Mags inclined her head to the staircase. 'She's been carving turtles out of melons since I arrived.'

'OK.' I nodded, racking my brains to think how we could prevent her panicking. 'We need to keep her out of the way until Tom gets back. Perhaps we could suggest she goes home for a few hours?'

Mags gave a bark of laughter then held out her perfectly painted nails and examined them.

'No chance. She won't relax until the cookery school is well and truly open at noon tomorrow.'

'Then we've got to make her relax.' My eyes glittered as a bright idea occurred to me. 'Let's tell her that as a surprise we've organized some pampering for her at the beauty salon in Plumberry.'

'My mate works there,' Pixie put in. She took off her glasses and breathed on them, polishing them on her T-shirt. 'She'll fit Gloria in as a favour.'

'She could have a lavender massage and a manicure,' Mags suggested. 'I always have those when I'm feeling low or tense.'

I flicked a curious glance at Mags; I couldn't imagine her ever being low.

'And what about a hair-do tomorrow morning before we open?' I added. 'We can tell her she needs to look her best for the photos.'

Mags blew me a kiss. 'Brilliant. She'll be made up. Who's going to tell her?'

'You!' Pixie and I chanted together.

Our plan worked, although Gloria took some considerable persuading to take the rest of the day off. But I was glad we'd done what we'd done. Tom rang me at lunchtime, full of apologies for letting the side down, but he was still too ill to leave the house.

'We'll cope,' I'd said staunchly and wished him a speedy recovery.

And for the next three hours I'd sat glued to my desk, doing my best to whip up a media frenzy in advance of tomorrow's launch.

Late in the afternoon, Pixie came to bring me a mochaccino. 'I'm getting the hang of this machine. As long as I only have to churn out one drink every ten minutes, we'll be fine.'

I inhaled the chocolatey aroma and took a sip. 'Mmm, I needed that, thank you.' I sighed.

She flopped down at Gloria's desk. 'You look like you've lost your winning lottery ticket.'

'I've just been chasing the press to see who's covering our open day.' I gave her a weary smile.

'And?'

'No one.'

She grimaced. 'No way? I'd have thought they'd be clamouring to come and have a look. Especially with Tom working here.'

I sat back in my chair and glanced down at my list. 'Yorkshire FM says they might do something next week if we can give them a juicy prize. I can't get a reply from the news desk at the regional TV station. The business journalist for the *York Mail* is at a meeting with the council about inward investment . . .'

We shared a how-boring-is-that look.

'And the entertainment person is at a press conference with Meryl Streep of all people.'

'There must be a food journo, can't he or she come?' Pixie frowned.

'*He*. And unfortunately not because he was at a tasting in York last night and has been tossing his cockles all night.'

'Isn't it supposed to be "tossing his *cookies*"?'

My lips twitched with a smile. 'Not when you've been to the Fresh from the Sea party.'

'Euwww.' Pixie leaned her elbows on the desk and grinned wickedly. 'I bet Tom's gutted. *Gutted*.'

I giggled. 'At least he'll be lighter when he gets on the *scales*.'

'Yeah and more crabby than usual tomorrow,' she countered.

'Or perhaps he'll still be tossing his cockles . . .'

And then both of us realized just how terrible that would be and the thought instantly wiped the smirks off our faces.

I awoke the next morning to a text from Tom. He was a dried husk of a man with nothing else to throw up, he said; however, he thought the worst was over. He'd be at the opening at noon, but didn't think he could manage to face food let alone prepare canapés. He was very, very sorry.

So was I.

My fingers trembled as I texted back 'OK'. We were expecting around one hundred people to turn up to taste the delights of the Plumberry School of Comfort Food in five hours. My mind flitted back to the canapés that Tom had presented to us on Wednesday. Somehow I was going to have to produce those with Mags and Pixie's help. And what about Gloria? If I admitted to her that Tom was ill and that I'd known about it yesterday, she'd probably start throwing up herself.

I threw back the covers, stood in front of the mirror and drew a deep breath. No more shying away from it, Verity Bloom, it was time to get back in the kitchen.

An hour later, the cookery school seemed to crackle with nervous energy as I beckoned Mags and Pixie up the beautiful wrought-iron staircase to deliver the news about Tom's continued absence.

I stood at the teaching workstation and cast my eye across the room. In four hours this space would be buzzing with expectant guests, all eager to sample, explore and hopefully sign up for a cookery course on the spot.

And everything was riding on the three of us.

I handed Mags and Pixie a brand-new apron with our logo on it and they eyed me warily. You and me both, I thought, my fingers fumbling with the ties as I wrapped the strings round my waist. Still, I was determined not to let them sense my nerves.

I'd left Gloria at home this morning still wrapped in her robe, sipping Earl Grey. 'I feel awfully guilty,' she'd protested. 'Swanning off to the hairdresser's while everyone else is slaving away.'

'It's all in hand,' I'd reassured her smoothly. 'And as the saying goes, "too many cooks . . ."'

Too many cooks wasn't going to be a problem for us this morning. I studied my team surreptitiously as Mags struggled to do up the apron round her ample curves and Pixie formed an 'O' with her mouth and began making Red Indian noises with a pink silicone spatula against her lips.

Mags was a competent if unrefined cook; Pixie was, well, *enthusiastic* at most and me, I was . . . How best to describe my own skills? Rusty? Dormant?

A sensation like the fizz of sherbet began to build in my stomach and I felt my body tingle. I could do this, I knew it.

There was another saying: if you can't stand the heat, get

out of the kitchen. And for two years that was exactly what I'd done. Only in my case, it was grief and not heat that had kept me away. But there was no time for dwelling on that today, no time for self-indulgent thoughts of how much I still missed Mimi and how life would have been different for me, Gabe and Noah if she'd still been here. Gloria needed me and if Mimi were here I knew exactly what she'd have said . . .

'Let's have some fun in the kitchen this morning.' I beamed at my fellow cooks. 'Let's show Tom what we're made of.'

'Phwoar,' said Mags. She leaned on the worktop and grinned. 'I'd love to show that boy what I'm made of.'

I was sure he could guess, I thought, trying not to stare at the deep V-shaped cleavage on display in front of me. Today's ensemble consisted of a pillar-box-red knee-length wrap dress, chunky pearls and, judging by the smell, a generous spritz of perfume.

'Sugar and spice and all things nice, I reckon, Mags. You are looking particularly gorgeous today,' I said, giving her a hug. 'Right, who's got the list of recipes?'

'Me!' Pixie piped up. 'Asparagus mousse, poached rhubarb with blue cheese on rye bread, crayfish pastry boats . . .'

Mags tootled backwards and forwards to the storeroom, fetching all the ingredients, while Pixie read through the instructions for each canapé. I felt my confidence begin to ebb away and my knees turn to jelly as the pile of complicated supplies grew. Tom had planned on whipping these magnificent mouthfuls up for a hundred guests. He was a professional, cooking his own recipes, which he'd perfected to a T. We didn't have a hope of producing all that lot. Yet the food was bought and paid for and looking at us reproachfully, and really what other choice did we have?

'Let's not bite off more than we can chew,' I said

decisively. 'Maybe we should adapt Tom's recipes to make them simpler?'

Mags clutched her chest gratefully. 'You took the words right out of my mouth.'

I looked at Pixie. 'What's your signature dish?'

She looked up from Tom's notes. 'Eh?'

'What do you think you could make?'

She screwed her face up. 'Er . . . In the cheese shop we do pieces of cheese served with a tiny smear of quince jelly. They always go down well.'

'OK.' I nodded, scribbling a note on the paper. Cubes of cheese on cocktail sticks. I suppressed a chuckle at what Tom would make of that.

'What about you, Mags?'

She cast her eye over the wealth of fine ingredients spread across the work surface and paled. 'I could always do a pan of scouse? Cheap, easy and good for feeding a crowd. And Tom loved it.'

A memory of Tom turning down a helping of Mags's pickled onions sprang to mind and I arranged my features into a diplomatic smile.

'It would be tasty,' I agreed. 'But it needs to be finger food. Do you think you could manage the asparagus mousse?'

She looked at me aghast and twisted her pearls. 'No.'

'Oh.' I stared mournfully at the ten fat bunches of delicate stems.

'But I could wrap the asparagus in Yorkshire ham and roast it?' she offered.

'Perfect,' I beamed. 'Now what can we do with all this rhubarb?'

'That is from the rhubarb triangle.' Pixie leaned forward conspiratorially and tapped her nose. 'Where strange disappearances happen.'

I didn't like to point out that she was getting Bradford confused with Bermuda.

'If it's *Yorkshire* rhubarb we must use that somehow,' I said.

'My granddad used to swear by stewed rhubarb every day with condensed milk,' Pixie went on. 'Said it kept him regular.'

'Rhubarb crumble!' I jumped in quick before we got another anecdote about Granddad's bowels.

'Now that's what I call comfort food. We can use those dinky little spoons Tom got for the asparagus mousse and serve it by the mouthful.'

'And I bet I could manage the meatballs, although I might give that plum sauce a miss. So we've all got a job,' said Mags, rolling up her sleeves. 'Ready, steady, cook!'

For the next couple of hours the three of us got stuck in. Pixie fetched a radio and we merrily chopped, stirred and whisked like fury along to the music until the first dishes were in the oven or, in Mags's case, prepped and ready to roast later.

'So far so good,' I said, fanning my face with the oven gloves. I checked the clock. 'We've still got time for another dish each.'

'Can I make gingerbread men?' Pixie asked.

'Sure.' I shrugged.

'Then I can decorate them all. No two men will be the same, just like the human race. Every one will be an individual. It'll be my statement. Rich or poor, black or white—'

'Or ginger,' Mags interrupted.

'We may all be different on the outside,' Pixie said philosophically, 'but inside we're just the same.'

'That's very deep,' Mags chuckled, 'for a biscuit. I think I'll make mini roast potatoes; we can serve them on sticks with some herby mayonnaise.'

'I tell you what I can't find,' I said over my shoulder while rummaging in the fridge, 'and that's those goose sausages.'

Tom had served them tapas-style dotted with a relish made from blueberries and sprinkled with parsley. I'd been

planning to grill them, chop them up and serve them on –
yes – yet more cocktail sticks. At this rate, everyone would
be thinking they'd stepped back in time to a seventies
finger buffet. All we needed was a potato decorated to look
like a hedgehog to complete the look.

'He made them from scratch,' Pixie pointed out. 'We've
got a sausage machine in the storeroom. Great it is. Tom let
me have a go. Reminded me of the time a lady came into
school to show us how to put condoms on bananas.'

I giggled, wondering whether she'd shared that particular
story with Tom.

'It reminds *me* of a TV programme back in the seventies. People competed for naff prizes by doing things like
making sausages.' Mags chuckled at the memory. 'It was a
scream. Sausages spewing out everywhere quicker than the
contestants could catch them.'

'TV was so weird in the olden days.' Pixie shook her
head.

'Sounds daft but the contestants loved it and it was great
to watch,' Mags insisted.

I slammed the fridge door and whipped round to face
them.

'Of course! Mags, that's it!' I cried. 'This is a cookery
school. Not a restaurant. And I've had an idea: let's give
our guests a hands-on experience. Why not let *them* make
sausages and roll out pastry and decorate their own
gingerbread men? It'll be fun! That's what cooking should
be about. Sorry, Pixie,' I added, spotting her crestfallen face
as she put the cookie cutters down.

'Verity's right,' said Mags. 'Let's concentrate on finishing
off the canapés that aren't entertainment-friendly and then
set up different stations around the room.'

'Gloria can do garnishes,' I said excitedly. 'Mags can
look after decorating biscuits, Pixie can be in charge of the
sausage machine . . .' Pixie punched the air. 'And I'll do
the pastry,' I finished.

'Gloria was right about you,' Mags beamed. 'This opening party is going to go with a bang.'

She and Pixie immediately sprang into action and I felt my heart swell with happiness.

Two weeks ago Rosie had asked me what made me happy and I hadn't been able to answer. But now I could. The Plumberry School of Comfort Food had reawakened my love of food.

Verity Bloom, the cook, was back.

Chapter 10

By eleven thirty, the three of us were pink-cheeked but ex-hilarated by our efforts. We had finished cooking, washed up and even managed to make ourselves look presentable. The cookery school was looking pretty good too.

Mags had gone to town in reception, polishing every surface until it shone and arranging jugfuls of lilies in each corner.

'Looks a bit like a tart's boudoir,' she'd commented, adding with a wink, 'but if the cap fits . . .'

The Aga kitchen was set out informally with trays of soft drinks and bowls of snacks dotted around the tables, and the cookery school leaflets spread casually among them. Pixie had retrieved some bread dough that Tom had made earlier in the week from the freezer and it was proving plumply ready to pop into the Aga any minute and entice people in with the smell of fresh bread. The doors to the deck were wide open and the sound of birds singing in the trees opposite and the gentle burbling of the river made the setting even more idyllic.

Upstairs, the teaching kitchen boasted the inviting aromas of coffee (Pixie had made some last-minute coffee granita following a YouTube video), gingerbread and vanilla, and the space was warm and welcoming, light and bright. The little pots of utensils stood to attention on every workstation and there were activities and food samples galore.

I left Pixie and Mags trying to work out how to use the cheese-making equipment and ran down to let the photographer in. Ellen was a stout Yorkshire woman with a bullet-proof hairdo and a reporter's notepad tucked into the waistband of her sensible slacks. My plan was for her to take shots of the cookery school in its 'calm before the storm' state: picture perfect and ready to party.

And the Plumberry School of Comfort Food was just that.

I briefed her quickly and left her taking arty shots of the Aga and just made it back into reception to see Gloria arrive, arm in arm with Gabe who was gawping at his surroundings in amazement.

'Look who turned up to chauffeur me here!' she beamed, her happiness shining out from her face. 'My handsome son-in-law!'

'Wouldn't have missed today for the world.' He rubbed a hand through his curls and grinned at me in a dopey way that I found impossible not to return. I reached up to kiss his cheek.

'Lovely to see you, Gabe.'

'Hey, Bloomers,' he whispered.

I tutted and pretended to look cross.

'No Noah?' I asked, feeling a stab of disappointment in my chest. I'd missed the little boy since being in Plumberry.

Gabe shook his head. 'He's with Granny. His other granny,' he corrected, shooting Gloria an apologetic look. 'I had some work stuff to do en route.'

'But they're both coming up to stay for a week soon, aren't you, darling boy?' she added.

Gloria was radiant, whether it was from the twenty-four hours of enforced relaxation or the nearness of her son-in-law, I couldn't tell. Her hair had been styled off her face in soft honey waves, her skin looked bright and her eyes sparkled. At some point I'd have to take her aside and explain the changes to the day, and about Tom's illness, but not quite yet. Everything had worked out beautifully and there was no need to worry her unnecessarily.

Gabe nodded. 'We've made a pact to see each other once a month from now on.'

'I'm glad,' I said, nodding fervently. 'And Mimi would be too.'

I know she regarded me as a daughter, but in reality Gabe and Noah were the only family Gloria had. It broke my heart that they had been seeing each other so rarely. Perhaps now that the cookery school was finally open, Gloria would allow herself a bit more time off; since I'd been in Plumberry, she'd consistently worked twelve-hour days.

Gloria swept us both in for another hug and the three of us stood in silence for a moment thinking of the darling girl who was missing from today's celebrations.

'Are you going to do an opening speech?' I asked, finally looking at my watch and then noticing her taupe peep-toe heels. 'You're looking fab, by the way. Those shoes are too cute.'

Gloria released Gabe and lifted up a foot. 'Thanks. Not at all practical and if I slip on a puddle of spilt milk, I'll know about it. But just for once I'd like to be able to look people in the eye and not the Adam's apple. I will give a speech, I just want to give Gabe a guided tour, before everyone arrives. Come on, Gabe – first the view of our river, to make you feel at home.'

He flashed me a grin as Gloria hooked her arm through his again. 'Catch up with you later, Verity.'

A small crowd had gathered already and several people were pressing their noses against the glass.

I popped my head outside. 'Five minutes, ladies and gentlemen, and we'll be open, I promise.'

'I hope you've got the kettle on, I'm parched,' called the cheeky old chap I'd met during our Plumberry market research day.

'We have indeed and it'll be worth the wait, I promise.' I grinned at the old man. 'See you shortly.'

Just then Tom pushed through the crowd and I stood back to let him in.

'You made it!' I exhaled with relief, taking Tom's arm and drawing him away from the entrance doors. 'How are you feeling?'

'Pathetic, to be honest.' He rubbed a hand across his face.

'I am *so* relieved to see you,' I said, laughing softly.

His complexion was on the yellow side and he was walking gingerly as if every muscle in his body ached but he managed a weak smile.

'I think that's the nicest thing you've ever said to me.'

'None of us can use the cheese-making kit.'

He blinked at me and nodded. 'Oh, right.'

He looked through to the Aga kitchen, I glanced down at my toes and for a moment neither of us spoke.

I cleared my throat. 'But apart from that, we managed. Mags, Pixie and I have been cooking all morning.'

'I bet that microwave has been doing overtime, hasn't it?' he said with a weak laugh.

'No,' I said a bit defensively. 'We've made everything from scratch. Not up to your standards, of course, but,' I lifted a shoulder casually, 'I hope you approve.'

My admission took me by surprise; but it was true. I wanted him to taste my food, I wanted his opinion and, more than anything, I wanted him to be impressed with what we'd achieved at short notice.

He rested a hand on my arm and gazed at me really intensely. 'I already approve. It was my job to cater for today and I let Gloria down. But I haven't managed to keep anything down yet and the thought of cooking. . .' He shuddered. 'Anyway, I know you're not a keen cook, yet you came to my rescue. I really appreciate that, Verity. Thank you.'

'My pleasure,' I said, going pink. And it had been a

pleasure. Spending time in the kitchen with Mags and Pixie had been fun.

'And is everything else OK, no other problems?'

I wrinkled my nose. 'I wanted at least one newspaper to attend today. We've got our own photographer, but it makes it more exciting for everyone when the press turns up.' I gave myself a little shake. 'Not to worry. There's still plenty to be glad about.'

'There is,' Tom agreed. He leaned down and pressed a kiss to my cheek. 'You've done a brilliant job, Verity, you should be proud.'

'Tom!' Gloria rushed forward to greet him. 'Let me introduce my son-in-law, Gabe.'

Gabe looked from Tom to me and raised a questioning eyebrow.

And then someone banged on the door to tell us it was noon and Mags and Pixie appeared. Gloria flung the doors back and suddenly the cookery school was open.

The great and the good of Plumberry flooded into reception and we all scurried into our hosting positions. Tom went up to sort out the cheese demonstration and Gabe became the unofficial leaflet distributor while Gloria stood at the entrance greeting each and every guest as they arrived.

Ellen the photographer was doing a sterling job recording the event and I even caught her balancing precariously on a swivel chair at the edge of Gloria's office, taking a wide-angled shot of the teaching kitchen.

The sausage machine, with Pixie at the helm, was creating much hilarity and Tom and I exchanged bemused glances when two women began a tongue-in-cheek competition about the size of their sausages.

Mags's gingerbread-men decorating activity went down a storm with children and adults alike and the photographer, having obtained their parents' permission, snapped away as a group of little ones chomped into their handiwork.

'No close-ups, please,' Mags informed the photographer briskly as she bent down, arms round some children posing with the mixing bowls. 'Those days are behind me.'

'You look all right from where I'm standing,' said Dave the accountant, who promptly turned a charming shade of pink.

'Oh.' Mags blinked at him, lost for an innuendo for once.

'Just in time, Dave,' said Gloria, handing him a spoonful of rhubarb crumble. (Almost as good as his own, Tom had said, perhaps add a touch of ginger next time?) 'I'm about to hold forth.'

Gloria made a speech about how thrilled she was to be opening a cookery school in Plumberry and that on Monday her dream would finally come true when she taught her first class. Her voice wavered when she said that sharing her love of food with people had begun when her beloved daughter was born and she'd been doing it ever since. At which point Tom stepped forward and proposed a toast to the Plumberry School of Comfort Food, Gloria kissed him lavishly in gratitude and we all raised our teacups and squash glasses. I hugged everyone, including Dave, who had managed to wedge himself in the corner with Mags, and Tom, who said that my crayfish pastry boats looked delicious but he wouldn't try one if it was all the same. In fact, he might not be eating seafood again for quite some time.

After a hectic hour, I snaffled one of Pixie's unadorned gingerbread men, poured myself a cup of coffee and headed to the deck for a breather. A large group of mums had commandeered the table nearest the door – their babies asleep in prams or on knees – and I edged past them to the end of the deck. I leaned on the balustrade nibbling my biscuit and stared up at the cookery school.

I spotted Gloria chatting animatedly in the middle of a crowd through the first-floor window and my heart melted to see her so happy.

I was happy too. Elated, in fact. Today was the most time I'd spent in a kitchen *actually cooking* since Mimi had died. And it made me feel whole again. I'd been an idiot to cut something out of my life that had made me so happy. Cooking was like therapy: while my hands were busy my mind unravelled its knots and made sense of things. Maybe if I hadn't abandoned cooking, it wouldn't have taken me so long to get over Mimi's death?

I turned away from the building and stared out across the river instead.

My time in Plumberry was nearly up. Although I wasn't privy to Gloria's finances, I was pretty sure she'd be glad not to have to pay me a salary for much longer. And she would be fine without me now that the cookery school was open. I'd shown Pixie how to update the website with new courses – she'd picked it up impressively speedily – and I could carry on getting the leaflets printed from Nottingham.

I'd go home. Soon. Perhaps next week. I'd start looking for jobs. And I'd cook every day. For Rosie and for Gabe, perhaps. I'd even start teaching Noah how to bake; it was never too early.

I felt a stirring in the pit of my stomach. There was a new start coming for me, I could feel it, and instead of shying away as I might have done a few weeks ago, I was ready. Bring it on . . .

Would that be OK, Mimi? If I spend more time with Noah? I'd hate you to think I was taking your place.

A flash of vivid blue caught my eye and I looked up to see a small bird on a branch in front of me. He was incredibly beautiful, with a bright orange chest and turquoise wings.

Dave joined me at the balustrade and whistled quietly. 'A kingfisher. A rare treat.'

I smiled at him and held my breath, watching as the little bird dipped down to the water and then returned to the branch. He repeated it a couple of times and then took flight, swooping low across the water and upstream out of sight.

'That was beautiful,' I breathed, turning to face him.

'Some people say that if you see a kingfisher, it's time to dive into a new activity or possibly a new love will enter your life.'

'That's funny, I was just thinking about a new direction.' I popped the last of my gingerbread man into my mouth and laughed. 'Not sure about the new love, though.'

Dave looked at me earnestly. 'Don't be afraid of trying the new. You won't drown.'

There was something other-worldly about Dave, as if he was some sort of guru. Perhaps there was something in that Ashtanga yoga. Whatever it was, I felt deeply touched by his words.

'Thank you, Dave.'

'I'll leave you to your thoughts.' He patted my arm. 'Namaste.'

He made to leave but I caught hold of his sleeve. 'I've always wondered what that means.'

He smiled softly. 'It means the spirit in me salutes the spirit in you. And you have a wonderful spirit, Verity. I can feel that.'

I felt quite emotional after that.

As soon as I'd dealt with the rush of tears that Dave's lovely words had produced, I wandered back inside and for the next half an hour I supervised the cooking of the home-made sausages next to Pixie's sausage machine. I flipped and prodded and shook the pan while sausages sizzled and then sliced them into pieces.

'Wow!' Pixie's eyes widened and she nudged me sharply. 'Girl crush at two o'clock.'

She motioned towards the top of the stairs with her head to where a girl with black hair and a turned-up nose stood poised, scanning the room and shoving her sunglasses up on to her head.

My heart squeezed and I felt my cheeks lift as I smiled my widest smile.

Pixie gasped. 'She's like something out of a chocolate advert.'

'Rosie!' I pushed the pan off the heat and darted through the crowd to hug her. Pixie followed close behind.

'Look at you!' Rosie flung her arms round me. 'I've missed you, oh tiny one.'

'Not so tiny now,' I said, pinching an inch from my waist.

'Rubbish,' Pixie laughed. 'As my granddad would say, there's more meat on a butcher's pencil.'

Rosie snorted and Pixie beamed with pleasure.

'So what do you think?' I extended an arm and waved it round the room. 'Gorgeous, isn't it?'

'Fab,' agreed Rosie, snaffling some chocolate from a plate. 'And do you know what's more fab?'

I shook my head.

'You.' She jabbed a finger in my chest. 'You've got your mojo back.'

A lump appeared in my throat so I simply nodded.

'Yum yum, pig's bum,' said Rosie, popping cubes of chocolate into her mouth one after the other like coins into a parking meter.

'Apple pie and chewing gum,' chanted Pixie and Rosie together.

'Twins!' yelped Pixie, throwing an arm round Rosie's neck.

At that moment there was a grinding crunch, followed by a howl of disappointment.

Pixie tutted. 'That soddin' sausage machine has jammed again,' she grumbled. 'Excuse me.'

And she stomped away to sort it out.

I looped my arm through Rosie's and led her to a couple of spare stools next to Mags's meatballs and we spent a lovely few minutes having a good catch-up. She told me all about the hush-hush project she'd been selected to head up at work and I admitted that being in Plumberry had worked its magic and I was ready to tackle life again.

'It was almost as if I'd been afraid to enjoy myself, afraid to be *me* without her. And that's wrong, isn't it?' I gazed at Rosie, who squeezed my hand encouragingly. 'I wouldn't have wanted her to do that, if I'd have been the one to go.'

'Course you wouldn't. Oh, hot diggity damn, look at that.' Rosie nodded her head to where Tom was leading a man with a microphone and another with a TV camera into the room. 'Sorry, Verity, I'll have to go: if I get caught on camera, I'll be fired. *Capisce?*'

'Not really,' I murmured, only half listening.

This was amazing. Where had the TV crew come from? The researcher had said categorically that no one would be able to make it. But who cared why; they *had* made it! This would put the cookery school on the map.

I grinned at her. 'This has made my day, Rosie. The cherry on my cake.'

'Not for me it isn't. I'm supposed to be at a conference in Harrogate. The boss will go crackers if he finds out I didn't go. Ciao, gorge.' She planted a kiss on my cheek and then held me at arm's length. 'Oh, by the way, I get it now.'

'Get what?'

'Your fixation with Gabe.' She nodded towards where he was chatting to Dave, both of them leaning on the window-sill, deep in conversation. 'He *is* very cute.'

Fixation?

'I do not . . . that's rubbish!' I gasped.

She cocked an eyebrow. 'Verity Bloom, you talk about him all the time.'

But before I could challenge her she kissed my cheek, skirted the room to avoid the TV cameras and made a speedy exit, shouting *arrivederci* over her shoulder.

By six o'clock, the party was over. The crowds, including Gabe, had gone and only the staff plus Dave remained. It had been a brilliant day – exhausting, but brilliant. We all gathered in the office round Mags's portable TV, which she'd popped home to fetch (along with Comfrey and Sage, who were now doing a fantastic job of hoovering up crumbs). The regional news crew had promised to squeeze the cookery school piece in at the end of the programme just before the weather report and there was a definite whiff of celebration in the air amongst us.

Gloria popped open a bottle of Prosecco and handed round glasses. 'While we wait I'd just like to congratulate Verity on securing the press coverage. Really, darling, I didn't expect TV, well done!'

'Oh, but it wasn't me,' I protested. 'I got a flat no when I phoned them.'

I noticed a secretive smile on Tom's face. And then he winked.

Of course! Tom was a Michelin-starred chef. He was bound to have good press contacts. One call from him and the media would come running. Silly of me not to have thought of that myself.

'It was—' I began.

'Shush, everyone, it's on,' Tom interrupted.

As many of you know, Plumberry is already a plum destination for epicureans and now a new cookery school in the village is set to raise the bar even higher . . .

The footage only lasted a few seconds, but it was enough to show the cookery school looking lovely, the open day in full swing, Pixie sharing a giggle with a group of old ladies as they taught her how to crimp pastry the old-fashioned way, a pale Tom chopping onions at the speed of light and ending with an excited quote from Gloria. And thankfully not a glimpse of Rosie. Gloria burst into tears. Happy tears, she insisted as she topped up everyone's glass.

We gravitated out of the office and back into the teaching kitchen and I sidled up to Tom who was perched against the teacher's workstation. He looked a lot better now, his skin was less yellow and the shadows under his eyes had begun to fade.

'Did you call up the TV people?'

'Yes. You did my job today, it was only fair I helped with yours,' he murmured. 'You can take the credit for that one. On one condition.' He waggled his eyebrows.

'Go on.'

'No more Princess Prick and Ping.'

'Deal,' I giggled. 'Although I do cook a mean fish finger sandwich.'

Tom shuddered. 'Not fish. Anything but that.'

We shared a laugh and then he leaned closer.

'Listen. A mate of mine wants me to buy his restaurant from him. I'm spending the weekend with him to take a closer look at the business. And if I can sort . . . things . . . the finances out, I'm sorely tempted. I'd need some help with marketing if you're interested?'

'I thought you said my ideas were tacky?' I grinned at him mischievously. 'Besides, I know you only planned on staying for a month, but realistically Gloria is going to need help with the teaching more permanently, I reckon.'

He sighed and raked a hand through his dark hair. 'I totally get what she's trying to do here, and I admire her for it, but teaching comfort food?' He exhaled and shook his head. 'I'm not sure it's for me. I'm used to fine dining. That's what I want to get back to.'

I peered at him over the rim of my Prosecco glass. Despite having worked in the same place for the past couple of weeks, we'd scarcely spent any time together alone and I was dying to dig deeper, to find out more about Tom's restaurant, Salinger's. Why had he left so suddenly and why did he seem to stumble over his words whenever he mentioned it?

111

I was just formulating a diplomatic question when Gloria waved another Prosecco bottle in the air.

'Is anyone in a hurry to get home?' she cried. 'Because if not, I've got a few more bottles of bubbly downstairs?'

'Let's not drink all the profits, though, eh, Gloria,' Dave joked, holding his palms up in a slow-down motion. At least, I think he was joking.

Gloria stalked towards the staircase in her high heels. 'It's a special day, Dave. I'm on a high and I want to celebr— Arrgghh!'

I jumped up helplessly as the sole of Gloria's shoe slipped on a morsel of food and in awful slow motion I watched in horror, a scream forming on my lips, while she tumbled down the first flight of stairs. She cried out, the bottle smashed as she landed and then there was silence.

Mags, Pixie, Dave, Tom and I raced to the stairs and almost fell down them in our haste.

Gloria lay on her side on the half-landing between the flights of stairs, surrounded by glass, her legs propped up on the lower stairs and her face the colour of uncooked pastry.

'Gloria!' Mags cried in a shaky voice. 'Don't move, chuck, stay still.'

But there was no response. I felt sick with worry and fell to my knees beside her. How could this happen now, just when everything was looking so rosy for her, for all of us?

Tom pulled his mobile from his pocket and called for an ambulance. Pixie and I began removing shards of glass from her hands and face and Dave gently patted her body to check for broken bones.

'It's on its way,' said Tom grimly.

'It's going to be OK, Gloria,' I whispered, unsure if she could hear me. Sobs choked my throat as I stroked her cheek. 'Hang on in there.'

Tom squatted beside me and laid a hand on my shoulder.

I looked at Gloria lying unconscious and then at him, his dark features pinched with concern.

After the conversation we'd just had, I wondered what was going through his mind. Would he still consider leaving the cookery school now? My stomach churned at the thought. And what about me? I'd just reached the conclusion that I was ready to return to Nottingham and to my own life.

But what would happen on Monday when the cookery school opened for its first day of business? Because there was precious little chance of Gloria being able to see her dreams come true any time soon.

The sound of approaching sirens put a halt to my thoughts. Right now my priority was Gloria and getting her to hospital. There was nothing anyone could have done to save Mimi's life, but no way was I going to lose someone else precious to me.

Cooking Up A Storm

Chapter 11

Even if I shut my eyes, I can always tell I'm in a hospital. The squeak of shoes along the corridors, the unmistakeable blended aromas of disinfectant and boiled cabbage, and the heat – I'm surprised more patients don't pass out from heat exhaustion. And then there are the plastic visitors' chairs, which are always so low that you can barely see the patient in the bed. Having said all that, as hospitals go, the one Gloria was in was relatively nice. It was a cottage hospital fifteen miles from Plumberry, small and friendly, surprisingly modern, and Gloria had been lucky enough to get a private room off the main ward.

The doctor wasn't overly friendly, though, despite Mags's best efforts. I sat at Gloria's bedside holding her hand while the doctor scribbled notes on his clipboard. Mags was arranging a bunch of flowers at the windowsill whilst trying to make conversation with him and was being largely ignored.

'Flowers do brighten up a lady's bedroom, don't they, Doctor?' she said.

'Hmm?' he grunted.

His badge read 'Mr Bryant', so he was a consultant rather than a doctor. Perhaps that was why he was ignoring her. I guessed he was in his late fifties; a tall jowly man with a thatch of white hair, extreme eyebrows and half-moon reading glasses, which he'd frowned over when he'd examined Gloria's hip.

'Do you buy your wife flowers? That is, if you're married?' she asked slyly.

The consultant exhaled somewhat heavily. 'No.'

'No, you're not married?' she persisted, with a tinkly hopeful laugh.

'She's allergic to pollen.'

'Shame,' Mags said flatly, and lifted her eyes heavenwards as if to say 'typical'.

Gloria and I smiled at each other. Well, I smiled. Gloria just softened her expression slightly.

'Excuse me a moment.' Mr Bryant opened the door and disappeared down the corridor.

Mags dropped into the other visitor chair and huffed. 'Talk about Frosty the Snowman. Would it kill him to smile?'

It was the morning after the night before. The night when Gloria had been whizzed through the Yorkshire countryside in an ambulance with sirens blazing.

What a traumatic way for our day to end. After the euphoria of opening the cookery school, watching our slot on the local news and then celebrating our success with a glass of bubbly, we had been brought swiftly back down to earth with a bump. Or in Gloria's case a broken lower leg and hip.

She had regained consciousness by the time the ambulance arrived. Two paramedics calmly took control and began transferring her to a stretcher to wheel her out to the ambulance. But even moving her from the half-landing between the two flights of stairs had been excruciating for her and poor Gloria had passed out again.

'My first ride in an ambulance and I can hardly remember a thing!' she'd said weakly when she'd woken up this morning.

But I could remember it all, and I could honestly say it was one of the most terrifying experiences of my life.

I squeezed her hand. 'Let's hope it's the last ride too.'

The interior of the ambulance had been dark because of the tinted windows and I had sat to one side, out of the way to let the paramedic do her thing. Gloria had looked so pale and tiny lying there with her eyes shut, and her lifeless body had been so corpselike that I'd been beside myself with worry. At that moment I'd felt Mimi's absence like a physical pain, a stab beneath my ribs. I would have given anything to have her sunny optimism reassuring Gloria that she'd be all right. Whereas I'd found myself swallowing great gulping sobs for most of the journey.

Luckily a combination of the ambulance siren and the clear roads meant that we arrived at Accident and Emergency in record time. A slot had conveniently opened up in the operating schedule and by the time Mags had arrived after locking up and taking the dogs home, Gloria had already been whisked away.

'Go home, ladies,' a brisk nurse had advised us. 'She'll be in theatre and then the recovery room and she'll be too groggy to talk to you. Come back in the morning when you've all got some rest.'

Mags and I had reluctantly obeyed her and had driven back to Plumberry in near silence; we had been so worried about Gloria.

Mr Bryant came back into the room accompanied by a nurse and I moved out of the way while she took Gloria's pulse and blood pressure. The two of them conferred, the consultant recorded the nurse's readings in his notes and the nurse left again.

My phone, which I'd put on silent, vibrated in my pocket and I moved away to the window to look at it.

'Gabe and Noah send their love,' I said, reading the text message. 'Gabe wants to know if they should come back up.'

Gloria shook her head and spoke in a dry, croaky voice. 'There's no need and I wouldn't want little Noah to see me

119

in hospital. Although I'll be able to go home soon, won't I, Doctor?'

He hooked the clipboard back on the end of Gloria's bed and frowned. 'Need to get you up and moving first. Your blood pressure is on the low side, too. I've asked for physiotherapy to put you on the list. But for now, rest, recover from the anaesthetic and get some sleep.'

'I can't languish in bed, Doctor; I've got a business to run.'

He pointed to her right-hand side and her leg, encased in plaster to the knee.

'Your hip was so badly damaged that we had to replace it. Your tibia, which had a nasty break, has been pinned and fixed with a metal plate, and you hit your head on a solid floor when you fell. You'll also be booked in for a scan to test for osteoporosis. I hardly think *languishing* comes into it.'

'And how long will I be in plaster?'

The consultant relaxed his steely expression for the first time and perched on the end of her bed next to her good leg. 'Six weeks minimum, probably more, I'm afraid.'

I slipped back to her side and took her hand as her face crumpled.

'Six weeks?' she said hoarsely.

Mr Bryant nodded. ''Fraid so. And you'll be on crutches for at least another month after that. Do you have someone at home to look after you?'

'Yes, me,' Mags and I answered together.

Mags crossed her legs. 'My bedside manner is legendary,' she added, seemingly unable to resist a little flirt.

'Oh well,' Gloria sighed, 'I suppose once I've got used to being on crutches, I'll be scooting about without any problems. I'm sure I'll only need a couple of weeks off from work.'

Mags and I exchanged anxious glances. Somebody was in denial . . .

The consultant leaned forward and patted her arm. 'It'll be much longer than that, Gloria. Possibly as much as twelve weeks. But don't worry about work today. I think you'll find that most of us are not quite as indispensable as we think.'

My heart began to thump. Gloria was quite indispensable. And so was Tom. With Gloria out of action, we'd need him to run every single cookery course. And he was spending this weekend in York looking at buying his friend's restaurant. What if he decided to go for it? Could we ask him to postpone it for three months?

Gloria turned her pale face away from Mr Bryant.

'But my cookery school,' she whispered. 'I've been waiting so long . . .' Her voice faded and tears began to trickle down her cheeks.

Mr Bryant patted her arm again. 'I'll see if a nurse can rustle you up a cup of tea.'

He stood, gave me an apologetic smile and left us to it.

Gloria's eyes swept from Mags to me and she attempted a brave face through the tears. 'Well, this puts us in a bit of a stew, darlings.'

A stew of colossal proportions, in fact.

'Mr Bryant's right,' I soothed. 'Don't worry about work today.'

My heart ached for her; she wouldn't be there to teach the first course at the cookery school and I knew how desperately upsetting that was for her.

Mags handed Gloria a tissue and pulled her chair up closer.

'Now, Monday's course, One Pot Wonders, is all taken care of,' she said briskly. 'I know you wanted to teach the very first course, but Tom is more than happy to stand in.'

'Oh, the angel.' Gloria sniffed, dabbing at her eyes. 'I've organized some lovely dishes for that beginners' course. Such a pity.'

Mags's eyes flicked momentarily to me. We'd called

Tom on the way to the hospital. He would happily teach the course, but on the proviso that he didn't have to stick too rigidly to Gloria's recipes. What Gloria didn't know wouldn't hurt her, Mags and I had agreed.

'There are eight bookings now,' I told her. 'Four friends who came to the open day emailed this morning.'

Gloria managed a smile. 'Eight is a good number to start with. The recipes for the course are in my drawer in the office; Tom'll want those.'

'I'll see that he gets everything he needs, don't worry,' Mags reassured her, not meeting my eye. 'I'll get in bright and early on Monday to give the students a Plumberry welcome. And Pixie will help, of course.'

'I'll be live tweeting our first course and taking some pictures for Facebook, and sending out press releases and Friday's launch-party photographs to all the glossy magazines,' I added.

'And meanwhile, I'll lie here like a completely useless old stick.' Gloria sighed.

'Not at all,' I argued. 'You can draw up the next three months' worth of courses to begin with. The current calendar only runs until the end of July.'

'I shall be back by then, that's for sure.' She tried to hitch herself up the bed a bit but gave up, exhausted.

Mags and I tucked a hand under each arm and lifted her gently upwards.

'But until you are, we'll steer the ship, won't we, Verity?' said Mags, and I nodded.

Gloria blinked at me anxiously. 'I quite understand if you need to get back to your own house. You've already been so kind.'

I lifted her hand to my lips and kissed it. 'As if I'd leave you *in a stew*.'

'It's times like these . . .' Gloria's voice faltered and tears began to cascade down her cheeks again. 'That I miss Mimi the most.'

'I know,' I whispered. 'Me too.'

Even though it was more than two years, the memories I had of the two of us shone as brightly as ever and it must have been even worse for Gloria. She had no family to speak of and having her daughter with her would have made all the difference. As it was, Gabe was her next of kin and I knew she would refuse to be any sort of burden to him.

Mags stood up and enfolded Gloria in a hug, which wasn't easy with tubes and monitors and drips surrounding her bed. I watched the two best friends together, wishing more than anything that Mimi was here to wrap her arms round me.

I sat back in my chair and let out a deep breath.

Yesterday at the cookery school, I'd taken stock and decided that cooking would become part of my life again.

I had decided that it was time to head back to Nottingham, but there was no way I could leave Gloria now. She'd need help at home for starters: goodness knows how she was going to get up and down the stairs, and what about showering? And then there were Comfrey and Sage to walk.

And the cookery school needed me, too. I might not be qualified to teach but I could help with other things, like drumming up sales and organizing the administration. And although bookings were beginning to trickle in, we'd need a lot more of them for Dave the accountant to stop doing that sharp intake of breath thing he did so well.

Mimi, if someone had said six months ago that I'd be looking after your mum and her cookery school, I'd have laughed in their face. Wish you were here to help . . .

A rush of steely determination propelled me forward on to the edge of my seat.

'Gloria, I know you're worried and I can't deny that this is a bit of a setback. But we all share your vision and we'll all help, won't we, Mags?'

123

Mags nodded obediently.

'There's no rush for me to get back to Nottingham,' I continued. 'Besides, being here will give me a chance to brush up on my cooking skills. After the fun I had with Pixie and Mags getting ready for the opening party, I'm itching to get back in the kitchen.'

I took her limp hand in mine and squeezed it gently, realizing how much I meant what I said.

Gloria looked at me, her blue eyes glittering with tears. 'Well, that's the best news I've heard all day, darling.'

'Three months,' said Mags with a low whistle as she drove us back to Plumberry from the hospital. 'Gloria will be going stir crazy by then. That woman never sits still for more than five minutes.'

The two of us contemplated the situation in silence for a few moments.

'I'd better call Gabe with the news,' I said reluctantly, pulling my phone out of my bag. I dialled his number and put the call on speaker phone.

'Poor Gloria,' Gabe sighed, when I relayed how long she would be incapacitated for. 'Perhaps she should close the cookery school,' he added. 'At least temporarily.'

Mags shook her head in horror. 'I know that's the sensible thing to do, Gabe, but getting back to work gives her something to aim for.'

'She's sixty-five, Mags, she should be aiming for an easier life!' said Gabe. 'Not putting her health at risk. I always thought she was too old to be starting a venture like this.'

'My mate isn't ready for the knacker's yard yet,' Mags harrumphed, shooting a vicious look at the phone. 'And she needs to see her dream come true.'

'Bloomers, talk some sense into Gloria, please,' Gabe begged. 'Sometimes things don't work out and we have to adapt, change direction. Look at me. Prime example. I was aiming to be a partner in my old law firm, remember? That was my dream. Amongst others,' he added quietly.

My heart melted for him and I felt a stab of guilt. He and Mimi had been blissfully happy together. Sometimes he appeared to be coping so well without her that I forgot his loss was far worse than mine.

I'd organize for him and Noah to come and stay as soon as it was convenient. My stomach flipped immediately at the thought. It would be lovely to see them; I'd barely had a chance to talk to Gabe yesterday and Noah would love taking the dogs on walks to the park and I could read him bedtime stories; I adored doing that and I hadn't done it for ages.

'I agree with Mags,' I said gently. 'The one thing that will help Gloria recover will be to see her cookery school up and running just as she wants it to be. We all need to help her do that.'

'I'm in,' said Mags straight away.

'Me too,' I agreed.

There was a small hesitation on the line and then Gabe sighed. 'Count me in too then. Anything – I mean *anything* – I can do to help, please shout.'

Mags and I beamed at each other complicitly until a worm of disquiet began to nibble at my confidence. It was all very well for the three of us to commit to getting Gloria's business off the ground, but without a chef, it was hopeless. And after spending a weekend contemplating purchasing his friend's restaurant, who knew whether Tom was 'in' or not?

Chapter 12

On Monday morning, I woke up bright and early and fizzing with nerves. Today the cookery school opened properly for business. It wasn't ideal, Gloria not being there, but I had every confidence that Tom, Mags, Pixie and I would make a brilliant team in her absence.

I was zipping up my raincoat in preparation for taking the dogs for a walk and inspecting the grey May morning when Gloria phoned.

'Just calling to wish you tons of love and luck for today, darling,' she trilled.

I brightened instantly at her cheerful tone.

'You sound full of the joys of spring,' I said, opening the front door.

Unlike the weather. The bright sunshine from last week had disappeared and had been replaced by a persistent soft drizzle. Comfrey and Sage pottered to the doorstep, their pointed noses sniffing the damp air despondently.

'I am! I slept like a baby, thanks to the drugs, and I even managed to go for a little walk last night. Well, a *hobble* and it did take two nurses, but even so – I made it!'

'Excellent!' I breathed a sigh of relief. 'You'll be home in no time. Comfrey and Sage will be glad; they've taken to sitting on the front windowsill on permanent lookout for you. They do miss you.'

'Oh, the darlings,' she said.

I heard her give a small sigh down the phone and my heart tweaked with disappointment for her. Poor thing; to have worked so hard at getting the cookery school ready for its first course and not even be there to see it. I pulled my hood up and shut the door behind me and the three of us set off down the path, heads bowed against the drizzle.

'The next few weeks will zip by,' I reassured her. 'You'll soon be back on your feet. But until then, we've got lots to do, you and I, and when I visit tonight we'll talk through some ideas I've got for summer.'

'OK, and I'll get my thinking cap on too. I'll want to hear all about our first course tonight. I hope all the students enjoy themselves. That's what the cookery school should stand for: sharing food and having fun.'

A sudden flashback popped into my head of an afternoon at Mimi's house when we had ridiculous amounts of fun spelling out rude words with piping bags of mashed potato.

'I hear you,' I replied, smiling down the phone. 'And I'll make sure the cookery school is exactly what you want it to be.'

Pixie and Tom were already there when I arrived with Mags and the dogs an hour later. Pixie was setting up the Aga kitchen with plates of pastries and pots of tea and coffee ready for the students to arrive and Tom was upstairs in the teaching kitchen, organizing ingredients for the morning's first dish.

Tom and I exchanged hellos as I passed through to the office, but he was so engrossed in his work that he barely made eye contact.

I watched him through the office windows while I waited for the computer to come to life. He certainly looked the part in his dazzlingly clean white chef's jacket and soft chambray cotton trousers. His dark hair was tousled where he'd been running his hand through it and his forehead was creased in concentration. From where I sat I could see his lips moving as he consulted a sheet of paper and darted from one side of the kitchen to the other.

I fetched us each a cup of strong coffee and sidled up to his teaching workstation at the front of the room.

'All set?' I asked casually, casting my eye over the array of dishes, plates and chopping boards he'd lined up on the counter.

Tom grinned and took the cup and saucer from me. 'Thanks. Almost ready. How's Gloria?'

'Doing well. She sends lots of luck and love for our first day, and says thank you again.'

He slurped at his coffee and smacked his lips together appreciatively. 'It's no bother. Besides it'll take my mind off wondering whether to buy this restaurant in York or not.'

'And? Are you tempted to buy it?' I mentally crossed my fingers and hoped he wasn't. I took a step backwards until I felt the windowsill behind me and perched on it.

'At the moment I'm a chef without a restaurant. And that makes me,' he shuffled his shoulders, 'edgy.'

My heart sank.

'So you are tempted.' I stared into my coffee, wondering how long these things take. If Gloria was going to be out of action for a couple of months, this could be a real headache . . .

'He's got a good business there.' Tom leaned forward and rested his elbows on the counter. 'The question is: is it the right business for me?'

'If you've got doubts, perhaps it isn't?' I said, brightening.

He nodded slowly. 'It's just that I vowed that next time around, I'd do it my way, create my own place, in my name, you know? And even though I could rename it, change the décor and the menu, I think there's something to be said for making a fresh start. Don't you?'

I thought back to three weeks ago – only three? – when I

thought I might be pregnant with Liam's baby, when I also thought I stood a chance of promotion in the marketing department of Solomon Insurance. And the feeling of relief I'd felt afterwards, that I was free to start again, to do something new. I'd certainly done that and even though none of it had been planned, and even though Gloria's accident was a terrible setback, the fresh start had done me the world of good.

'I do,' I agreed with gusto.

'I'll take my time, I think. Anyway, at the moment my money is still tied up in Salinger's so I couldn't make any hasty decisions even if I wanted to. I'll stay here until Gloria's fit to return, if that will help?'

'Oh phew!' I let out a breath and reached out to touch his arm. 'That is such a weight off my mind. I'll ring Gloria and let her know.'

'That's twice you've been nice to me now, Verity Bloom. People will talk,' he laughed, holding his coffee cup away from us as it wobbled in its saucer.

'I thought for one awful moment that if you left, I might have to teach a course or two.' I grinned and fanned my face.

Tom pretended to shudder. 'Heaven forbid.'

I raised an eyebrow haughtily. 'I'll have you know I do a mean *cod goujon au pain* with tomato reduction.'

He raised his eyebrows. 'I stand corrected . . . Hold on, isn't that a fish finger sandwich with ketchup?'

'Oi, don't knock it until you've tried it,' I laughed.

A clumping sound coming from the staircase distracted us and we both turned towards it.

'Here comes the Sugar Plum Fairy,' chuckled Tom under his breath as Pixie appeared, shod in her Doc Martens boots as usual.

'They're here!' she said. 'All eight of them, having a cup of tea and mingling. Mags is sorting them out with name badges. She told me to fetch you two.'

'No cancellations?' I asked happily. 'That's brilliant.'

'Where are your whites?' Tom asked her, pointing to her faded black Judas Priest T-shirt. 'We've spoken about this before. Professional, please, Pixie.'

'Sorry, Chef.' She bit her lip. 'I'm just excited. This is it, we're really opening!'

I grinned at her, sharing her exuberance. 'And any last-minute allergies we should know about?'

There was a lengthy form for each student to fill in, but you never knew, someone could have developed an intolerance to something since submitting the form. It was Pixie's job to check.

She took off her glasses and polished them on the bottom of her T-shirt. 'One woman can't stand the word "clotted". Says it gives her dithers.'

Tom stared at her. 'The word *clotted*. Just the word?'

'Shush!' Pixie looked over her shoulder. 'Yes, apparently.'

He shook his head. 'Jesus.'

'Thanks, Pixie. Come on, Tom,' I said briskly. 'Let's go and introduce ourselves.'

I led the way back downstairs and tried to ignore Tom, who was muttering something that sounded like 'give me strength' under his breath.

'Have you ever taught anyone to cook before?' I whispered as we strode across reception towards the Aga kitchen where our students were waiting to begin their One Pot Wonders course.

'Of course, I've trained my own staff in the Tom MacDonald way of doing things. Which, as you can appreciate, is the only way to do things.'

He was smiling. So that was a joke. I hoped.

'You do know that . . .' I paused, wondering how to put this diplomatically, 'well, that for most people, cooking is a form of relaxation, don't you?'

He looked at me as if I was crazy. 'Food is a serious business. I won't have people messing about in my lesson.'

130

'Tom.' I laid a hand on his arm as we reached the door. 'You will make sure our first paying customers have a nice time, won't you?'

'Of course,' he said, laughing softly. 'They'll have never had an experience like it.'

Hmm, that was what I was afraid of.

Tom pushed open the door and gestured for me to go in ahead of him.

I stepped into the Aga kitchen and my breath caught in my throat. The Plumberry School of Comfort Food's first ever course was about to commence and I was both jittery with excitement and sad that Gloria wasn't there to see it. Nor Mimi. She would have loved this and for a second or two the notion that I was stealing their moment threatened to overwhelm me.

I felt a hand on the small of my back and turned to find myself looking into Tom's dark brown eyes twinkling with confidence and warmth.

'Show time,' he murmured. 'Let's do Gloria proud.'

My heart melted with gratitude; whether he realized it or not it was the perfect thing to say.

I nodded and walked towards the Aga at the head of the kitchen.

The room was fragrant with the aroma of sweet pastries and freshly brewed coffee. The tables had been arranged in a U-shape and the doors were open to the sound of the river, which was flowing faster today because of the rain. The students were all women and even though some of them had only just met, they were all chatting away merrily to each other and already looked as if they were enjoying themselves.

They ranged in age from the young mums who'd come to the open day last Friday up to an older lady called Nora, who Mags informed me was Dave the accountant's mother. Allegedly Dave had booked it as a present for her, but I couldn't help but wonder if it was his way of helping Gloria out in her first week. Either way, it was a lovely gesture that endeared him to both Mags and me even more.

'Good morning, everyone, and welcome to the Plumberry School of Comfort Food,' I said, handing out aprons to all the students.

'Oh, I love it!' exclaimed one, shaking her apron out of its plastic bag.

'Mine won't go round,' chuckled a plumper lady.

'Borrow mine,' said Mags, with a wink. 'It's specially adapted for women of a more curvaceous build.'

I mouthed my thanks to Mags and made a mental note to get a couple adjusted for customers with more generous proportions.

I smiled and cleared my throat. 'Ladies, I'm delighted to introduce Tom MacDonald, who won a Michelin star for his restaurant, Salinger's in Manchester.'

One of the ladies shot up her hand. 'I've been there. Had the scallops with lime foam. Out of this world.'

Tom and I shared a smile.

Everyone started chatting again about posh restaurants and whether or not they liked seafood when Tom, who'd been waiting with his hands on hips, put his finger and thumb to his lips and gave a shrill whistle. I flinched and caught Mags's astonished expression, Pixie snorted and several of the women gasped, but then the room went quiet.

Tom held up a hand and smiled.

'Hello, ladies. As Verity said, I'm Tom MacDonald and I'm your tutor for today. When I give you an order, you respond with "Yes, Chef!" OK?'

An order. Seriously?

The women looked stunned but most of them managed to nod.

'You are kidding me,' Pixie murmured close to my ear.

'Come on, ladies.' Tom gave them a wolfish grin. '"Yes, Chef" is the answer I'm looking for. Let's try that again. Is that understood?'

He cupped a hand to his ear and my stomach fluttered nervously. This was so not what Gloria had in mind when she'd dreamed about sharing good times in the kitchen.

'Yes, Chef,' they all responded hesitantly.

'Then please all follow me upstairs to the teaching kitchen.' He marched to the door and held it open. 'Ready?'

'Yes, Chef!'

I sank down on to a bench at the back of the room not even daring to catch Mags's eye when I heard one of the women whisper to another, 'I think I'm in love.'

Which surprised me almost as much as her friend's reply: 'Me too.'

I had to admit, Tom was certainly very commanding when he wanted to be.

'What just happened there?' Mags said, shaking her head. 'It was like *Dad's Army* meets *MasterChef*.'

I looped my arm through hers and giggled. 'Then we're all doomed, I tell you, doomed.'

The morning session appeared to go without a hitch, although Tom hadn't used Gloria's recipes after all. Her lamb hotpot had been replaced with his Navarin of lamb and the chicken supreme had become a Moroccan chicken using the lovely terracotta tagines. It was essentially the same but slightly more sophisticated, he had explained during his students' coffee break. The smoked haddock chowder was now sweetcorn chowder, because Tom still couldn't face fish after his food poisoning last week.

But even though my office overlooked the teaching kitchen, I was scarcely aware of the students. I was so caught up with the aftermath of last Friday's opening activities that before I knew it, the students had gone back downstairs to eat lunch. I nipped down to the ladies' loos and had just locked my cubicle door when two of the students came in, hooting with laughter.

I smiled to myself; it sounded like they were having a whale of a time.

'It's like being back at school,' one of them giggled.

'Yeah. *Military* school!'

'I can't believe you got told off for talking.'

I squeezed my eyes shut. *Please tell me Tom hadn't done that.*

'I know! I only wanted to know whether to use a sieve or a colander.'

'He is hot, though.'

'Oh God, yeah. I'm going to talk on purpose this afternoon, just so he comes over . . .'

I opened the door and sneaked out before the women saw me. Hot or not, it sounded like Tom was taking his teaching role a little too seriously. And according to those two, his style was a lot more Gordon Ramsay than Gloria Ramsbottom . . .

At four o'clock the course was finished for the day. We waved the students off armed with their new aprons and boxes of the food they'd prepared and I made Tom and Pixie some tea while they finished clearing up.

'That went well; we only needed the first-aid box once and only two people cried.' Tom grinned and began to stack pans under the teaching station.

'Two out of eight,' I said pointedly, handing him his tea. 'That means you made a quarter of our customers cry.'

'Me?' Tom said, half-laughing. 'One said she had sensitive eyes and the other one was chopping onions.'

I gave him a sideways glance. 'According to Pixie, you told her to throw away her sautéed onions and start again. In fact, *shouted* was the word she used.'

'Yup, you definitely shouted, boss,' Pixie piped up. She was refilling the pots with the brightly coloured utensils at each workstation.

'Amateurs.' Tom rolled his eyes over his teacup. 'What can I say? They can't take simple instructions.'

I folded my arms. 'That's the whole point of them being here. Because they are amateurs.'

'But I'm in charge of the kitchen and I'm a professional. With a reputation to uphold.'

'And I'm in charge of marketing. With the ethos of Gloria's cookery school to uphold.'

We stared at each other for a few seconds as the tension crackled between us. Pixie tiptoed away.

'Fair play,' Tom acknowledged finally. 'I suppose I'm used to shouting orders and getting an immediate response. Was it really bad?'

He looked as sad as a sunken soufflé; I felt quite sorry for him.

'It's only natural for you to have high standards. But perhaps you could just try to . . . lower them a bit so that our customers have fun?' I grinned at him. 'This is a day out for our students. We want people to go home just as happy when they leave as if they'd spent the day, I don't know, at a spa, or walking in the Yorkshire Dales.'

Tom thought about that for a few moments and then set his cup down. 'I disagree,' he said with a frown. 'People expect to learn and they can't do that while others are whooping and squealing around them, like two of the time-wasters we had today. The day needs to be challenging and I think giving them a taste of being in a pro kitchen makes it more memorable.'

'*Memorable?*' I retorted, feeling my heart race. 'Well, you certainly made it memorable for the two women who spent half the day in tears.'

He tutted. 'Next you'll be saying that we should have the radio on and they can all dance around the kitchen to music.'

'Cool!' said Pixie, coming over to collect her tea. 'Shall I bring my wireless speakers in?'

'No way!' Tom snapped.

'Excuse me,' she muttered. 'Just a suggestion.'

'The students found it difficult enough without any distractions,' he said.

'Well, we need something to lighten the atmosphere with *Mein Führer* stressing everyone out with his orders,' said Pixie. 'I'm going to unload the dishwasher. Again.'

I watched her disappear downstairs and took a step closer to Tom.

'She's right, we should allow people to enjoy themselves, share good times. We want them to fall in love with the cookery school so that they come back and bring all their friends.'

'I agree with wanting repeat business.' Tom's jaw clenched as he wiped a cloth over the already immaculate work surface. 'But food should be about respect and reverence and doing justice to the ingredients. It has nothing to do with caring and sharing. When I cook, it reflects who I am, which means I create the best plate of food I can. Every time. Either people like my food or they don't.'

He flicked the cloth over his shoulder and his face softened into a smile. 'Fortunately plenty of them did or my restaurant wouldn't have earned such a good reputation.'

Big head. I blinked at him incredulously.

It was on the tip of my tongue to ask why he'd left Salinger's; he'd just given me the perfect lead into the topic. But I didn't want to change the subject right now. Because what he'd just said was so fundamentally opposed to my views on cooking that his words had sent a shiver down my spine.

'Cooking for someone else is a sign of love. It shouldn't be about you,' I argued.

'*Love?* Love has nothing to do with it. You're wrong.' He shook his head and smoothed his fingertips over his neat beard.

I tilted my chin and stared at him. 'No, *you're* wrong. And I'll prove it.'

'Will you, now?' He looked at me from under dark eyelashes, an amused smile playing at his lips. 'How?'

There were a thousand examples I could share with him about times I'd cooked with Mimi or cooked for someone I cared about, even making the canapés for the cookery school open day had been out of love for Gloria. But looking at his cynical expression I realized that this was something Tom needed to experience for himself.

Perhaps being at the cookery school would teach him what he needed to know; it had already done wonders for me. I felt happier and more connected to the real me than I had in two years.

Tom was still waiting for an answer.

I smiled at him mysteriously. 'Just watch this space.'

Chapter 13

The next course on the calendar was Wednesday's Teatime Treats: three hours in which to make Yorkshire tea loaf, mini chocolate éclairs and crumpets to take home, topped off with a sumptuous afternoon tea. The students had arrived looking damp after having run through heavy rain from the car park and now the upstairs windows had steamed up with condensation. But despite the grey clouds outside, the ambience inside the cookery school was every bit as warm and welcoming as Gloria wished it to be. Even Tom seemed to be behaving himself.

After our disagreement on the place (or not, in his case) for fun and love in the kitchen, I resolved to keep a close eye on him during this course. I positioned myself near the door of the office ready to leap into action in case he started to bellow at the students like an army sergeant licking his recruits into shape.

Mags and I had reported back to Gloria after the One Pot Wonders course, focusing on all the positives: the camaraderie of the students; the delicious smells that had wafted through the entire building as the aroma of cinnamon, ginger and cumin began to escape the Moroccan tagines; how a certain pair of students had declared Tom 'hot' and had rebooked for the Perfect Pasta course.

'Well, he is very attractive,' Gloria had whispered, the corners of her mouth lifting in a twinkly smile. She inched herself up her hospital bed, wrinkling her bottom sheet as she reached out for her glass of water. 'I knew as soon as I met him that those Irish eyes would add a certain charm to the cookery school.'

Mags, who'd been munching her way through the tub of tangy black olives that Tom had sent for Gloria, passed the glass to her after taking a swig herself.

'He certainly has a commanding presence,' she'd said, tipping me the tiniest wink.

I'd nodded. We had omitted to tell Gloria that those same Irish eyes could glare fiercely enough to turn her students' legs to jelly.

Tom was a bit of an enigma to me: away from the kitchen he was a charmer. He'd certainly charmed me on my first day in Plumberry when he'd rescued Comfrey and Sage with a crumb of fancy cheese. But when he donned his chef whites, he seemed to take on a harsher, colder persona, as if being in the kitchen sapped all his sense of humour.

'What's the real story behind him leaving Salinger's?' I'd asked her, reaching forward to smooth the sheet underneath her.

Gloria had remained tight-lipped. 'Darling, I would tell you, but you know what he's like – intensely sensitive about these things. I'm sure he wouldn't mind you asking, but I won't break his confidence. All I'll say is that he had an irreconcilable difference with his partner in Salinger's and leaving was the only option.'

That was a bit worrying; he and I had had pretty irreconcilable differences on Monday. I hoped he wasn't considering leaving us . . .

There were nine students on this afternoon's Teatime Treats course, including a man who wanted to learn to cook for a surprise birthday party for his wife, three women from the local Women's Institute who said they'd let the side down at previous WI events, and a newly married vicar's wife in her forties.

The course was now halfway through, and from what I could make out from my desk overlooking the teaching kitchen, the éclairs were cooling, the Yorkshire tea loaves were in the oven and Tom was giving the students instructions on how to cook crumpets.

'Make sure you grease the crumpet rings,' he reminded them, as one student valiantly tried to scrape burnt-on batter from an unoiled ring. 'And wait till all the little bubbles have burst before flipping them over. No, not like that!'

I looked across to the furthest workstation to see Tom trying to take over from someone whose crumpet-flipping skills were clearly below par.

I needed a quick word with Mags about Friday's course and was about to phone downstairs, but decided to go and see her in person instead. Not that I was checking up on Tom. Well, not much. I left my office and skirted round the edge of the kitchen.

'Let me help you,' I said, spotting the vicar's wife waving a crumpet about on the end of a spatula. I rummaged through the drawer to find a cooling rack.

'Thanks,' she said, sliding her golden crumpet on to it. 'There's just so much to remember.'

'Are you enjoying yourself?' I asked, watching as she ladled more batter into rings.

'Oh yes!' She nodded, cheeks pink from standing over a hot griddle pan. She was a mousy sort of woman with a pointed chin who looked ready to flee at the slightest calamity. 'Although next time I'll bring a friend, much more enjoyable to cook with someone else.'

'I agree, I always enjoyed cooking with a friend.' I smiled at her.

She narrowed her eyes at me and I realized I'd spoken in the past tense. Bad habit. I'd cooked canapés on Friday with Mags and Pixie and I'd made prawn and pea risotto for Mags and the dogs on Sunday. I suppose that meant I was officially cooking again.

My chest heaved with a lightness I recognized as pleasure.

'*Enjoy*, I mean,' I said, making a mental note to speak to Gloria about cooking with friends. Perhaps we could offer a discount if you booked two places.

'I'm so thrilled with my éclairs,' she confided. 'My husband has got the parish council coming round this evening; last time I only offered them ginger biscuits. There's something a bit special about serving something that you've made yourself, isn't there?'

I agreed again and left her to it, walking past the sole male student, who had already clocked up a tall stack of rather singed crumpets.

'Watch the temperature of your griddle pan,' Tom said loudly to the room. 'Low and slow is better than hot and fast.'

He caught my eye and made a beeline for me, raising his eyebrow just a fraction. I was so glad Mags wasn't there to make an innuendo out of that comment. Oh damn, I swallowed, now I'd thought of it anyway and my face was going red . . .

He leaned down to whisper in my ear. 'Better, wouldn't you agree?'

'If you say so . . .' I gave a nervous laugh.

'I'm being much more mellow and I haven't made them say "Yes, Chef" once,' he continued.

'Absolutely.' I nodded firmly, pressing a palm to my face to hide the worst of my blushes. 'Much better.'

He grinned at me. 'So you can stop spying on me now. You've worn a groove in the floor this afternoon walking backwards and forwards from your office.'

'That's not true. Well, maybe a bit.' I laughed, tweaking a packet of tissues out of my pocket to show him. 'Just a precaution, in case I came across a blubbering wreck in the kitchen.'

'Tom, is this OK?' called a wavering voice.

We both looked across to the teaching station, where Pixie was obscured behind a cloud of smoke rising from her griddle pan.

'There, ladies and gentlemen, is a prime example of too hot and fast,' Tom said loudly, and with a roll of his eyes, he pinched one of my tissues and strode across to help her out.

Later that afternoon, Pixie was eating leftover crumpets for tea before her shift at the pub and I was boxing up slices of buttered Yorkshire tea loaf and mini éclairs to drop into the hospital for the nurses. (They deserved a treat; Gabe had phoned this afternoon to say that Gloria had been caught packing her case in secret and trying to book a taxi home.) Both Pixie and I were listening to Tom's justification for spending a ludicrous amount of money on Italian flour.

'It has to be Tipo 00 or the pasta won't be—'

'Verity! Are you there?'

We didn't find out what the pasta would or wouldn't be because Mags came thudding up the stairs from reception. Strands of her bright blonde hair had stuck to her red lipstick in her rush to share her news. She pressed a hand to her heaving bosom and panted. 'Verity, you'll never guess, there's a girl on the phone from the telly asking for you. They want to come and film. Here. On Saturday.'

'Television? Oh my goodness!' I gasped. 'I'll take it on the office line.'

All four of us scampered to the office and I grabbed the phone.

This was it; this was what I'd been hoping for, all those press releases I'd sent out to the BBC. This news would cheer Gloria up no end; in fact, I might bribe her with it to stay in hospital.

'Verity Bloom speaking,' I said, widening my eyes excitedly at Tom. 'Marketing manager of the Plumberry School of Comfort Food.'

'Hiya, this is Cheryl from *Challenge Chester?*' said a gum-chewing female voice.

I'd never heard of it. I crossed my fingers. 'Oh yes?'

'What show is it? *MasterChef?*' Tom scooted closer and pressed his head to mine so he could hear the person on the other end.

'*Challenge Chester,*' I hissed, covering the mouthpiece with my hand.

Tom's shoulders sagged and he slouched away to lean against the doorframe.

'Cool.' Pixie popped the end of a buttery crumpet in her mouth while Mags perched on the edge of Gloria's chair. 'Love that show.'

'He must be a new chef,' Mags whispered, peeling her hair off her lipstick. 'I've never heard of him.'

'Someone passed on your press release,' Cheryl continued. 'So Chester Fulwood, the presenter, yeah? He gets challenged to do wacky stuff every week and the producer thought it would be cool to make a loaf of bread in the shape of the Eiffel Tower. And I got your press release and thought, "Cookery School, sorted". Interested?'

'Er, a loaf of bread in the shape of the Eiffel Tower?' I repeated for the benefit of the room.

Tom covered his face with his hands and his shoulders drooped further towards the floor. I twisted my body away from him to avoid the negative vibes.

'Well, that does sound like fun,' I beamed. 'We'd be delighted.'

I sorted out a few details with Cheryl and ended the call.

'That is perfect,' I said, clapping my hands together and trying to ignore Tom's thunderous expression. 'And it will prove how fun cooking *should* be. Tom will teach this presenter Chester Fulwood to make bread and then turn it into the Eiffel Tower and we get prime-time TV coverage. Sorted, as Chewing Cheryl would say.'

'Verity.' Tom folded his arms. 'Remember when I accused

your BOGOF idea of being tacky, saying it cheapened the product more than any other strategy?'

I nodded nervously. He sounded really cross.

'I take it back.' His dark eyes blazed at me. 'This one takes the biscuit.'

'Or the loaf,' Pixie piped up.

Tom made a noise like a bear who'd had his porridge pinched and began to untie the strings of his apron.

'Lighten up, chuck,' said Mags, plucking a nail file out of a pot on Gloria's desk. 'Just think of the publicity.'

'Yeah, use your loaf.' Pixie sniggered through her fingers.

Tom dumped his apron on the desk.

'It's the publicity I am thinking of,' he muttered. 'So count me out. In fact, count me out of the cookery school completely. This just isn't going to work.'

'Tom?' I gasped, my jaw flapping. 'What about Friday? What about your Knife Skills course? We've got four booked in for that.'

But Tom strode across the kitchen, ran down the stairs and disappeared.

'Oh my God, he's walked.' Pixie blinked her heavily kohled eyes at me. 'That's a bugger, isn't it?'

I gulped. Just a bit.

'But he can't leave now,' I stuttered. 'He promised to stay.'

I charged down the staircase after him and saw the doors to the Aga kitchen still swinging.

My stomach fluttered. At least he hadn't left, which meant I still had a chance to persuade him to stay. I pushed through the double doors. He was out on the deck in the rain, leaning over the balustrade, head hanging low.

'Tom?' I said. 'Come back in. Let's talk about this.'

I pulled the collar up on my jacket to avoid the worst of the drips and hunched my shoulders against the chill wind.

He didn't move a muscle, simply stared at the flowing river, which had been gaining in speed all week. It gushed and splashed against the rocks now, compared to the meandering burble it had made when I'd first arrived in Plumberry.

'I'm sorry. I'm being a complete tosser,' he muttered.

Privately I agreed. But as it wasn't a question, I decided to neither confirm nor deny it.

'You probably think I'm being precious—'

'Noo!' I protested. *Yes. Totally.*

'But being a chef is a profession. I've battled, literally battled—' he turned to me, his dark eyes searching mine, 'to get where I am, or was. I served under Jordi Rocha at La Casa in Barcelona for two years; I worked unpaid as an intern at the Ritz in Paris for six months. Do you know how hard it is to get into those places?'

'I can imagine,' I said sympathetically.

'A few weeks ago I felt on top of my game. Now I'm reduced to this: being seen making a giant phallus out of bread on some ridiculous TV show that doesn't give a fig about food.'

Phallus? I stared at him.

'It would make me a laughing stock.' He shook his head. 'As if I'm not already.'

'Hold on a minute.' My eyes narrowed. 'Working here shouldn't make you a laughing stock.'

'It doesn't,' he snapped.

The two of us stared at each other through the rain: me breathless with indignation and him looking like he had the weight of the world on his shoulders.

He wiped a hand across his wet face and sighed.

'I didn't mean working here,' he said curtly. 'I was referring to my exit from Salinger's . . . Look, forget it. I'll stay, OK?'

If my housemate Rosie was here, she'd pin him down until he spilled the beans. But she wasn't and I was too polite to push for details. But the pain on his face told me all I needed to know for now: something or someone had damaged his professional pride. And if forcing him to work with Chester Fulwood made life even more uncomfortable for him, I wouldn't push him to do that either.

'Thanks, and Tom,' I reached a hand out to touch his arm, 'if you ever want to talk . . .'

There was a cough from somewhere behind us.

Tom and I span round to see Dave standing in the doorway, hands in pockets, jingling his change.

'Sorry to intrude, but Mags insists that you come in out of the rain.' He shrugged sheepishly. 'And the kettle's on.'

'Tell her we're on our way,' I said, giving him the thumbs-up as he turned back into the Aga kitchen.

Tom gave me a weak smile. 'She who must be obeyed.'

I looped my arm through his and led him inside. 'Look, don't worry about *Challenge Chester*, we'll sort something out.'

'Like what?' He chuckled. 'You take my place in front of the camera?'

'What's so funny about that?' I retorted.

'You?' he repeated with a snort.

And before my brain had a chance to filter out what had to be one of my most ridiculous ideas ever, my mouth took over.

'Yes, actually, Tom,' I said haughtily. 'If it means that the cookery school makes national TV, that is exactly what I propose to do.'

Back inside the Aga kitchen Mags was waiting anxiously with a tray of tea. My hands shook as I accepted a cup from her.

'Sorted?' she whispered, inclining her head to Tom, who was showing Dave the difference between the Aga's two ovens.

'Kind of.' I swallowed. 'I've volunteered to take part in *Challenge Chester* in his place.'

'Good for you, chuck,' she beamed. 'You'll do us proud.'

There was one problem with this particular idea: I'd never made bread in my life.

146

Chapter 14

'I just dropped by on my way to visit Gloria,' Dave said, before sipping the camomile tea that Mags kept specially for him. 'Is there any post or anything to give to her?'

I shook my head; I'd be going myself later. I needed a crash course in bread-making, or at least pointing in the right direction towards a really good cookery book. But Mags didn't need asking twice.

'Give her this from me.' She crushed Dave to her, pressing her lips to his noisily. 'A big kiss and a hug from Mags. I can't visit tonight; I've got my art class.' Adding with a wink, '*Nude* art class.'

'I didn't know you painted.' Tom grinned.

Mags sashayed in front of him and peeled the neckline of her dress down to reveal a freckled shoulder. 'I don't.'

Pixie and I exchanged amused glances. We already knew Mags was a life model. The men's red faces indicated that they didn't.

I came to Dave's rescue. 'Did your mother enjoy being at the cookery school on Monday?'

'Very much.' He shot me a look of gratitude. 'We ate the hotpot—'

'Navarin of lamb,' Tom corrected.

I examined my toes to hide my smirk. Tom was a stickler for the proper name for dishes.

'Yes, we ate that on Monday night and Mother's put the chicken thing . . .?' He looked at Tom.

'Moroccan chicken tagine,' Tom supplied.

'Yes, that, in the freezer for next week.'

'And did she enjoy the actual course?' I asked.

'Um, she, er . . .' Dave hunted round for the right phrase. 'She said you were old school, Tom.'

'I'll take that.' Tom folded his arms. 'There you go, Verity, Nora appreciates me. Firm but fair.'

'Wait, I got that wrong,' Dave remembered suddenly, sticking his finger in the air. 'You reminded her of her old schoolmaster. A bit handy with the cane, apparently.'

'Fantastic,' Tom murmured drily.

Pixie exploded with a coughing fit and I leapt up to relieve her of her cup.

'Evening all, I'm off to my other job. Say hi to Gloria for me,' said Pixie when she got her voice back.

We bid Pixie goodnight and Dave started his usual probing about how business was going. Mags began clearing away the tea things.

'We are going to be filmed for national TV on Saturday,' I announced proudly. 'So expect bookings to go through the roof.'

'Cheap gimmick,' muttered Tom, 'which will do nothing for the long-term reputation of the school.'

I huffed at him. 'It wouldn't hurt to be a bit more positive now and again, surely?'

'Sounds like fun,' said Dave.

I could have kissed him.

'Settle an argument for us, please,' I said and told him about the disagreement Tom and I had had about the place of fun in the kitchen.

'I believe food is deeply connected with our well-being,' Dave said earnestly. 'Feed the person and you feed their soul.'

'Exactly,' I said, nodding at Tom. 'Sharing is caring.'

'And food is also a sign of respect,' Dave continued.

'Which is what I said,' Tom said smugly.

I glared at him. That was stretching the truth a bit.

'I have every faith you'll find a middle ground,' Dave said diplomatically, looking to Mags for assistance. Unfortunately, the phone rang in reception and she dashed out to answer it.

Tom and I regarded each other doubtfully. I couldn't see him budging an inch and I wasn't going to because . . . well, because I was right.

'Although it may all be immaterial,' said Dave, plunging his hands back in his pockets and rocking on the balls of his feet. 'The classes need to be much fuller to cover our costs.'

And Gloria would have to cover my salary for a little longer, although it wasn't a huge amount seeing as I was living at her house rent-free. But it all had an impact on the bottom line.

I swallowed. 'We'll make it work, won't we, Tom?'

Mags reappeared. 'That was a lady wanting to know if we do kids' cookery classes. I said we had nothing in the calendar, but I've taken her details.'

She bustled back to the washing-up and Tom and I looked at each other. I braced myself, expecting him to say he'd only have children in the kitchen over his dead body.

'Why not?' He lifted a shoulder. 'I love kids.'

'You do?' I blinked at him. Which reminded me, I needed to sort out a date for Gabe to bring Noah up. I missed that smiley little face with the scruffy sandy hair and eyes that were full of questions and laughter and mischief. And Gabe too, actually.

'Oh yeah, I have a god-daughter, Saoirse, back home in Ireland. She's a cracker.'

Tom smiled proudly as he spoke about her and I felt an unexpected rush of warmth towards him. He might be gruff in the kitchen, he might take his food a tad too seriously, but here was proof that somewhere underneath he was a good man with a kind heart.

Mags popped her head back out, caught me gazing at Tom and pressed a hand to her bosom.

'Tom MacDonald: a demon in the kitchen and he loves kids, that's what I call husband material, eh, Verity?'

'If the idea of marrying a demon appeals,' I said airily, trying not to blush.

'I didn't know you were looking for a husband, Mags.' Tom grinned.

Dave stood tall and puffed out his chest but Mags missed the signs.

'If I was ten years younger you'd know about it,' she chuckled.

Dave's face fell and Tom cleared his throat.

'Teach a child to cook and they've a skill for life,' he said. 'So yeah, I'm up for that.'

Dave checked his watch. 'Visiting hours are about to start; any other messages for Gloria?' He glanced at Mags in case she tried to jump on him again. I couldn't quite make out whether he was hoping she would or not.

I ran and fetched the food parcel for the nurses – better for them to have it while everything was still fresh – and walked Dave to the door.

'I won't tell Gloria about the TV thing, I'll leave that to you.' He tucked the box under his arm and smiled at me. 'Remunerative issues aside, you're doing a grand job, Verity.'

I sighed. I hoped he'd still think that after I'd made my first ever loaf of bread. In the shape of the Eiffel Tower. On national television.

'Tom doesn't think so. We disagree about everything. Well, most things. And neither of us is officially in charge, so I can't make him do things my way,' I added grumpily.

'Competition sometimes adds a bit of spice,' Dave said, patting my arm.

I watched Dave run across the car park in the rain. A

competition: now that might raise our profile a bit. Food for thought. Definitely.

The weather the next morning was as unsettled as me. I gave up trying to sleep at six and decided to make an early start at the cookery school. I had quite a challenge on my hands if I was to be Plumberry's bread-making expert in front of a TV camera in three days. It was only flour and water and a bit of yeast, though, I thought, as I dropped bread into the toaster. I was sure I could get the hang of it before then.

I poured a mug of tea while I waited for my toast to brown and thought about Rosie. She had phoned me last night just as I arrived home from the hospital.

'I miss you,' she'd complained. 'There's no one to eat toast mountains with and I miss the ping of the microwave.'

'I miss you too,' I'd said, letting myself into Gloria's cottage.

Mags had left a dish of chicken curry keeping warm in the oven for me and the kitchen hummed with the aromas of garlic, ginger and garam masala.

'Although there's much less pinging going on these days. I'm a changed woman. I'm a *bigger* woman, come to that,' I said, undoing the button on my jeans as I sat down to eat.

Both Mags and Gloria had pointed out that I was looking much healthier now that I had regained my appetite. I felt healthier, too; I had more energy, more of a spring in my step, and with that came a certain contentment. But sometimes I had a crisis of conscience and instantly felt bad that my life was moving on and I was leaving Mimi behind. I'd get there eventually, I knew I would, but it was hard not to feel guilty when I was beginning to feel so at home in Plumberry.

'By the way, Liam came round yesterday.' Rosie had snorted with laughter at the memory. 'He wouldn't believe me when I told you were still away; he even came

151

into the house to check for himself. Not a happy bunny. I thought he was actually going to cry when I said you weren't coming back for ages.'

'Really?' Not that I wanted him back. I could never trust him again. But I was flattered that he was missing me.

'When *are* you coming back?' Rosie had asked. 'It's the middle of May already. Summer is on its way.'

'Not sure,' I'd replied. 'But summer might arrive in Nottingham before me, that's all I can say.'

Summer didn't look like it was on its way to me, I thought, peering out at the charcoal sky over the back garden as I sipped my morning tea. I'd packed an optimistic suitcase full of lightweight clothes, assuming I'd be here for a month, and now it looked like I'd be here for the entire summer – a *cold and wet* summer. Today I had borrowed one of Gloria's jumpers, goodness knows what I was going to wear for the filming of *Challenge Chester*.

The toast popped out of the toaster and I felt a wave of nostalgia for a cosy catch-up with Rosie.

'I'm glad you're here,' I said, scooping up the dogs for a cuddle. 'Or I'd feel very lonely indeed.'

Comfrey and Sage licked their lips and eyed up my toast hopefully.

'OK, just this once.'

I set them down on a chair at the table and shared my toast with them, cheered by their comforting presence.

'This can be our little secret, don't tell a soul,' I added with a wink.

There were no courses on today, which meant that Mags and Pixie had the day off and in theory Tom didn't need to be in either. But when I arrived with the dogs, the lights were on and the smell of fresh coffee drifted down the stairwell to greet me.

Comfrey and Sage scampered on ahead of me and had burrowed their way under the blanket I kept under my desk until only their noses were poking out by the time I'd reached the office.

Tom was sitting in front of the computer screen at Gloria's desk, scribbling notes on a pad with one hand and nursing a mug in his other.

'Wasn't expecting you to be in at all, let alone this early,' I said brightly.

'Just watching *MasterChef* on catch-up TV. Now that's the sort of thing I'd like to see going on here.' He stretched his arms up above his head and rolled his neck from side to side like a boxer. His denim shirt rose up to reveal a taut stomach and a line of hair, shockingly dark against his pale skin.

I dragged my eyes back to his as he lowered his arms. 'Sorry? What?'

'A course for serious foodies, who want to take their amateur skills to another level. What do you think?'

I shucked off my dripping raincoat and pulled a face. 'They always look so stressed on that show. I prefer *The Great British Bake Off*; it's more light-hearted somehow, even though it's very competitive. I don't know,' I finished with a shrug, 'it just looks more—'

'Fun?' Tom finished wryly.

'Quite.' I exhaled, refusing to get drawn into that debate again. Besides, I had other fish to fry this morning, or should I say, dough to knead.

Tom chuckled to himself as he refilled his coffee cup from the ancient percolator that Mags had donated to the office. The fancy Italian machine downstairs made the best coffee, but we all agreed it was a bit of a faff for every day.

'You're in early too,' he said, 'seeing as we don't have any courses today. Coffee?'

I nodded and he took a clean mug from the shelf and poured some for me.

'I thought I'd get some practice in for Saturday,' I cleared my throat, 'making bread.'

'Oh yes, your TV debut,' he said with a slight snigger.

'Only because you won't do it,' I retorted crossly. 'Gloria is over the moon about it.'

He fetched the milk from the fridge with a grunt and muttered something under his breath about not all publicity being good publicity.

Thank goodness I'd had something exciting to talk to Gloria about when I visited her last night; she had needed a distraction from thinking about her injuries. She was thoroughly fed up with being in hospital and her leg was very painful. She'd been allowed out of bed in the afternoon, but she'd found using the crutches very tiring and admitted that ordering a taxi and trying to discharge herself had been foolish.

On a lighter note, the nurses had raved about the cakes Dave had taken in, which had gone some way to repairing her relations with the ward staff. The only downside was that Gloria had been so thrilled to hear about the *Challenge Chester* programme that I hadn't had the heart to admit that it would be me rather than Tom joining Chester Fulwood in front of the camera. And that meant I couldn't pick her brains about baking bread. Instead, I'd stayed up half the night watching 'How to Bake Bread' videos on YouTube, so now I knew the theory, I just had zero experience.

And as much as I didn't like to admit any weakness to him, I was going to have to ask Tom for help.

I cleared my throat. 'Tom, don't laugh but—'

He looked at me, an amused frown playing across his face.

'I've never actually made bread,' I confessed with a gulp.

Chapter 15

'Haven't you? Oh. *Oh!*' His eyes widened as the implications of my admission formed furrows across his forehead. 'So why offer to do it?'

I shrugged. 'I couldn't let the opportunity pass the cookery school by.'

Tom was still staring at me. 'I don't know whether you're brave . . . or mad.'

'Can you teach me?' I said, opting to ignore that comment. 'Before the film crew turn up.'

He handed me a piping-hot mug of coffee. 'Smell that.'

My eyes closed and I inhaled the rich sweet aroma. 'Very zingy.'

Tom's face flickered with pleasure. 'Made with my secret stash of coffee beans from Panama. Quite floral, isn't it? The beans are grown slowly at high altitude—'

'Tom, the coffee is great,' I interrupted with a smile. He was such a food-geek. 'Now, about the bread?'

He swept an arm towards the beautifully appointed kitchen with its twenty student workstations gleaming under the halogen spotlights.

'Choose your spot.'

We washed our hands and gathered bowls, whisks, flour and yeast, sugar and salt in efficient and companionable silence. I hoped I wouldn't live to regret this; there was no doubting Tom's bread-making skills – I'd tasted his bread before – but wherever food was concerned he and I always seemed to clash.

However, needs must. I'd just have to be ultra-diplomatic and avoid getting into a row whatever the cost.

'OK, what next?' I asked.

He whacked the oven up to full heat and smiled. 'When I give an order, you say . . . ?'

My stomach fizzed dangerously.

I looked at him. 'Not in this life, Mister.'

We stared at each other for a moment before bursting out laughing and then got down to work. He showed me how much yeast and sugar to add to hot water, judging the temperature with the tip of his finger. He handed me a whisk and I whipped the cloudy water until it was frothy and then while I stirred until I thought my arm would drop off, Tom poured the yeasty liquid into the bowl until the mixture had formed a sticky beige ball which left the sides of the bowl clean.

He flicked a pinch of flour expertly over the work surface and indicated for me to tip the bowl up. The dough landed with a pleasing 'bouf' sound.

'And now you knead it.'

'OK.' I nodded confidently, thinking back to the You-Tube tutorials I'd watched last night. Push, pull, quarter turn, lift and fold. Simple.

I plunged my hands into the dough and . . .

'Eww, it's clinging to me,' I said, looking down at my fingers covered in sticky goo.

I heard him huff and I glared at him. 'What's wrong now?'

'Put your body weight into it. You can't over-knead. And find a rhythm. Like this.'

He positioned himself behind me and reached round to place my hands on the dough. My pulse leapt; he smelled lovely: spicy and sweet like toasted teacakes.

'Now let me do all the work,' he said, adding in a lower voice, 'shouldn't be too hard.'

156

I could have retorted. I could have said something really witty. But the warmth of his breath on the back of my neck and the feel of his fingers against mine were doing amazing things to my insides. I hadn't expected that. So I kept my mouth firmly shut.

His hands covered mine and he pushed down with the heel of his left palm and curled my fingertips around the edge of the dough to pull it back to the centre. We changed hands and did it again on the right, pushing away and bringing it back. Left, right, left, right . . . our bodies swaying slightly with each turn of the dough.

'This is fun,' I said, surprised.

Actually, it was more than fun; it was mesmerizing. And soporific and mildly sensual. Feeling the fluid movement of our arms, our fingers intertwined as we pushed back and forth, back and forth. My eyes were beginning to close when suddenly a vivid image popped into my head of that scene in *Ghost* with Patrick Swayze, Demi Moore and a potter's wheel. That really erotic one . . .

I let out a gasp and jumped, stepping back on to Tom's toe in the process.

'What did you do that for?' Tom grunted, releasing my hands.

'Sorry. It's done,' I said breathily, shaking my hands from the dough. 'I think.'

I was used to giggling my way through recipes, laughing at my mistakes, to cheering my achievements, not getting all hot under the collar and quivery. Exciting though it was.

'It's not.' He smoothed a loose strand of my hair behind my ear.

I swallowed. 'Isn't it?'

He shook his head. 'We're looking for silk. When you feel silk between your fingers, smooth and cool to the touch, then and only then is it ready to rise. Feel it.'

My head flipped to thoughts of 'Fifty Shades of Dough'

157

and my pulse began to race. I swallowed and patted the soft smooth ball of dough gently. Like a bottom.

'Now whip it into shape, on your own this time.'

Stop with the innuendos now, please. I pressed a hand to my hot face and blew out a breath.

He moved to the other side of the kitchen worktop to watch. 'There's flour all over your nose.'

'I know.'

'You look quite cute.'

'Shush.' I circled my shoulders round, followed by my wrists and prepared to start again.

'Quite a workout, isn't it?' he chuckled.

I nodded and wiped my forehead, aware that that probably meant I was even more floury. I dropped my gaze and began to knead until I was perspiring and my breath was coming in short pants. Finally, the dough was deemed 'silky' enough. Tom chopped off a piece of it and, following instructions, I popped the rest in a bowl and covered it with a clean cloth.

'An hour to prove,' said Tom, stretching his small lump of dough into a rough triangle. 'But in the meantime, we can enjoy a little *fougasse*. If you fancy it?'

'Sure.' I shrugged, not wanting to admit I'd never heard of it.

He flipped the triangle on to a baking sheet, slashed it several times and fanned it out into a leaf shape.

'*Et voilà.*' He held out the baking sheet to show me before slipping it into a hot oven. 'It doesn't need any proving so it's great to make with kids.'

I nodded. 'Noah would love to have a go: all that kneading and stretching it into shapes.'

'I was thinking it was something we could make in a kids' class, actually.' Tom peered sideways at me. 'Noah is Gloria's grandson, isn't he? Are you close to him?'

'Very. He's my godson,' I said, my voice catching in my throat. 'His mum, Mimi, and I shared everything. And now she's gone, he's all I've got left of her. Well, him and Gloria.'

We began to clear up, Tom scooping the excess flour from the surfaces while I filled the sink with hot water.

'You must miss him, being so far away?'

I nodded. 'We speak on the phone and I love hearing his little voice but it's not the same. Plus, conversation is a bit limited with a three-year-old.'

'I'm the same with my goddaughter, Saoirse. Whenever I go home to Ireland, she's doubled in size.'

'Like our bread dough?' I caught his eye and he nodded. 'Exactly.'

We smiled at each other and then went back to our cleaning. He was easy company today, more like the man I'd met on my first day in Plumberry, and I felt like I was getting to know the real Tom.

'And Gabe?' he asked a minute or so later as he carried the ingredients we'd finished with back to the store cupboard. 'Are you close to him?'

The question made my skin tingle.

Were we close?

How did I even begin to answer that? Gabe and I were bound eternally; we had been through so much together, shared and lost so much. The only other person I'd ever been closer to was Mimi.

'Mimi met him when we were sixteen.' I plunged my hands into the washing-up water, scrubbing the sticky dough from the utensils, conscious of the tremor in my voice. 'We've grown up together, I suppose.'

'Gloria said you and Mimi were never out of the kitchen when you were growing up?'

'Nor as adults,' I said, shaking my head softly as memories zipped through my brain. 'We always hung out in the kitchen; it was our favourite place.'

I remembered back to when I'd bought my house in Heron Drive with Chris, my fiancé; it had been Mimi who'd come with me for a second viewing, pointing out what a lovely light kitchen it had, perfect for cooking up a storm in. And it had been at that kitchen table a couple of years later that Mimi had doled out tea and sympathy when Chris called off our engagement, stating in a defeated voice that I'd never put him first and I probably never would.

Tom touched my arm. 'Tell me to mind my own business if I'm being nosy.'

I shook my head. 'It's fine. Happy memories, most of them.'

'And yet you arrived in Plumberry as Princess Prick and Ping?' He grinned, picking up a clean tea towel.

'Yes, well,' I said primly, 'I lost my passion for cooking for a while.'

Tom began to dry the wet things on the draining board.

'If I lost that, then . . .' A shadow of vulnerability passed across his face. I could have hugged him. But then he shook himself and smiled again. 'But that'll never happen to me. Losing someone you love makes us do odd things, though.'

I nodded. 'A hole opened up in my life when Mimi died and instead of filling it in, I tiptoed round it until it got bigger and bigger and then I found I was cutting out bits of my life that I loved just because it reminded me of her. I forced myself to see Gabe and Noah, even though it hurt to do so, because . . . well, because I suppose they need me. And I need them.'

I felt shy all of a sudden; I'd never said that out loud before. And now I'd told Tom. I hoped I hadn't gone too far.

'But now you're cooking again, so you must be moving on?' he said softly.

'Slowly,' I agreed. 'I've rediscovered my love of food, but the other side to my grief – that twist of guilt, as real as a sharp pain between the ribs – is still there. Even this, preparing for the TV show, despite my nerves, deep down I'm excited about it and it's exactly the sort of thing she'd have loved doing. That makes me feel sad.'

And there were lots of things like that.

Icing cupcakes, trips to the park, bedtime stories . . . All the things Mimi had dreamed of doing with her own little boy would be done by me instead. And now that I was so involved with Gloria's life – living in her home, helping run her business – the feelings of guilt were always there under the surface.

'Now, *me*,' he grinned, lightening the mood, 'when things don't go my way, I become more determined than ever to improve, to cook better, be more competitive . . .'

'I hadn't noticed,' I said, cocking an eyebrow.

'Ha ha. Talking of which . . .' Tom checked his watch and pulled the piping-hot *fougasse* out of the oven. 'This crusty little number will take some beating, I promise you.'

The bread smelled so good my mouth watered and as soon as it was cool enough to touch, Tom broke it into pieces, piled it on to a bread board with a bowl of extra virgin olive oil and a pile of sea salt.

'Here,' he said, pulling up a stool and shoving the bread board towards me. 'Sit and enjoy.'

I sat, popping a piece of still-warm bread into my mouth. The crust was nutty and chewy and totally set my taste buds alight.

'Oh.' I widened my eyes. 'That is good.'

'Told you.' He dunked a piece of crust in the oil and dabbed it with salt.

The rain was still beating a tattoo on the old mill windows and there wasn't as much as a sliver of blue to cheer up the sky. It was very intimate in the silence of the empty cookery school: just Tom and me, with the warmth of the oven heating the space around us, the comforting aroma of freshly baked bread. The moment felt right to dig into his story.

'So. Tell me about Salinger's,' I said softly. 'You obviously miss it, so what happened?'

He stared at me for such a long time that I felt a blush creep from the neck of my jumper up to the tips of my ears.

'It was my dream to open my own place,' he began. 'And after Rebecca and I got together, it became hers too. She gave up being a maths teacher, started looking for premises and before I knew it, we were in business. There was no stopping her.'

I blinked at him. Gloria had mentioned a partner; I hadn't realized it was *that* sort of partner. 'So you went into business with your girlfriend?'

He nodded. 'I won't be making that mistake twice. I dictated the direction for the food . . .'

Dictated. I could imagine. I hid my smile by shoving a hunk of hot bread into my mouth.

'But she took over the interior, the décor, the bar, even the name,' he added darkly. 'I've wanted my name over the door of my own restaurant since I was a wee boy growing up.'

'You didn't put up a fight about the name? That's not like you,' I teased.

'She's very persuasive, or as I now see, manipulative,' he continued. 'And her surname is Salinger, which she argued worked better than—'

'MacDonald's!' I let out a snort and then caught sight of his stony face. 'Sorry.'

'We could have called it Tom's.' He flashed his eyes at me, filled with humour. 'Anyway, it all went well for the first couple of years. And then . . . Will I tell you the whole miserable story?'

I nodded. So while I finished up the *fougasse*, secretly wishing I could have chocolate spread on it instead of olive oil, he did. And it was quite miserable.

Business at Salinger's was brisk, especially after they'd

162

won the much-coveted Michelin star. But also because of his sublime food, Tom hastened to add. He was confident about business and even started looking at venues to open a second restaurant, which Rebecca thought was a great idea. And then he started dropping hints about them having a baby: they were comfortable financially, the right age, in love . . . what better time? Rebecca apparently thought it was a terrible idea, declaring that having a family and a restaurant were mutually exclusive; the demands of a business and the long unsociable hours plus a small child didn't add up. Tom accepted it reluctantly, right up until he came across Rebecca in the wine cellar late one night with Ryan the sous chef.

'No,' I gasped. 'And were they . . . ?'

He looked at me from under his dark brows. 'Well, they weren't discussing corkage.'

'But how can she possibly have been unfaithful with Ryan when she had you?' I said, full of indignation on his behalf.

Tom laughed and I felt my face heat up.

He told me that Ryan's father was the CEO of a giant pharmaceutical company and had offered to fund a much larger venture than Salinger's could ever hope to be.

'Rebecca had done the maths,' he said drily, 'and decided she was better off with Ryan. And she had the audacity to claim responsibility for Salinger's' success. So I left them to it, sloped off like a wounded bear with the entire staff probably laughing at me behind my back.'

He checked the time, took the cloth off the bowl and turned the huge fluffy ball of dough out on to a clean surface. He punched it a couple of times. Hard.

'You just walked away? Letting them get off scot-free?' I couldn't believe that of him. It seemed so . . . defeatist.

'I loved Rebecca. Really loved her.' He gazed into the middle distance and my heart twisted for him. I was beginning to understand why he had such a touchy side: his professional pride was wounded but not only that, his heart was broken too.

'But I'm over her. If she walked back in here now, today, I wouldn't even flinch,' he said matter-of-factly. I wasn't sure I believed that. He sat down and raised his eyebrows at me. 'Your turn.'

'OK.' I swallowed, taken aback by his directness. 'His name was – *is* – Liam.'

I told him about Chris, and how after he'd called off our engagement it had taken me quite a while to dip my toe back in the water, until I fell for Liam's charms. And then I told him about my job at Solomon's and how Liam had used the office party that I hadn't gone to as an opportunity to cheat on me with Melanie, then present my ideas to our boss and steal the job from under my nose.

'So I suppose you and I have had similar treatment at the hands of our loved ones,' I finished with a shrug.

'Bloody hell.' He whistled and then pointed to the dough. 'Actually, I meant your turn to knock it back.'

'Oh,' I said, going pink. I took his place in front of the floury work surface.

'Punch it like you mean it. Take out all your anger on it.'

I picked up the dough and threw it down a couple of times, trying to be angry.

Take that, Liam, I thought, mustering up an inner feistiness. How dare you pass my *One, Two, Three Plan* off as your own? But it was no good. My beef with him for losing me my job and cheating on me seemed to have evaporated. It was as I'd suspected: I'd never really let myself get too attached to either him or my job at Solomon's. My grief over Mimi had numbed my nerve endings for a while and I'd been going through the motions without properly loving or feeling. Which explained why, when Rosie tried to make me fight for that promotion, I couldn't be bothered.

So actually, thanks, Liam, you did me a favour . . .

I pursed my lips and squished the dough into the shape of a smiley mouth.

'I didn't just walk away from Salinger's.' Tom scratched his beard. 'I bust Ryan's nose first. Then I walked away. And then a few hours later I got a call from the police. They'd drop the charges as long as I promised to be a good lad. Straightaway the jungle drums starting beating through restaurant-land about me having left Salinger's and I got a call from Gloria. So here I am.'

I pressed my knuckles daintily into the dough while Tom greased some tins.

'But you can start again, you'll have another restaurant and call it MacDonald's or Tom's or whatever you like and meanwhile you're passing your passion and talent on to others. Come on, cheer up,' I said, punching his arm with a floury fist.

He brushed his sleeve and a little white cloud drifted to the ground. 'I know all that. It's just a bitter pill to swallow.'

'And that's why you don't want to be on *Challenge Chester*, because it's a blow to your ego?'

'I had it all back there for a while. And now Ryan has it: my restaurant, my woman and my Michelin star,' he said, his voice getting a little bit shouty. 'And making giant phallus-shaped bread on TV in front of millions, but especially in front of those two, would make me feel like a total knob.'

'OK, OK,' I soothed, patting his arm, wishing he'd stop referring to the Eiffel Tower like that. 'That's why I'm doing it.'

I set the three tins aside and left them to their final proving.

'Thank you; I mean that,' he said, adding quietly, 'Even though I think you're mad for volunteering. And brave.'

'I am, aren't I?' I laughed. 'But it'll be—'

'Fun, yes, I'm sure it will.' He smiled a smile that lit up his entire face and the room. And me.

He wrapped an arm loosely round my shoulders and squeezed. 'And you're right, I will run a restaurant again. On my own. My way.'

I looked up and gave him my most sparkly grin. 'Yes, Chef.'

Chapter 16

By lunchtime I was heading south to pay a whistle-stop visit to Nottingham, with two loaves of fresh crusty bread on the passenger seat. I'd dropped off Comfrey and Sage with Mags for the day, delivered a clean nightdress and a thermos of Tom's special coffee to Gloria and now I was battling the elements to stay afloat on the motorway.

Today was the perfect day to schedule in a quick trip home: there was nothing urgent to do at the cookery school now that I'd mastered bread-making. I'd been missing my little house for the last day or so and it would be good to sort out a few boring jobs like paying bills.

My phone began to ring from the depths of my handbag as I passed an articulated lorry. I ignored it – safety first, and all that – and flipped my windscreen wipers up to maximum as the spray from the lorry's rows of wheels cut a swathe through the surface water and threatened to wash my little car off the road. I stopped at the next service station, treated myself to a skinny latte and a cookie, and saw a missed call from Gabe.

'Verity! Gloria's been on the phone,' he said when I called him back; he sounded worried. 'She wants to come home to watch some TV film on Saturday.'

'Ah,' I said, sliding into a little booth at the busy coffee shop. 'That'll be the TV filming at the cookery school. Not the actual TV.'

I told him about my on-screen debut and he laughed. 'That makes sense. I'd quite like to see that myself.'

'I'd rather you didn't; I'll be nervous enough without an audience, thank you very much.' I blew a hole in the froth of the latte and took a sip.

'Where are you anyway?' Gabe asked. 'It sounds noisy.'

'Motorway services on my way home for a few hours. I'll come over to the boat if you like, I'd love to see Noah. And you.'

'Verity Bloom, I could kiss you. In fact, I will kiss you. How quickly can you come?'

'I'm flattered,' I laughed, breaking off a piece of cookie and dunking it in my coffee. 'An hour, bit more depending on the rain.'

'Rain? It's brilliant sunshine here. And it's Noah's first sports day at nursery.' He paused and I heard him swallow. 'All the mums will be there.'

And Gabe would be flying solo.

I fumbled to get the lid back on my takeaway coffee cup in my haste to leave. 'I'm on my way.'

Gabe was right, by the time I'd passed the sign informing me that I was now in Nottinghamshire, the sky ahead of me was forget-me-not blue dotted with marshmallow clouds. And at two o'clock when I squeezed the car into the nursery car park and stepped out into the bright May sunshine, I'd almost forgotten about the Yorkshire rain completely.

The children, some looking far too small to walk, let alone run, were gathered at one end of the field, sitting cross-legged on the floor in teams. Brightly coloured plastic crates of beanbags, balls and other assorted equipment were lined up ready at the starting line. Two long rows of chairs had been set up on the grass alongside a makeshift running track. All appeared to be taken, and the audience, almost exclusively female, had cameras poised to record the fun and games.

'Aunty Vetty!'

I held my arms out as Noah, in shorts, T-shirt and a green baseball cap, broke ranks and came barrelling towards me.

I caught him mid-leap and swung him round, placing a kiss on his hot pink cheek. I squeezed him as tight as I dared, breathing in his little boy smell of biscuits and sun cream and fresh grass.

'I have missed you more than chocolate,' I said, lowering him to the ground.

He giggled and I caught him looking at my bag surreptitiously. I wished I'd brought him some chocolate now; somehow I doubted he'd be impressed with my homemade white loaf.

'I've got my trainers on, look.' I held up a Nike-clad foot. 'When do I get to race?'

Gabe's head appeared above the sea of spectators. He waved and pointed downwards to the seat next to him.

'I'm in the green team. You can tell by my hat. My favourite is the egg and spoon race,' explained Noah, taking my hand as we made our way to Gabe.

'Oh, me too.' I smiled, wrapping my fingers round his.

'But they're not real eggs so no eating them,' he chanted with a wag of his finger.

'I'll try to remember that.'

'And grown-ups have to wait till the end for their go. There's Daddy! Bye, Aunty Vetty.' Noah spotted his teacher waving frantically at him and he ran off to join the rest of his team.

Gabe lifted his jumper off the empty seat next to him. 'I am so glad you're here,' he murmured, running a hand through his scruffy sandy hair. 'I'm feeling grossly outnumbered.'

'Me too,' I beamed, wrapping my arms round his neck and kissing his rough cheek. 'I wouldn't have missed my godson's first sports day for the world,' I added for the benefit of the curious women who'd instantly stopped all conversation as soon as I'd arrived.

'Thanks.' He grinned and held out a packet of sweets. 'Have a wine gum.'

I took a black one and we chatted while we chomped, catching up on each other's news and discussing Gloria's predicament in hospital.

'I thought Noah and I might come up to Plumberry in *The Neptune* and moor up somewhere nearby. That way we can be around to help out without being a burden.'

'She'd love that. Although you could always stay next door with Mags.'

Gabe shuddered. 'Only if there's a lock on my bedroom door.'

I laughed. 'She's all talk; you'd be quite safe.'

He shook his head. 'Even so, I'll come under my own steam. I might set off at the weekend; it'll take us about ten days to get there. Noah will love the adventure and a few days out of nursery won't hurt.'

I glanced at him sideways, marvelling as I always did at how dramatically he'd changed his life since losing Mimi. He used to have a sporty BMW and drove like a rally-car driver, always in a rush to get places. Now, he was content to meander along England's waterways for as long as it took. He was an incredible person on so many levels and a brilliant father.

'What?' he asked, noticing my warm smile.

I helped myself to another wine gum. 'Ten days,' I chuckled. 'Gloria will definitely be out of hospital by then; I don't think the nurses can wait to get rid of her.'

'PARENTS, GRANDPARENTS, FRIENDS, BOYS AND GIRLS!'

A tall willowy lady dressed in a tracksuit began to bellow into a loudhailer. Gabe and I jammed our fingers into our ears as the sound system screeched with feedback.

'Welcome to the annual Ashdale Nursery sports day. The

children have been training hard all week . . .'

The races were soon under way and when Noah came second in the skipping race, I clapped and cheered until I was red in the face and my hands stung. My heart was in my mouth during the egg and spoon race and when he passed close by and I saw the concentration on his face, I clutched Gabe's hand with nerves. And when he came first in the hula-hoop race I wept tears of unabashed joy and pride and absolute love. So did Gabe.

'AND NOW LET'S SEE ALL THE MUMMIES JOIN IN,' squeaked the lady with the loudhailer.

I felt Gabe's hand cover mine and squeeze it tight. Neither of us spoke. We didn't need to. The heartache we both felt wrapped itself around us like fog.

The women around us groaned and got to their feet slowly. Although one or two of them, I noticed, did slip on some very professional-looking footwear and started doing a few limbering-up exercises.

'Aunty Vetty!' Noah had both arms in the air trying to attract my attention. 'Now you can have a go.'

Gabe and I gazed at each other and the sadness in his grey eyes broke my heart. This should have been Mimi's moment. She would have been the first up there, probably still wearing her high heels, her jokes, aimed at herself, raising a smile even amongst the most serious competitors.

'Shall I?' I said, squeezing Gabe's hand.

He nodded, tears blurring his eyes. 'You're all he's got.'

Cheer me on, Mimi, I'm doing this for you. And for Noah. If you could send down some celestial good luck that would be great.

'Yes!' Noah punched the air as I swallowed the ginormous lump in my throat, got to my feet and made my way to the starting line with the rest of the game-for-a-laugh girls.

'Is that your mummy?' a little girl next to Noah wanted to know.

He shook his head. 'She's my godmother, but she loves me just the same.'

171

'READY, STEADY, GO!' yelled the only male member of staff, adding a toot on his whistle for good measure.

I flicked the tears off my cheeks and ran as if my life depended on it.

'Some people take things so seriously,' I said later that evening, rubbing my ankle where a bruise had appeared.

'Says the girl who has given me a full ten-minute rundown of how you were robbed of first place.' Rosie lifted an eyebrow before taking another generous mouthful of my most excellent crusty white bread. 'And shown me all the pictures.'

After hot dogs and fried onions aboard *The Neptune* with Gabe and Noah, I'd finally made it back to Heron Drive at eight o'clock. Rosie and I were making the most of the setting sun in the narrow strip of back garden with a cafetière of coffee and slices of my bread and jam.

'I'd better be getting back soon,' I said with a yawn.

According to a text from Mags, the rain in Plumberry hadn't let up all day and I really did not relish driving back in the dark along those windy roads with the wipers going at full pelt.

'Stay the night,' Rosie insisted. 'Then we can have too much wine and regret it in the morning. Please. It's ages since I did that.'

'But what about the lodger?' I said, already calculating what time I'd have to be up in the morning. 'What's his name?'

She flapped a hand. 'Joe. Don't worry about him. He'll be at the gym for ages yet.'

'Yes, but doesn't he sleep in my room?'

She flashed her dark eyes mischievously. 'Not often.'

'Rosie!' I squealed. 'Just how old is this intern?'

'Old enough,' she said smugly, getting to her feet. 'White or rosé?'

*

She came back with blankets and wine and we proposed a toast to girls' nights in. I told her all about *Challenge Chester*, realizing as I did so that for someone who'd refused even to open a cookery book for the last two years, I'd made a pretty remarkable recovery in the last few weeks.

'I know I'd originally said I'd be away for a month,' I said, 'but Gloria is going to need a lot of looking after when she comes home.'

'Don't worry about it. The Yorkshire air suits you. Well, something does, anyway; I don't think I've seen you so sparkly since I met you.'

I sipped at my wine thoughtfully. I did feel sparkly. I'd had a fabulous day: making bread with Tom had been fun and it had brought a new understanding to our relationship. Being there for Noah and Gabe at their first sports day had been fun too and it had warmed my heart to be part of their lives, even if the occasion was tinged with sadness. But it was more than that.

'Plumberry suits me,' I replied. 'I didn't think it would because it's such a foodie place. But I feel alive and happy. And even though it has only just opened, I adore the cookery school. Being there makes me excited for the future.'

'Then stay as long as you can, girlfriend. Even though I'll miss you.'

'Come and visit me in Plumberry and learn to cook then.' I grinned. 'Nonna would love that.'

'She would. How you gonna keep a man happy if you can't even-a make-a pasta?' said Rosie, doing a mean impression of her Italian grandmother, complete with eye-rolls and sharp shoulder-shrugs.

'We're doing Perfect Pasta soon, as it happens,' I said with a sudden shiver. I pulled the hood up on my hoodie and tucked a blanket over me, doing my own little-old-lady impression.

'I'll bear it in mind,' said Rosie, humouring me. She leaned across to top up our glasses just as the doorbell rang.

'Sorry,' she said flatly, returning two minutes later with a tall, broad-shouldered figure behind her. 'The bad penny is back again.'

It was Liam, looking handsome in a navy suit and a white shirt. I, on the other hand, looked like one of those all-night fishermen you see on riverbanks all hunched up in their deckchairs.

'Hi, Verity.' Liam's bemused eyes flicked over my co-cooned body. 'You're looking . . . cosy.'

'I'll go and sort your bed out,' said Rosie, throwing me a look of apology.

'That's very generous of you.' Liam grinned and lowered himself into her deckchair.

'Not yours, tosser,' Rosie growled and stomped off into the kitchen.

'Verity,' Liam began. His face was one of total contrition as he attempted to hold my hand.

I dodged him, picked up my glass and took a big swig.

'You stole from me, Liam; you stole my ideas and my trust.'

'I know, I know, and it's been keeping me awake at night ever since.'

'Really?' I cocked an eyebrow. That and Melanie, probably.

He had the good grace to look sheepish.

'It is lovely to see you. I've missed you, you know. And you had such a lucky escape at Solomon's. There have been even more redundancies and Ruthless Rod is such a cretin to work for.'

I couldn't help but feel a teensy bit pleased. Liam had made his bed, now he could lie in it, as far as I was concerned. 'But you got the promotion you wanted, so you must be happy, no?'

His shoulders slumped and he raked a large freckly hand through his copper hair.

'I'd only admit this to you, but . . . I'm out of my depth.

174

I've got twice the amount of work to do and now that I'm the marketing manager, Rod expects me to just cope with it.'

I shrugged my shoulders. 'So you've got more responsibility. What's this got to do with me?'

'I'm presenting the marketing strategy to the board next week. Please, help me out,' he pleaded. 'Explain your *One, Two, Three Plan* to me. Or else I'm toast.'

We stared at each other for a long time. He pulled his cute schoolboy grin and I kept my poker face. Finally I exhaled.

'If I tell you will you leave me alone?'

He nodded.

'All right. Have you got something to write with?'

'Yes!' His eyes shone. 'I'll put it straight into my new phone.'

He pulled his latest gadget out of his pocket and flashed it around. I tutted; that was so very Liam. He had the looks and the patter, but none of the substance to back it up.

'OK.' I cleared my throat. 'Take note.'

His finger hovered over his touchscreen.

'One. Never be unfaithful to your girlfriend. Two. Never cheat your girlfriend out of a job. And three. Get your own sodding ideas.'

He dropped his head in his hands and groaned. 'I guess I deserved that.'

'You did.' I raised my glass and took a swig. 'Cheers.'

Liam dragged himself to the back door.

'I'm finished,' he said flatly. 'You were my last hope. Goodbye.'

Revenge is a dish best served cold and all that but I thought of the work I'd put into developing those marketing plans for Solomon's. I could take it to my grave, I supposed, let my brilliant idea go to waste, but where was the harm in letting him have it? Not because I wanted to help him out, I told myself briskly. Although he did cut a pitiful figure with his dejected smile and hunched shoulders. But at least I'd have the satisfaction of knowing that my ideas were good enough, even if Rod had chosen not to hear them from me when he had the chance.

'Wait,' I said. 'I'll email you my PowerPoint presentation.'

Liam's face lit up. 'You, Verity Bloom,' he said, pointing at me, 'are the bomb.'

'I know, Liam,' I said earnestly. 'I know.'

Chapter 17

By dawn the next morning the wet weather had found me again. Not as heavy as the rain I'd left behind in Yorkshire, but nonetheless as I packed my car with enough clothes to cope with every possible climate, water was running down the neck of my sweatshirt and soaking into the toes of my Converses.

I hastily kissed Rosie, whispered my goodbyes to the mound of duvet next to her (which she assured me was Joe) and made an early start back to Plumberry.

We hadn't had too late a night last night after all, nor drunk too much wine; Joe had come back from the gym with fish and chips (rather counter-productively, I thought), which Rosie forced him to share with us. Then the two of us had retired to her room to style me for my TV debut, with me wishing I'd not eaten quite so many of Joe's chips and her berating me for agreeing to help Liam out.

Joe was a sweetie. At twenty-three he was several years Rosie's junior and had a baby face to match. He'd finished his degree in computing and was working in the IT department at Rosie's place temporarily, storing up experience ready for his gap year of travelling, which he planned to fund by mending computers on his way round the world from September.

Both of them were realistic about the longevity of their

relationship, but were happy to enjoy it while it lasted if the bumps in the night were anything to go by.

So I was somewhat bleary-eyed as I made the journey northwards and had to stop off halfway for coffee at the motorway services. I sat down with a double espresso and called Mags.

'Plumberry house for retired sex-goddesses?' she panted as she answered the phone.

'Retired?' I said with a chuckle. 'Since when?'

'Verity! It's the crack of dawn!' she cried. 'I'm still in my birthday suit. Hold on, you've woken the dogs. I'll have to let them out.'

I heard her feet slap on the tiles on her way through to the kitchen and the dogs squeak excitedly as she opened the back door.

'Wee wees! Good boys. No, don't dig there, Sage; stop! Oh no,' she groaned.

'What's he doing?'

'Stick-mad that dog, trying to pull my bamboo wigwam up again. My poor petit pois don't stand a chance. If it isn't the torrential rain, it's him stealing the canes. I'll have to go out there.'

'But aren't you . . . ?'

'Hold on a minute, love.'

I heard rustling noises and muffled grunts and more excited barking.

'Jeepers, this rain is wet. And cold. Avert your gaze, Len,' I heard her yell. 'It's an emergency.' Len Banbury was Mags's other next-door neighbour and must be pushing eighty.

'Len? What is he doing outside at this time of day?' I asked. 'In the rain?'

'Putting his nuts out on the bird table. Put those binoculars down,' I heard her shout.

The mind boggled. I sipped my espresso and waited dutifully.

'Sage Ramsbottom, come back here with that cane.'

I squeezed my eyes shut to block out the image of Mags chasing the dog round the garden in all her morning glory.

'Please go back inside, Mags, before poor old Len reports you for indecent exposure,' I said when I heard her heavy breathing at the end of the line again.

'Pah! He loves it. Why do you think he took that fence panel down and replaced it with trellis? The saucepot.'

'Well, if nothing else, you'll catch your death,' I said. 'And one invalid is quite enough, thank you.'

'Come on, you two, back in.'

I held the phone away from my ear as Mags shouted to the dogs. There was a patter of little paws and then the kitchen door closed with a bang.

'We're all back in,' she gasped. 'Talking of invalids, good news. Gloria is coming out of hospital today.'

'Is she? Oh, that is good news.'

She gave me all the details and I rang off, agreeing to meet her at the cookery school later on. I swallowed the rest of my espresso in a single gulp and got up to leave.

I was pleased for Gloria, of course, it must have been awful for her spending a week in hospital while goodness knows what was happening at her brand-new cookery school. But it did mean that my day had become even more hectic. She was going to need a lot of looking after when she arrived, as well as a makeshift bedroom sorting out downstairs. Plus, I had to prepare for the arrival of the *Challenge Chester* crew in the morning. My stomach lurched; only twenty-four hours to go . . .

I arrived at the cookery school in time to greet the students and pinch a fresh pastry for my breakfast. Today I planned on using my new bread skills to attempt a loaf in the shape of the Eiffel Tower before my trip to hospital to collect Gloria. Tom was running the morning Knife Skills class

179

for a small group of students so I decided to base myself in the Aga kitchen downstairs.

I tied on an apron, gathered together my ingredients and began to mix the dough, trying to remember everything that Tom had taught me. An hour later, I'd pummelled and punched it into submission, covered it with a clean tea towel and set it aside to prove.

'Can I borrow you for a moment?' Mags's head appeared round the door of the kitchen. I followed her out into reception.

'Listen.'

I frowned. 'I can't hear anything.'

'Exactly.'

She jerked her head towards the staircase and the pair of us tiptoed halfway up to peep into the teaching kitchen. Pixie was scraping vegetable peelings into the bin, Tom was patrolling the aisles like an officer of the law and the students were bent over their workstations, chopping root vegetables as though their lives depended on it. No one made a sound.

My heart sank. I wanted our customers to gush with enthusiasm to their friends when they left us, not mop their brows and declare they hadn't felt under such pressure since school exams.

We crept back down and pulled grim faces at each other.

'It's like a morgue up there,' Mags muttered.

'I know,' I whispered.

'What are we going to do?'

I sighed. 'His heart's in the right place, Mags. And he is very talented. He was brilliant at helping me knead bread yesterday.'

'I've no doubt he's good with his hands.' She raised her eyebrows knowingly.

'Mags!'

'But it's not the Plumberry School of *Cold* Comfort, is

180

it?' she hissed. 'We've got to find a way of getting him to lighten up.'

I nodded. 'Leave it with me.' I stifled a sigh. Along with everything else.

By lunchtime the students had gone, Pixie had popped out somewhere and Mags and Tom were clearing up while I took the most ridiculous loaf of bread the world had ever seen from the oven.

Having Googled a picture of the Eiffel Tower, I'd moulded the dough into three sections: the bridge-shaped base, an upper-case A for the middle and a long thin bit with a bobble on the end for the top.

I held the baking tray with my oven gloves and stared at my creation; it did look a bit suggestive. That bobbly bit on the top wasn't helping. The loaf fell to pieces as I slid it on to a cooling rack, and at that moment the doors swung open and Tom appeared, a streak of red across the front of his chef whites.

'Don't worry, it's my blood.' He held up a thumb wrapped in a blue plaster.

'Phew. As long as we haven't maimed a student.'

He grinned at me and my stomach fluttered.

It had been a long time since a man had had that effect on me. I certainly hadn't felt that way about Liam, and I wasn't even sure Chris had made my insides quiver quite so deliciously either.

I remembered my promise to Mags earlier to ask him to lighten up when he was teaching, but it could wait. There was a new intimacy between Tom and me since yesterday and I was enjoying this moment too much to spoil it.

He examined my bread, leaning his head first one way then the other.

'Is that meant to be the Eiffel Tower?' he asked.

'It's a complete cock-up,' I admitted.

Tom stared at the floor, but I could see he was struggling to keep a straight face. Pixie burst in, her dark hair plastered to her head and rivulets of water running off her waterproof coat.

'Have you heard— Ooh, that looks a bit, er . . .' she began until she noticed my glare. 'I mean a *lot* like the Eiffel Tower.'

'Thank you,' I said briskly.

The two of them exchanged mischievous grins and I coughed. 'Have we heard what?'

'About the storm.'

Pixie took off her steamed-up glasses and blinked wide eyes at us. 'It says on the news that people should avoid unnecessary journeys tonight. This rain is going to get worse.'

'Is that even possible?' I said, peering out of the window at the rain drumming on the glass like hailstones.

'Yep. A storm of colossal proportions is on its way from the north. Floods, gale-force winds, the lot.'

'That's it, I'm coming with you to fetch Gloria and I won't take no for an answer,' Tom announced, folding his arms. 'Mags told me you were heading off there later.'

Pixie looked from him to me, her eyes dancing. 'Cor, that was masterful, wasn't it?'

Very. I swallowed and managed a nod, trying to ignore the fluttering in my stomach. 'Thanks. But perhaps we shouldn't go at all if it's dangerous?'

Tom laughed. 'You could try telling Gloria that, but I wouldn't dare. Give me a shout when you want to go,' he added, sauntering off to reception with a whistle.

'What about the *Challenge Chester* lot?' Pixie said, chewing her lip. 'Do you think we should cancel? I mean, if they're driving up from London or something, they might not be able to get through if the roads are flooded.'

That was a thought. I took my phone out and dialled Cheryl's number.

'Chill, Verity,' Cheryl said when I explained about the local precipitation problems. She was chewing gum, as usual; I could hear it in her voice. 'We've been filming somewhere in Yorkshire today anyway and the boss's mum only lives in Thickleton, so we're all sleeping over tonight.'

'You wouldn't consider postponing?' I suggested, trying to keep the glimmer of hope out of my voice. A few more days to perfect my bread tower wouldn't go amiss.

'Nah. With such a tight filming schedule, we can't afford to miss a day. Your show will go out next week.'

'Oh, right,' I said, swallowing my disappointment. The village of Thickleton was only a few miles away, between Plumberry and the motorway; they would be able to walk it if they really had to. 'Great. Well, see you tomorrow, then.'

'By the way,' Cheryl added with a chomp on her gum, 'we're hoping to make the Eiffel Tower at least a metre high, just so you know.'

'You mean *long*?' I said in a wavery voice. I looked down at the baking tray. If it hadn't fallen apart it would be about forty centimetres long, which was as big as I could fit in the oven.

'No, *high*,' she said impatiently. 'It's a tower, isn't it? We want it to stand up like a tower. So you'll have to bake it in sections and, I dunno, stick it together with something?' And with that she rang off.

Stick it with what – chewing gum? I thought crossly, wishing I'd followed Tom's example and given the whole thing a wide berth.

'Let's take mine,' he yelled as we splashed across the car park through the rain later that afternoon. 'It'll cope better with this weather than your little Fiat.'

I stared at his battered Volvo estate. 'Why, does it have oars fitted as standard?'

He was right, though; it was twice the size of my car and Gloria would be able to stretch her legs out properly. The passenger-side door handle was broken and he had to let me in from the inside.

183

'It's very lived-in,' I said, searching for something nice to say about his car.

'That's because I have lived in it.' He started up the engine, which rattled like a bag of loose spanners. 'I like to chuck my stuff in the back and take off. I camp if the weather's good enough; otherwise I just fold down the seats and kip in the back. Just me, a camp fire and a deserted field. Perfect.'

I peered sideways at him. His dark hair was shiny with water droplets and there were tiny curls clinging to the nape of his neck. I fought the urge to reach out and touch them. 'Didn't have you down as an outdoorsy guy.'

'Me? Brought up on a sheep farm in Northern Ireland.' He put the car into reverse and we sloshed through puddles and out of the car park. 'Have you heard of the Giant's Causeway?'

'Of course.' I was impressed. 'I've never been but the pictures are beautiful.'

'Well, it's nowhere near there.' He grinned.

I laughed. 'You know you're quite . . .'

'Quite what?'

'Good company when you relax, let your guard down.'

'Thanks. I think.'

Now was my chance to tackle him about his teaching style. Mags's comment about the morgue popped into my brain. As much as I didn't like to be the one to point out his failings, I'd promised Gloria that her cookery school would be exactly what she wanted it to be: a place for sharing her love of food and having fun.

I decided to bite the bullet. 'If only you could be a bit more like this when you're teaching.'

He groaned. 'Not this "cooking should be a barrel of laughs" thing again. Can't you just accept that we're all different? Agree to disagree?'

'We definitely disagree,' I confirmed. 'Those poor students looked on the verge of committing hara-kiri this morning.'

'You'd rather they were rolling around the floor clutching their ribs hysterically whilst in possession of six inches of Japanese steel, I suppose.'

'No, but—'

'Good. So that's settled. Now can we drop it?'

'You're impossible, Tom MacDonald.'

'Thanks.' His eyes glinted with amusement.

Rain drummed on the car roof and the windscreen wipers batted backwards and forwards at top speed and neither of us spoke for the length of Plumberry high street. I bristled with irritation, although Tom seemed oblivious as he concentrated on driving. But when we hit the country roads the silence was too much to bear.

'Any plans for the weekend?' I said eventually to break the mood.

He shot me a sideways glance.

'I'll be at the cookery school offering assistance to new bread bakers in case they have any problems with their Eiffel Towers.'

It took a second to sink in.

'You will?' My face broke into a smile.

Oh, the relief! Just knowing he'd be there tomorrow when the TV crew arrived made me feel better. And you never know, perhaps I'd persuade him to take my place with Chester Fulwood in front of the cameras after all . . .

'Indeed I will.'

He stared ahead and I studied his handsome profile. He was impossible and irritating but I couldn't help but like him.

'You have no idea how ecstatic I am to hear that.'

I was tempted to hug him but after the mood of only a few moments ago, I didn't dare. I punched his arm instead.

'Ouch. I think my new bruise is a bit of a clue,' he said drily.

*

It took us an hour to manoeuvre Gloria from the ward into the car. We had to wait for her drugs to be dispensed, hunt down a wheelchair and go through copious lists of dos and don'ts from the ward sister before she'd let us leave with the patient. But eventually we got her settled in the passenger seat, with the chair pushed back as far as it would go and me wedged in the back with her crutches across my lap.

'You're sure you're OK?' said Tom for the umpteenth time, reaching across and doing up the seatbelt for her.

'I'm fine,' she said with a weak smile.

She looked a little grey to me and her forehead looked moist. It could have been rain, I supposed, but she certainly wasn't a picture of health. My stomach churned with worry; I was sure another couple of days in hospital would have been the best thing but she wouldn't hear of it.

'I've made a bed up for you in the living room. Mags and I carried a spare one down from upstairs, but are you absolutely sure you want to come back home?' I said, unable to stop fussing.

'Bliss.' She sighed, closing her eyes as she sank back against Tom's upholstery. 'I've never been more certain of anything in my life, darling. Now tell me everything I've missed.'

'We've got eleven booked on to Perfect Pasta next week,' I began.

'And the Knife Skills course went well today,' Tom added. 'In fact, I was demonstrating how to *brunoise* when—'

Gloria made a soft snuffling noise and her head dropped forward. I peered round to look at her face. She was fast asleep.

'It's the way you tell 'em,' I said with a grin, catching Tom's eye in the rear-view mirror.

Chapter 18

Gloria only awoke for a few seconds during the next hour or so and that was when we helped her to hobble from the car through the rain and into her cottage.

Comfrey and Sage, who'd spotted her from their perch on the windowsill, whimpered with heart-warming joy when she came in and soon the three of them were snuggled up in bed together in the living room.

I closed the door, leaving only the low glow of a table lamp to light the room, and joined Tom in the kitchen.

He was standing at the door, looking out at the garden where the wind was flattening Gloria's poor rose bushes. 'So much for the spring weather; I'm used to heavy rain in Northern Ireland, but this is awful.'

'Tea?' I asked, automatically reaching for the kettle.

'Please.' As he checked his watch, his stomach let out a piteous growl and he pressed a hand to it.

'Or maybe I should get going; we're getting into "essential journeys only" territory out there, and if you hadn't already guessed I'm hungry.'

'Stay for a little while. Please,' I added. 'I don't fancy an evening on my own, watching the storm clouds gather. And I can feed you.'

He looked back at the skies doubtfully and at the cooker, also doubtfully.

'It won't be up to your usual standards, of course,' I said, scanning the cupboards for inspiration, 'but I can offer you toast and a tin of soup?'

'A feast,' he said with a grin.

I was about to clamp the tin opener over the edge of the can when the back door opened and Mags appeared wearing a rain poncho and red stilettos.

'Cooee! Meals on heels!' she trilled, brandishing a large casserole dish. 'I made us a chicken and chorizo stew.'

I abandoned the soup.

Mags dished up three generous portions of the stew, while I uncorked a bottle of Spanish red wine and Tom sliced some crusty bread. I checked on Gloria in case she was peckish but she was still out for the count.

I inhaled and my mouth watered. It smelled Mediterranean and spicy and warming and perfect for a stormy English night.

Tom took a mouthful and closed his eyes. 'Mags, this is a bowl of sunshine.'

She patted her hair. 'Flattery will get you everywhere.'

'Now, while the three of us are together,' I said, sipping the Rioja, 'I've had my best idea yet.'

'Does it involve making bread into rude shapes?' Mags winked at Tom.

'So childish.' I tutted. 'No, Dave said something to me the other day and it got me thinking.'

'Was it a way to ameliorate profit margins?' Tom asked, tweaking an eyebrow.

'Sort of,' I said carefully. 'In the long term. After bank holiday Monday next week, we have two days without courses. How about we open up the cookery school and run some competitions? I'll run one and Tom, you run the other.'

'What for?' Tom frowned.

'I love this idea already,' said Mags, scooping up sauce with a crust of bread.

'Firstly because it will give people a chance to try our facilities for nothing,' I explained.

'I can't see Dave going for that one,' Tom doubted. 'What about the cost of all the food?'

'The entrants have to bring their own ingredients. So no outlay for us. And secondly, it gives you and me a chance to test our theories.'

'What theories?' Mags and Tom said together.

'I think people would like a day of fun, like on *Great British Bake Off*, don't you?' I gave Mags a please-help-me-out look. This would be the ideal way to demonstrate to Tom that the courses at the cookery school would be more enjoyable if the day was more relaxed.

Mags caught my drift. 'Definitely.'

'So I'll run the Plumberry Bake Off,' I continued. 'We'll invite contestants to come along and bake their very best cake, then we judge it.'

'Like the show-stoppers round!' said Mags. 'Brilliant idea.'

'Exactly. Tom, on the other hand,' I said slyly, '*quite wrongly*, thinks people want a challenging, stressful environment while they cook up some complicated signature dish topped with a smear of this and a dribble of that.'

He flashed his eyes and I held his gaze with a challenge.

'I'm not wrong,' he said confidently, helping himself to seconds. 'That is what keen cooks want.'

'We are all on the same side, remember,' Mags pointed out.

'Of course we are!' I reassured her. As long as I won.

'But if it gets punters in, I'm all for it,' she added.

I looked at Tom. 'And? What do you think?'

'I'm all for a *MasterChef*-style contest, something to push the boundaries of everyday home cooking.' He nodded. 'I like it. It could be the Plumberry Signature Dish competition.'

'And winners get to attend a course of their choice as a prize,' Mags said.

'With a friend,' I added. 'So are we all agreed?'

Tom smirked. 'If I do it, will you stop with the whole "food is fun" thing?'

I had a sudden flashback to my conversation with Liam last night about helping him: *If I do it, will you leave me alone?* I really must email him that presentation tonight before I forgot. At least that would be one thing off my mind.

Tom was still waiting for an answer. 'Do we have a deal?'

I tuned back into the conversation and stuck my hand out. 'Deal.'

By nine o'clock, the kitchen was clear, I'd designed a flyer, Tom had drawn up some competition rules and Mags had done a sterling job drumming up some actual contestants. Gloria had woken up and eaten two slices of cheese on toast, which she'd shared with Comfrey and Sage, and the three of them were asleep again. The rain was still coming down in diagonal sheets.

'Pixie says two of the other barmaids are definitely up for entering and she's sure the manager of the cheese shop will want to take part in Tom's competition,' said Mags. 'And the pub landlord has agreed to put a poster up.'

'Excellent,' I beamed, standing up to put on the kettle.

Both competitions were beginning to take shape and I was glad I'd suggested the idea. Next week would have seemed a bit flat otherwise after all the excitement of filming the *Challenge Chester* show.

Eek, what was I thinking? I'd completely forgotten about the metre-high bread tower I was supposed to be baking in the morning. It wasn't exciting; it was terrifying.

My hands trembled as I poured water into the kettle. It was too late for second thoughts now. I was going to have to style it out, come up with a bright idea to make slabs of bread and piece them together like some sort of gigantic Jenga . . .

'No tea for me, thanks,' said Tom. 'I'd better head off.'

'Me too,' added Mags.

The wind had picked up and the window panes were rattling in their frames as the two of them made for the door.

I waved them off as an enormous clap of thunder broke overhead. Comfrey darted between my legs, relieved himself against the fence and scurried back inside.

'Be careful, you two,' I shouted above the noise of swirling wind.

I poked my head into the living room to see Gloria still dozing in the dimly lit room. The sky was leaden with angry-looking storm clouds and not a chink of light penetrated them. I sent up a silent prayer that Tom would get home safely and closed the curtains.

Suddenly the sky was split in two by a crack of lightning that ripped through the clouds and cast a momentary flash of light over the houses opposite.

Comfrey and Sage sprang to their paws and immediately burrowed to safety beneath Gloria's duvet.

Gloria stirred and opened her eyes. 'What was that?'

'Thunder and lightning. The storm must be right above us.' I knelt down beside her and Sage poked his trembling nose out from under the covers for me to stroke him.

She patted the covers. 'Keep me company for a while and tell me your news. I want to hear all about Noah's sports day,' she asked, nestling her head back against the pillows.

'He was a superstar,' I laughed softly, remembering his little face beaming when the nursery teacher had put a medal round his neck.

'I'd love to have seen him.'

She had lost weight since being in hospital and her eyes looked huge, staring up at me sadly.

'Hold on, I'll fetch my bag,' I said, getting to my feet. 'I took photos on my phone.'

Gloria shuffled herself up to look at them. My action shots weren't great but she could get the gist. She chuckled at the one of Noah holding his egg firmly on to the spoon with his thumb.

191

'Here's one of Noah and Gabe when the races had all finished.' I showed her the screen.

'Look at the pair of them enjoying themselves,' Gloria marvelled.

Without Mimi. The words were left unsaid, but I knew what she meant.

Noah was demonstrating how to hula-hoop to his dad, who hadn't been able to master rotating his hips. I swiped the screen to the next picture. It showed Noah and me hugging. His pudgy arms wrapped round my neck, both of us were laughing.

My heart twisted as I remembered standing in for Mimi in the mums' race.

'Goodness me,' Gloria gasped, 'what a beautiful boy he is . . . that face . . . and such lovely eyes. Oh, gosh.'

Suddenly she pushed the phone away. 'Thank you, I think I've seen enough.'

'What's the matter?' I frowned as she brushed a tear from her eye.

'Nothing, nothing at all. It's been a long day, that's all; I think I need to rest.'

I nodded, slipped the phone into my pocket and stroked her hand.

'Can I get you anything?' I asked softly.

A second burst of thunder, even louder than the first, rumbled across the sky and Sage's nose retreated further down the bed.

Gloria fiddled with the neck of her nightdress and wiped a tear from her cheek. 'Just my tablets, please.'

I fetched a glass of water and tipped out some painkillers for her.

'Can you put the TV remote on this side,' she asked, patting the table next to her bed.

'Of course.' I smiled.

'And move the little lamp over here.'

I obliged.

'On second thoughts,' she decided, 'I think I preferred it where it was.'

I suppressed a smile; I could almost hear Mimi's voice in my head telling her mother to make her mind up. The two of them had always got on brilliantly and I knew instinctively that Mimi would have moved up to Plumberry like a shot to look after Gloria if she'd been alive.

The thought brought a familiar niggle of sadness and I tried to shake it off.

I moved the lamp back and smiled. 'There. Better?'

She nodded. 'You are good. Mimi would have lost her patience with me by now,' she said wistfully, reading my mind. 'She was a terrible nurse.'

'Nothing to do with you being a terrible patient,' I laughed, pressing a kiss on to her soft cheek. 'I'm going up to bed myself now, I've got a bit of work still to do and I'd better get some beauty sleep before tomorrow.'

'Goodnight, darling,' she said, waving me out of the room.

'Shout if you need me; I'll leave the door open.'

'Verity?' Gloria called, as I got to the top of the stairs.

I ran back down.

'Yes?' I said breathlessly.

'I don't want to be a burden, you know, so just say if I'm being a nuisance, won't you?'

Her blue eyes blinked at me dolefully. She looked little and old all of a sudden and I felt a lump form in my throat.

'Don't be silly.' I put her mobile phone where she could reach it and kissed her again. 'Living here with you and the dogs, with Mags next door and working at the cookery school with Tom and Pixie . . . I feel very privileged. I can't think of anywhere else I'd rather be.'

'Not even back in Nottingham with Noah,' she paused, 'and Gabe?'

I took a deep breath and shook my head. Much as I loved being with them I had to start forging my own life.

'I'm glad.' She smiled gently and closed her eyes. 'I'm glad.'

I ran back up the stairs, listening to the rain hammer against the windows and the wind whistling down the chimney, my heart beating a tattoo in my chest. Despite my nerves about tomorrow and the horrendous storm churning up everyone's gardens, I was telling Gloria the truth. There was nowhere I'd rather be than Plumberry.

You see, Mimi? Even your own mum reckons you'd have made a terrible nurse. So why do I still feel bad that I'm the one here looking after her and you're not? When is this permanent shadow of guilt going to allow me to enjoy every happy moment instead of apologizing for it?

The storm continued to shake and rattle the cottage for the next half an hour, but by the time I was ready to turn out my light, the worst of it had passed and only the wind and rain remained. I pressed my head into the pillows and with my mind swirling with images of edible Eiffel Towers, I eventually dropped off to sleep.

A terrible noise woke me in the night. My eyes sprang open and my pulse throbbed loudly in my ears. I stared at the display on my alarm clock. Two twenty. The noise was coming from the back garden: a gut-wrenching, painfully slow creak followed by an almighty crash. And then the display on my clock disappeared. I snapped on my bedside lamp. Nothing: there must be a power cut.

I jumped out of bed and pressed my face to the window. The rain had stopped, but the wind was still raging. I couldn't see anything at first: the whole of Plumberry was in darkness. Then a little light appeared in Len's garden. And then another in Mags's garden. Two figures lit by torches moved towards their shared boundary. Now I could see what the crash had been: Len's old apple tree had blown over, its trunk had smashed straight through Mags's fence and its roots had left a huge crater in Len's garden.

The torches flickered for a few more seconds and then went out. Mags and Len must have gone back inside.

I snuggled back into bed, waiting for my heart rate to slow, and pulled the duvet up around my ears to block out the sound of the howling wind. I closed my eyes and tried to go back to sleep. Plumberry seemed to be fighting a losing battle with Mother Nature tonight and only tomorrow would reveal who the winner had been.

Chapter 19

I woke the next morning to complete silence. The wind had dropped, the clouds had vanished and the sun beamed cheerfully from a pale blue sky, as if to announce that normal service would now be resumed. But the total silence wasn't normal, even for a Saturday.

I padded downstairs through the kitchen and opened the back door. The dogs bombed past me and sniffed the air inquisitively before performing their usual morning business. I wandered down the path and peered into Mags's garden. The fallen apple tree took up the full width of the lawn and the fence and trellis lay splintered underneath its trunk.

'What a kerfuffle!' Len called from his garden. He was wearing a white vest and had bright green braces keeping up a baggy pair of trousers. His wispy white hair swirled about the top of his head like candyfloss.

'What a night!' I called back, shielding my eyes in the low sunshine. 'Such a shame to lose your lovely apple tree.'

He flapped a hand dismissively. 'Pshh. The storm did me a favour; I can't eat apples with my teeth these days. Besides, I get a better view of Mags now,' he said with a wheezy chortle. 'No, it's the power cut that bothers me. I wanted to watch Formula One racing this weekend.'

So that was why the house seemed so quiet: the power

was still off. No humming fridges or clicking on and off of hot water.

'It won't be long till it's back on, though, surely?'

'Might be ages.' Len shrugged. 'We lost electricity for three days last winter. Nobody bothers with us little villages. And I was listening to the news on my wireless, another tree has come down and blocked the main road between Thickleton and Plumberry, so nothing and no one will get through, including the engineers.'

This was not a good start to the day. The village could be cut off for ages and we were without power. The *Challenge Chester* team would have to walk to the cookery school. And what about Tom? And, I remembered suddenly, the fridges at the cookery school would be full of food. If the power wasn't turned back on soon, it would all have to be thrown away. On top of all that I was supposed to be being filmed this morning for national television . . .

I'd have a cup of tea, I decided. Everything seems brighter after a cup of tea.

'I can't even make myself a brew,' Len said. 'The kettle's electric.'

Damn, I'd forgotten that.

'Oh well, every cloud has a silver lining,' he said, rallying suddenly.

'Oh yeah?' I eyed him dubiously.

'Do you fancy a whisky?'

An hour later, I was walking briskly along Plumberry high street, mentally juggling a hundred to-do lists and taking deep breaths of fresh summery air to clear my head. I'd left the car at home just in case there were any roadblocks between here and the cookery school and the exercise was serving to calm me down.

Despite the lack of electricity, Plumberry was positively sparkling this morning, as if completely washed clean by the storms of the night before. It was impossible not to feel uplifted as I passed the lovely old-fashioned shops with their striped awnings. The flowers in large wooden planters had been changed since I'd first arrived at the end of April, from spring bulbs to summery bedding plants. They had taken a bit of a battering in the night, but the frothy pink fuchsias and purple petunias still managed to provide bright pops of colour along the pavements.

This was my silver lining, I mused, as I waved to a couple of the shop owners who were comparing storm damage on their doorsteps: blue skies, warm sun and cheerful flowers.

As I turned off the high street towards the old mill, Gabe phoned me.

'Is that Verity Bloom, soon-to-be TV star?'

'Oh shush,' I laughed. 'Don't remind me. Besides, my plan is to stay as much in the background as possible.'

'Remember those films you and Mimi used to make?' He sounded wistful.

'How could I forget?'

The YouTube cooking videos we used to mess about with had been on my mind since waking up. Mimi had been the lead 'presenter' with me as her sidekick. Much as I would be today. I felt my stomach churn; sometimes I wondered how I got myself into these situations, I really did.

Gabe cleared his throat. 'Anyway, Noah and I are setting off in *The Neptune* this morning so we should be in Plumberry in about ten days, depending on how many stops we make. There are one or two antique dealers en route. I might call in and advertise my furniture restoration skills.'

I smiled to myself as he outlined his journey along the canals, through the Midlands and up to Yorkshire. He had been in such a rush to get everywhere once; now he was happy to take his time, enjoy the journey and take in his surroundings.

'Gloria will be thrilled and probably much more mobile by the time you arrive,' I said. 'Is Noah there?'

I had a quick conversation with Noah about his new pyjamas and signed off.

Gloria had enlisted Mags to help her get ready this morning. She was still insisting on coming to see the filming, even though she'd got exhausted simply travelling up one flight of stairs on her bottom to the bathroom, and my heart ached with sympathy for her. As much as I wanted her to feel part of our exciting day, I didn't want to put her recovery in any jeopardy either.

The district nurse was due to visit her early this morning and part of me hoped that she might ban her from leaving the house – at least then I wouldn't have to worry about her doing herself an injury at the cookery school.

Across the car park I could see the boys from the microbrewery next door sitting outside in the sunshine. There were three of them: Simon, Bruce and Rick. But because they all had beards large enough to provide habitats for woodland creatures and all dressed the same in tight jeans and checked shirts, I could never remember who was who. As I got closer I saw they had rigged up a camping stove with a small tin kettle balanced on top of it. Two of them were sitting on upturned crates and one on a beer barrel. I raised my hand and waved, hoping they'd offer me a hot drink. I'd turned down Len's whisky and had only had orange juice so far this morning and my caffeine levels were dangerously low.

I hardly ever saw them; their business was only small and according to Pixie, who was always first with the gossip, they ran the brewery in their spare time alongside day jobs and generally spent the whole weekend here.

The kettle began to whistle.

One of them jerked his head towards the mill. 'The power's off and the landlines are down.'

'The phone lines too? Oh no.' I grimaced; stupidly I hadn't thought to give Cheryl my mobile number.

'We were supposed to be bottling today,' said another, folding his arms.

The third one did a fake sigh. 'Guess we'll just have to sit and drink beer in the sun instead.'

Then they all laughed.

'Bruce is making tea,' said one of them, pointing to his friend. I made a mental note: Bruce's shirt was grey and white. At least I could now identify one of them. 'You can have some but you'll have to fetch your own mug.'

I thanked them and went inside to find Cheryl's number and a mug. Bruce's industrial-strength tea was nectar. I slurped half of it down and took my phone out to call Cheryl.

But before I could even dial her number everyone arrived.

Mags, driving at a snail's pace, had managed to stretch Gloria across the back seat. She parked in front of the cookery school doors and the brewery boys helped Gloria out. Tom had come on foot – he'd had to abandon his car near the toppled tree – while Pixie had cycled in on her brother's bike. Next, a group of strangers strutted towards us like a rock band. There was a James Dean lookalike complete with leather jacket and shades, a girl whose jaw chewed constantly and a man with the thickest glasses I'd ever seen. They all seemed to be carrying bags and aluminium cases of varying sizes, except for a plump man in a tracksuit, bringing up the rear, who had a large camera perched on his shoulder.

'Welcome to the Plumberry School of Comfort Food. I'm Verity Bloom,' I said, waving my arms about nervously. My voice had gone all high-pitched too. It seemed that I'd gone camera shy before the thing had even been turned on. I cleared my throat and introduced the rest of the team.

The man with the glasses stepped forward to shake my hand.

'I'm Goggles, the director. This is Chester Fulwood, presenter, obviously. Cheryl, our researcher, and Jonno the cameraman,' he said, pointing to each member of the *Challenge Chester* team in turn.

'We've all been so looking forward to your visit,' I said, studiously avoiding Tom's eye as I shook hands with everyone. 'I was worried you wouldn't get past the fallen trees.'

According to the local news, the road was blocked at both ends of the village so at the moment no vehicles could access Plumberry from either direction.

'We left the van near the roadblock,' said Goggles. 'There was a team of blokes with chainsaws attacking a fallen oak tree, so the way should be clear soon. We've carried everything we need for the shoot.'

'Hey, I'm Pixie,' said Pixie, pushing herself in front of Goggles to get to Chester.

'Cool name.' He stretched out a hand to shake hers and then pulled her in close to kiss her cheek. She went pink and grinned goofily.

'I loved the show this week,' she said. 'When you went commando.'

Chester threw his head back and laughed, running a hand through his perfectly styled hair. He looked like an advert for expensive aftershave. Or jeans. Or toothpaste.

Mags, who'd settled Gloria on a chair next to the camping stove, perked up considerably. 'Oh, I missed that episode. Will it be on catch-up?'

'I think you mean training with *the Commandos*,' said Cheryl.

Pixie went pinker.

'Anyway, shall we get set up?' Cheryl added with a yawn.

'In a minute,' said Goggles, rubbing his hands together. 'Any chance of a cuppa?'

It was the most random tea party ever: the cookery school team, the brewery boys and the TV crew, sipping from an assortment of mugs in an empty car park under a gloriously sunny sky. It was almost impossible to imagine the torrential wind and rain from yesterday.

'Now,' I said assertively, feeling as if I should try to corral everyone into action, 'the power cut does provide us with a challenge. No pun intended, Chester,' I said with a nervous laugh.

'We're all self-sufficient,' said Jonno. He'd been wandering round the building 'panning' with his camera. He gave it a pat. 'Battery-operated.'

'Sadly, we're not,' I said. 'We can make the dough for your Eiffel Tower but none of our ovens works on gas. So until the power comes back on we can't bake it, I'm afraid.'

Hurrah. I even managed to look disappointed.

'Shame we haven't got an outdoor clay oven,' said Tom, scratching his chin.

His beard was more like stubble and was neatly groomed, adding a rakishness to his face rather than the full-on hairiness of the brewery beards. I much preferred his.

'We had a cracking wood-fired oven at Salinger's. Brilliant for bread and pizzas.'

'Can't we build a makeshift one?' Gloria suggested.

'I could build a fire good enough to cook on, I suppose,' Tom offered. 'I was a Boy Scout in my youth.'

'Shame you don't still have the uniform,' Mags murmured. 'I'd pay good money to see that.'

'Er, just a minute.' Cheryl chewed on her gum frantically. 'This is primetime TV, love, there's no makeshift about it.'

'Well, that's me told,' Gloria mumbled and turned her head away.

'Psst,' I said to Mags, jerking my head for her to join me away from the others. 'What did the district nurse say when she came?'

'She phoned to say she couldn't make it because of the power cut,' Mags whispered. 'There are tonnes of emergency cases apparently. I heard Gloria say she'd taken all her medication and that she felt fine.'

I glanced over at her sitting next to the brewery boys. She did look all right, I just hoped she stayed that way. On top of everything else, the last thing we needed was for her to end up back in hospital.

'What are you two muttering about?' Gloria narrowed her eyes.

'Mind your own biscuits, Glor,' Mags tutted. She trotted back over to her. 'Now, let's get that leg propped up.'

Just then two transit vans with electricity company logos on the sides pulled up into the car park and four men clambered out. One of them had his legs crossed.

'Any chance I could use the toilet? We've been stuck in a hold-up because of the tree and I'm desperate.'

Tom took him inside and I quizzed the others about the power failure.

'Will we be reconnected soon, do you think?' I fretted. 'It's just we're trying to film a TV show. And we've got food we'll need to rescue from the fridges too.'

There was much sucking in of air and shaking of heads. Hard to say, seemed to be the consensus. Apparently the lines were down in several places, including one a little further downstream where a cable was dangling in the river.

'Oh, bumbags. Poor Granddad,' Pixie exclaimed. She was staring at her phone and chewing her lip.

'What's the matter?' I asked, crossing my fingers that given the present company, Granddad's dilemma wasn't bowel-related for once.

'I'm going to have to nip up to him later. Mum says his Meals on Wheels service has been cancelled. Poor old sod. It's sausage and mash on Saturdays.'

'There'll be loads of people in the same boat,' said Rick (or Simon). 'Hardly anyone in Plumberry has gas. And we haven't got a pub that serves food any more.'

Hmmm, that was true.

Everyone started talking at once about the pub that went bust because it only served microwaved food (Tom looked pointedly at me), and about the old people they knew who

203

wouldn't be able to boil a kettle and all the food that the shops would have to throw away if the refrigeration systems didn't come back on soon and I could scarcely hear myself think.

'Quiet!' I yelled. 'I've got an idea.'

Gloria clapped her hands together. 'I knew it! Verity has the best ideas. She's a marketing whizz, you know.'

'However, it doesn't involve bread or the Eiffel Tower because, under the circumstances, I don't think that's doable,' I continued. 'Goggles, what about changing Chester's challenge?'

Cheryl butted in before the director could even open his mouth.

'No way.' She flicked her hair over her shoulder. 'We've already announced in the last show what the next challenge is.'

Goggles frowned. 'I don't see that we've got much choice. Unless we cancel completely?'

'You can't do that,' Mags squeaked. 'I didn't give my best mate a strip-wash for nothing this morning. *Challenge Chester* is what's kept her going, even when she got a carpet burn on her bum from the stairs. You've got to do it.'

There was a whimper from Gloria.

Jonno swung his camera round to Mags. 'Can you just say that bit again? Starting from strip-wash.'

'Nooo.' Gloria sank lower in her chair and buried her face in her hands.

'OK,' I said grimly. It'd certainly be a challenge. 'Here's what we'll do . . .'

After a bit of lateral thinking, I'd allocated everyone a task. Well, all except Cheryl who'd gone for a look round the brewery with Rick, Simon and Bruce. Pixie and I were hunting through the cupboards to see what food we could use. Mags had gone up to the village to beg some spare meat and vegetables from the shop owners in return for a free lunch and Tom was leading the TV crew in building the largest outdoor barbecue grill I'd ever seen with sheets of stainless steel purloined from the brewery.

'We need something we can make in one pot,' Gloria had mused, hunting through her recipe bible, which I'd retrieved from her desk for her. 'Something that won't take too long to cook.'

Mags had pulled a face. 'I was going to suggest a big pan of Scouse with all the pickles, but that tastes best when you leave it cooking for ages.'

'Oh well, never mind,' Tom jumped in hastily. 'What about some sort of risotto?'

Pixie scuffed the toe of her Doc Martens on the floor. 'We've, er, got plenty of rice.'

So it had been decided we'd make something rice-based and once Mags returned from her local foraging spree, we'd finalize the exact recipe.

Upstairs in the storeroom, I opened a cupboard and two giant bags of rice fell out. There were another three bags behind them.

'Who ordered all this rice?' I wondered aloud.

'It was on offer.' Pixie shrugged sheepishly. 'Stock up on the basics and you'll never go without, that's what my Granddad always says.'

'I bet Granddad never runs out of loo paper,' I said wryly, lugging ten kilos of rice downstairs with Pixie carrying her body weight in tinned butter beans behind me.

We set up a makeshift kitchen at the side of the old mill, with the waterwheel in the background. We'd originally started off on the deck at the back of the cookery school but the river was running so fast because of the previous day's rainfall that Chester had to shout at the top of his lungs above the torrent of water cascading past and Jonno had complained about the poor sound quality.

Twenty minutes later Mags arrived back with Dave in tow, both of them carrying bags full of food. 'Look who I found wandering the streets,' she said proudly, putting her arm through his.

He rubbed his neck, which had turned a bit pink. 'You make me sound as if I've been sleeping rough.'

She laughed and smacked his arm playfully. 'I'd always find a bed for you, David, or squeeze you into mine.'

'OK, listen up,' I said, clapping my hands once Tom and Gloria had had a chance to survey the food we'd cobbled together and I'd conferred with Goggles.

'Chester, your new challenge will be to feed the whole village with a giant Plumberry Paella.'

'Nice one,' Chester said, lifting his shades up and giving me a cheeky wink. He was leaning on the edge of the table we'd set up and had managed to keep himself perfectly clean during the barbecue build. I suspected he didn't do much unless the camera was running . . .

'Does that include us?' shouted one of the beards, who by now were all lolling around, drinking beer in the sunshine.

'Everyone,' I confirmed.

Now that I looked closer, Gloria was swigging from a beer bottle too. I suppressed a smile; someone had wrapped a blanket over her legs, she had two pink spots in her cheeks and she looked the most relaxed I'd seen her since her accident. I'd have to keep an eye on her and I wasn't entirely sure she should be drinking alcohol on top of her tablets, but I wasn't going to be the one to spoil her fun.

'Mags, your job is to tell as many Plumberry people as you can to get here for a free lunch at one o'clock. Oh, and if you get a chance, spread the word about next week's competitions too. There's no landline, so you'll have to use your mobile and drive round in the car.'

She tapped her nose. 'I can do better than that. Leave it with me.'

'I'll assist,' Dave offered, raising a hand.

I smiled my thanks and then asked Pixie to show Chester

206

where he could freshen up ready to start cooking.

'So then, um, I just need to go through the filming part with you, Goggles,' I said shakily, rubbing my fingers under my eyes in case of mascara streaks. Shouldn't I have a team of hair and make-up artists to ensure I look my best . . . ?

'Great, I'll be right with you,' Goggles nodded. 'Jonno, what I thought was . . .'

The two of them wandered off to where Tom's huge grill was beginning to burn vigorously. Cheryl joined Gloria to make a note of all the ingredients we were using so she could put it on the *Challenge Chester* website and I walked over to our makeshift kitchen, conscious that my legs had begun to wobble.

This was the bit I'd been dreading. Any minute now I'd be on camera, cooking with Chester. At least we no longer had to bake the Eiffel Tower; a giant paella couldn't really go wrong.

I hoped.

My lungs felt tight all of a sudden and my palms had gone clammy. I shook out a new apron from a plastic packet and tried to tie it round my waist but my hands were shaking.

'Fiddly thing,' I tutted. My mouth had gone so dry I could hardly speak.

'Let me do it,' Tom's voice murmured softly against my neck.

He turned me round and tied the apron strings in a bow at the front.

'Thank you,' I murmured. I held my hands out in front of me; they were jumping around so much, I doubted I'd even be able to hold a knife. 'I'm a nervous wreck.'

'I'll do it,' he said softly.

'You've done it,' I replied, looking down at my apron.

'I mean, I'll do the filming; I'll show Chester how to cook paella.'

'Really? Are you sure? I mean, after all you said . . .'

He grinned at me, nodding. 'I'm sure.'

Thank God. I felt my shoulders relax for the first time in what felt like weeks.

'You've made my day,' I said, undoing my apron instantly.

'Cooking paella on an open fire for the village is a totally different proposition to cooking that stupid bread thing. Besides, I think it's time someone did something nice for you. In all the time I've known you, I've never seen you put yourself first. You are one of the nicest people I've ever met.'

He smiled at me and I glowed inside.

'Stop being kind,' I said with a little sniff. 'I'm not used to it from you.'

Given a choice I'd have preferred 'lovely' or maybe 'wonderful' to *nice*. But under the circumstances I was grateful for small mercies. I happily relinquished my cooking duties and stepped away as Chester and Tom got down to business.

It took two hours with all the stopping and starting and re-shooting various bits but eventually the thirty large roasting trays that we'd slotted on to the enormous barbeque were all as full as could be with steaming rice, chicken, butter beans and assorted local Plumberry vegetables.

'Bloody hell!' exclaimed Chester, pushing his shades to the top of his head.

'Cut!' shouted Goggles. He glared at Chester. 'Language, mate.'

'Bloomin' Nora,' said Chester again, pointing this time.

We all turned to see what Chester was staring at. I blinked twice and let out a squeak. A massive crowd of people was gathering in the road leading to the cookery school. It looked like the entire village of Plumberry was descending on us for lunch.

'Gloria,' I said in a wavering voice, 'how many bowls do we have?'

Chapter 20

Pixie and I ran inside and rustled up stacks of plastic bowls plus bags and bags of plastic spoons, which we'd bought for the open day last Friday. But it was Bruce who came to the rescue with hundreds of sturdy plastic cups they'd bought to use at festivals. They were the perfect size for a portion of paella. Pixie, Tom and Mags organized a serving system and Goggles insisted that Chester be a part of it too.

'FHB, folks,' said Pixie, handing Chester a serving spoon.

'What does that stand for?' He winked. 'Fulwood's hot body?'

'You wish,' she said, raising her eyebrows until they disappeared under her fringe.

'Family Hold Back,' said Tom with a laugh. 'I haven't heard that for ages.'

'It's what my mum always says when extra guests turn up and she panics that we haven't got enough food,' Pixie explained to a bemused Chester. 'The family has to hold back until all the guests have eaten before tucking in. My brother was fifteen before he got a slice of pork pie.'

'Good plan,' I said, casting my eye across the queue of people snaking through the car park all waiting eagerly for their free lunch. 'Although I don't think the few portions that our little family would take would make much difference to this lot.'

Talk about the feeding of the five thousand; I hadn't known Plumberry had so many residents. But even though I'd only been here for less than four weeks, I recognized quite a few people: the old couple I'd met when Mags and I were doing our research were there, some of the staff from the greengrocer's, Pixie's colleagues at the cheese shop, as well as some familiar faces I'd encountered when walking the dogs. I spotted Len amongst the crowd too.

'Bloody hell, Mags, how did you manage it?' I said, pouring her a drink of water. The sun was beating down and we were getting very hot standing next to the ginormous barbecue. 'The world and his wife have turned up!'

'I called the radio station, Yorkshire FM.' She wiped her hands on her apron and took a grateful sip of water. 'They added it to their morning news bulletin as part of the storm update. They're going to give our Plumberry Bake Off and Plumberry Signature Dish competitions a plug later too.'

I beamed at her. 'You're brilliant! You know that, don't you?'

'I am good in a crisis,' she agreed. 'But then so are you. Gloria was singing your praises earlier, telling me what a good nurse you are.'

I searched through the crowd to see where the patient was. She was sitting by Dave and they looked deep in conversation. I hoped he wasn't worrying her with things like cash flow so soon after her accident.

'I love her like a second mum, but I must admit I'd rather she was safe in hospital being looked after by professionals.'

I'd spoken to my own mum earlier in the week and she'd suggested Gloria go into a convalescence home, which in theory might be a good idea if we couldn't cope. But I knew Gloria would refuse point blank to leave her own cottage now she was back home. We'd just have to manage.

'She's fine; stop fretting.' Mags gave me a bowl of paella

and stuck a spoon in it. 'Here, give this to Len. Don't tell him it's paella, he'll say it's foreign muck.'

I found Len standing alone staring at the old waterwheel.

'Lovely to see you here, Len. And you're looking so smart!'

He had dressed for the occasion in a double-breasted jacket that had three shining military medals pinned to the chest.

'Heard on the radio you were doing free lunch for villagers and seeing as my Sky isn't back on yet I thought I'd have a stroll down.'

'We are indeed. Here you go.'

He lifted his glasses up and squinted at the bowl. 'What is it?'

'Pae . . . chicken and rice.'

'Funny-looking pie.' He took it from me and nodded at the assembled crowd.

'This is grand, young lady. I haven't seen people gather together like this in Plumberry since VE Day.' He puffed out his chest to better display his medals and flicked a butter bean out of the bowl.

'Foreign muck,' he muttered. 'Except that on VE Day we had dripping sandwiches and beer.'

I glowed with pleasure. 'Well, we've done better than that today.'

He grunted. 'I miss dripping. Since my wife died I don't get it any more.'

I pointed him in the direction of the brewers and sent him off for a beer to make up for the disappointment.

Pixie had given up serving and was darting in and amongst the crowd of happy lunchers, taking photos on her phone for the cookery school website, and a queue had formed in front of Chester for selfies and autographs. Two of the brewery boys set up a trestle table selling plastic cups of beer straight from the keg and Annabel from the Plumberry Wine Merchants arrived in her small van and set up another table for wine tastings.

People from the other small businesses had come out to join us, too: I spotted the lady from the candle shop and the two artists who shared the art studio. Len was right; there was a real street-party atmosphere developing and it warmed my heart to think that it was the cookery school that had pulled the community together in such a lovely way after that terrible storm. I stood silently, happy for a moment, hands on hips, soaking up the scene and feeling inordinately proud of what we'd achieved under extremely trying circumstances.

Suddenly burglar alarms on the outside of the buildings all began to flash and ring in unison.

'Jesus, what's this – a mass hold-up?' said Chester, looking worried.

'The power must have come back on,' said Tom, sprinting inside.

He turned the cookery school alarm off and gradually all the other bells stopped ringing too.

'Such a perfect day,' said Gloria happily, taking a swig from her beer bottle. 'The weather's perfect, my cookery school is perfect and Tom's perfect. Don't you think Tom's perfect, Verity?'

'Well, I . . . he's very . . . um,' I stuttered, conscious of Dave watching our exchange with interest.

She squinted at me, shielding her eyes from the sun.

'I always thought Gabe was perfect too, what do you think?' she continued.

'Mimi thought so and that was what mattered,' I said briskly, wondering how much beer she'd had. 'Would you like a cup of tea?'

The landline in reception began to ring out and Mags scurried in to answer it.

Fabulous! The phones were obviously reconnected, which meant that the internet would be back on too. My emails had kept on coming through via my phone, luckily I hadn't lost service on that this morning, but I made a mental note to check the cookery school computer before I left. Hopefully we'd have more bookings for the Perfect Pasta course next week.

Mags reappeared, holding the phone out to Gloria. 'It's Yorkshire FM. They want to interview you.'

Gloria gasped with delight and handed me her beer bottle before grasping the phone in both hands.

'Gloria Ramsbottom, the Plumberry School of Comfort Food,' she trilled.

She told whoever it was on the end of the phone about the *Challenge Chester* filming and the great Plumberry paella and then yelped when she realized she was live on air. She cleared her throat for her parting shot.

'I set up the cookery school to pass on my love of cooking to others. Food is about sharing good times with the people you care about. Plumberry has proved just how true that is today.'

Tom caught my eye and gave a tiny nod, his face breaking into a warm smile.

I care about you, I thought unexpectedly, feeling my heart flicker.

He held my gaze and the two of us smiled a smile that got bigger and bigger. I'd got to know the man underneath those chef whites this week and I liked what I'd found. A lot. He'd shown me his softer side as well as his passion for cooking spectacular food. And for the first time in a long time, I'd begun to feel passion as well – not only for food, but for life and possibly for love too . . .

'Right, I think we're ready for the final shot, folks,' Goggles shouted.

Chester made a show of stirring one of the roasting trays, touched the back of his hand to his forehead and blew his cheeks out with mock exertion. 'You challenged Chester to feed an entire village with the famous Plumberry paella.'

I grinned widely; Plumberry paella might not be famous

yet, but this time next week, who knows.

Chester then raised his spoon triumphantly. 'Challenge complete.'

The crowd cheered and clapped. Mags put her fingertips in her mouth and whistled like a pro.

'And now for the moment of truth.' He slung his arm round Tom's shoulders and took a mouthful. He whooped with pleasure and banged the spoon loudly on the edge of the grill. 'Oh man, that is the bomb!'

Cue more cheering and merriment.

'We're good,' shouted Goggles. 'Chester, you're done.'

'Part-ay,' yelled Chester, arms in the air.

Someone had set up some speakers and music blared out across the car park, adding a certain something to the atmosphere. Tom seemed to be enjoying it – his head was nodding to the beat as he served yet more paella, beer in hand, sleeves rolled up. Chester and Goggles had finished filming, but Jonno was still wandering round zooming in on conversations and plates of food and right now, the camera was focused on Tom.

'Are you sure you don't mind being filmed?' I whispered, standing out of shot.

His dark eyes glittered with humour. 'Just try and stop me, I'm having a whale of a time. I've even had a few people asking for an outdoor cooking course in the summer. I haven't had this much fun since . . . well, since I split up with Rebecca.'

Jonno moved away and I stepped closer and nudged him gently in the ribs.

'See,' I said with a hint of smugness.

'What?'

'You see how much better life is when you let your hair down and have some fun when you're cooking?'

He groaned. 'Yes, OK. You win. Jesus, will you ever stop going on about that?'

214

Just then my phone buzzed with a text message. I whipped it out of my pocket and read it.

It was from Liam.

Got the email. Thanks, Verity, you're a mate. I'll leave you alone now. Promise.

'Good riddance.' I shoved my phone back and sighed happily. Hopefully that would be the last I heard from him.

'Nuisance caller?' Tom raised a concerned eyebrow.

'You could say that.' I laughed. 'It was a text from my ex.'

His face darkened. 'The unfaithful, two-timing cheat who nicked your chance at promotion?'

I nodded.

'What does he want?'

I suppressed a giggle at Tom's indignation on my behalf. 'Nothing. Any more.'

I explained to him about Liam's panic and my offer to send him the plan that I'd done.

'You should have let him sort out his own mess. He took your livelihood from you, your trust . . . He can't have his cake and eat it.'

Tom reminded me of Rosie for a second. They were quite alike now that I came to think about it: both ambitious, competitive and, it seemed, highly protective of me. My heart gave a little skip.

'You're probably right,' I said with a shrug. 'But what does it matter whether I get the credit for it or not? Solomon's has had enough redundancies just recently. What if my plan could help improve the company's fortunes? If I can help save even just one job with my marketing plan, then it's really me who comes out on top, regardless of who knows it.'

Tom stared at me admiringly. 'I wish I was more like you, Verity. I hate to say this, and excuse my language, but

I wouldn't piss on Salinger's if it was on fire. I'm done with the place. You genuinely are—'

'Do not say *nice*,' I interrupted. 'I'm beginning to wonder if that's not quite the compliment I thought it was. Anyway, that's the last time I come to Liam's rescue. If he asks for help again he'll be sorry. He's history as far as I'm concerned.'

Tom's eyes locked on to mine and he took a step closer. My heart pounded with anticipation.

'In that case—' he murmured.

But before he could finish, Mags squeezed herself between us.

'*Pardonnez-moi* for breaking in on your *tête-à-tête*,' she said, lowering her voice, 'but I think Gloria's had enough for one day.'

Tom and I whipped our heads round to see Gloria fast asleep, her leg still propped up on a second chair and an empty beer bottle dangling loosely from one hand.

'Whoops,' I said with a sharp intake of breath. 'I feel awful for not taking better care of her. She could have got sunstroke sitting there. I hope she hasn't passed out from drinking in the sun.'

No,' Mags chuckled. 'Rick only gave her one low-alcohol beer. And this has been the best tonic for her; seeing her cookery school – well, the car park, at least – being part of Plumberry. She's had a lovely day. And those china-blue eyes of hers sparkled for the first time in days. Before they closed.'

'I'm pleased.' I hugged Mags. 'I only came to help her fulfil her dream of opening the cookery school and so far it seems she's the only one who hasn't been able to enjoy it properly.'

Mags leaned closer. 'I had my reservations about letting her come today too, but I'm made up that she did. She said it's been one of the best days of her life.'

I looked over at Gloria again and I felt a surge of love for her. Mimi would have loved it too. I felt a bit emotional so I simply nodded at Mags.

'Can you manage Gloria on your own?' Tom asked her.

'Dave's coming home with me to help,' she said, her hand fluttering to the gold chain round her neck. 'So if you pop round later, Verity, don't forget to knock.'

And with a final salacious wink, she scampered off.

'What are *you* doing later?' asked Tom nonchalantly.

'Nothing,' I replied equally casually.

'We could, er, go somewhere?'

'We could,' I agreed, focusing on keeping my cheeks under control as my smile threatened to take over my whole face.

Within a couple of hours, all thirty trays of paella had been hoovered up by the good folks of Plumberry and Annabel's free wine samples had run out. I'd remembered to put a portion aside for Pixie's granddad but had had to protect it several times from Dave, who also thought his mum might like it. The *Challenge Chester* crew had packed away and were kicking back outside the brewery with the three beards, listening to Chester boasting about the time he had got stuck in the lift with film star Emma Stone at the Oscars. Judging from everyone's expressions, no one believed him but they were enjoying the tale nonetheless.

'Cheryl's coming with me to take Granddad his food. I've phoned ahead and checked he's got his teeth in,' said Pixie.

Cheryl giggled as Pixie helped her up on to the handlebars of her bike. Wait – Cheryl *giggling*? Wonders would never cease.

I packed Granddad's paella into the pannier on the back of the bike and watched Pixie steer the wobbling bike towards the exit of the car park with both of the girls squealing with laughter.

From nowhere a smart, low-slung white car sped into

the car park, taking Pixie by surprise. She panicked and the bike tipped over and crashed to the ground. The girls screamed, landed in a tangle of limbs and were showered with chicken and rice from an exploding tub of paella.

The car screeched to a halt and a woman jumped out and ran to them. Goggles, Jonno and I did the same. Tom either hadn't noticed or had decided enough of us had gone to their rescue.

'Oh my goodness,' cried the woman in a trembling voice, 'I am so, so sorry.'

'Are you OK?' I panted.

Cheryl rubbed her leg and Pixie gripped her arm. Both of them moaned, but they were still smiling.

Goggles and Jonno picked up the bike. One of the wheels looked a bit skew-whiff.

'Totally my fault; I was trying to turn the satnav off,' said the woman, pressing both hands to her cheeks. 'I'll pay for the damage to the bike and to you. Oh, this is not at all how I planned it.'

'Planned what?' I frowned at her.

'My grand entrance. What an idiot.' She sighed.

Perhaps she was from the media? Perhaps Yorkshire FM had sent her down for an 'at the scene' report?

The woman knelt beside the two girls and began a futile attempt to pick paella out of their hair.

'What is this?' she said with a sniff.

'Granddad's Meals on Wheels,' Pixie murmured.

I regarded the woman surreptitiously. Her hair was a deep glossy auburn and with bouncing curls at the end of her pony tail. She had a striped Breton T-shirt under a navy blazer and her skin was so luscious she oozed healthiness. I'd got beer down my dress and my glow was more of the sweaty kind from the barbecue, and I also ponged of woodsmoke.

'Pixie, Cheryl, are you OK?' I repeated.

Cheryl staggered to her feet and nodded; Goggles put an

arm round her and led her away to sit down.

'I'm fine. I think. Ouch,' said Pixie, circling her shoulder.

'Am I too late; are you still open?' the woman said, peering across the car park towards the cookery school. She was still kneeling on the ground and grains of rice had stuck to her jeans.

'Yes, the paella's all gone, I'm afraid,' I said, assuming she'd come for a free lunch, 'but if you're hungry I could always find you something in the kitchen.'

She blinked at me.

'I'm not here to eat. I've come to see Tom.'

'Oh.'

A cold finger of fear traced a line down my spine and I sensed Tom's presence beside me even before I heard him.

'Rebecca?' he growled. 'What are you doing here?'

'Oh baby!' She leapt to her feet and flung her arms round his neck, pressing kiss after kiss on his face as tears sprang from her eyes.

Tom strained away from her, but she tightened her grip. I stared, aghast yet riveted to the spot.

'Tom, I've made a terrible mistake. I've missed you so much. Salinger's is nothing without you. *I'm* nothing without you.'

Tom peeled himself away and then wiped a tear from her cheek with his thumb. It was such a tender gesture that I had to look away. For about a millisecond, and then I stared at them again. There was an ache in the pit of my stomach at the sight of Tom with another woman.

'I thought you were Ryan's girlfriend without me?' he said, folding his arms, his dark eyes blazing as they bore into hers. 'There's a well-known saying about too many cooks, you know.'

Rebecca licked her lips nervously and reached her hands out to touch his arms. He took a step back and shook his head.

I should really have tiptoed away, but my feet were glued to the spot.

'I'll leave you in private,' I said half-heartedly.

'No need,' said Tom. 'This won't take long.'

'OK.' I shrugged, inwardly gladdened by that.

Rebecca flicked a look in my direction and then focused on Tom.

'Forget Ryan,' she pleaded. 'That was a silly mistake. A very silly mistake. Please, Tom, give me a second chance. Salinger's can't manage without you. Bookings are down already.'

A flash of annoyance passed over Tom's face. I felt dreadfully sorry for him, knowing how hard he had worked to build up the restaurant's reputation. I was intrigued too; only a few minutes ago he'd said he wouldn't – ahem – pee on Salinger's if it was on fire. I wondered whether he'd really meant that. I guessed I'd soon find out.

'Define "bookings are down",' he said, narrowing his eyes.

'Last night we only had four tables in. On a Friday. Imagine that. When you were there we were full every night. You and me, we were invincible.'

'Until you had an affair with Ryan.'

'If you come back, I'll sack Ryan,' she promised.

'Oh, so he's still there?' Tom looked livid.

'Of course.' She looked at him blankly. 'I need a head chef.'

I sucked in a breath; she truly was a piece of work.

Tom shook his head in disgust. 'All those hours I put in to earn that Michelin star.'

'I know.' She stared at her feet. 'And you should read what they're saying on Trip Advisor.'

'Oh God.' He covered his face with his hand.

'Then help me?' she pleaded, gathering the front of his shirt between her fingertips. 'If not for me then for Salinger's, for the rest of the staff.'

He removed her hands from his chest and gazed at me.

'Verity, what do you think?'

He wanted my advice. My heart swelled; I was torn. Rebecca didn't deserve a second chance, not with the restaurant and certainly not with Tom. But after the conversation we had just had about me helping Liam, it would be hypocritical of me to say that, wouldn't it? Oh hell, I wished right now I hadn't been so . . . *nice*.

Rebecca whipped her head round and stared, studying me properly for the first time. She looked from me to Tom, incredulity etched into her pretty face.

'Are you two . . . ?'

'Excuse us.' I tilted my chin up, grabbed Tom's arm and led him a few steps away out of earshot and tried to assemble some answers.

Tom's face was grey. 'I was moving on. I'd got over her. Now what?'

I could see the turmoil in his eyes. I didn't like the way this was heading one bit. If I asked him to stay then I was making him choose between Rebecca and me, between Salinger's and the cookery school. And the thing was, I wasn't confident that I'd be on the winning side and after my recent humiliation with Liam, I had no desire to put myself in that position again.

'What do you want to do?' I whispered.

'Kill her. I am so mad with her. That restaurant was the best in Manchester a month ago,' he hissed. 'But . . .'

But. The word hung between us for a long moment.

Rebecca jingled her keys.

'A few hours ago you said you were done with the place,' I reminded him, unable to resist a little dig.

'I know, I know; I said I wouldn't piss on it. Jesus.' He exhaled and rubbed a hand through his hair, making it stand in wild peaks. 'We have never had a bad review. Never. And even though I'm not in charge of the kitchen any more, people will think I might have been when these reviews were written. I'm still associated with the place.'

'Then I think you should go,' I said briskly.

He looked taken aback. 'You do?'

'Obviously I want you to stay here,' I murmured pragmatically. 'The cookery school needs you. But ask yourself this: would you regret it if you didn't go and help her out?'

'You are lovely.'

He took my hand and squeezed it and I heard Rebecca gasp. The gesture took my breath away too.

I watched as he walked over to her and outlined his conditions. He'd go back, sort the kitchen out and get the restaurant on an even keel.

'But as far as you and me are concerned—' he began.

'Baby!' she squealed and threw her arms around his neck. 'Thank you, thank you. Come on, we need to hurry if we're going to make it in time for service tonight.'

She dashed to the car and jumped into the driver's seat, revving up the engine, ready to depart without giving me a second glance.

I felt a lump form in my throat.

What if he fell in love with her all over again? What if he didn't come back? What about me?

I was dying to yell that I didn't mean it, that I didn't want him to leave, but I was too stubborn, too scared to face the possibility of rejection. Besides, my throat felt tight and I couldn't say a word now if I'd wanted to.

'I'm sorry about later,' Tom said as he reached the passenger door. 'We were going to do something.'

'Oh that.' I laughed gaily, lying through my teeth. 'Don't worry. I'll probably be too tired after I've finished here anyway.'

'Oh.' He blinked. 'Right then. Bye.'

Tom folded himself into Rebecca's car and waved as she put the car into reverse. I stood and watched them leave with a heavy heart.

What was that phrase, if you love someone let them

go . . . ? I swallowed my own sadness and felt mounting panic take its place.

Had I done the right thing, giving him my blessing to go, or had I just made the biggest mistake of my life?

Taking Stock

Chapter 21

It was the last week in May, the Tuesday after the bank holiday, and the teaching kitchen was bathed in spring sunshine and bursting with activity. Unfortunately, my mood wasn't quite so sunny. Maintaining a welcoming smile was proving so difficult that my cheeks ached and I was worried about rigor mortis setting in to my face. I performed another circuit of the room, pausing in front of the row of windows to scan the car park. Again.

Sometimes you just get out of bed the wrong side and you have no one to blame for your own grumpiness. At other times, the blame can be very justifiably placed at the feet of others.

In my case, Tom's.

A wave of panic swelled inside me; how were we going to get through today without him? Where on earth was he?

He had disappeared with Rebecca on Saturday afternoon, like a knight in shining armour dashing off to save the restaurant he'd claimed not to care about any more, and no one had seen him since. I'd even called the friend whose flat he was staying in but he was none the wiser either.

Not a word from Tom. Not one.

And even though I'd given him my blessing at the time, now I was an uncomfortable mix of livid and nervous.

I mean, of all the days he could have chosen to leave me in the lurch, he had to pick the day when a room full of keen-as-mustard amateur chefs had gathered to compete for the Plumberry Signature Dish competition.

So much for 'shall we do something later?', which he'd murmured to me after the *Challenge Chester* crew had finished filming. The only things I'd done all weekend were look after Gloria and answer cookery school queries while he was presumably getting his feet back under the table at Salinger's.

The giant paella that we'd fed the entire village with on Saturday had created a flurry of publicity. Which was amazing, of course, but a little bit overwhelming to deal with singlehandedly.

Not only had the *York Mail* sent a photographer over yesterday, bank holiday Monday, but there had been huge interest in the two competitions Tom and I had organized. There were eighteen contestants for today's amateur chef competition and we would be at capacity for the Plumberry Bake Off competition tomorrow.

But even the fact that more people had applied for my competition than Tom's failed to raise a smile this morning.

I worried a tiny loose piece of skin on my lower lip until I made it sore. What if he didn't come back? What if the 'everydayness' of the Plumberry School of Comfort Food proved no match for the lure of fine dining and the love of the absolutely gorgeous Rebecca Salinger . . . ?

Oh God. Don't torture yourself.

I cast my eye round the room and looked at the amateur chefs. They were a mixed bunch: I recognized Annabel from Plumberry Wine Merchants and Jack from the village butcher's, along with Pixie's boss, Harriet, from the cheesemonger's. Pixie had also introduced me to Merrin, who she worked with behind the bar at the pub, but the others were all new faces to me.

Normal routine had flown out of the window this morning; none of the contestants were interested in idle chitchat over coffee and pastries in the Aga kitchen. As one man put it to Mags, 'I'm not here to make friends, I'm here to win.'

They had all arrived early, had spent the last hour stressing and generally driving Mags, Pixie and me round the twist with their queries and questions, and now they were chomping at the bit to get cooking.

It was a shame Gloria didn't feel well enough to come in this morning and see her cookery school so packed. As a former food stylist, she would appreciate the standard of today's cooking. Although at this rate – I glanced at the large clock on the wall – she might have no choice, aching hip or not, because unless our esteemed Michelin-starred chef turned up, we were without a judge. And when he did arrive he was going to wish he hadn't because when I got my hands on him I'd . . .

Ouch. I looked down at the red marks on my palms; I'd been digging my nails into them again.

Mags caught my eye and came bustling over. She was dressed for summer today in a fuchsia dress with lipstick to match. Her cheeks were also a flustered shade of pink and some of her hair had already escaped from its chignon.

'I think we'll have to start soon,' she hissed out of the side of her mouth, 'or we'll have a riot on our hands.'

I nodded. 'They're taking it so earnestly. And Mr Serious Chef himself isn't even here to witness it. He'll be kicking himself. After I've kicked him, that is,' I added in a low mutter.

'Still no word from him?'

I slipped my phone out of my apron pocket and checked it again. 'Not a peep. Anything on the answerphone?'

She pulled a face. 'Not had a chance to check, this lot were queuing up outside when I arrived to open up at eight o'clock. It's been non-stop demands ever since.'

'What are we going to do?' I whispered.

'Don't worry, chuck.' She patted my arm. 'If push comes to shove, I'll be the judge. I might not be able to tell my partridge from my pigeon, but I went to a lot of cookery book photo shoots, so I know what looks nice and I'm more than happy to test everything.'

'Thanks.' I managed a smile, but my heart wasn't in it. This lot had come to be judged by Tom, not Mags, who as far as they were concerned was just the receptionist.

'I feel such a fraud,' I continued. 'The contestants are far more knowledgeable about food than me, and yet here I am asking them questions about what they're cooking and nodding away as if I've got a clue what they're talking about.'

'Ditto,' breathed Pixie. She stood between us, a hand on both of our shoulders. 'That bloke over there with the black-and-white bandana just freaked out when he realized he'd forgotten to bring his boning knife and could I please find him one or he'd have to withdraw. I mean, what the hell does a boning knife look like?'

'What did you do?' I asked her.

She shrugged. 'I opened the knife drawer and told him he could borrow anything he wanted. Let him find his own.'

'Tell me about it,' Mags grumbled. 'One woman had a meltdown when she found out we didn't have a blast chiller and I thought the young lad with bright pink ears was going to cry when he couldn't find any truffle oil in the store cupboard.'

That was the other thing; some of them had brought their own equipment, from leather rolls containing flashy knives to complicated grinding machines, and those that hadn't were demanding we supply them with things I hadn't even heard of. I was completely out of my depth.

No wonder my head was already throbbing.

'Have they all got name badges?' I asked and Pixie nodded.

'OK, here goes,' I murmured.

I shook my hands out to release the tension, plastered on a bright smile and cleared my throat. The room fell silent,

230

the contestants staring at me with anticipation, and I felt my palms go clammy.

'On behalf of the Plumberry School of Comfort Food, I'd like to welcome everyone to our very first Signature Dish competition. I'm Verity Bloom, marketing manager; this is Mags, a former cookery book publisher, and Pixie, our—'

'Where's Tom?' shouted the man with the bandana.

'I knew he'd be trouble,' Pixie muttered from behind her hand.

Suddenly all heads swivelled towards the corner of the room at the sound of rapidly approaching footsteps as the man himself came into view at the top of the staircase.

Tom did up the last popper on his chef's tunic and grinned as he caught my eye. I nearly fainted with relief. His hair was more wild-looking and windswept than normal and his neatly trimmed beard was not quite so neat but he was here. Thank heavens.

'Last but not least, I'm delighted to introduce the immensely talented Tom MacDonald.'

I stared pointedly at him and hoped nobody noticed I was gritting my teeth.

'Tom has worked at top-class restaurants all over the world and what he doesn't know about fine dining isn't worth knowing. He will be presiding over today's competition, which judging by the atmosphere in this room is going to be pretty fierce.'

Everyone in the room erupted into applause. Except me. I might be relieved to see him, but he had some explaining to do before I'd be fanning his already monstrous ego.

'Thank you.' Tom held his hands up modestly. 'Ladies and gentlemen, your job here today is – if you'll pardon the pun – a piece of cake. All you have to do is impress me.'

He paused while the contestants laughed.

'This is about your signature dish, your very best cooking.

I'll be looking carefully to see what your food says about you.'

He checked his watch and then looked at me. I nodded.

'OK, the boss says you can start,' Tom continued. 'You have two hours. Off you go, I'm expecting some great plates of food!'

He clapped his hands and the contestants leapt into action. Saucepans clattered, machines whirred, knives chopped and sliced, and Jack the butcher whipped out a whole rabbit complete with fur, which made Pixie squeak.

As soon as I could, I marched across the teaching kitchen, down the stairs and out on to the deck.

I stood at the balustrade, staring down at the water as it sparkled in the sunlight, my chest heaving as I caught my breath. How could he just breeze in and grin at me like that? The *MasterChef*-style competition had been his baby, not mine, and yet I'd been the one running round like a headless poussin until he swanned in at the last second like . . . like a flippin' swan.

He was so infuriating . . .

I heard a soft laugh behind me. 'Verity, did you just growl?'

I turned to see him standing in the doorway, a nervous smile playing at his lips.

'Where the hell have you been? Why didn't you ring? The cookery school is full with *your* contestants,' I demanded, a sob catching in my throat. 'I've been so—'

Worried, I was going to say, but before I could even get the words out, he'd covered the distance between us and scooped me up in his arms so tightly that all my protests were literally silenced. I could hardly breathe let alone talk.

I closed my eyes for a second and forced back the tears and the exhaustion that had threatened to engulf me over the weekend. It would have been so easy to relax against him and it did feel good to be held again.

But I mustered all my indignation instead and struggled

out of his arms. I needed to show him how mad I was, how hurt that he had disappeared and not even thought to get in touch. Now was not the time to go all gooey.

He looked blankly at me. 'Why are you mad? You knew where I was.'

The thoughtless, selfish lump . . . Right now I'd cheerfully tip him over the balustrade into the river.

'When I didn't hear from you, I thought . . . I thought you might not come back,' I managed to croak.

He groaned and ran a hand through his hair. 'I'm sorry. I left Plumberry with just the clothes I stood up in and nothing else. My phone had died by the time we reached Manchester and Rebecca has got some Sony thing so I couldn't use her charger. I couldn't even turn my phone on to find your number. I left a billion messages on the cookery school line, didn't you get them?'

I shook my head. That made me feel better at least. I wanted to ask where he'd been staying; he didn't look like he'd had much sleep. But I didn't like to; it wasn't any of my business and I was pretty sure that I wouldn't like the answer.

The last seventy-two hours had been awful. This weekend, looking after Gloria, not just providing meals and drinks but supporting her while she did her exercises, making sure she had everything she needed, helping her to wash and dress . . . being at her total beck and call, in fact, had been non-stop. And much as I loved her, it had niggled a little bit when the district nurse had phoned offering assistance and Gloria had refused, saying that I could give her all the help she needed.

As well as my nursing duties, there had been the cookery school to deal with: sorting out the aftermath of the power cut and answering the emails and website enquiries that our *Challenge Chester* stunt had generated. On top of that I'd had to wash thirty large paella pans. For the first time since I'd been in Plumberry things had begun to get on top of me and I had felt lonely and taken for granted.

Something Tom had said to me on Saturday had been playing on my mind too: *I've never seen you put yourself first.*

Well, that was going to change. Tom clearly wasn't afraid to put himself first. He might be apologizing now, but look how quickly he'd left me on Saturday. Even Mags had been conspicuous by her absence over the bank holiday weekend, going to visit her sister in Liverpool. So why shouldn't I start looking after number one a bit too?

'That explains a lot,' he said. 'I repeat, I am sorry. Come here.'

He held out his arms and this time I stepped into them. I didn't return the hug, but rested my cheek against the crisp cotton of his chef whites.

'We don't normally do this,' I said grudgingly.

'No.' He placed my arms around his waist and forced me to hold him. 'It feels good, though.'

I didn't reply. But yes, it did.

Seconds later, he released me and took a step back.

'You've got great eyes.'

Not pretty, or beautiful, but great. It was such a 'Tom' compliment. I blinked self-consciously. 'Thanks.'

'They're as green as summer grass, but there are amazing tiny specks of amber in them that flash like fire when you're angry.' He leaned forward to examine them. 'And I seem to make them flash quite often.'

And he had two tiny creases between his eyebrows that met when he frowned and long, long eyelashes that swept his brow bone when he blinked. I held my breath, not sure what to say, but liking the sensation his words were having on my stomach. Like sipping brandy, I thought absent-mindedly. Intoxicating and fiery and definitely something worth getting used to.

'Whose fault is that, I wonder,' I replied finally.

'Verity, this weekend . . . Being away from Plumberry has given me time to think.'

He stared at me, his watchful eyes registering every flicker of emotion that passed across my face.

'Me too.'

I glanced up at him again; he didn't need to tell me what *he'd* been thinking about. This was exactly what had been going through my head on and off all weekend. It was obvious; he was going to leave the cookery school. Rebecca and his posh restaurant had won him back. Part of me wasn't surprised; the other part was heartbroken.

'Will you give me a chance to explain?'

I took a deep shuddering breath; I wasn't ready to hear this. Not yet.

'You should get back upstairs,' I said. 'There are eighteen chefs up there, all trying to impress you.'

Maybe they could succeed where I had clearly failed.

He nodded. 'You're right. But can we talk later? Out here again once all their food is in the ovens?'

I blinked at him and swallowed, my mouth dry. 'Of course.'

Chapter 22

Tom strode away and disappeared from view. I stood for a moment, breathing in the fresh late-spring air and listening to the burble of the river and the song from the birds in the trees and eventually the gentle rhythms of nature calmed my thumping heart.

I went back inside, determined not to panic. Tom hadn't left yet. What was the use in worrying about how I'd manage without him or about how we were going to cope without anyone to teach the courses? There'd be plenty of time to panic later . . .

I stopped off at the fancy coffee machine, made two lattes for Mags and me and meandered into reception where she was hunched over her desk.

'Ooh, thanks,' she said as I set a mug on a coaster near her keyboard. 'Look at all these.'

She swivelled her computer screen so that I could see her email inbox.

'Lots of lovely enquiries?' I said, blowing the froth on my coffee.

Mags nodded. 'And these, look.'

She tapped her pad to where she'd made a list of the messages that had been left on the answerphone since I'd checked it on Sunday.

'Including five messages from Tom asking you to ring him on this Manchester number.'

So he had tried to get in touch. Good. My heart gave a little bounce.

'Word is getting round about our cookery school,' I said, scanning through the other messages. 'Just imagine what it will be like once our episode of *Challenge Chester* has gone out; we'll be swamped!'

'We're already doing well.' She took out several sugar packets from her drawer and tipped them into her mug. 'Gloria will be thrilled to see that bookings are up.'

'She will. Goodness, is that the bookings list for Perfect Pasta?' I gasped, looking at the computer. 'Nineteen students?'

Mags chuckled. 'It's because people are trying to register for the Plumberry Bake Off competition. I've managed to persuade a few of them on to a course instead; the Cakes and Bakes course is getting close to fully booked too. I think we might have struck gold with the competitive element, I've been turning people away in their droves today.'

'Hmm,' I said. 'We just need to find a way to make money from competitions.'

'We could advertise to companies to run their own competitions for staff,' she suggested. 'Dave said that cooking could be the new paintballing, you know, team building, that sort of thing.'

He might have a point there. I for one would much rather spend a day at a cookery school learning a new skill with my colleagues than chasing each other round a muddy field with camouflage paint plastered across my face.

'Good idea. And?' I probed, nudging her with my elbow. 'How did you get on with him? I left you alone as requested on Saturday after *Challenge Chester.*'

She flapped her hand. 'Nothing to report on that front,' she said gloomily. 'Once he'd helped me get Gloria inside he scuttled off home.'

Odd; I was sure there was a spark there on both sides. 'Did you actually invite him in?'

A flush rose to her neck. 'I wanted to . . .' She swallowed. 'But when push came to shove, I lost my bottle.'

I blinked at her. 'This is not the brave and bold Mags that I know and love.'

'Yes. Well.' She began to fuss with her hair. 'That's all a front. I'm actually quite shy when it comes to men.'

I burst out laughing. 'Are you having me on?'

To my horror, her lip began to wobble. 'I'm my own worst enemy, Verity. Scared of being on my own for ever, but too scared to do anything about it. And then I spent the rest of the weekend at my sister's, worried that I've missed the boat.' She sighed and my heart went out to her.

'Oh, Mags, I'm sure you haven't,' I said, giving her shoulders a squeeze.

She produced a tissue out of her drawer. 'Don't listen to me. You're far too young to worry about missing any boats.'

Out of the corner of my eye I saw Tom jogging down the stairs towards us, a determined look in his eye.

'I'm not so sure,' I murmured.

Tom grinned as he approached, and for a moment I felt my heart stop.

'Have you got time for that chat now?' he said.

'Sure.'

Mags raised a curious eyebrow as I followed Tom back through the Aga kitchen and out on to the deck. The sun was higher now and the air smelled fresh and bursting with life after all the rain over the last few days. I rested my elbows on the wooden ledge overlooking the river and watched as a tawny mallard leading three fluffy ducklings bobbed past on the river. Tom joined me, mirroring my body language.

'So how's Rebecca?' I blurted out. 'Good, I'm guessing, seeing as you stayed so long?'

He nodded thoughtfully. 'She's happy, I think. I had originally planned to come back on Sunday night but we spent the day locked behind closed doors yesterday. Exhausting but worthwhile.'

I closed my eyes, to shut out the image of him and Rebecca . . . together. Oh God, this was going to be worse than I thought.

I swallowed. 'So you're back together?'

Tom looked at me sharply. 'Jesus. Not. A. Chance.'

'Oh,' I said in a neutral tone and resisted punching the air.

He stared down at his hands and twisted the leather strap round his wrist.

'I'll be honest, when I left with her on Saturday my heart was beating like the clappers. I was angry with her, but I was flattered too, and she always did have the power to bend me to her will. As we drove out of Plumberry, I wondered whether I'd been too hasty to walk away from her in April. Maybe I should have fought harder for her. For the restaurant.'

'What happened to change your mind?'

'We hadn't gone far when she reached for my hand. I thought, this is the moment. Do I want this?'

'And?' I prompted, swallowing hard.

'I realized I didn't,' he said simply. 'When something so fundamental has been broken it can never be fixed. Like my trust in her.'

I nodded. I knew exactly how he felt. I remembered the first time I'd seen my fiancé Chris after we'd split up. We had hugged and I'd told him how much I missed him and he'd said the same. But when he'd tried to kiss me, I'd hesitated and the opportunity to make up had slipped away. And although it was sad, I had no regrets because deep down I realized that we didn't love each other enough to accept each other's choices. And if we couldn't do that before we were married, what chance did we have for a happy future?

'I didn't take her hand and the moment passed.' He

shook his head and gave a hollow laugh. 'You can imagine the atmosphere in the car after that. And before we'd even reached Manchester I knew I'd made the right decision. You heard her apologize, right?'

I nodded. Rebecca had vowed that her affair with Ryan had been a silly mistake.

'That didn't last long; she started reeling off all the ways *I'd* pushed *her* into being unfaithful, which included – I'm not kidding – the time I'd not come out to say hello to a table of her old teacher colleagues. We were full that night, and short staffed . . .'

I shot him a quizzical look. 'She was unfaithful because you were busy in the kitchen?'

'That and several hundred other alleged misdemeanours on my part,' he said in disgust.

'So why did you stay away so long? What have you been doing all this time?' I asked.

He left here on Saturday. It was now Tuesday. That was three days. And three nights.

'I remembered what you said about helping Liam. So I decided to help her and Ryan out.'

'So they are still together?' I exclaimed.

He nodded. 'She hadn't ended it with him, just in case I turned her down.'

'Charming.'

'Part of me wanted to gloat and leave them to it. But I kept thinking, What would Verity do?' he said with a shy grin.

'*Me?*' I stared at him. Inside I glowed with pride.

'You said that you'd sent that marketing plan in to your last place to help your ex out even though no one would ever know it was your work.' He gazed at me unwaveringly and I felt my cheeks go a bit warm. 'That really stuck with me. And when I saw the mess they'd made of the restaurant I decided to try to do something kind and selfless. Like you would.'

I was flattered beyond measure. And blushing like mad.

'Excuse me while I polish my halo,' I said, rolling my eyes.

He grinned and looked away over the water.

'Whether I like it or not, I'll always be associated with Salinger's. Even though it might not have my name over the door, it received that Michelin star under my leadership, my menu. It would be a crime to let that reputation go to waste.'

I studied him surreptitiously. He'd changed since I'd first met him when he'd said that his food was about him; he'd started to lose that hard edge and I liked him all the more for it.

'So what did you do?'

He lifted one shoulder casually. 'I simplified the menu. Took out a couple of my signature dishes.'

'No more scallops with lime foam? Shock horror.'

He laughed. 'No. Although I left them with a minted pea purée.'

'Ah, that was kind.'

'Well,' he pulled a guilty face, 'yes and no. I'm giving Rebecca and Ryan a month to buy me out. So it's in my interests to help it succeed.'

'So you're really putting the restaurant behind you?' I held my breath, willing him to say he wanted to stay in Plumberry.

He nodded. 'While I still part-own it, it's like she has permission to come running every time they get into trouble. And I don't want that. It's time to move on. I actually came away feeling a bit sorry for Ryan, if I'm honest. He has big shoes to fill.'

He waggled his eyebrows self-deprecatingly and we shared a smile.

I felt a weight lift off my shoulders and with it, the remains of the black mood I'd been carrying round with me ever since he'd left with Rebecca on Saturday. I knew that at some point Tom would still want his own restaurant, and he deserved to reach his own goal, but right now the cookery school needed him. Oh, who was I kidding? I was just grateful that he hadn't got back together with Rebecca.

'You're all heart,' I said, pressing a kiss to his cheek.

'You leave my heart out of it,' he said drily. 'It's taken a battering this weekend.'

Instead of stepping away from me, Tom moved his hands until they were resting lightly on the tops of my arms and I felt my heart leap.

'I'm proud of you, you know,' I said, looking into his eyes, the colour of espresso. 'When you said on Saturday that you wouldn't pee on Salinger's even if it was on fire, it made me sad to see you so bitter. But you're a bit like crème brûlée: a tough shell to crack on the outside, but underneath you're a sweetie.'

'Shush, don't let that get out.' He grinned. 'Anyway, as much as I hate to admit it, Ryan is a talented chef. I think he just got out of his depth; he realized running a professional kitchen wasn't as easy as I made it look. And Rebecca . . . she knows which side her bread's buttered. She'll stop at nothing to get what she wants. She'll never change, but I have.'

'I can see that; I'm impressed,' I said, shaking my head.

'I know, I blame you, you've mellowed me.' He laughed as I raised my eyebrows in surprise. 'You managed in only four weeks what Rebecca failed to do in years. So I'm rid of her.'

'And I'm rid of Liam,' I added.

'So . . .' Tom began.

'So?'

'We were going to do something on Saturday after *Challenge Chester* until I behaved appallingly and left you in the lurch.'

'*I* did do something,' I laughed. 'I cleaned up after the world's biggest barbecue.'

He cringed. 'Sorry. Again. I'll make it up to you, I promise.'

His watch started beeping and he turned off the alarm.

'That's my cue to go back up. Come on, let's go and see how the contestants are doing. You can tell me who you fancy to win.'

'I might even offer them a few pointers,' I said, tickled pink that he seemed to value my opinion.

He scratched his head. 'Er, I don't think any of them are doing fish finger sandwiches.'

Upstairs in the teaching kitchen the air was tight with adrenalin and activity, and a mêlée of sweet and savoury aromas, of caramelized sugar and roast meat combined to give an almost fairground atmosphere.

'How's it going?' Tom asked Pixie.

She was standing at the teaching station at the front of the room, holding a stopwatch.

'So so,' she said. 'Jack the butcher and that bloke Brian with the bandana nearly came to blows at one point, and she might need a motivational chat.' She pointed to the woman who'd requested the blast chiller earlier.

Tom chuckled. 'Leave it with me.'

We walked up to the first aisle where Jack was looking very professional, a small frying pan tipped to one side while he basted meat with butter. He was an athletic-looking man in his early forties with a broad chest and huge sausagey fingers; the frying pan looked like a child's toy in his hands.

'I've only used the loin of the rabbit,' said Jack, grinning at Tom. 'You can keep the rest if you like. Very fresh? Free?'

Tom threw his head back and laughed. 'Thanks, although it won't get you any extra marks.'

Jack shrugged sheepishly. 'Worth a try.'

'And have you and Brian sorted out your differences?' I asked.

The butcher rolled his eyes. 'Yeah, it was something and nothing. He'd never seen anyone skin a rabbit before. Told me I was a barbarian.'

Tom winced. 'It can be a bit of an eye-opener if you're used to buying your meat wrapped in cling film ready to cook.'

'And how do you skin a rabbit?' I asked.

'You hook its ears over the taps and tug its coat off,' Jack said matter-of-factly.

I swallowed. 'Oh.' I wished I hadn't asked. Poor Brian would probably never get rid of that image.

We left Jack making his sauce and moved along to blast-chiller woman, whose name was Michelle. She was a few years older than me and had looked quite smart when she walked in but now her hair had gone limp from the steam and was hanging in damp curls around her face and she had flecks of purple all over her face. In fact, now that I looked closer, everything around her was flecked with purple too.

'Gosh, you look . . . busy!' I said brightly. 'And what a lovely colour.'

'It's supposed to be a coulis to go with my espresso crème brûlée. But nothing's going right. Nothing,' Michelle said in a wobbly voice as she tried to jam the top on the food processor. Her hands were dripping with juice.

I pressed my lips together to hide a smile; not five minutes ago I'd compared Tom to a crème brûlée. Her signature dish was effectively Tom in edible form. She might well be my winner.

Tom took over and screwed the lid on for her.

'What do you love about cooking, Michelle?' he asked, reaching for a paper towel.

She took a deep breath and looked like she was swallowing a large lump in her throat before she spoke. 'It's a good way to unwind. I get in the kitchen and lose myself for an hour.'

'And are you unwinding now?'

'No,' she said in a small, high-pitched voice.

'Then try and calm down,' said Tom in a kind voice that I'd never heard him use at work before. 'Who do you normally cook for?'

'My two lovely boys.' Her face softened. 'They are such good kids. I'm a single working mum, but I always cook from scratch for them every night. I think it's much better than feeding them processed rubbish.'

Tom nodded with approval and I half expected him to give me a pointed look. But he rested a hand on Michelle's shoulder. 'Then imagine you're cooking for them rather than me. I'm sure if your food is good enough for two demanding kids then it'll do for me. Relax, have fun with it.'

We walked away from her and I pressed a hand to his forehead. 'Relax and have fun? Should I be worried?'

He smiled sheepishly.

'I lost touch with what mattered for a while. And that is heart. There has to be heart in cooking.' He stared at me so intently that I felt guilty for teasing him.

'So from now on,' he continued, 'I'm focusing on that.'

Heart. Something inside me pinged.

'Suits me,' I murmured.

We continued round the room, offering encouragement and in Tom's case dipping spoons in every pan until we came to the youngest contestant, Aaron, who looked about sixteen and whose ears had gone red under pressure.

'What made you enter today, Aaron?' Tom picked up a teaspoon and tasted some sort of cheesy mix.

'Two reasons.' Aaron looked up briefly from his task of placing small mounds of filling on to circles of fresh pasta. 'I like doing magic. Take the simple sweet potato – a boring, lumpy everyday thing. But with a bit of magic it turns into something special. In this case sweet potato and goat's cheese ravioli.'

Tom grinned at him with approval. 'Why vegetarian?'

'Because we could never afford much meat growing up so the veggies became the star of the show. My mum has always made the most of what we had. She's shown me that cooking is about making the best of things. Just like life.'

I changed my mind; he was my new favourite. Aaron blushed furiously and stared at his chopping board.

'And what is your other reason?' I asked, barely holding myself back from giving the boy a hug.

'I need a job and I thought if I could win this, it would be good to go on my CV.'

'Good man.' Tom clapped him on the back. 'Good luck.'

'Oh my God, I love him so much,' I muttered under my breath as we walked on.

'He's got grit; I like him,' Tom agreed. 'If I was to open a restaurant, he's exactly the sort of lad I'd want on my team.'

I shot him a panicky look.

'But I'm not.' He laughed and checked his watch. 'You carry on round handing out words of wisdom, I just need to make a quick call.'

He strode across to the office and shut the door. I wandered over to Annabel from the wine merchants who had a pile of discarded honeycomb pieces that looked in need of sampling.

It was a tough job, I sighed contentedly to myself, crunching into golden pieces of honeycomb a few seconds later, but someone had to do it . . .

Chapter 23

Ten minutes later I joined Tom in the office. He dropped the phone in its cradle immediately and stretched his arms above his head.

'Who was that?' I asked, slipping into the chair behind my desk.

He grinned and tapped his nose. 'A surprise.'

'Suit yourself.' I shrugged, pretending not to be bothered. I scooped my hair up into a pony tail and turned my computer on. 'By the way, have you ever done any team building?'

I told him about Dave's idea for running cookery days for corporate clients and how it might be a way to make this sort of competition profitable for the cookery school.

'Hmm.' Tom rubbed his chin thoughtfully.

'You don't sound convinced.' I turned to look at him. He was close enough for me to see purple shadows under his eyes. He looked weary; he'd probably not had a moment to himself since leaving Plumberry on Saturday.

'Forget it,' I said with a smile. 'We can do this another time. Have you eaten today?'

He wrinkled his nose. 'Er, only what I've tasted in there.'

'Right, sit down; I'll go foraging.'

I returned a few minutes later with a glass of milk and a cheese sandwich.

'Thanks, Mum,' he said.

We were quiet for a few moments, each engrossed with our task: he ploughed his way through his food and I responded to my emails.

'I took over service on Saturday night at Salinger's,' said Tom eventually, brushing the crumbs from his hands over the plate. 'Ryan went back to being my underling.'

I winced. 'That must have been awkward.'

'I can't deny feeling a certain satisfaction.' He grinned, leaned back and propped his feet up on Gloria's desk. 'But it was strange being back in that heated environment; all that bent double over food nonsense, making every vegetable look perfect. I see it in there today.' He nodded to the teaching kitchen through the glass panel. 'I can feel their passion, and I admire them for it, their skills, the techniques, and the commitment to making the very best plate of food possible.'

'They are certainly going for gold,' I said with a laugh, catching sight of Annabel whisking something in a copper bowl as if her life depended on it.

'But I can't help feeling . . .' He hesitated.

'What?' I prompted.

'That I'm a bit over it.'

'*What?*' I said again.

'I realized on Saturday that I got more satisfaction from teaching you to make bread last week than serving intricate dishes to discerning diners in Manchester.'

'Do I know you?' I cocked an eyebrow at him.

What had happened to the pretentious chef who'd insisted we taught students how to confit eggs and make the perfect fondant potato?

'To tell the truth, I hardly recognize myself,' he said with bewilderment. 'But now I get it. I get why Gloria has invested in this cookery school to pass her love of food on to others. I think that for the moment, being in Plumberry where food is about taste and enjoyment and sharing is right for me; it's somewhere to take stock and plan my next move.'

I studied his face; his strong jaw with its dark beard contrasting starkly with his pale Irish complexion, those brooding eyes that mirrored every emotion so clearly, and I felt my heart flutter. He looked up and caught me staring, but rather than look away I held his gaze.

'That's exactly how I feel too,' I said. 'Like I'm taking stock and that Plumberry and the cookery school are giving me the time and space to do it.'

'So basically we feel the same way.' He grinned.

Little bubbles of happiness fizzed and popped inside me.

'We do,' I laughed.

He leaned forward, reaching his fingertips towards my desk. I did the same until quite suddenly we were holding hands.

'Time's up,' Pixie yelled, appearing in the doorway.

We leapt back in our seats, me red-faced and Tom finding the floor of the office very interesting.

'I didn't mean you two,' she sniggered. 'Although you might want to go somewhere more private. The contestants have had their two hours and I think most of them are looking this way. Can I dismiss them?'

'Of course,' I said, clearing my throat. 'Mags will be putting drinks out in the Aga kitchen while Tom does the judging.'

'OK.' She turned back into the room. 'Please make your way downstairs for—'

There was a stampede as the contestants made a bid for freedom.

'They're all desperate for the loo,' Pixie laughed.

'It smells heavenly up here,' Mags announced, appearing at the top of the stairs. 'Hey, do we get to taste this food like on *MasterChef*?'

'We do.' Tom switched immediately into professional mode. 'I'll get each of them to come and present their dishes. Then they can relax while we select the top three between us and then I'll choose the overall winner. Does that sound good?'

The three of us leapt to attention army-style. 'Yes, Chef.'

Tom went out to examine the entries while Mags went to deliver the instructions to the contestants. I gestured to the chair recently vacated by Tom and Pixie dropped into it.

Pixie was last seen disappearing off to her granddad's house on Saturday with Cheryl from the *Challenge Chester* team. Her bike was too bent to ride, so Mags had called her a taxi while I'd gone inside the cookery school to rustle up some lunch for her granddad. I hadn't had a chance to speak to Pixie properly about it.

'Good weekend?' I asked casually.

Pixie went pink and nodded. 'Cheryl came over to mine on Sunday and we just, you know, hung out.'

I was surprised; she always talked about her home as if it was stuffed full to the rafters with siblings. I didn't think there would be room to hang out comfortably.

'You seemed to get on well.' I was surprised about that too, if I was honest. Pixie was such a happy-go-lucky character whereas Cheryl seemed to give off an air of permanent boredom.

'I really like her.' She began worrying a loose piece of fingernail and shrugged. 'We swapped numbers and she says she's going to invite me to London, so . . .'

I blinked at her as the penny dropped. 'Pixie, am I being extremely dense? Are you gay?'

She exhaled and her lips twitched. 'I've kept quiet because, well, you know, you're so conservative.'

My jaw dropped. 'Me? I'm far from that. You'd be amazed at some of the things I've done in my time.'

Her eyes held mine and she grinned broadly. 'Go on then, amaze me.'

I pressed my lips together. It would be tempting to bust her image of me as conservative, but my past wasn't something I should bandy about just to win points in the 'how broad-minded is Verity Bloom' competition.

Instead, I got up and pulled her in for a hug. 'You can think I'm boring if you like, I don't mind. And I'm happy for you both.'

'She's so cool.'

'You certainly seemed to bring out the fun side in her,' I said diplomatically.

'Now we need to get you hooked up.' Pixie folded her arms and tapped her chin. 'What about Jack the butcher? He's good with his hands.'

I nudged her. 'Stop it.'

'OK, OK.'

I rolled my eyes. 'Please don't say you're one of those annoying types who, as soon as they've got a date, think that everyone else needs fixing up?'

'Ooh, touchy.'

'No, seriously,' I said, holding my palms up. 'I've only just managed to get myself unhooked from my ex in Nottingham.'

'Pity.' She pressed her lips into a smug smile.

'How so?'

'Because Mags just took a phone call confirming Tom's reservation for a table for two this Friday night at Platform Six. I was hoping the lucky lady might be you.'

Platform Six was probably the swishest restaurant in the area, set in a converted Victorian railway station. I'd never been but I'd heard the food was amazing.

'Really?' I said in a squeaky voice, mulling over the phone call I'd walked in on a few minutes earlier.

Hmm, I was sort of hoping it might be me too . . .

'I like this one,' said Pixie stubbornly, tapping a large dish of spaghetti flecked with tinned crab and some unidentifiable green herb.

'Only because he'd set himself a five-pound budget,' Tom retorted. 'It looks like a dog's dinner.'

'I have to agree,' said Mags. 'It's not the most attractive plate of food.'

'I think setting a budget is a brilliant idea.' Pixie grimaced under her heavy fringe. 'And it's the sort of thing people can make at home.'

'You're right, we should encourage people to make the most of cheaper ingredients,' I said diplomatically, squeezing Pixie's arm. 'But in this case, I think other contestants have done a more inventive job. This is their signature dish, after all.'

Besides, I wanted Aaron to win in case it helped him find work. The spaghetti man already had a job with the council.

I'd been hoping Harriet's twice-baked stilton soufflé would be a contender for a place in the top three, but unfortunately she'd had an issue with steam and it looked more like a crustless quiche, quivering apologetically under a rocket garnish. Annabel's zabaglione with poached apricots and a honeycomb topping had shown initial promise too, but something had gone wrong in the whisking and it had pieces of cooked egg in it.

Nonetheless, overall the contestants had far exceeded my expectations (and my capabilities, come to that) and we'd narrowed it down to three: Jack's loin of rabbit with wilted greens and a cream sauce; Aaron's ravioli (minus truffle oil); and from the chairwoman of the Women's Institute, a pan-fried pigeon breast with crispy croutons, a red wine jus and a cauliflower purée.

The cookery school team had sampled every dish and Tom was having a final taste and scribbling notes as he did so. I was impressed as usual by his attention to detail and utter professionalism in everything he did. Finally, he lifted his head, put his notebook in his breast pocket and nodded. 'Bring everyone back in, Mags; we've got our winner.'

The contestants filed back in and took seats in rows in front of the teaching station. Credit where it was due, they had all cleared away after themselves beautifully and the kitchen was spick and span ready for tomorrow's Bake Off. Just as well: I'd already got enough to do this afternoon. I'd bought some props to decorate the room with; we wanted it to look as much like the warm and welcoming set of *Great British Bake Off* as we could.

A hush fell across the room as Tom took centre stage to announce the results.

'Thank you all for entering the inaugural Plumberry Signature Dish competition. Given the tradition of good food in this village, it's no surprise that today's cooking has been of an exceptionally high standard. You should all be proud of yourselves and what you've achieved. But of course there can only be one winner and that's . . .' Tom paused in the spirit of every game show across the world and the tension in the room was palpable, 'Aaron for his sweet potato and goat's cheese ravioli.'

We all applauded Aaron whose face turned as beetroot as his ears. And then gradually conversation began again as people swapped recipes and disaster stories and generally allowed the morning's tension to seep away.

'Oh, this is much more what we're used to,' said Mags, pressing a hand to her bosom. 'All that competitive banter this morning gave me heartburn.'

I wrapped an arm around her shoulders. 'I'm hoping tomorrow will have more of a village fête feel about it. I've got bunting and flowers and I've even ordered some pretty tablecloths.'

'This has been the most brilliant day of my life,' said Aaron, coming to join us.

He had been wandering around numbly shaking hands and being kissed. His eyes still looked dazed with disbelief and he had the sweetest smile that showed up his dimples. 'I've never won anything before today.'

'And it's going to get better,' said Tom, stepping forward to shake his hand. 'I've arranged an internship at Salinger's for a month, if you'd like it? It might not pay much, but I guarantee you'll learn a lot.'

'Oh, man! Are you serious?' Aaron's eyes filled with tears and he grabbed hold of Tom and hugged him.

My heart squeezed for him; he really was a deserving winner. And as for Tom . . . What a thoughtful thing to do.

The phone rang and I scurried into the office to answer it. It was Gloria.

'Now you're not to worry,' she panted, 'but I've had an accident.'

'Don't move,' I yelled. 'I'm on my way.'

Chapter 24

I raced home at top speed with a pulse rate to match to find Gloria sprawled out, half in the downstairs loo and half in the hall, with Comfrey and Sage licking her face and whimpering. She was lying on her side, luckily not on the hip she'd broken. Her ivory linen dress gave her such a ghostly appearance that I let out a huge sigh of relief when she turned her head to look at me. Her features were screwed up and her blue eyes seemed huge against her porcelain skin and hollow cheeks, but at least she was conscious.

'I'm sorry to be such a nuisance, darling,' she said weakly.

A shudder of guilt slithered down my spine; Gloria had been released from hospital on the proviso that she had someone looking after her. She simply shouldn't be left on her own all day; it was too dangerous. Things like this – or worse – were bound to happen.

I knelt down beside her. 'No, I'm sorry. You poor thing. Where does it hurt?'

'Nowhere really. I bumped my head on the door handle and I think there's a lump somewhere.' She prodded the side of her head above her ear gingerly. 'Ouch. There.'

'What happened?' I slid my arm under her shoulders and propped her up to a sitting position.

'I was opening the door to come out of the loo and one of my crutches slipped. I didn't dare move in case I damaged something by struggling.'

'And *have* you damaged anything, do you think?'

She wriggled her toes on the leg that had been plastered to the knee.

'Only my pride,' she said, half-laughing.

I carefully helped her up, taking all her weight while she got her balance, and fitted her crutches to each arm. All the while Comfrey and Sage bounced round us, frantically yapping as if telling me how worried they'd been.

We made our way unsteadily into the living room and Gloria lowered herself gratefully on to the sofa. I made us both a drink and returned from the kitchen with the lunch I'd prepared for her before I'd left in the morning.

'Gloria,' I said hesitantly, 'I really don't think you should be here on your own . . .'

She nodded. 'I agree. Tomorrow I'll come into the cookery school.'

'I meant that perhaps you could have some convalescence somewhere lovely,' I chided.

'What?' She looked at me, horror-struck. 'Sit in a bath chair all day with a blanket on my knee until it's my turn for a push round the grounds? No thank you.'

'It wouldn't be that bad,' I said half-heartedly.

Mimi, what am I going to do with her? If she was my mum, I could be firmer, but it doesn't seem fair to insist. Wish you were here.

I could hardly force her out of her own home even though she had shunned all offers of help from the district nurse. She had grudgingly made an appointment with the physiotherapist for Friday, but I think she had only agreed to that because she wasn't given any choice. She was so damn stubborn; just like Mimi had been, never taking the easy option, never accepting defeat for one second. And whilst I admired her independence it frightened me to death on a daily basis.

She spread a napkin on her lap and took a tiny bite from her cheese and pickle sandwich.

'Please let me come into work. I'm so bored here, I can't

get out into the garden without help because of the steps and I need a change of scene.'

She blinked her blue eyes at me.

'All right.' I nibbled my lip. 'But I still think we should call the doctor to take a look at you after that fall.'

A look of fear flashed across her face before she pulled herself together. 'There's little point. They're closed now for the afternoon, so we wouldn't get an appointment today, even if I needed one, which I don't. So . . .' She patted the chair beside her. 'Tell me all about your morning.'

I did as I was told and gave her an edited version of the morning's events. I hadn't told her that Tom had spent the weekend with his ex, nor that I'd been beside myself with worry when he hadn't turned up this morning, so instead I told her all about the full-to-bursting cookery school, the fabulous food that had been produced under her roof and all about our winner, Aaron, and the fantastic opportunity Tom had arranged for him at Salinger's.

It did the trick; she was thrilled to bits and by the time I'd finished I could see her eyelids beginning to droop. I made sure her crutches and phone were in easy reach, pressed a kiss to her cheek and left her to have an afternoon snooze.

Back at the cookery school, Tom was holed up in the office on the phone to suppliers, ordering food for the next few days' courses, and Mags and Pixie were arguing about who should reprise Mary Berry's role in tomorrow's Plumberry Bake Off competition.

'Older doesn't necessarily mean wiser,' said Pixie, very boldly, I thought.

'Correct. But I'm both and besides, I've been to her house for an Aga cookery demonstration. So I win.' With that Mags smiled smugly and folded her arms. 'She was charming and said she liked my nails.'

'Actually, there are three of you in the running to be lady judge,' I announced. 'Gloria is planning on being here.'

Mags lifted an eyebrow. 'Is that wise given her recent falling-out with the toilet door?'

I shrugged. 'No. But you try telling her that.'

'How will she get up the stairs?' Pixie asked. 'On her bum?'

Mags pointed to the fire escape door on the far wall. 'That leads to the brewery and a lift shaft that used to serve this half of the mill too. I think Gloria did some sort of deal with the landlord to use the lift as and when required.'

Pixie went off to investigate and I tiptoed into the office so as not to disturb Tom and retrieved the box of pretty Union Jack bunting.

'Have you really met Mary Berry?' I asked five minutes later as the two of us stretched the stream of flags across the room.

'Oh yes. I met all the greats while I was in publishing. Lovely lady.' She gazed wistfully out of the window. 'Good times.'

My phone vibrated and I looked at the screen to see a text message from Rosie.

When's that pasta making course and is there any room left on it?

I ran downstairs to Mags's computer in reception and opened up the bookings screen on the website to check; there was one remaining space. I reserved it and sent a text message back.

Friday afternoon, one spot, who wants it?

Rosie replied instantly.

ME!!

I laughed softly to myself and typed another question.

And will you be able to stay over?

Her reply pinged back quickly.

On a Friday night?? Naturalmente!

Friday? My stomach flipped. Tom had a table booked at Platform Six on Friday. If Pixie was right and he was planning to ask me, I wouldn't be able to go. Never mind, a catch-up with Rosie was exactly what I needed after the stress of the last few days.

I beamed as I sent her a text back.

A girls' night out! I'll chill the prosecco!

By six thirty I was back at Gloria's cottage serving supper. I'd made a Cheesy Cod Casserole with jacket potatoes and a huge bowl of sugar snap peas, which someone had left behind after the Signature Dish contest. Haute cuisine it was not, I thought, ladling it on to three plates, but it was quick, easy and above all, comforting after a tiring day.

'Dinner's ready,' I called down the hallway to Mags and Gloria.

It was a sunny evening but too cool to eat outside so we opened the French doors to the garden and sat at the kitchen table. Comfrey and Sage lolled on the patio like little bookends, keeping guard and barking if a butterfly dared to come too close.

'It's so lovely to see you cooking again,' Gloria said, helping herself to vegetables.

'This is one of the few recipes my mum taught me,' I said. 'Not like you and Mimi, Gloria. In fact, I think I learned more from you than I did from Mum.'

Gloria and I shared a smile.

'Your mum was a secretary, Verity, working long hours, whereas my job was also my passion,' she said generously.

'Cooking and styling food comes as naturally to me as eating. "Don't play with your food" was one of the first things I can remember my mother saying to me. "I'm not playing; I'm making it pretty," I used to reply.'

'"Get your hand out of that cake tin" was what mine said to me,' Mags said with a chuckle. 'Although she was a big girl, so I think I inherited my love of food from her.'

'I don't think I've inherited too much from my mother other than Cheesy Cod Casserole,' I said with a lopsided smile, 'and I don't think that's much to boast about. Ooh, your pills, Gloria.'

I passed her her tablets and she shook some out into her hand.

'I disagree,' Mags declared, scooping the centre out of her jacket potato and loading the skin with butter. 'It's lovely to have family recipes passed down. You must miss your family over in Canada?'

I shook my head. 'I love my parents dearly, but we've had a turbulent relationship in the past. Mum and I get on much better now we're on different continents.'

Mags cocked a quizzical eyebrow. 'I can't imagine you falling out with anyone.'

I squirmed in my seat, conscious of my face heating up.

'My brother has done everything by the book in my mother's eyes: met a nice girl, settled down and procreated,' I said, passing her the vegetable dish. 'Unfortunately, I've fallen short of her expectations.'

'Oh?' Mags stared, consumed with curiosity, her loaded fork poised in front of her mouth.

I went redder, wondering just how deep a hole I could dig before falling in completely. Fortunately, Gloria was miles behind the conversation and still talking about food.

'Anyway, darling, it was a pleasure passing that love of cooking on to you and Mimi. I always looked on it as my legacy.'

She stopped and her eyes welled with tears. I guessed

what she was thinking: that she should have gone before her daughter and not the other way round. That was the natural order of things. What good was having a legacy if you had no one to pass it on to?

'I think about legacy a lot,' Mags admitted, 'not having children of my own. What will be left of me when I go? What can I leave behind to remind people that *Mags was 'ere?*'

'I don't think you'll be forgotten for a very long time,' I said, trying to jolly her along a bit. 'Besides, surely you don't have to have children to leave a legacy?'

'I hope not because otherwise that would leave me in a bit of a pickle,' said Gloria in a wobbly voice.

Mags and I exchanged glances as she put her knife and fork together neatly and stared out of the window. As if sensing her change in mood, the dogs trotted into the kitchen and pushed their noses against her leg.

'You've got Noah,' Mags soothed, patting her arm.

Gloria swallowed. 'I know, and lovely Gabe, but I so loved every stage of Mimi's life from baby to adulthood and I can't help but think about all the mother-and-daughter things we've missed out on since.'

Her words touched a nerve with me and I felt a lump swell in my throat. If only Mimi were still here . . .

'I would never dream of trying to take her place.' I faltered for a second, unsure of myself. But wasn't that exactly what I was doing? I pushed away the uncomfortable thought. 'But I'll be here to pass on your legacy. If you'd like me to?'

She took both of my hands and squeezed them gratefully.

'Thank you, darling. Thank you. Life is so short, Verity.' Gloria's tone was suddenly urgent. 'Promise me you won't waste a single chance to be happy.'

I felt tears pricking at the back of my throat and I managed a small smile.

'Promise. Anyway,' I said, determined to jolt my two

lovely friends out of their melancholy, 'we don't need to worry about any of that just yet. You'll be as fit as a fiddle before you know it.'

'Unless you carry on chucking yourself off the loo,' said Mags with a chortle.

'Let's drink to our health.' I fetched a bottle of wine and poured us each a glass; only a small one for Gloria, who wasn't strictly allowed alcohol with the painkillers she was on.

'Cheers.' Mags downed half of hers in a single swallow.

'Tom called me earlier,' said Gloria brightly. 'He was asking for Friday morning off. Naturally I said he could; the Perfect Pasta course is only on in the afternoon.'

My ears pricked up.

'Did he say why?' I asked nonchalantly.

Her brow wrinkled. 'Er, a solicitor's meeting in Manchester, he said; something to do with selling Salinger's.'

That was very speedy of him; it seemed that once he'd made up his mind he got straight on with it. I liked that in a person.

'Which reminds me,' Gloria continued, 'I must give my own solicitor a tinkle. I've got some paperwork to catch up on. I think it's important to keep on top of your affairs when you're single.'

Mags topped up her glass.

'Here's to affairs,' she said, lifting her glass. 'And staying on top.'

We all laughed and the mood was instantly lighter.

'To affairs,' I echoed, sipping my wine.

A warm sensation came over me as the alcohol hit my bloodstream. Or maybe it was the image of a gruff Irishman that had popped deliciously into my head?

Later that evening I took the dogs out for a walk through the village. The sun was low in the sky and the shops along Plumberry high street were bathed in a golden glow. We had slowed to a snail's pace outside the butcher's shop as Comfrey and Sage sniffed the closed door and scoured the pavement for meaty treasure when my phone rang.

'Verity, it's us,' said Mum in a shouty voice.

'Dad as well,' said Dad more discreetly.

My heart swelled. I'd always had an easy relationship with Dad, and had done with Mum, I supposed, until we had our big clash a few years ago. But now, whether it was having been away from Nottingham for a month, or perhaps the stress of looking after Gloria on my own over the bank holiday weekend, it was lovely to hear their voices.

'We're on hands-free!' Mum trilled.

'Your mother's had a gin and tonic,' said Dad in a loaded voice. 'We're having lunch out. What are you doing?'

'Walking off supper. Which *I* cooked. Actually, it was your recipe, Mum: Cheesy Cod Casserole.'

'Hasn't Gloria suffered enough?' Dad muttered. 'Ouch.'

'Cheek,' Mum tutted. 'And the cookery school? How is it doing?'

'Very well!' I said happily. 'Big day tomorrow . . .'

The dogs were on the move again, so I followed behind them while I filled my parents in on the Bake Off competition and how overwhelmed with enquiries we'd been since our day in the limelight on Saturday when the *Challenge Chester* team had been in Plumberry.

'A baking competition?' Mum sighed. 'I'd love to enter one of those. There's nothing like that over here.'

I smiled to myself; I think I could count on one hand the number of times Mum had baked a cake.

'Since when have you been a keen baker?' Dad chortled.

'I have my moments.' Mum sniffed. 'Anyway, love, it sounds like you're in heaven.'

'Yes, it was a good career move,' Dad added.

At that moment a teenage boy slouched past, dragging a reluctant Yorkshire terrier behind him on a lead. Sage decided to skip round the little dog in circles, possibly to cheer it up, and before we knew it our leads were tied together.

'Oh, I am in heaven,' I said fervently.

The youth stared at me uncomfortably and picked up his dog.

'But my career doesn't come into it,' I said, threading Sage's lead through the teenager's legs whilst trying to keep Comfrey out of the tangle. 'I'm only here temporarily until Gloria is back on her feet.'

As soon as the words were out I felt a pang of sadness. As much as I wanted Gloria to get well, I didn't want my stay in Plumberry to end.

'She's sixty-five,' Mum piped up. 'That might be months.'

That would be awful for Gloria. Not so awful for me.

A major fact hit me between the eyes and I gasped.

'You're free,' I said to the relieved youth, who slouched on his way smartish.

'Do you know, Dad? You both might be right,' I laughed.

Only this morning, I'd been telling myself that it was time to start looking after number one, put myself first for a change. And suddenly I realized that I'd already found what I'd been looking for. This. This life. Plumberry, the village, the cookery school. All of it.

I'd agreed to come as a favour for Gloria, but somewhere along the line, the Plumberry School of Comfort Food had become my own dream.

'Thanks, Mum and Dad. You've really helped,' I said, picking up my pace. I wanted to get back to Gloria, talk to her before she fell asleep.

'I know we didn't always see eye to eye in the past,' said Mum, lowering her voice finally, 'but we're here for you.'

I swallowed hard. 'Thanks, Mum.'

'And we have always only wanted what's best for you,' she continued.

I tensed at that but now wasn't the moment to argue.

'Don't drag me into it,' Dad grunted.

'So you don't want the best for your only daughter—'

I managed to interrupt their bickering long enough to say goodbye and hung up. We'd walked as far as the boarded-up pub and the dogs were beginning to flag so I turned back in the direction of home, my mind whirring.

In my head I'd sort of assumed I'd be here until the end of the summer, until Gloria was back on her feet, and then I'd have to go back home and kick-start my career. But maybe there was an alternative . . . I had a sudden flashback to the open day when I'd stood with Dave on the deck watching the kingfisher.

If you see a kingfisher, it's time to dive into a new activity or possibly a new love will enter your life . . .

Despite my initial fears about coming to Plumberry, I'd enjoyed connecting with food again and I cared passionately about making a success of the cookery school. Being close to Gloria was a bonus too, even if she was a handful at times. But could I do that? I wondered, a sudden shiver prickling the hairs on the back of my neck. Could I finally let go of my guilt about being alive without Mimi and choose the life I wanted to lead?

I turned into Hillside Lane and took a deep breath. I guessed there was only one way to find out.

Twenty minutes later, I handed Gloria a cup of camomile tea and settled beside her on the sofa.

'Gloria, I've been thinking about the future.'

She leaned back against her cushions and smiled her thanks. 'I'm all ears.'

Chapter 25

The Great British Bake Off had come to Plumberry!

I stood back, hands on hips, and surveyed the room, feeling extremely proud of myself. My research had paid off and the props I'd assembled captured the look of the hit TV show perfectly.

We couldn't quite manage the canvas walls of the giant marquee, of course, but we'd pinned Union Jack bunting in pastel shades of pink, yellow and mint green across the wooden beams. I'd ordered huge enamel jugs of flowers from the village florist and borrowed some wicker hampers from Mags and stacked them in a corner. I'd even covered the teaching workstation in pink and white polka-dot tablecloths for the day to give a softer look to the room.

Pixie had helped me every step of the way, and she had been in since the crack of dawn getting everything ready for our bakers. She'd assembled a side table with a plethora of bits and pieces in case anyone had forgotten anything, from baking beans to greaseproof paper, icing bags to cake boards, as well as a row of essences and food colourings.

We'd done Plumberry proud and if I managed to persuade the local paper to print pictures of the winner and a few action shots from the day, I was sure we'd get some great publicity for all our efforts.

The fire escape doors opened and Tom wheeled Gloria in. I felt my stomach tighten as he approached. He wasn't wearing his chef whites today and looked very trim in a tight-fitting charcoal-grey shirt and black trousers and his shoes looked like they'd been shined specially.

'May I present Plumberry's very own Mary Berry,' he announced, bringing the wheelchair to a halt next to the teaching station.

We'd bought the wheelchair second-hand from Pixie's granddad first thing this morning. He'd been quite keen to sell Gloria his commode chair too (good condition, one gentleman owner) but she'd been mortified at the suggestion and had reassured him that she hadn't any need for such an appliance.

Privately I thought that after yesterday's toilet kamikaze pilot incident, she perhaps did, but I didn't like to remind her in company so I'd loaded the wheelchair in the back of the car and we'd driven straight here. She'd spent the last hour in reception going through the bookings with Mags while I'd put the finishing touches to the teaching kitchen.

'Oh, what a sight; it looks wonderful. Verity, you've surpassed yourself.' Gloria clapped her hands, her bangles tinkling as they slipped up her arm.

'Thank you. It was a team effort and you look wonderful too.' I grinned and bent down for a hug. Her face felt warm as I pressed my cheek to hers, but then the weather was sunny again and it was nearly June after all. She'd put make-up on today and dressed carefully and looked far more like the Gloria I was used to. Apart from her mode of transport.

'I'm glad we did this,' I said, patting the wheelchair. 'A lot safer than having you scooting round on crutches.'

'I suppose so,' she grumbled. 'But I'm going to stand when I make the welcome speech otherwise no one will see me at the back.'

'That's fine,' I conceded. 'I'll bring your crutches up, but no overdoing it.'

'Better do it now, V,' said Tom, peering down to the car park through the window. 'It looks like the contestants have started to arrive.'

V. Tom had called me V.

Gloria glanced at me and I felt my heart thump. Mimi used to call me V. I always corrected everybody else who shortened my name. Especially Melanie the secretary, who called me Vee-Vee. But hearing Tom say it felt good. My face softened into a smile. It felt very good.

'Will do,' I said and scampered down the stairs to fetch them.

At ten o'clock precisely Pixie opened the doors to let the twenty contestants in. Mags and I stood at the top of the stairs ready to welcome them and to direct them each to a workstation. A crowd of women, as I'd suspected, came tip-tapping up the stairs, chatting animatedly and oohing and aahing as they reached the teaching kitchen.

'Look at the bunting!' exclaimed a yummy-mummy type in a Cath Kidston dress. 'To die for!'

'Morning!' I smiled. 'Hello! Follow Mags please, she'll show you where to go.'

'Lovely flowers,' said a pretty girl with shoulder-length curls and lovely long eyelashes. She gave me a twinkly smile.

'Aren't they just.' I winked at her; she was Plumberry's florist and had been so helpful and friendly when I'd popped in to order the flowers. 'Good luck!'

'And all the little pots of utensils – so cheerful.' A middle-aged woman with a long neck and a very severe haircut pressed a hand to her chest.

'We do our best.' I sighed a happy sigh; that was just the reaction I'd hoped for and even though I was sure there'd be a competitive edge to the day when things started hotting up, already I could tell that the atmosphere was a lot more relaxed than yesterday. I pointed her towards a workstation near the window.

'Stick me in a corner please,' said a low voice, close to my ear.

I whirled round to see Dave clutching two bulging carrier bags.

'Dave! I didn't know you were coming.' I gave him a hug.

'I knew,' Mags piped up, appearing as if by magic at my side. 'You're the only man here.'

'Thought I might be.' He smiled shyly. 'But there's a special lady that I'm endeavouring to impress and I thought that a cake might ameliorate my prospects.'

For the first time since I'd met her, Mags went silent. And a bit pale. Poor thing. She obviously didn't think for a second that Dave was referring to her. But judging by the flush that was creeping gradually from the top of his shirt to his rosy cheeks, I had my suspicions.

'Over here, Dave,' I said, looping my arm through his. 'Let's put you by the office; that's nearly in your comfort zone.'

Within fifteen minutes every contestant had a workstation and had assembled their ingredients in front of them. Pixie and Tom scooted round the room demonstrating the ovens and pointing out the spare supplies in case anybody had forgotten anything, and then we were ready to begin.

Mags, Pixie and I positioned ourselves near the office out of the way and Gloria, at the front, pushed herself up out of her wheelchair, hooked her hands into her crutches and beamed.

She'd begun to put on a bit of weight, I noticed; her face had filled out and her collarbone wasn't quite as prominent as it had been, but it suited her – she had always been as tiny as a bird before. She still had all her elegance and poise, though, even on crutches.

'If you're as big a fan of *GBBO* as I am,' she began, her eyes shining as she looked round the room at her audience, 'you'll understand exactly how honoured I feel to be holding our very own version in Plumberry. Tom

MacDonald, our resident Michelin-starred chef, will help me with the judging and he will be along to talk to all of you about what you're baking for us today. On behalf of the Plumberry School of Comfort Food, good luck, but above all have fun!'

'Thanks, Gloria,' said Tom, resting a hand on her shoulder. 'We are looking for something extra special today, something that will put a smile on our faces. We know you're not professionals, but we are looking for excellence.'

'No pressure then,' Dave murmured, loosening the collar of his shirt.

'The prize for today's competition is two places on any cookery course,' said Gloria, taking up the baton from Tom.

Pixie nudged me and we shared a smile. I knew what she meant; they were working exactly as a duo should: sharing the introduction, each of them delivering part of the information that the contestants needed. They truly were Plumberry's answer to Mary Berry and Paul Hollywood.

'In addition, you have each received one of our lovely aprons, designed by our marketing director Verity.' Gloria paused and sought me out in the crowd.

I raised my eyebrows at her and smiled.

Gloria had been overjoyed to hear my proposal to stay on as marketing manager last night. So overjoyed that she had promoted me instantly to director and admitted that she'd been worried about how she was going to cope when she finally did come back to work. I'd called Rosie too, who'd whooped with delight and declared that we'd have even more to celebrate when she came to stay. I still had to sort out what to do with my house, but the knowledge that I'd be staying in Plumberry indefinitely had put a permanent beam on my face ever since.

'Your wonderful food will be featured on our website and in our press materials over the coming weeks,' Gloria continued. 'Right, you have three hours to make your show-stopping cake.'

Three hours was a long time, but given that cakes had to be completely cool in order to be iced, we'd decided to give the contestants plenty of time. And once again Mags and Pixie had been busy arranging refreshments in the Aga kitchen for people to help themselves to as and when they had a free moment in their baking schedules.

'OK then, ladies.' Tom paused. 'And Dave.'

'Woohoo!' someone shouted suggestively.

I craned my neck to see who it was.

Two women in their early forties were alternately gripping their sides with laughter and elbowing each other, so my money was on one of them.

Dave looked at me and my heart melted for him. He was such a lovely and thoughtful man. Admittedly, he did manage to turn most conversations into a discussion about balance sheets, but even that was just because he cared about his clients. I so hoped that the special lady he was baking for was Mags. I linked arms with Mags and squeezed it.

Tom gave the women a hard stare and cleared his throat. 'I'm very honoured to be assisting the lovely Mary Berry – I mean *Gloria Ramsbottom* – in today's competition.'

'Does that make you Paul Hollywood, then?' tittered a lady in the front row who had come with her friend.

'I bet he has a show-stopper,' the friend said out of the side of her mouth.

'Yeah, I wouldn't kick him out of bed for dropping crumbs,' snorted another.

Tom clapped his hands loudly. 'Good luck, everyone. You may start cooking!'

Gloria waved to Pixie who went over to help her into a chair. Tom caught my eye and made a beeline for Mags and me.

'They're a lively bunch,' I whispered.

'They're nymphomaniacs,' he muttered, wiping an arm across his forehead.

'I'm not,' Dave put in, over his shoulder.

'More's the pity,' Mags murmured.

I chuckled to myself and went for a wander round the room.

'Does Tom know I was in early to help set up?' Pixie whispered in my ear a few seconds later.

I thought about it. 'Not sure. Probably.'

'Will you tell him to make sure?' She pushed her fringe out of her eyes. 'I'd really like to impress him. I mean, *really* impress him.'

I looked at her quizzically. 'Any particular reason?'

She scuffed the toe of her Doc Martens on the floor and then polished it on the back of her black jeans. I didn't know how she coped in this hot weather, top to toe in black. The sunshine seemed to be doing overtime this week after all that rain and I was feeling warm, even in my denim dress.

'Aaron,' she muttered.

'Yesterday's winner. What about him?'

She folded her arms and stuck out her bottom lip. 'I want an opportunity to work in Salinger's too – why hasn't Tom got me a gig there?'

I looked over at Tom, who was chatting to one of the contestants. She was very pretty, dressed in a navy vest, white skinny jeans and flip-flops. Her curly hair was the colour of spun sugar and she'd scooped it up loosely to reveal gold hoop earrings. She and Tom had their heads together trying to read the writing on a tiny pot of something.

'Who's that Tom's with?' I said, trying to act cool.

Pixie looked up briefly. 'Chloe. One of the barmaids from the pub. Fit, isn't she?'

I shrugged. 'I guess, although in an obvious way, if you know what I mean.'

She grinned at my expression. 'Jealous? Don't be. Chloe is great. She has a little kid who she's devoted to and she works two jobs to get by: behind the bar with me and then as a cleaner while the toddler is at nursery.'

Tom and Chloe burst out laughing, which made my heart sink another notch.

'I'm surprised she can spare the time to be here baking cakes then.' Miaow. Even to me that sounded catty. 'With all that going on,' I added hurriedly.

'Oh, she was determined to come; she took the morning off from her cleaning job to be here. Something about a grudge match.'

I frowned. That sounded ominous. And there was me thinking that today's event would be all sweetness and light . . .

'But to go back to your question, Pixie, I think if Tom knew you wanted work experience in a pro kitchen, he'd help you organize that.' I took her arm and led her towards the window where it was more private. 'How long has that been your goal?'

'Since yesterday. Seeing those normal people' – Pixie shook her head and I stifled a smile at the word 'normal' – 'cooking all that fancy food was like opening a door to a secret world. I always thought posh food was for posh people. But anyone can make food look beautiful, can't they?'

'Of course they can,' I retorted. 'Whatever made you think otherwise?'

She took her glasses off and rubbed them on the corner of her apron.

'There was this girl at my school whose mum baked her a cupcake for her school snack every day. *Every day.*' Pixie stared at me with those big eyes. 'At half past ten we'd be turfed out into the playground come rain or shine. And I'd try and stand near to her to see what was in her lunchbox. Gorgeous they were, these cakes: topped with a giant swirl of icing, or dipped in melted chocolate, or covered in hundreds and thousands. Know what me and my sister had?'

I shook my head.

'An apple,' she said in disgust, popping her glasses back on.

'Fresh fruit is far better than sugary cakes,' I said diplomatically.

'*One* apple.' She rolled her eyes. 'To share. A bite for her and a bite for me. So embarrassing. I used to think that that girl must have been so rich to have a snack like that.'

My heart went out to her; I could just imagine her and her sister looking longingly at Cake Girl over their apple core.

'And really, how much does it cost to whip up a few fairy cakes and make them pretty?' Pixie shrugged. 'So that's what I want to do from now on. Make food that looks as good as it tastes. Or better perhaps, in my case.'

'Pixie, you are such a hard worker, I have no doubt you can achieve anything you set your mind to. And I'm sure you already impress Tom.'

She pulled a sceptical face.

'There's nothing Gloria doesn't know about making food look lovely,' I said, inclining my head to the office where Gloria had just gone for a sit-down. 'She was a food stylist, remember. Go and pick her brains.'

While I go and pay the ultra-fit Chloe a visit, I added to myself. I nipped back to the office, collected my phone and a notepad, checked Gloria was comfy and passed Mags badgering Dave.

'Hey, good looking, what you got cooking?' She peered into his mixing bowl, stuck a finger in the pale yellow mixture and tasted it.

Dave hastily shoved a sheet of paper under a bag of flour. 'It's, er . . .' he began croakily. He cleared his throat and tried again. 'It's top secret.'

'Oh,' said Mags, sounding injured. 'In that case, I'll be in the office.' And she swept off to sit with Gloria.

'Whoops,' said Dave, pulling a face.

274

'Don't worry,' I said, patting his arm. 'I'm sure it'll be worth it.'

Chloe was humming to herself as she greased two cake-pop tins when I went over to her station.

'Chloe, isn't it?' I said, making a show of reading the name badge on her vest top. 'Do you mind if I take your picture for Facebook?'

'Verity? Course you can, we can do a selfie if you like?' She beamed rather disarmingly at me, wiped her hands on a cloth and pressed herself to me ready for a close-up.

'No, just a shot of you will be fine,' I said, easing myself away.

She giggled. 'Pixie is always going on about you lot here, about all your funny little ways.'

I raised my eyebrows, not sure if I wanted to know what she meant.

'So,' I said with my best welcoming smile while I snapped away, 'what brought you here today?'

Chloe's smile faltered. She began sifting flour into a glass bowl and glanced sideways at me.

'I'm here because I want to make my son proud of me.'

'Oh, that's nice,' I said, jotting a note on my pad.

'Every couple of months at nursery they have a little cake sale. I used to just take in a packet of chocolate mini rolls or something, just to show willing, you know. But then we had a letter come home saying no shop-bought stuff allowed.'

'How ridiculous.'

'I know, yeah? So I did my best, made a batch of butterfly cakes and took them in. They got a bit squashed on the bus because I didn't have a tin big enough so I had to use a tray covered in tin foil. Bloody nightmare.' She shook her head at the memory. 'As I got closer to nursery the foil wouldn't stop flapping in the chuffin' wind. Helen . . .' Chloe paused to point out the yummy mummy I'd spotted earlier in the Cath Kidston dress. 'Her over there, she pulled up in her big flash car, lifted some white cardboard boxes out of the boot, the sort you get at a cake shop. And as I got level with her car the foil lifted and there were my butterfly cakes, all smashed up like they'd been punched, and you know what she said?'

Chloe's voice had lowered to a whisper and her lips were pursed like she might cry.

I shook my head mutely.

'She laughed and said, "Oh bless." I felt that big.' She pinched her thumb and forefinger together.

'Oh dear.'

'I didn't let her see me cry, I took my boy into nursery and dumped the squashed cakes at the back where nobody would see them and I've been practising baking ever since.'

'Well done you for not being defeated by her,' I said. This Helen sounded like a terrible snob.

'So now I'm going to make my boy proud,' Chloe said with a gleam in her eye. 'And I've bought some new cake tins.'

I took one more photo of her cracking eggs over a bowl and then left her to it.

Before long I arrived at Helen's workstation. She seemed to have had some sort of accident with the flour, or maybe the icing sugar. Either way, everything was coated in white powder, including her lovely dress.

'What's that girl making?' she hissed, pulling me to one side and gesturing towards Chloe with her head.

'I couldn't tell from what she's done so far,' I replied. Which was true.

'I'm sure I spotted ice-cream cones in her bag,' said Helen, narrowing her eyes.

'What if she has?' I sniffed, thinking that if Helen was going to be snooty about Chloe's choice of ingredients then I was going to nip it in the bud straight away.

'It won't matter anyway,' she said with a heartfelt sigh.

She dropped a whole packet of butter into a pan of boiling water. 'Chloe can make anything look good. Even her squashed butterfly cakes tasted delicious.'

'How do you know?'

'Her little boy is at the same nursery as my daughter,' she explained. 'We both made cakes for a cake sale. Mine tasted like cardboard and hers were as light as a feather.'

I suppressed a smile, making a mental note to tell Chloe, and lifted my phone up in camera-mode. 'Do you mind?'

'Sure,' she said, brushing the powder off her dress half-heartedly for the picture. 'I think I try so hard to make nice cakes that I beat all the life out of them. My little girl gets through beakers of milk when she tries to swallow my sponge. But Chloe . . .' Helen gazed at her rival. 'Seriously, that girl can't put a foot wrong. She's so naturally beautiful. Do you know I don't think she even wears foundation? Flawless skin, absolutely flawless. And as for her figure, she'd look good in a paper bag. Her son has the most adorable manners I've ever come across and my husband fancies the pants off her. I envy her so much.'

'Why don't you tell her, then?' I said softly, thinking that with a bit of prodding these two could be friends.

Helen gave a sigh. 'I've tried to be friendly towards her but she just seems to take it the wrong way. I'd really like, just the once, to do something to impress her.'

I began to laugh. 'Helen, you won't believe this, but I think she feels pretty much the same about you.'

'Me, but . . .' She blinked at me furiously. 'Really?'

I looked through the white flour and icing sugar haze and caught Chloe shooting worried glances in our direction.

'Look, I've got an idea,' I said with a sudden flash of inspiration.

The person sharing an oven with Chloe had already complained that she'd prefer to be near a window because of her hot flushes, so it wasn't difficult to persuade her to swap with Helen.

Chloe glared at me when I helped Helen move her things across. 'You are kidding?' she muttered.

'Trust me on this,' I whispered, 'and go easy on her, her husband is apparently your biggest fan. After Helen herself, that is.'

Her eyes flickered at that and she smiled stoically as Helen began to unpack her ingredients again.

'Oh, my word,' I heard Helen say as I left them to it, 'those roses are adorable. How did you do those?'

Oh, I'm good, I mused, smiling to myself. I should be some sort of ambassador for world peace . . .

By the time the contestants had had their allotted three hours, the air was filled with the mouth-watering aroma of vanilla, cinnamon, ginger and lemon, mixed with the irresistible smell of freshly baked sponge cake. Mags ushered them all downstairs for a well-earned cup of tea and one of Tom's delicious petits-fours, giving us the chance to look at all the finished cakes.

'Look at this three-tiered thing covered with glitter,' said Pixie.

'Hmm, very sparkly,' I agreed. 'What about this one?'

I pointed to a gingerbread house studded with hundreds of different types of sweets.

'It's a good job smells don't have any calories,' murmured Gloria dreamily as she passed me on the way to the front. 'Otherwise I'd pop.'

She'd abandoned the wheelchair because she couldn't see anything, she'd claimed. So she was hobbling on her crutches and I held my breath, hoping that she didn't slip on any greasy blobs on the floor.

'Dave's looks interesting,' said Pixie with a grin.

I joined her to look at it. It was tall and round and

covered in meringue that he'd browned with a blowtorch.

'Some sort of baked Alaska?' I guessed.

Pixie shrugged. 'Don't know but it's a beast.'

Chloe had made a row of cake pops in the shape of roses in pots. She'd made the pots from flat-bottomed ice-cream cones and the red roses themselves were beautifully decorated in ornate icing and edged with glitter.

But the winner wasn't hard to spot. A lady called Carey had recreated the tea party from *Alice in Wonderland* in cake form. The circular cake had a table in the centre set with tiny teacups and plates piled high with party food. There was even a dormouse peeping out of a teapot. Everything was made from fondant icing in vivid colours and each detail was true to the story. It was the most intricate and beautiful cake I'd ever seen and even Tom was hesitant to cut into it for spoiling the look of it.

'Some of these cakes are incredible,' he said to me as he wielded a knife over a giant cupcake iced to look like a basket of flowers. His eyes glittered with possibilities. 'And today has sparked off loads of ideas. I can't wait to get in the kitchen and do some experimenting.'

'I'm glad.' I smiled, happy to see him so enthusiastic. He was a chef first and foremost, not a cookery school teacher. And while he might stay here for a while, his heart would always beat for the frenetic pace of a restaurant kitchen. The cookery school simply didn't test his skills like fine dining did and I'd just have to accept that. I rested my hand lightly on his arm and squeezed. 'Your eyes dance when you're happy, it's good to see.'

We smiled at each other and for a second the noise of the room faded away until Gloria coughed loudly and asked Tom to cut her a sliver of Dave's creation.

Pixie dragged me off to see Helen's towering *croquembouche* laced with spun sugar and decorated with tiny fresh flowers. I didn't know what she had been worried about; it was amazing. Pixie and I snapped a loose piece of caramel off the side of the plate and licked our fingers like guilty kids in the corner.

Once Gloria and Tom had dutifully cut into and tasted everyone's entries, Pixie was dispatched to bring the contestants back up to hear the result.

Half an hour later, Carey had sobbed with joy and made the longest winner's speech outside of the Oscars. And for a short while the contestants lingered, chatting and tasting each other's cakes. When they finally left, I spotted Chloe and Helen laughing and talking away across the car park, at which point Helen had pointed to a black Range Rover and both women had jumped in.

Dave was still mooching about, taking an age to pack his things away.

'Are you sad you didn't win, Dave?' Pixie asked, leaning her elbows on his workstation.

'Not at all, I've had a lovely day.' He grinned.

'Well, I'm sure your special lady will appreciate it,' said Mags with a sniff, examining her nails.

Dave turned as pink as Mags's dress.

'I hope so, Mags, because this is a raspberry and lemon cloud cake. I chose this recipe because it reminded me of someone I admire greatly. The lemon is sweet but with a delicious sharpness, which makes me all of a tingle. The swirly meringue on the outside reminds me of her lovely hair, all feminine and swept up like every day is a celebration. And the cloud part . . .' He cleared his throat and shuffled from one foot to the other. 'Well, it's because when I'm with her I feel like I'm on cloud nine.'

My chest heaved hopefully; that was the longest speech I'd ever heard him make. I crossed my fingers behind my back.

'Who is this virtuous creature?' said Mags sourly.

'Oh and lastly,' he added, reaching for her hand, 'I've used the raspberries to represent your lovely red nails.'

'My nails . . . *Me*? You made this cake for *me*?' Mags stuttered, looking down at their joined hands.

He nodded, a wide smile spreading across his face.

'Oh Dave, come here.' Mags puckered up and launched herself at him.

'I think this makes me the winner,' said Dave in a muffled voice, barely visible through a sea of pink chiffon.

Chapter 26

On Thursday afternoon Gloria gathered us in the Aga kitchen for a meeting. Even though the cookery school had been operational for a week and a half, we hadn't had a chance to sit down together since the open day. And after two days of competitions and this morning's Chinese Cuisine for Beginners, it was a relief to have the cookery school to ourselves for a few hours.

It was a warm afternoon and Mags had smothered her freckly shoulders and nose in sun cream in the hope that we could sit outside, but Gloria was suffering with a headache so we'd compromised. The doors to the deck were open wide, letting in a gentle breeze, and we'd turned the tables from a lecture-room style to a more convivial meeting-room arrangement.

'Probably as well,' Tom joked, pouring water from a jug topped with ice cubes and lemon slices into several glasses. 'I trade on my pale and interesting look.'

I grinned at him as he handed me a glass; he was so white that his skin was almost blue. 'You told me you were the outdoors type.'

'I am – my complexion just didn't get the memo; five minutes in the sun and my shins look like streaky bacon.'

'Ooh, bacon,' Pixie moaned, clutching her stomach. 'Don't, I'm starving.'

'Have a spring roll,' I laughed, pushing the plate of extras from this morning's course across the table to her. 'You'll pass out at this rate.'

Since meeting Cheryl, Pixie had decided that the love handles (her words) had to go and had imposed an impossibly difficult regime on herself. Impossible in the sense that she worked here, in a cheese shop and at a pub, none of which were ideal if you were trying to avoid calories. She chewed her lip for a second, eyeing up the crisp pastry.

'They're not much bigger than a mouthful really,' she said, convincing herself more than anyone. 'If you've got a big mouth.'

'Remember Mags's principle of pleasure,' said the lady herself with a wink.

The corners of Pixie's mouth lifted up slowly. 'Or as my granddad would say, "Eat now or forever hold your peas."' And she took an enormous bite of a spring roll.

'I don't think I've heard your pleasure principle,' said Dave, opening his notepad.

'Life is for living so take pleasure where you can,' Mags said gravely, and then leaned across and added in a stage whisper, 'and I'll explain that in more detail later.'

Dave chuckled and turned pink, probably wishing he hadn't asked, or at least not in public.

Mags had been busy modelling at her nude art class last night, so sharing a slice of the cloud cake with Dave had been postponed until tonight. And to make the occasion even more special, Dave was treating her to dinner at a nearby hotel first. No wonder she'd been frothing with excitement all day.

She had popped round last night before going out and had gushed about Dave and his lovely cake-baking gesture and shared with us her hopes for a less lonely future. And Dave seemed to be on top form this afternoon; he was normally so serene and laid-back, but he had a perky spring in his step too. It was early days, of course, but it warmed my heart to see their happiness and I was keeping everything crossed that love would blossom between them.

'I'm not getting too much pleasure at the moment,' said Gloria breathlessly. 'So shall we get on?'

She was poking a chopstick repeatedly down her plaster cast as if her life depended on it. The toes that were peeping out looked chubby and red.

'Should you be doing that?' I asked.

'The itching is torture,' Gloria puffed.

Mags looked at her sharply. 'Glor, are you OK?'

'It must be twenty-two degrees out there and my leg is trapped in a plaster of Paris prison. It's hot, *I'm* hot. So no,' she sighed, 'not really.'

'Oh chuck, you poor thing.' Mags tipped more ice into Gloria's water glass.

'Are you sure you're up to this?' I whispered as discreetly as I could. 'I can take you home if you'd rather. You don't look very comfortable.'

Gloria shook her head adamantly.

'I'm too hot and irritable and my head hurts. But at least here I've got company, which distracts me a little.'

I smiled at her sympathetically and she squeezed my hand.

'Here,' said Mags, passing Gloria's handbag to her. 'Why don't you take some painkillers?'

Gloria nodded, and took two tablets with a sip of water. 'Right, sorry, everyone, whinge over. Do start, Dave. Let's have the figures.'

Dave coughed importantly. 'Firstly, I'd like to say congratulations to you all on such an auspicious start to trading. There are teething troubles to be expected in any new business, but in all my years of working with new companies I can honestly say I've never come across such a team that manages to be harmonious, supportive and united in the goals of the business as this one.'

'What *are* the goals of the business?' Pixie asked, wrinkling her nose.

'To share our love of cooking,' said Gloria. She pressed her cold glass to her forehead and sighed. Condensation ran from the glass down her face. 'Oh, that's marvellous.'

'And to teach people how to make better food,' Tom added.

'Don't forget giving them a good time,' Mags chimed in.

'As well as being profitable,' I said, looking at Dave. 'Thought I'd get in there before you.'

'Ah, I'd say that's the goal that still needs some work.' He frowned, scanning his notes.

'So how are the figures looking so far?' Gloria asked.

Dave began to talk about the numbers and I half-listened, but I was more concerned about Gloria. She seemed to be having trouble breathing, although that could have been due to the constant bending and scratching she was doing with that chopstick. And she was complaining of being hot. It was warm for May, but not overly so – I was wearing more than her and I felt fine. Perhaps it was just because her leg was confined in that hot plaster cast. Even so, as soon as this meeting was over, I was going to take her home, whether she liked it or not. The cottage was cooler than the cookery school and she could sit in a bath of cold water if she so desired.

'So what I'm saying is: carry on doing what you're doing, but perhaps look for some other revenue streams.'

I noticed Pixie glance outside at the river with a look of confusion on her face. I sucked my cheeks to stop myself from giggling at her and caught Tom's eye. He shook his head ever so slightly and grinned and my body responded with a ping.

A delicious warmth began to spread through me as if my body was waking up after a long, long sleep. Over the past month, I'd had so much to occupy my head: splitting up with Liam, moving to Plumberry, opening the cookery school and then looking after Gloria, that I'd put my heart on hold. But now I knew I was definitely staying and Tom was definitely over Rebecca . . . well, that changed things.

I studied him secretly as he turned his attention back to Dave. His eyelashes were amazing, I mean really amazing, almost as if he wore mascara. Most girls would kill for lashes like that. And his eyes weren't just dark brown; they were ringed with black. And there was a tiny scar above his left eyebrow . . .

'Well, I've got a revenue stream, straight off. This little lot are books that I worked on back in my publishing days. I thought you might like to see them,' said Mags, retrieving a stack of cookery books from under her chair. She opened the top one, entitled *Indian Suppers*, and stroked the pages. 'I could spend all day reading cookery books. Being at the cookery school has reignited my love of recipes.'

'Ditto.' Tom grinned.

'Oh, me too,' exclaimed Gloria, so sincerely that it broke my heart.

We'd been open for ten days and she had only just attended her first course, one she'd been looking forward to teaching herself. I thought back to my first few days here when she'd reverently shown me her recipe bible and gone misty-eyed with excitement for the future.

'I'd like to borrow a few of these some time if I may?' Tom asked, reaching for the next one on the pile: *Italian Suppers*.

'Of course.' Mags went pink and preened. 'My *Suppers* series was the most successful cookery book collection Saffron Publishing produced in the nineties.'

'And I can see why,' interrupted Dave diplomatically, 'but can we stay on topic? We were talking about profitability?'

He softened his words by gazing at her with a gooey expression and Mags seemed to melt down into her chair.

'A suppers course?' Gloria cocked her head to one side. 'That could work. Scintillating Suppers or . . . Sophisticated Suppers?'

Mags chuckled. 'I wasn't thinking of new courses. I mean

publishing our own Plumberry School of Comfort Food recipe book. That would be another string to our bow.'

Dave sucked in a breath. 'Sounds expensive, Mags.'

'Oh Dave, not everything should be about money,' said Mags, folding her arms.

Except this was a financial meeting, I mused, catching Tom's eye again. We shared a smile and he passed me the recipe book. His fingers brushed mine and it sent a tiny shiver through me.

'Well . . .' Dave opened his mouth to argue but apparently thought better of it. 'That's true.'

'We looked into a cookery book for Salinger's, Mags,' said Tom. 'Dave's right; it's pricey to do a good job, but it is worth thinking about once we're more established. We could list some of the recipes from our courses, perhaps?'

Mags looked suitably mollified. 'One for the back burner then,' she said, offering round a plate of raspberry and white chocolate shortbread.

'Ooh, pudding,' said Pixie, diving straight in.

At which point I had a light bulb moment.

'Oh, I've just had an idea for a revenue stream!' I wriggled forward in my chair excitedly. 'We could cook *actual* suppers at the cookery school. Open it up like a restaurant in the evenings!'

'Interesting.' Tom leaned forward, resting his lovely strong arms on the table. 'Go on, I'd like to hear this.'

'Would you?' I said, feeling all the eyes in the room turn to me, but especially his.

He nodded encouragingly. My brain whirred and I wished I'd thought it through a bit more before opening my mouth.

I don't wish to blow my own trumpet or anything, but I've always been one for coming up with ideas. Some of them more successful than others, of course. But right now, with Tom's full attention on me, this idea suddenly seemed extremely important. I thought about yesterday and Chloe and Helen trying to impress each other and Dave desperate to impress Mags and even Pixie trying to impress Tom, and I realized that I was exactly the same: I wanted to impress Tom too.

I couldn't pinpoint when exactly, but Tom had become someone special to me. I wanted him to look at me in awe, unable to tear his eyes away. And not only that, I wanted to make him happy. Happy enough to stay in Plumberry for as long as possible.

My pulse quickened as I began, rather tentatively, thinking on my feet.

'On days when we're not running courses, we could run a Supper Club right here in the Aga kitchen. We have seating and spare capacity; what's to stop us opening in the evenings? Tom could demonstrate and cook a three-course supper, which the diners then eat – no cooking involved on their part. It would also give you a chance to cook the more experimental stuff that you love doing, Tom.'

'Plumberry needs a restaurant,' said Pixie, brushing crumbs from a second spring roll off the front of her T-shirt. She regarded me mischievously for a second before adding, 'Like Platform Six.'

My stomach whirled with embarrassment as Tom glanced at her sharply and then looked back at me. If Tom was planning to ask me out tomorrow evening, he was certainly playing it very cool. Perhaps he had never intended to invite me at all, maybe he already had a date?

I grabbed the water jug and replenished glasses to look busy.

'And I could cook anything?' Tom asked thoughtfully, stroking his chin.

I nodded, pushing all thoughts of his mystery dinner date out of my head.

'The fancier the better, probably. That way our offering would stand out as unique. I'm sure there are plenty of places to get standard pub food.'

288

'What do you think, Gloria? Dave?' Tom asked.

'I adore it!' exclaimed Gloria, spreading her arms out to encompass the room. 'And what a perfect setting for supper; imagine it lit with a hundred candles!'

'Imagine the health and safety risk,' said Dave. 'But fire hazard aside, it would certainly maximize our revenue streams.'

'And I get to cook restaurant food.' Tom pushed a hand through his thick hair, folded his arms and grinned at me. 'Top idea.'

That smile lit me up inside like an Irish coffee, warm and delicious with a soupçon of naughtiness.

'Tom gets to cook fine dining; the cookery school earns more money. Two birds. One stone.' *Go me*, I added inwardly as I stood and took a bow.

'I'm humbled,' said Gloria. 'I don't know how I've done it but somehow I seem to have recruited a wonderful team of people. *Wonderful*. You don't know how much seeing you all here means to me.'

And then she burst into tears, a reaction so completely out of character for feisty, nothing-gets-me-down Gloria that for a second Mags and I simply stared at her. Mags put her arm round Gloria and handed her a tissue, Dave shuffled his papers and Pixie started clearing the glasses and plates.

'Gloria and I are going home now,' I announced smoothly, getting to my feet. 'Unless anyone has anything to add?'

'Just one thing.' Tom stood and hesitated, raking his hand through his hair. 'Only that . . .'

'Yes?' I held my breath and anticipation bubbled through me. A brief fantasy popped into my head where he asked me out to dinner and everyone in the room clutched their hearts romantically, even though I'd have to let him down as Rosie was coming . . .

'I know I said I wasn't bothered about it,' Tom shrugged

sheepishly, 'but I was going to suggest anyone who wanted to could come over to the flat and watch *Challenge Chester* with me later. My flatmate is away so we'll have the place to ourselves.'

My stomach flipped. '*Challenge Chester!* Oh my goodness, I'd completely forgotten about that. Our episode is airing tonight!'

Tom looked at Pixie. 'Pixie?'

'I'd love to,' she groaned in despair, 'but I'm working at the pub. I'll make sure the TV is tuned to it. It'll make a change from the sports channel.'

'I've asked Mother to set the video recorder,' said Dave proudly, 'because Mags and I will be at dinner.'

'I doubt I'd stay awake for the whole programme,' Gloria mumbled, dabbing at her tears. 'So I think I'm better off at home.'

Which left me.

We'll have the place to ourselves . . .

'I was planning on live tweeting through the show – you know, hashtag Plumberry,' I said airily.

'Before you forgot it was on,' Tom said, barely containing his mirth. 'So? I can offer you WiFi.'

'Sounds like an offer I can't refuse,' I smirked, looking him in the eye.

He didn't need to know that my heart was knocking at my ribs like a hammer on particularly stubborn toffee. But it was.

Chapter 27

I was not happy with the Gloria situation one bit. She insisted on hobbling to the car herself, refusing to use the wheelchair, which I stowed in the boot of my car. But once she was in the passenger seat, her breathing was ragged and her face was contorted.

'You know I'm only asking this because I love you,' I said softly, reaching out for her arm, 'but you wouldn't hide it from me, would you, if you felt poorly?'

Gloria flashed me a look of panic. 'It must be getting on your nerves, mustn't it, looking after an old croc like me? You should be out having fun with people your own age. I'm such a burden.'

'Stop right there, Gloria Ramsbottom,' I said briskly, before she dissolved in another flood of tears. I fastened her seatbelt for her and started the engine. 'You're not preventing me from doing anything. I'm popping over to Tom's tonight, aren't I? If you're well enough to leave.'

I was aiming for casual, but my face must have given me away. Gloria blinked at me, her blue eyes gazing solemnly from her flushed face.

'And I'm only saying *this* because I love *you*,' she said gravely, 'but I don't think Tom is the man for you. He's on the rebound. So are you, come to that.'

'Gloria!' I laughed. 'I think we're getting a bit ahead of ourselves here; I'm only going round to watch TV with him.'

'OK,' she sang as if she didn't believe me for one second and then looked out of the window.

Why was she being negative about him? She thought the world of Tom. Did she know something about him that I didn't? On the other hand, Mags was having dinner with Dave, I was going to Tom's . . . Perhaps it was simply a bit of good old-fashioned envy on a day when she wasn't feeling so great. Poor thing.

I focused on the road as we drove along the high street. 'I appreciate your concern, but I can look after myself, I promise. And Tom's a nice guy.'

'He *is* a nice guy,' Gloria agreed, smiling at the children who crossed the road in front of us while a jolly lollipop lady held up the traffic. 'But when I interviewed him for the job only a few weeks ago, he was very bitter about his ex-girlfriend. He told me that he would never, ever, put his job at risk again by mixing his love life with his professional life. I don't want you to get your hopes up or your heart broken, darling. That's all.'

Fleeting images flashed through my brain as I let Gloria's words sink in, snatches of conversations, smiles, body language . . . I could have sworn that I'd seen a flicker of interest on Tom's part. But one thing was for certain: I'd obviously got the wrong end of the stick about that table at Platform Six tomorrow night. Thank goodness I hadn't made a fool of myself and mentioned anything to him.

'Thanks for the warning,' I said, deliberately hiding my disappointment and keeping my tone light, 'but I'm a big girl and I truly believe he is a lovely person, just understandably cautious.'

'There are plenty of other lovely men out there, without some axe to grind.' Gloria turned her head away from me and waved to Harriet from the cheese shop as we drove past. 'Unattached men. Like Gabe. Maybe while he's staying here you could spend some time together, just the two of you?'

Gabe? My heart swelled to three times its normal size and threatened to burst out of my chest completely. She wasn't suggesting . . . not Gabe and me . . . ?

'Gabe is lovely.' My cheeks were aflame. I swallowed hard. 'But he'll always be Mimi's husband to me, Gloria.'

She harrumphed at that and there was an awkward silence in the car for the rest of the journey.

The cottage felt a bit stuffy so I settled her in the garden in the shade for a snooze.

I was still worried about her, despite her reassurances that she was just tired. Even getting her from the car into the house and then out to the garden seemed to have totally drained her. And she was constantly out of breath. Gloria was a slim, fit thing and even though I accepted that using crutches was hard work, I had a suspicion she was feeling worse than she was letting on.

After checking she was comfortable, I took the dogs for a walk down the hill and along the river and when the three of us returned panting an hour later, there was just time for a cool shower and to get changed before leaving for Tom's flat.

I wasn't bothering with dinner; I'd had plenty of the Chinese leftovers. Besides, my stomach was far too busy whipping itself up into a frenzy at the prospect of meeting up with Tom. Outside of work. Just the two of us.

I threw a cardigan over my printed summer dress, pulled on my Converses and ran down the stairs. All I needed to do now was help Gloria in from the garden and then I'd be off. But as I reached the kitchen my phone rang. It was Gabe. *Lovely, unattached Gabe.* My stomach flipped as I remembered Gloria's words.

'Hey, Gabe.'

'Bloomers! How you doing, dude?'

'I'm good.' I grinned. Whatever hare-brained scheme

Gloria might be conjuring up to get Gabe and me together, she'd have a job on her hands convincing him to see me as girlfriend material.

'Guess what!' he continued. 'Noah and I should be with you some time on Saturday. We've made better time than I thought; we're already nearly at the River Ouse.'

'Aunty Vetty, a heron landed on *The Neptune*!' I heard Noah shout in the background, followed by Gabe shushing him.

I perched on a chair in the kitchen, my heart revelling in listening to their banter. It would be great to have the Green men here. The responsibility for Gloria was beginning to weigh heavily on me and it would be brilliant to be able to talk things over with Gabe. And having Noah around would do Gloria the world of good.

'I can't wait.' I let out a sigh. 'The sooner the better.'

I heard him suck in a breath. 'What's up?'

I bit my lip, unsure as to whether to bother him. It wasn't as if he could do anything to help until he arrived.

'Verity?' he probed. 'Come on.'

'I'm worried about Gloria. She doesn't seem well to me.'

I described her symptoms. She hadn't managed to shake off the headache, her hip and leg were throbbing and she was constantly scratching inside her cast.

'Poor old bird.' Gabe tutted. 'I had my arm in plaster once on a family holiday to Spain, never been so uncomfortable in my life, I know how she feels.'

'So it's fairly common to be hot and irritable, then?' I asked doubtfully.

'I think so, but call the doctor if you're worried.' He paused. 'Or should I? I'm her next of kin, after all, and you've done everything so far.'

'She's forbidden me to call the doctor. But I suppose I could phone the nurse? Or she's got a physiotherapist coming round to the cottage tomorrow afternoon so I could just wait to see what she says.'

'Mimi was just the same when she was ill, never made a fuss,' Gabe said softly.

And look what happened to her.

There was a beat of silence.

'I'm calling the nurse,' I blurted. 'Right now.'

'Good idea.'

'Call me when you get here. Where are you mooring? I'll come and fetch you,' I said.

'Just above Knaresly lock. We've brought bikes, so we might cycle over. Oh, just say hi to Noah.'

I had a quick chat with my favourite boy who told me that if he was good tonight, he'd be allowed to stay up and see Jupiter and Venus in the sky and would I make him a chocolate cake. Just thinking about wrapping my arms round him and inhaling his soft warm skin made me feel all glowy. I promised to make him the cake, blew him a kiss and rang off, immediately calling the nurse's mobile number, but her voicemail said she was on annual leave.

'Well, lucky old you,' I tutted, dropping the phone back on to the kitchen table. Now what?

Gloria clambered gingerly up to the open French doors.

'Who were you ringing?'

I squirmed in my seat and wondered whether I dared fib. But Gloria's gimlet-eyed stare warned against it. 'The nurse.'

'Verity, darling, there's absolutely no need. I promise I'll take better care,' she said, pausing to catch her breath. 'I've just been overdoing it. Probably should have stuck to the wheelchair on Wednesday instead of stomping round on crutches so I could poke my nose into people's baking. Tomorrow I will sit as still as a sphinx and I won't move a muscle until the physio gets here.'

'And you're absolutely sure you've been taking all your medication?'

'Of course!' she retorted. 'Now please try not to worry about me, you know I abhor being a nuisance.'

She was on morphine for the pain and had a box of heparin in the fridge, which she had to inject into her leg to prevent blood clots. I'd seen her take the tablets, and she'd assured me she was taking the heparin too, but I always gave her some privacy for that.

I hooked a hand under her elbow for extra support as she hopped up the step and into the kitchen. Together we manoeuvred her into a kitchen chair and she fanned a hand over her pink face. The dogs came in from the garden too. Sage flopped on the cool tiles in the shade and Comfrey pushed his nose into the back of my leg, reminding me that it was his teatime.

I frowned at Gloria, unconvinced, and bent to stroke Comfrey's ears.

'I still think I should call the doctor,' I pleaded. 'If nothing else to tell him about your constant poking with that chopstick. You might have done some damage.'

She produced the chopstick from her pocket and laid it on the table. 'Guilty as charged.'

'I'll take that,' I said sternly, putting it out of reach.

'If you ring the doctor I might end up back in hospital.' She caught hold of my fingers and gripped me tightly as if her life depended on it. 'I don't think I could bear the heat in there again.'

I was with her on that one; the hospital had been incredibly airless. But what if it was the best place for her? What if something wasn't healing properly down that cast . . . ?

Gloria must have sensed my apprehension. She patted her lap and Comfrey jumped straight up.

'If there's anything drastically wrong the physiotherapist will pick it up tomorrow, won't she?' She kissed the top of Comfrey's bony head. 'Now go on to Tom's before you miss the start of the programme.'

'Ooh, yes,' I said as I picked up my bag. 'Mustn't be late for our big night.'

Gloria pinched her lips together and looked down at her wrist, twirling her bangles round agitatedly.

'I meant the cookery school's big night being on *Challenge Chester*,' I said, feeling a blush rise to my cheeks. 'National TV coverage will be massive publicity. Just think of the bookings it'll bring in!'

Gloria opened her mouth to say something and then appeared to change her mind. 'Of course, darling, you go,' she said wearily. 'Have fun.'

I kissed her cheek and let myself out of the cottage. But her words had unsettled me. Why did she suddenly seem against Tom and me getting to know each other better? What on earth was on her mind?

Chapter 28

I followed the satnav's clipped instructions to the address in Pudston that Tom had given me, a long two-storey block of flats. I left the car at the roadside, collected my bag from the back seat and set off in search of number eleven.

The closer I got to his flat, the more jittery I felt. This was the first time I'd been alone with a member of the opposite sex since I split with Liam.

Mimi, get me. I'm off to a boy's house. Wish me luck!

Then a thought struck me. What if Gloria was right? What if the idea of getting friendly with a colleague was a total no-go zone for Tom? Perhaps he'd been secretly gutted when no one else could make it this evening except me?

There was no doorbell at number eleven. I lifted my hand to knock and hesitated, my body gripped with indecision.

Maybe it would be more sensible all round if I left now before he saw me, made up some excuse about Gloria being too ill to leave. Then I wouldn't be putting him in a difficult position.

On the other hand, I was sure the two of us could have a perfectly nice time watching *Challenge Chester* together and just getting to know each other. It wasn't as if I was planning on throwing myself at him.

Good. Fine. I'll knock.

My hand struck out boldly just as the door opened. My

fist flew through thin air and I stumbled over the threshold straight into Tom.

Wow. In a white linen shirt rolled up at the sleeves, worn jeans and barefooted, he looked nicely rumpled, as if he'd just woken up. My stomach performed a loop-the-loop.

'Hello,' I said, taking a step back and out of his personal space.

'Welcome.' He laughed softly and rubbed his neck. 'I'd invite you in but you already are.'

'I'm all set for our TV debut,' I said, jiggling my bag. 'I've bought beer and lemonade and snacks.'

'I haven't had a chance to eat dinner yet. Are you hungry?'

Starving. During the drive over I'd regained my appetite but as he hadn't officially invited me for dinner, I felt awkward admitting it.

'No, no,' I said. 'But you go ahead and eat. Don't mind me.'

He stood aside to let me in properly and as I squeezed past him my stomach produced a rumble worthy of the *Hogwarts Express.*

'Goodness, no idea where that came from,' I said, feeling my face grow hot.

He laughed again and gestured for me to follow him into the kitchen. Three paces away.

In my head I'd pictured a typical bachelor pad: a minimalist monochrome space with wooden floors and wall-to-wall technology. But this flat was nothing like that; the hall was small and windowless, the carpet was a vision in paisley swirls and the walls were decorated in a Regency-striped paper. The cramped kitchen had wall tiles patterned with peppers and aubergines and the dated cupboards had sunflower door knobs.

'Not quite the facilities I'm used to.' He grinned, nodding towards an elderly electric oven that looked like it was straight out of a 1950s TV commercial. 'But hunger is the mother of invention, I always find.'

'Ditto,' I said, leaning back to watch him. 'That was how I invented the perfect fish finger sandwich.'

He opened cupboards and took out some glasses. 'I'm a fan of comfort food too, I just prefer mine with a bit more finesse.'

'Oh well, if it's *finesse* you're after, look no further,' I said, producing a bag of cashew nuts, another of chocolate-covered raisins and a third of chilli-flavoured crisps from my bag. I set them on the counter. 'I bought the posh ones. Not that I'm hungry, obviously.'

'Obviously.' His lips twitched.

'But these are for watching TV with,' I explained.

'Really. And all these years, I've been doing it with my eyes.'

'And my mother taught me never to arrive anywhere empty handed.'

'Your mother did a very good job,' he murmured. He leaned forward, his fingers brushing my cheek as he hooked a stray strand of hair behind my ear. In the silence that followed I could feel my heart thumping.

'I'll tell her,' I said hoarsely. At which point my stomach let out a second thunderous growl.

'I think we'd better deal with that noise, or we won't be able to hear *Challenge Chester* on the TV.' He grinned and then squatted to look in the fridge. 'I know you're not very hungry but how about Eggs Benedict?'

I pretended to think about it. 'I could manage that.'

'Great.' He retrieved a saucepan and a mixing bowl with a clatter from the depths of the cupboards. 'Do you want to poach the eggs or do the hollandaise?'

'Neither. I'm a guest,' I quipped.

No way was I going to show myself up in front of him. I could never get poached eggs right, I always ended up with a pan of white water. Mimi and I used to say it looked like I was cooking ghosts. And I'd never produced a glossy hollandaise sauce in my life. To his surprise I levered myself up to sit on the end of the Formica kitchen worktop. 'I'll just sit here.'

I tore open the nuts, popped a handful in my mouth and offered him the bag.

Tom shook his head.

'Did your mother never tell you it's rude to stare?' He moved constantly while he talked, taking out more bowls and another smaller pan, eggs, butter and lemon juice.

Actually, I think she said that if a man ever offered to cook for me, first check he wasn't gay and second, marry him instantly. But I had no desire to alarm him.

I shook my head. 'I'm pretty sure my mother would approve of me staring at you.'

He gave me a sideways glance. 'Oh?'

'My hollandaise sauce is rubbish.'

He chuckled. 'Watch and learn, then, my girl. Watch and learn.'

He melted butter, separated eggs and whisked lemon juice. It was a pleasure to watch; he was so skilled and effortless and besides, I couldn't drag my eyes away from his wild curls and the curve of his mouth and the way he muttered instructions to himself under his breath.

'So today, ladies and gentlemen,' he began in a jolly, exaggerated tone, 'we're making a classic American dish featuring a smooth and tangy hollandaise sauce, free-range eggs and a lightly toasted muffin.'

My eyes widened in surprise at this change in personality.

'My guilty pleasure,' he said in a stage whisper and began to add the melted butter to his beaten eggs. His face broke into a boyish grin. 'Pretending to present a cookery show. I've done it since I was a kid.'

'Really? Me too!' I pressed a hand to my chest. 'That was my favourite thing to do. Well, with Mimi, of course. We set up a video camera in Gloria's kitchen and took it in turns to do the talking.'

His eyes lit up. 'I never filmed myself. Just focused on

trying not to chop my fingers off while I talked and waved a knife around.'

My heart skipped a beat and a warm sensation filled my chest; how lovely to think we shared such a precious part of our growing up.

'I still wave knives,' he laughed. 'When I'm alone I get quite flamboyant.'

'Now I'm alone, I don't do it at all.'

I felt my throat tighten and gently set the bag of nuts back down. There were tears lurking, I could feel them. I squeezed my eyes shut.

For a while after Mimi died, I'd heard her voice in my head giving me instructions. But lately she had been silent. Then again, lately I'd been so busy simply getting on with life and my head had been so full with other things that perhaps I'd stopped hearing her.

When I opened my eyes Tom had set his whisk down. He took my hands in his.

'Well, that's a terrible shame,' he murmured. 'I'll have to see what I can do about that.'

I swallowed and dropped my chin to my chest. 'There's nothing to be done. It's just the way it is.'

He placed a feather-light kiss on the back of my fingers, which cheered me up no end, and then released them.

'The kitchen is out of ham this evening, so we'll be serving our Eggs Benedict with bacon,' he said in his presenter's voice and lowered a couple of rashers on to a griddle pan.

For a simple supper, there certainly seemed to be a lot of pans.

'But we shall be serving them on lightly toasted muffins, if my assistant would be so kind?' He nodded towards an enamel bread bin.

'Me?' I tapped my fingertip on my chest. But I was *Mimi's* assistant . . . I blew out a calming breath. I *had been* Mimi's assistant. Maybe I should start doing the things we'd loved doing without her. Start living and loving and celebrating every single moment like it's a delicious feast.

Despite Gloria's warning, I could feel my body responding to Tom. And why not? He had a lot going for him. He was passionate. He had a good heart – look how he'd gone back to help Rebecca at Salinger's even though she'd cheated on him. And right now those deep, dark eyes were inviting me in. All I had to do was jump . . .

Tom made a show of searching the tiny kitchen for other people. 'Yes, you.'

He held out a hand to help me down and I took it. His forearm was lean and muscular and flecked with dark hair, his hand was warm and there was a smear of butter across his knuckles. I stared at the leather thong around his wrist, the one he wore every day.

'Are you looking at my mangle?' He grinned.

'Your *what*?' I stuttered.

'My man bangle. I read in a magazine it's called a mangle.' He twirled the leather strap round his wrist. 'My goddaughter made it for me and said if I ever took it off a fairy would lose her wings.' He shrugged. 'I can't have that happening, can I?'

What do you think of him, Mimi? I hope you approve, because I think . . .

'Absolutely not,' I agreed.

Because I think he's lovely . . .

We had been together nearly every day in the month I'd been in Plumberry and in that time I'd seen him soften like a peach. From those first flinty-eyed days when he'd berated us all for not appreciating his sophisticated canapés to revealing his soft and sweet nature when he'd offered our winner, Aaron, a foot up the ladder on Tuesday. And now this. I mean, *fairy wings* . . . How adorable was that?

Holding on to his hand, I jumped down and planted a kiss on his cheek. 'That's on behalf of . . . what's her name?'

'Saoirse.' Tom touched his cheek where I'd kissed him.

'On behalf of Saoirse for being such an excellent fairy-wing protector.'

'Thank you . . . Oh, damn, I forgot about the hollandaise.'

He began to whisk it off the heat furiously while I fetched the English muffins.

I held up the packet.

'Not homemade?' I said, feigning shock.

'Whisk this and don't stop,' he said with a grin, handing me the whisk, 'while I start on the eggs.'

'Yes, Chef,' I said, tongue in cheek. And then I took a deep breath. 'Now the secret to a velvety hollandaise sauce, ladies and gentleman, is to get lots of air in and to not over-cook it . . .'

Five minutes later we carried our supper into the living room and sat down, balancing our plates on our knees. On the wall opposite the sofa was the biggest TV I'd ever seen. Tom turned it on and found the right channel. 'Just in time, *Challenge Chester* starts after these ads.'

I inhaled the lemony scent of the hollandaise. 'This smells amazing, thank you.'

'Thank *you*,' he said. 'For bringing that sauce back from the brink. And for joining in with my TV show game.'

'I enjoyed it.' I shrugged a shoulder casually but inside I was glowing with happiness.

It probably seemed like a small thing to him, but for me, recreating the fun I used to have with Mimi with someone else was a huge milestone. One that I admitted was long overdue.

'Oh wow,' I groaned, putting a mouthful of Eggs Benedict into my mouth. 'I've died and gone to food heaven. Food is definitely the way to my heart.'

Tom smiled lazily at me for a long moment before murmuring, 'Mission complete.'

I didn't know where to look.

'You'll have to give me the recipe,' I said in between mouthfuls to cover my embarrassment. 'This is amazing.' Oh God, now I sounded all Women's Institute.

'No, I won't,' he murmured. He took both of our plates and set them on the floor. 'A recipe is just a list of ingredients, but what brings it to life is the memory, the people, the mood. I think that's what makes a dish amazing.'

He took my face in his hands. My heart literally forgot how to beat.

'That's true,' I managed to say.

I'd never eat hollandaise sauce again without remembering the touch of his rough skin against mine, the way he made my pulse race with just a look and his scent of lemons and spice and warm sexy man.

'I was nervous before you came,' he said, reaching for my hand. 'It's been a long time since I was alone with a girl. Rebecca and I were together five years.'

I nodded. 'I felt the same.'

We shared a smile and I squeezed his hand.

He ran the tip of his tongue round his lips nervously. 'I told myself not to get my fingers burned again. Not in love and not in business either.'

And then my heart began beating again, squeezing fast as adrenalin, mixed with disappointment, began to pump through my body.

'Absolutely. Very wise. I understand. It's understandable.' I was nodding a lot and his mouth twitched into a smile. 'Me too.'

'I thought I'd find it very hard to trust someone again.'

'Again, very wise,' I agreed. 'Although I'd like to point out that I'm completely trustworthy. The name Verity means truth in several different languages.'

He was laughing softly now and I closed my mouth, aware that I was in danger of overstating my case.

'The thing is,' he murmured, 'I think you had me the

moment I saw you tearing along Plumberry high street shouting "sausages".'

We both laughed at the memory of me racing after Comfrey and Sage on my first day in the village.

'So what I'm trying to say is . . .' He squirmed in his seat, struggling to find the right words.

I stared at his full mouth, and the way he caught his bottom lip between his teeth when he paused and I wished he'd . . .

'Kiss me,' I said. My eyes widened in shock. 'Oh gosh, that just slipped out.'

But I was glad it did because it was all the encouragement he needed. A smile crossed his face and as the opening titles of *Challenge Chester* began to roll we kissed, gently at first and then more deeply, and I stopped holding my breath, I closed my eyes and forgot all about live tweeting, because live kissing was way much more fun.

I let myself into the cottage later that night, checked that Gloria was asleep and let the dogs out for their bedtime wee. I didn't care that I'd got a bit of a rash on my chin from Tom's beard, I didn't even mind that my stomach was rumbling (the Eggs Benedict had been abandoned indefinitely), because there was a hope and happiness in my heart that I hadn't felt for a long time.

I lay in bed and left the curtains open so that the stars could twinkle at me in the night sky. There was no moon to be seen and a million tiny pinpricks of light decorated the inky blackness. Two brighter dots caught my eye, a big one and a smaller one: Jupiter and Venus, I thought automatically. My mind wandered to Gabe and Noah. I imagined them lying on the banks of the River Ouse staring up at the same sky, gazing into infinity, Noah asking endless questions about how far away they all were and did anybody live there.

I love them, I thought simply. And I always would. But it

was time for Gabe to move on, for me to move on and for all of us to find the right person to love.

The Plumberry School of Comfort Food had given me so much in such a short time: I had a new zest for life, I was part of a community who shared a love of food, and now that I had recaptured my passion for cooking, I never wanted to lose that connection again.

And Tom . . .

I sighed a happy sigh and closed my eyes. It was too soon to tell whether there was a future for the two of us. But the taste of his lips was still on mine and for now that was enough to guarantee me the sweetest of dreams.

Chapter 29

It was Friday morning, nearly the weekend. Rosie was arriving today, Gabe and Noah tomorrow, and on Sunday, Tom had asked me to spend the afternoon with him 'in the wilds of Yorkshire'. The prospect of all of these things had put me in the very best of moods.

'I've thought about it long and hard . . .' I paused, waiting until I had Gloria's full attention at the breakfast table. Her face was screwed up in concentration and she was breathless again, although that could have been the frustration of retrieving the last sliver of lime peel from the bottom of the jar. That was easily solved; I'd pop into the little supermarket in Plumberry and buy her a new one for tomorrow's breakfast.

'I'm going to sell my Nottingham house. Then my life will truly be here.'

'Oh, darling!' Gloria's eyes glittered as she squeezed my hand. 'That's wonderful news. You've made me the happiest woman in Plumberry.'

I might contest you for that honour, I thought, remembering last night when Tom's lips had pressed a line of sizzling kisses from my collarbone to that soft ticklish spot just below my ear.

'And I can see how happy you are too.' She smiled but then instantly pressed a hand to her chest with a wince.

'Gloria?' I frowned. 'Are you in pain?'

'Silly me.' She managed a weak smile that didn't quite fit with the look of discomfort in her eyes. 'Swallowed a sharp bit of crust, that's all.'

I eyed her beadily. 'If you say so. But please be sensible today, don't overdo it.'

Comfrey was curled up near the foot that was supposed to be raised. Her little toe was hidden by the end of the plaster cast and the others were vivid red. I nudged an empty chair out from under the table and nodded at it to make her lift up her leg.

'Your toes look a bit puffy to me, do you think they're swollen?'

'Verity,' Gloria soothed, cutting me off by touching my arm, 'don't worry about me. I shall keep off my leg all morning. I won't have much choice, anyway; the physio is coming later and before that my solicitor is calling round to make some changes to my will. Lovely chap, divorced and totally in love with me, poor soul.'

'You dark horse, Gloria Ramsbottom!'

'Oh, yes.' She sighed dreamily, fanning her face with a placemat from the table. 'Percy took me to dinner a couple of times, but I knew pretty quickly we weren't compatible.'

'How?'

She wrinkled her nose. 'No appreciation or savouring of his food. He treated me to chateaubriand at a smart hotel in York once. The most expensive meal I think I've ever had.' She closed her eyes at the memory. 'It melted in the mouth, I remember it vividly. But he gobbled his dinner down so fast I doubted he even tasted it. Literally. Worse than Sage.'

Sage, who was sitting statue-like under Gloria's chair, nose quivering hopefully at the prospect of a dropped morsel, pricked his ears up and yapped.

Gloria obliged and dropped a piece of marmalade toast for him.

'Oh dear, I can see that wouldn't have worked,' I said with a cringe. If that was the secret to a happy relationship,

Tom and I must be extremely compatible: we both adored food. I hugged the secret to myself; Gloria hadn't been particularly encouraging last night and it was still early days with Tom. Far better to wait.

'Never mind,' she said practically. 'He makes house calls and gives me a discount, so I mustn't grumble.'

I glanced at my watch. Tom would be on his way to Manchester now to instruct his solicitor on the sale of Salinger's.

'You'd better be off,' said Gloria wistfully, noticing my gesture. 'You'll no doubt have a busy day dealing with enquiries following *Challenge Chester* last night. Was it good, by the way? I fell asleep before the start.'

'Brilliant. Amazing. Great publicity,' I said, not meeting her eye.

At least that was what Tom had said in a text last night after he'd stayed up late to watch it on catch-up.

I screwed the top on to the blackcurrant jam and fed the last crust to Comfrey to cover up my pink cheeks. 'With any luck the phone will be ringing off the hook.'

Watching *Challenge Chester* on my laptop was top of my morning's agenda. I just hoped I'd get through the first hour in the office without having to answer any awkward questions, like why I hadn't seen it last night and in that case what *had* I been doing at Tom's.

My heart sang a merry tune as I cleared the breakfast table, made Gloria a second cup of tea and topped up the dogs' bowl with fresh water.

'Verity?' Gloria called as I reached the kitchen door. She still had a hand pressed to her throat and I could see her chest rising and falling rapidly.

'Yes?'

She held out her arms and I returned to the table for a hug.

She squeezed me tight, pressing her soft cheek to mine. Gloria gave great hugs. She smelled of Pears soap, lime

310

marmalade and . . . my heart leapt as I realized it . . . home. Gloria, Plumberry, the cookery school . . . it had all become my home.

Finally, she pulled back to look at me.

'I love you like a daughter; you know that, don't you?' she said with a sniff. 'You, Gabe and Noah are all the family I've got. You're what I live for. I can cope with the inconvenience of this stupid plaster cast and the constant throbbing of my stupid leg because I know I've got you.'

'You soppy thing.' I kissed her cheek.

'Having you living here with me and seeing my cookery school finally open,' she swallowed and there were tears sparkling in her eyes, 'this has been my happiest time since Mimi died.'

We stared at each other for a moment.

'For me too, Gloria,' I said, 'for me too.'

'I thought you were going to be live tweeting last night?' Pixie leaned against the door of the office. 'I searched for the Plumberry hashtag and nothing came up.'

She was chewing gum, which she only dared do because she knew Tom was out.

I took off my headphones.

'Internet went down,' I said in a businesslike tone that didn't invite comment.

I minimized the screen, which was playing *Challenge Chester*. I'd watched nearly the whole hour of it and I was thoroughly enjoying it. Tom was a natural in front of the camera. All those years of pretending to present a TV show had paid off, I thought, my heart pinging as I remembered last night. And when he twinkled his dark eyes at the camera I felt my stomach flutter as if he was looking just at me.

I would have finished the programme by now, but Tom had rung earlier from his car to tell me that he'd arrived in Manchester and we'd chatted for ages.

'A couple of my chef mates have phoned already this morning,' he'd said. 'They saw the programme last night and have volunteered their services if we ever want guest chef appearances. That might add something to your Supper Club idea, what do you think? Imagine the possibilities, V! It could be the start of something really exciting.'

He had been so fired up and full of enthusiasm that I'd been both touched and carried away with the idea myself. I'd already pencilled in our first Supper Club for the last Friday in June.

Pixie took a seat in Gloria's chair and span round and round, blowing her fringe up out of her eyes as she turned.

'Tom was a star; I think he could be a TV chef himself, don't you?'

In spite of my best efforts to control it, my mouth lifted at the corners. I couldn't get the sound of Tom's voice out of my head from last night as he carried on a running commentary of our Eggs Benedict supper. He would be brilliant on TV, just as he was brilliant in the kitchen, and on the sofa, come to that . . .

'Probably,' I said vaguely. 'But what struck me was how happy everyone was, and what a lovely thing it is to get together and share food and flavours and recipes. Making memories . . .' I finished with a sigh.

Pixie arched an eyebrow. 'Get you, all romantic for ten o'clock in the morning.'

My phone rang. I looked at the screen. Tom. Again.

'Excuse me, Pixie,' I said pointedly, choosing not to answer the call until she took the hint.

She heaved herself up off the chair, muttering under her breath about being the only one doing any work around here, and whipped her head round with curiosity as I answered the phone.

'Tom!' I smiled down the phone. 'Long time no speak.'

'I know, I know, I'm turning into a stalker,' he laughed. My heart went gooey at the sound of his lovely Irish accent.

It sounded stronger over the phone. 'Have you watched it all yet?'

'No, because I keep getting interrupted,' I teased.

'Well, hurry up because everyone else has,' he urged. 'Anyway, you'll never guess who I've just had on the phone?'

'Jamie Oliver?' I idly flicked through my emails.

I'd had twenty-five messages from advertising people and thirty from Chester Fulwood fans who wanted to know if we had any signed souvenirs – actually, I was a bit cross with myself about not having any of those – plus tons of new Facebook likes and Twitter followers.

He hesitated. 'OK, not that exciting. Fresh from the Sea. That new seafood company.'

'Whatever the question, the answer's no,' I said briskly. 'Remember how ill you were last time?'

On the other hand, as stressful as his illness was it had forced me back into the kitchen, so the company wasn't entirely without its merits.

'They were very apologetic about that and managed to trace a duff batch of langoustines back to . . . Anyway, the good news is that they want to run an event at the cookery school on June the ninth for bloggers.'

'Here?' I flipped to the diary screen on my laptop. 'I thought they'd got their own venue. Don't you think that's a bit . . . fishy?'

'Ha ha.'

He explained that their building had been flooded in last week's storms and the repairs hadn't happened as quickly as expected. Fifteen food bloggers were expecting a Cooking with Fish demonstration, plus a three-course fishy lunch and they had nowhere to put them and were prepared to pay a handsome sum for our facilities.

As it turned out we didn't have a course running on that day, so as Dave would say the booking was a useful extra revenue stream. Providing they didn't poison all the bloggers who'd then blame the cookery school and blog all about it . . .

I took the details from Tom over the phone and promised to phone Fresh from the Sea's PR person, Rachel, and give her the good news.

After I'd finished watching *Challenge Chester*, I spent the rest of the morning sorting out admin and liaising with the printer for some new Supper Club leaflets until it was almost time for Rosie to arrive. Mags had been conspicuously quiet this morning and I was dying to know how her dinner with Dave had gone last night. I turned off my laptop and picked up my phone in preparation to go and wait for Rosie in reception when my phone beeped with a message.

It was Tom again. I laughed to myself; at this rate he'd never make it back to Plumberry before the start of the Perfect Pasta course.

Gosh, long message. I read it as I descended the stairs.

You know what you said last night about being
trustworthy? Well I am too. I know this might not be
the most romantic text you'll ever get but it's true.
Talking to my solicitor about Rebecca has brought
it to the fore. I won't cheat on you like she did and
I won't steal your ideas like Liam did. But I can't
promise not to steal your heart. T x

Wow; I think he may have already done that.

'Fifteen new bookings this morning,' Mags cried as she saw me coming downstairs. 'June is going to be a busy month.'

It was still May. Sometimes I forgot that I'd only been here since the end of April, it felt like much longer.

'Brilliant!' I dropped my phone in my cardigan pocket and squeezed behind the desk. 'Gloria will be thrilled!'

'I called in on her earlier,' said Mags.

'How did she seem to you?' I said, smoothing the skirt of my dress as I perched on the end of her desk. 'She was clutching her chest this morning as if she was in pain. Denied it, of course,' I added ruefully.

'I didn't see her.' Mags took a diamanté hairclip out, tucked a stray blonde wisp into her bun and repinned it. 'I called up the stairs but I could hear the shower running, so I left her a note instead.'

'I helped her to have a bath this morning,' I said. 'That means she's crawled up the stairs by herself. She'll be exhausted.'

Mags frowned. 'And isn't it odd that she felt the need for a shower?'

I nodded. 'Very. Maybe she's suffering from the heat again?'

My stomach lurched. Going upstairs was a major event for Gloria: up on all fours and down on her bottom. She avoided doing it if she could and rarely went upstairs without Mags or me to help her.

'Let's ring her,' we both said together.

Mags grabbed the phone but before she could even dial Gloria's number, her mobile rang.

'Gloria!'

She mouthed *Phew* to me and I gave her the thumbs-up.

'Everything OK? Did you see my note?' Mags asked.

Gloria's voice was too tinny and faint for me to catch.

Mags chuckled. 'He *would*. Yes, I'll tell her.'

She paused and frowned. 'All right, but not too far. Bye, chuck.'

'Well?' I asked as Mags replaced the receiver.

'The solicitor has been and scoffed all the biscuits. She's going to walk up and down Hillside Lane to mobilize her hip a bit. The physio has rescheduled the appointment to half past five. Also,' she added, 'she says we're to stop fretting about her.'

I felt my shoulders relax from their hunched position under my ears. I nodded slowly. 'I'll try.'

'Her biggest concern is being a burden.' Mags sighed. 'I keep telling her not to be daft.'

'Anyway, she's fine for now. So?' I nudged her shoulder. 'How was your date with Dave? Did it live up to all that anticipation?'

She blushed and clasped her hands in her lap demurely. 'He was a perfect gentleman.'

Pixie pushed her way backwards through the door from the Aga kitchen with a pasta machine tucked under her arm. She took one look at us and put the machine down on the desk.

'You're talking about Dave, aren't you? Is he a good kisser?' She winked at me.

Mags, who was normally the first to enter into a lewd discussion involving anyone else, seemed extremely reticent now that the boot was on the other foot.

She tilted her chin up. 'A lady never divulges such things.'

'You didn't get any action last night, then,' Pixie snorted. 'We were relying on you for some juicy gossip, weren't we, Verity?'

A rosy feeling crept across my cheeks as I tried not to think about my own 'action'; I'd no wish to divulge either.

'Your friend's here,' said Mags with a touch of relief.

I fanned my face; her and me both . . .

She nodded towards the car park where Rosie's car was drawing to a halt. The car door opened and a foot encased in an impossibly high heel touched the tarmac.

'How can she drive in them?' Mags marvelled.

'Because she's a goddess,' Pixie said breathily.

A slender, tanned leg appeared. Rosie was dressed in a crisp white fitted blouse, tight black skirt and red shoes. She shook her black hair off her face and shut the door with her bottom. She was on the phone, waving her arms about animatedly as usual, and even from this distance I could see she was frowning. But she raised a hand in a wave when she saw us.

'Go and make her one of your special caramel lattes, Pixie,' said Mags. 'She looks like she needs cheering up.'

I scurried out into the car park to greet her as Rosie ended the call and we squealed and hugged our hellos.

'I've got so much to tell you!' I exclaimed. 'We've been on TV, the cookery school is fully booked, and—'

I broke off, not wanting to mention Tom yet. There was time for that later, away from the cookery school.

'You have been busy.' She raised an eyebrow at my exuberance. 'It's only a week since I saw you.'

I nodded gravely. 'A lot can happen in a week. An awful lot.'

'What a relief to step out of the rat race for a day,' said Rosie, sinking on to one of the picnic benches on the deck and gazing out over the river. 'You don't know how lucky you are, spending your days in a beauty spot like this.'

I did actually, I thought with a secret smile.

'Tough morning at work?' I asked. Rosie was never averse to a bit of drama. She blamed it on Nonna whose motto was 'sing when you're winning and wail when you're not'.

'You have no idea.' She rested her elbows on the table and dropped her chin into her hands. 'My place is having to make redundancies and my boss has asked me to draw up a list of candidates for the chop.'

My heart went out to her; after escaping from Solomon's only a month ago, I knew how stressful the workplace could become when jobs were under threat.

'I'm so sorry.' I laid my hand on hers. 'How awful to be put in that position.'

She shrugged wearily. 'Let's just say I'm about as popular in the office as the Grim Reaper at the moment. Anyway,' she waved a hand, 'let's talk about something happier.'

Pixie approached, carefully carrying a tall latte glass with four caramel biscuits balanced on the saucer. We normally served it with one.

'I've added extra caramel syrup,' said Pixie, blushing as Rosie crossed her legs, revealing a lean thigh and a flash of gold ankle chain.

Rosie picked up the tall glass and slurped. 'Oh, sweet Madonna, this is better than sex.'

Pixie beamed and I thought for a second she was going to curtsey. 'You looked like you needed a sugar hit.'

'Spot on.' She grinned, sticking her thumb up as Pixie made her way inside. 'Unlike Verity Bloom who looks like she's won the lottery.'

My turn to grin like a loon. 'I've got loads to tell you, Rosie, but—'

Out of the corner of my eye I saw Mags usher two women into the Aga kitchen.

'The other students have begun to arrive for your course. I'd better go and see if Tom is back. You can let off some steam punching pasta dough and we'll catch up later.'

Rosie dunked one of the biscuits in her latte. 'Can't wait. And Nonna will be so proud of me for finally learning how to be a proper Italian.'

'Don't eat too much, though.' I stood and gave her a quick hug. 'We're going for an early dinner.'

She rolled her eyes. 'I don't mind where we go as long as there's alcohol.'

'There will be,' I laughed. 'After dinner we're going home for cocktails; Mags has invented a cocktail called the Plumberry Pucker. You have to try it.'

Rosie gave a hoot. 'Thank the Lord you don't live in Flumberry.'

I could still hear her laughing at her own joke when I reached the office upstairs.

Chapter 30

'Would Nonna approve of Tom, your tutor, do you think?'
I asked as we settled ourselves into the back of a cab on
the way to Platform Six later that afternoon. I maintained a
neutral expression for as long as I could, but my eyes were
already beginning to crinkle at the corners.

'Who cares?' Rosie pretended to fan her face. 'I very
much approve. He looks as dark as an Italian from the
back and then he turns and does that cheeky Irish smile.
Phwoar. I wouldn't mind a trip to the Emerald Isle if they
all look like that.'

'He's delicious, isn't he?' I fidgeted in my seat, like Noah
when he's too excited to contain himself.

She stared at me. 'Are you and he . . . ? Is that the reason
for the I've-won-the-jackpot sparkly eyes?'

'It's still very new,' I said, trying to keep a lid on my glee.
'Less than twenty-four hours. We haven't even been on a
date. In fact . . .'

I stopped short of telling her that tonight was to have
been mine and Tom's first date. I didn't want Rosie to feel
guilty. Our first date would be on Sunday instead. Sometimes looking forward to something can be just as spine-
tinglingly exciting as the thing itself.

I allowed my mind to flash back to our goodnight
kiss yesterday when Tom had asked me out to dinner at

Platform Six. When I'd explained that I couldn't, he insisted on me taking Rosie in his place. We'd changed the booking to make it earlier, though, because I didn't want to leave Gloria on her own for another evening.

Hence the reason that we were trundling through Plumberry at half past five.

'In fact,' I said, changing tack, 'I haven't even told Gloria yet.'

'Wow.' She flashed her dark eyes and gave me a sly sideways glance. 'You know, I really thought . . .'

'What?'

'Don't bite my head off.'

'Spit it out,' I ordered, laughing.

'I really thought you and Gabe might . . .' Her voice petered off, allowing me to fill in the gaps.

Not her as well. I rolled my eyes.

'Stop. Seriously. Just – stop.' I folded my arms. 'Gabe Green is a no-go zone. End of. Imagine what Mimi would think?'

Rosie huffed softly. 'I'll tell you what I think. She'd see two people who care about each other. And I don't see how she could be anything but pleased?'

'Rosie,' I said sharply, 'you don't understand.'

'Whose fault is that?' she retorted.

'Just drop it. Please,' I said through clenched teeth.

She held her hands up. 'OK. Dropped.'

There were very few people who knew the truth about what happened four years ago. Rosie knew that Chris and I had ended our engagement over it and that Mum and I had rowed about it too. And although I knew it hurt Rosie's feelings that I'd never confided in her, I always thought she understood my reasons. Now, it seemed, Rosie was siding with Gloria and hoping Gabe and I would become an item . . .

As much as I adored him, that was unthinkable for both of us.

I sneaked a look at her. Her hands were clenched in her lap and her eyes were closed.

I suppressed a sigh. How had we even got into this conversation? This was supposed to be a girlie chat about me and Tom. I looked out of the window, racking my brains for a less controversial topic of conversation.

Luckily the taxi pulled into the car park of Platform Six only a few minutes later.

'Here you go, ladies. Fifteen pounds please.'

'Cute,' said Rosie, peering out of the window at the converted Victorian railway station.

I took my purse out of my bag to pay and Rosie climbed out, dragging my bag with her.

'Sweet Jesus, Verity, what have you got in here, rocks?' she said, pretending to stagger under the weight of it.

The bad atmosphere between us evaporated instantly. It was Friday, I had hours of fun ahead with my completely mad friend and a glass of chilled Prosecco with my name on it at the bar.

'A jar of marmalade and two packets of biscuits,' I said with a giggle.

'Who's joining us for dinner,' Rosie snorted, 'Paddington Bear?'

A smiley waiter showed us to our table, pulled out chairs, handed round menus and the wine list and poured us each a glass of iced water from a carafe. Rosie and I were the only diners apart from two men in suits who looked like they were in a meeting.

Platform Six was not at all like the dark Victorian Gothic interior I'd imagined. It was kitsch and quirky with lots of bright colours: a fused glass wall behind the bar, mismatched velvet dining chairs in jewel shades and a collection of eclectic art above our table, including a lime green stag's head. I loved it and felt a warm rush of tenderness towards Tom for wanting to bring me here.

'We have our resident mixologist ready to make your bespoke cocktails at the bar,' said the waiter, extending an arm to where a barman paused from polishing a glass to give us a smile.

Rosie jumped up straight away. 'I love it here already.'

'Does everyone get a bespoke cocktail?' I asked, tucking my bag safely under my seat.

The waiter shook his head and smiled more broadly. 'Somebody rang to include it in your booking. Your dinner is also paid for, madam.'

Rosie's eyes widened and my heart swooped; it could only be Tom. She looped her arm through mine as we approached the bar.

'Has Tom got any single brothers, by any chance?'

I glowed with happiness. I had a good feeling about Tom and me. I was independent enough not to need my girl-friend's approval on my choice of men, but it was nice to have it all the same.

The barman – or mixologist, as he liked to be called – was from Brazil and his name was Luis. He had dimples to die for and sparkling white teeth. He gave us the cocktail list and instructed us to choose one or if we'd prefer, he'd make one for us.

'I read the body,' he said in heavily accented English. He ran his eyes over Rosie appreciatively. 'I know exactly what are the flavours that will excite your mouth.'

'That is a challenge that no woman could refuse,' said Rosie, batting her eyelashes. 'Surprise us.'

We settled ourselves on bar stools and watched as Luis crushed ice, squeezed fruit, plucked fresh herbs and shook and stirred our drinks elaborately. It took him a while, but it was worth the wait. Our cocktails were as different as our personalities and we both loved what he'd made for us.

Ten minutes later and halfway down our cocktails, we thanked Luis for the entertainment and returned to our seats at our table.

Rosie raised her eyebrows as she sucked on her straw. 'This is mouth-puckeringly sour, but I love it.'

Luis had made her his own version of a Brazilian caipirinha but I preferred mine. I'd already forgotten what it was called but it had a big sprig of rosemary in it and tasted fresh and exciting and I could feel the alcohol zipping through my bloodstream.

I shimmied with happiness. That was my life at the moment: fresh and exciting. I felt like a bubble, all shiny and light and iridescent with joy.

'Let's take a selfie and send it to Tom!'

I scooped up my bag and found my phone. And at that moment the bubble popped.

I stared at the screen in disbelief: in the fifteen minutes or so that we'd been at the bar I'd received a slew of calls, voicemails and texts. The cookery school, Tom, Mags and Gabe . . .

My heart turned to lead as I read Gabe's text:

I'll meet you at the hospital

And Tom's:

I'm on my way to fetch you

My first thought was that Noah had had an accident and my blood ran cold, but then I realized who *hadn't* called me: Gloria. It had to be . . .

'Oh my God,' I whispered. I'd known there was something wrong. I'd never forgive myself if . . .

'Verity? You've gone chalk-white.' Rosie's eyes searched mine.

'I think Gloria might be ill.' I gripped her hand as I called Tom back.

'Tom?' I gasped as he answered the phone. There was the sound of an engine and road noise in the background.

'Stay calm, I'm on my way.' I shut my eyes and suppressed a sob; how could I possibly be calm?

'What's happened?' I stammered.

'I'm afraid Gloria has been taken into hospital. The physiotherapist arrived, took one look at her and called an ambulance.'

'Is it serious?' I said, barely louder than a whisper.

There was a beat of silence before he spoke.

'The paramedics informed next of kin from Gloria's cottage. That's all I know.'

Gabe. And he called me. My heart thumped. While I was laughing over cocktails.

'We'll get a taxi,' I said, getting to my feet. 'It'll be quicker.'

I couldn't sit here waiting, I needed to do something.

'No need. I'm almost there, come straight out.'

With cries of apology to the restaurant staff, Rosie and I ran outside just as Tom pulled up to the entrance. I jumped into the front and Rosie dived on to the back seat. I met Tom's eyes and my heart bounced at his grim expression. We didn't waste time with words; as soon as our doors were shut, Tom put the car into gear and drove.

As we sped out of the car park, Tom's mobile rang. He chucked it into my lap without reading the display.

'No hands-free in this car, put it on speaker phone, would you?'

I touched the screen to accept the call, a York number by the look of the code. The hospital? I held my breath.

'Tom MacDonald,' Tom said loudly. He pulled on to the main road towards York. I couldn't see the speedometer, but the G-force thrust me back against my seat.

'It's Nige,' came the gravelly voice of a man who sounded like he gargled whisky for breakfast.

Tom shot me an anxious look and groaned softly under

his breath. 'Can we do this later, Nige? Only I'm on my way to hospital.'

'No,' said Nige blithely. 'You chefs might be masters of your own destiny, but us journos are on deadline. I'll keep it quick. OK. Got the email and the pic. Looks like you've fallen on your feet there, mate. Especially after the Rebecca fiasco.'

'Er, I think so,' said Tom. His eyes slid briefly towards mine and then back to the road. His eyebrows had scrunched together to form one long one and if I wasn't mistaken there was a flush to his cheeks; was this Nige person talking about me?

'I have to say, it's a great idea. I was in Liverpool recently and went to a Supper Club there. Packed out it was.'

I sat up straighter and stared at Tom who muttered something rude that I didn't quite catch.

He cleared his throat. 'So you've got everything you need, Nige?'

'Just the date, mate. When's your first one?'

Tom looked utterly uncomfortable. 'Um, Verity, when's the first Plumberry Supper Club event?'

I held his gaze unflinchingly. ' June the twenty-sixth.'

'Did you get that, Nige?'

'Sure did, mate. It'll be in next week, don't forget you owe me a—'

Tom grabbed the phone out of my hand and ended the call before the journalist could finish. He grimaced.

'Sorry,' he murmured. 'I didn't want you to hear that.'

'I can't think why.' I turned and faced the window. We passed a road sign for York. Ten miles to go.

'It's not as bad as it sounds, trust me.' He reached a hand towards my thigh but I inched away.

'Can we go any faster?' I asked.

Rosie's hand snaked through from the back seat and squeezed my arm. She wouldn't have a clue what that whole

325

conversation had been about. She didn't need to; you could cut the atmosphere in the car with a knife.

Tom sighed. 'Verity—'

'Just drive, Tom. Now's not the time.'

He nodded grimly and pressed his foot down on the accelerator.

It was obvious what had happened. He'd called a contact of his at the York newspapers and was passing off the Supper Club idea as his own before I had had a chance to do so. My heart thudded angrily against my ribs.

Why would he do that to me? And after that text he'd sent me this morning about being trustworthy. He was just as bad as Liam. No – worse, because at least Liam had always been upfront about pinching my ideas, whether I approved or not.

What it all boiled down to was this: Tom's ego was bigger than his promise to me and that made my stomach curdle.

I pushed thoughts of him aside for now. All that mattered was getting to the hospital. Poor Gloria. My hands twisted in my lap. Please, please, let her be all right . . .

The journey to the accident and emergency department of York's major hospital seemed to take for ever, although in reality it was probably only half an hour.

Thankfully, Tom didn't speak again and I spent the entire trip dialling numbers – Gabe, the cookery school, Mags, even Gloria's cottage . . . I was desperate for information but no one picked up.

Tom pulled up outside a pair of double glass doors just as a trolley was unloaded from an ambulance. It was instantly surrounded by an army of medics in blue uniforms and whisked inside.

Rosie and I jumped out and Tom drove away to find the car park.

Rosie exhaled sharply and grabbed my hand. 'OK?'

I couldn't answer; I felt like I'd got a lump of fudge

lodged in my throat. So I simply shook my head and together we made a dash for the entrance.

A receptionist checked her computer before giving us directions to the ward in which we'd find Gloria. The pleasantly fuzzy sensation that my cocktail had given me had evaporated. In its place was one of cold terror; it tightened around my lungs and left me gulping for air.

'This way,' I said, pulling Rosie behind me.

The hospital was busy; there were visitors milling around, patients being wheeled about with tubes and drips attached, cleaners emptying bins, people at vending machines . . . Rosie and I ran blindly past, looking for the ward number we'd been given.

Finally, we rounded a corner, pushed through double swing doors and there they were in the corridor immediately in front us: Noah crouched on the floor playing with dinosaur toys and Gabe, a hand pressed to his mouth, talking, or rather listening, to a doctor. By his side was another woman in a navy uniform, tears staining her cheeks, an envelope in her hands.

'Gabe,' I yelled.

I released Rosie's hand. Out of the corner of my eye I saw Noah jump to his feet and spring towards me.

'How is she?' I cried.

Gabe turned his face towards me, both hands caught in his hair. He looked distraught. A rush of nausea rose up in my throat and I forced it down.

Every aspect of the scene in front of me screamed the news: Gabe holding his arms out to me, his face creased in pain; the doctor shaking his head; the woman's shoulders trembling. But even so I couldn't take it in. This was not – *could not* – be happening.

'No! No!' I stumbled forward into Gabe's arms.

'Aunty Verity, are you sad?' Noah wrapped himself round my legs, his sandy hair standing in soft peaks, his green eyes curious.

Verity. He'd pronounced Verity properly. I gazed down at him and blinked away my tears.

I stroked his hair and nodded, forcing a smile. I couldn't speak. Not yet, not until I'd heard it for myself.

I looked up into Gabe's face, vaguely aware of Rosie hovering behind me. 'Gabe?'

'Gloria, she—' He broke down, his shoulders racked with grief.

The doctor stepped forward, a softly spoken Indian man with kind eyes.

'I'm afraid there was nothing we could do for Gloria. She suffered a pulmonary embolism. A blood clot. By the time she arrived here it had reached her lungs and it was too late. She couldn't survive. I'm very sorry.'

She couldn't survive . . .

The room began to spin and I stuck a hand out and gripped Gabe's arm.

'A blood clot?' I stuttered.

The doctor explained that this sometimes occurred in patients who had had leg surgery but that Gloria should have been given anti-coagulant drugs to prevent it.

'But she *was* given medication!' I wailed. 'She had heparin to inject herself with.'

'Inject?' Gabe shook his head. 'Gloria had a fear of needles; no way would she have injected herself.'

The doctor murmured his apologies, touched our shoulders and told us where to find him if we needed him.

I felt heavy and numb: my legs, my shoulders, my heart. This couldn't be happening. How could she be dead?

I burst into tears and dropped my face into my hands. When Gloria had been released from hospital last week, it had been me who'd told the nurse I'd be there for her. Me who should have been checking that she had taken her medication.

'This is all my fault,' I sobbed.

'Verity?' said the woman in navy. Her cheeks were

streaked with mascara and her nose was red.

I tried to focus through my tears and nodded.

'I'm Tina, the physio who came to see Gloria today. I travelled in the ambulance with her. She was . . . poorly . . .' She glanced at me, and I could see she didn't want to frighten me with facts. 'But she blamed herself for not taking the heparin and for hiding how ill she was from you. She didn't want to be any trouble.'

Tina told us how Gloria had been in distress when she'd arrived, short of breath, with chest pains and feeling clammy. She'd called an ambulance straight away, thinking that Gloria was having a heart attack.

'I'm only sorry my appointment wasn't earlier in the day, then perhaps she—' Tina bowed her head and backed away, dabbing her tears with a tissue.

My head felt like it was in a vice, too tight for my skull. I wanted to scream with frustration. She was sixty-five, I wanted to yell. She was too young to die.

I dropped my head on Gabe's shoulder and let my tears flow. Poor little Noah, not really understanding the situation but recognizing my sorrow, tightened his grip around my legs. Rosie picked up his dinosaurs from the floor and Tina stood and held out the envelope she'd been holding.

'I'm going to leave you and your family now,' she said. 'But Gloria was most insistent I gave you this, Gabe, it was in her handbag. She got quite agitated about it.'

'Thank you, Tina, and thanks for everything.' Gabe took the envelope from her.

That was how Tom found us: Gabe, Noah and I wrapped up in our grief in each other's arms. Bound together once again by the loss of someone close. Despite the harsh words we'd had in the car, my heart swelled when I saw him.

'Verity?' he panted, pushing through the doors. 'How is she?'

I wriggled free from Gabe's embrace and stepped blindly

into his arms. 'She died, Tom; Gloria died,' I sobbed, barely able to believe my own words.

'Jesus. I am so sorry.' He hugged me to him and I leaned against him gratefully, letting my sorrow bubble to the surface.

Tom pressed his lips to my forehead and rubbed at my tears tenderly with his thumb.

'Thank you for fetching me from the restaurant,' I murmured. 'I'm so glad you're here.'

'What happened?'

I began to tell Tom how Tina had found her when a noise like a wounded animal cut through my words.

I stared at Gabe.

'Oh God, no.' Gabe's face had turned completely white. He stared at me with grief-stricken eyes. In his hand was the single sheet of paper he had taken from the envelope. 'Verity, she knew.'

'What? What are you talking about?' My heart froze and fear spread through me like splinters of ice.

'Gloria knew about . . .' Gabe's gaze flickered nervously to Noah and back to me. 'About us.'

'No,' I gasped, pressing a hand to my mouth. My body began to shake. 'Oh no.'

Gabe's shoulders sagged. He gathered Noah to him and squeezed his eyes tightly shut, rocking from side to side. Out of the corner of my eye I saw Rosie's eyes narrow, flicking from each of us in turn.

Tom released me and took a step back. 'You and Gabe?'

His eyes searched mine. I wanted to tell him the truth, the whole story, but I couldn't, not now and perhaps not ever.

'It's not what you think. Truly,' I stammered.

I extended a hand to him. He looked at it and swallowed hard.

'I'm intruding. This is a family moment. I'm . . . I'm sorry for your loss.'

And with that he turned and walked away, leaving a whoosh of air as he slammed through the double doors.

'Tom, come back, let me explain,' I shouted, but he carried on walking.

If I'd had the strength, I'd have followed him but instead my knees gave way and I sank to the floor. My heart was so full of pain that I could scarcely breathe. I loved Gloria so much and the future without her seemed unthinkable. In a matter of minutes, the new life I thought I'd built for myself in Plumberry had crumbled. I'd lost Gloria, just like I'd lost Mimi two years ago, and now it looked as if I'd lost Tom too.

Mimi, I wish you were here to help me. The promise I made to you seems to have done more harm than good. Should I continue to keep it, or share our secret with the man who has stolen my heart? What should I do?

I dropped my head in my hands and sobbed, for Gloria, for Mimi and for what might have been with Tom. What did the future hold for any of us without the ones we loved?

The Magic Ingredient

Chapter 31

It was Monday morning and fingers of golden June sunlight poked through the curtains and teased me awake. I rubbed my eyes, feeling the salt from dried tears on my lashes.

Come on, Verity, best foot forward. Time to get up and face the day.

Comfrey and Sage didn't stir as I clambered out of bed. They were curled up in such tight cosy balls that I couldn't even see which end was head and which was tail. I bent to stroke their sleek fur, biting back the temptation to lift the covers, dive back in and hide from the real world for a little longer.

I'd feel better after a shower, I told myself firmly, and ventured into the bathroom.

Last week had been much easier. Modern life provided the perfect coping mechanism for the days following the death of a loved one: a huge mountain of jobs to be done. I'd had experience of it before when Mimi died. But then, of course, Gabe had had Gloria to help him as well as his own parents. This time I was in the thick of it. Gabe, Mags and I, with more restrained help from Percy, Gloria's solicitor, had formed a team of dogged 'doers', tackling our tasks with gusto, relieved to be occupied because it gave us an excuse not to dwell on our broken hearts too much.

'Well,' Mags would say briskly, pushing herself off the

sofa, 'I'm too busy to sit around here moping, I've got people to ring.'

'Cremation,' an email from Percy announced efficiently, 'and a humanist service. Good old Gloria got it all down in writing. Such a worry for relatives if they don't know these sorts of things.'

'I'd better get on to the funeral director,' Gabe would say, tapping his watch sharply. 'Lots to do if we're to have the funeral on Friday.'

'Order of service,' I'd pipe up. 'And flowers. I'll ask that lovely florist in Plumberry to do them. Or charity donations, what does everyone think? And catering. Leave the catering to me, I'll speak to Tom.'

And so it had gone on.

But now the funeral was over and we'd spent the week-end clearing up and then collapsing with exhaustion. But now Monday had come round again and with it a heaviness in my heart and a tremble in my breath.

I chose a smart dress and heels, the sort of outfit I used to wear to Solomon Insurance, tugged a brush through my hair and despite my mood felt reasonably pleased with the result.

Since coming to Plumberry, I hadn't had that Monday-morning feeling that had often assailed me when I'd worked at Solomon's. That slumping sensation that coincided with the early-morning alarm. For the last month I'd leapt out of bed, head full of ideas and to-do lists and body propelled by a lightness that I'd naively assumed would stay with me for ever.

Gloria had been responsible for that new zest for life. And Gloria, unthinkably, had gone.

The ten days since that terrible day had flashed by in a blur. I was still dizzy with shock from her death, still struggling to accept that she had truly left us. As Gabe had put it in his brave speech in the packed little crematorium chapel, she'd be reunited with her beloved daughter,

336

catching up on all the news. She'd be in a happy place, I knew, but the aching gap left by Mimi, only so recently patched up, had opened again and I was constantly having to remind myself how to smile.

It seemed that the whole of Plumberry had turned out to bid farewell to Gloria as well as old friends and colleagues from the newspaper in York and even far-flung acquaintances from her time at the TV studios in Nottingham.

A lovely lady, the messages of condolence read, a *much-loved face of Plumberry. We will miss her gentle ways and kind words.* Stacks of cards lined the reception desk at the cookery school, closed now for a time out of respect, but also because we simply didn't know which way to turn.

Maybe seeing Percy today, hearing Gloria's plans for a world without her, would help me to see a way forward, give me some stepping stones across my river of emotions.

Gloria had been right about Percy, I'd mused, watching him gnaw through the buffet Tom and Pixie had prepared in the cookery school after the funeral. He was a lovely chap, and I'd caught him dabbing at his eyes with a handkerchief several times during the course of the day, so he was obviously fond of Gloria, but he ate as if he were against the clock. I could see why that would have annoyed her, such a lover of food as she'd been. But he had been one of the few to stay and help and as the mourners had thinned out, he'd reached into his jacket pocket and handed me and Gabe an envelope each.

'Gloria changed her will on . . .' He'd stumbled over his words and pulled his handkerchief out again. 'The day she died. This letter is simply to say that you are both beneficiaries. I'm free on Monday morning if you'd like to pop in for a chat. Together or separately, as you wish. Nicer to discuss these things face to face, I always think.'

So that was what Gabe and I had arranged to do today at eleven o'clock, together.

I pulled a navy jacket from the wardrobe, slung it on and

left my bedroom. The dogs sprang awake and bombed past me down the stairs and I trudged after them.

I seemed to move more slowly now, as if grief had sapped my energy; the sensation of wading through treacle with reluctant limbs felt like the norm. My world had become more muffled too, as if it had been covered with a thick layer of icing, which blocked out the outside world and its sounds and mundane concerns. Neighbours still pottered about in their gardens, the little shops on Plumberry high street were still open, cars and pedestrians went about their everyday business and the news was still full of atrocities around the globe. But my routine had ceased to exist and the notion that other people could carry on as if nothing had happened had the power to shock me on a daily basis.

Don't you realize? I'd wanted to shout at the window cleaner last Thursday, when he'd casually told me to 'cheer up, it might never happen'. But I didn't. I merely opened the door wide enough to hand him his money and murmur my thanks.

Now it was time to snap out of it and pull my socks up; Gloria wouldn't want me to act this way, she'd want me to plunge back into life again, to seize the day.

I opened the back door to let out the dogs and busied myself with the kettle and a teabag while I waited for them to return. I wouldn't bother with breakfast; I didn't feel hungry, there was a nasty taste in my mouth, as though I was licking metal.

I'm falling out of love with food again, I thought with a pang.

I couldn't have felt more bereft if one of my own parents had passed away. In fact, Mum had called last night and the sound of her voice, laced with sympathy and love, made me long to jump on a plane to Canada and escape to the mountains for a couple of weeks.

But I couldn't do that; there were too many loose ends

in Plumberry to sort out. Not only of Gloria's but of my own.

I was acutely aware that Tom and I needed to talk. Properly talk. That Friday when Gloria died, Tom had broken my trust by pitching my Supper Club idea to the newspaper, but in his eyes, I'd lied too. It was obvious that he thought Gabe and I had had an affair and I hadn't been able to set him straight. We'd discussed funeral details instead and decided on catering for the wake and arrangements for the temporary closure of the cookery school.

His manner had been respectful and kind but it was clear he hadn't wanted to discuss 'us'. And at the time I'd been sort of grateful for that; my grief had been all-encompassing and I hadn't had the strength left for anything else.

I would put it right this week, I decided, as soon as I got the opportunity. Because even though it seemed that our blossoming romance wasn't to be, Tom was an important part of the cookery school and at the very least we needed to be amicable.

The dogs were still outside, so I took my tea into the garden to join them, inhaling the perfume of the lavender as the hem of my dress brushed past the purple fronds.

'Morning, chuck, don't you look a bobby dazzler.' Mags was leaning over the garden fence, tweaking dead heads off Gloria's roses. 'Sleep OK?'

My face softened at the sight of her. Not for Mags the black shades of mourning. Today's outfit was a kaftan printed with tropical birds and turquoise hairclips; a seam of bright colour, which served to lift my mood a notch.

'Not bad,' I said, smiling. 'Although I think I've been talking to myself.'

'Tell me about it.' Mags chuckled. 'It's when you start answering your own questions that you really need to worry.'

Being in Gloria's house without her was bittersweet. I missed her gentle presence so much that on several occasions I'd found myself straining for her voice as if I'd heard her calling my name just as she would do when she needed something fetching or carrying. Yet at the same time, there was a comfort in being in her cottage, as if the thick stone walls held echoes of her voice, the tinkle of her bangles and her gentle laugh.

But the night-time was the worst. That was when guilt crept up on me, burning like acid in my stomach. I should have spotted the signs of her illness, I muttered, should have insisted on calling the doctor, swept away her protestations.

And if I had, maybe Gloria would still be here.

Comfrey and Sage jumped up excitedly at the fence, knocking each other out of the way as Mags made cooing noises and produced a packet of dog treats and I couldn't help laughing at their antics. Sage, always the greediest, shoved his dark chocolate body in front of Comfrey and pawed at the fence.

'What's going to become of you boys, then, eh?' she tutted, giving me a sideways glance.

The dogs missed Gloria incredibly but in her absence they had attached themselves to me; they'd become my mini shadows, following my every move, joining me as I walked from room to room, even sitting as grim-faced sentries outside the door when I went to the loo.

'I'll adopt them,' I said rashly. Gloria had rescued them; no way was I sending them back to be rescued again. I didn't quite know what the future held for us over the next few months. But whatever happened, we would all stay together.

Mags beamed. 'That's good of you, love. I was going to offer, but Dave's mum's allergic . . .'

Her plump cheeks flushed and she dipped her head coyly. My heart squeezed happily for her. Dave had been an absolute rock since Gloria died, not only taking on the job of sorting out her financial affairs, but also being a shoulder for the big-hearted Mags to lean on. She was going to miss her friend so much in the coming months; I was glad she'd got Dave, even if his mum was allergic to dogs. I wished I'd got someone to lean on. My thoughts automatically turned to Tom and I gave myself a shake. No point stirring up those feelings today.

'I couldn't bear to live without you two now anyway,' I said, scooping them both up and kissing their silky heads, laughing as they tried to lick my face.

So that was one decision made, only three million to go.

'Right, I'd better go and get ready for the onslaught,' said Mags with a wink, and she disappeared back inside her own house.

She had offered to look after Noah while we were at the solicitor's office and he and Gabe would be here any second. They had stayed over that first awful night with me at the cottage, as had Rosie, but the next day Rosie had left for Nottingham and the Greens had returned to *The Neptune*. They were happier in their own space, Gabe explained, and he had commandeered Gloria's car to get around in, offering to stay close by as long as needs be.

I settled the boys in their basket, doling a chew stick out to each of them as a consolation prize for leaving them on their own as the doorbell rang.

My stomach churned; this was it.

Gabe, his face etched with concern, smiled grimly and held his hand out to me.

'Ready?'

I swallowed hard and nodded. I slipped my hand into his and hoped he didn't feel it trembling.

She knew about us.

The look of panic on Gabe's face when he'd read that

letter from Gloria and the look of disappointment on Tom's had haunted my nights. The pain of that evening would be seared on to my memory banks for ever.

I hoped whatever Percy was going to tell us today wouldn't make matters worse. If they could get any worse, that is . . .

Chapter 32

We walked towards the car, still holding hands. Gabe looked nice, smarter than usual in clean jeans, a checked shirt and black trainers. Gone were his floppy locks, too; he'd had a haircut before the funeral – something else to keep him busy. He opened the door for me and I climbed in.

'Any word from Tom?' he asked nonchalantly, sliding into the driver's seat.

I concentrated on fastening my seatbelt and shook my head. 'Not since the funeral.'

'Are you and he, er . . . ?' Gabe raised an enquiring eyebrow.

'He went back to Manchester after the funeral,' I said, avoiding a direct answer. 'On business.'

Rebecca and Ryan had made him an offer for his share of Salinger's and his solicitor and accountant were battling it out to secure him the best deal. Tom had decided to take advantage of the cookery school being closed to wrap up the negotiations as swiftly as possible. He was probably already planning his next move. Without me. My heart plummeted at the thought.

Gabe nodded and started the engine, not meeting my eye.

'It's probably for the best.'

'Why?' I said sharply.

He shrugged sheepishly. 'Who knows what's going to happen at the cookery school now? Perhaps he'll decide to leave Plumberry altogether. An ambitious bloke like him won't hang around for long.'

The skin at the back of my neck prickled. Gabe had summed up my worries exactly, although unlike me, he didn't sound particularly concerned at the prospect. But I'd miss Tom enormously. Even though things hadn't quite gone to plan between us, I liked him a lot and he was undoubtedly an asset to the cookery school.

Noah and Mags stood in the window of her front room waving us off. I smiled and waved back, my heart swelling with love for them both. Noah's hair was still long and wavy; he'd escaped the barber's chair last week and I was glad, there'd be plenty of time for short hair when he started school. But for now he could run free and wild and have hair as long as he wanted.

He and Mags would have a great time together; Mags had planned a fishing expedition at a shallow point in the river at the bottom of Hillside Lane. She'd bought some fishing nets especially and had tied string round jam jars to put their catch in. No doubt he'd be full of their exploits by the time we got back.

'Let's see what Percy has to say first before we jump to any conclusions, shall we?' I said tartly, drawing the topic to a close.

Gloria's solicitor had a smart little office above an antiques shop in the pretty village of Thickleton. Within half an hour of leaving home, we'd found a parking spot and arrived with a few minutes to spare, which Gabe used to drop a business card into the owner of the antiques shop. He might as well take on a bit of French polishing work if he was staying for a while, he told me.

'I love my job,' said Percy, waving us into his two visitors' chairs bang on eleven o'clock. 'Love the job and the job will love you, someone far cleverer than me once said. And by and large the two of us have got on just great.'

'I love *my* job,' said Gabe and I unison. We grinned at each other, the shared moment dissipating the cloud that had hung over us on the journey here, and I felt my spirits lift a little.

'Sometimes, though,' Percy continued, sitting on a leather swivel chair and wheeling himself close to his desk, 'a client will get under your skin and jobs like this one, well, I don't mind telling you, it breaks my heart to think I won't see those beautiful blue eyes again.'

He shook his head glumly and stared down at the pile of papers in front of him.

I stretched across the desk and patted his hand. 'Gloria always spoke of you very fondly, Percy.'

'Did she really?' He pulled a handkerchief out and blew his nose. 'Sorry about this. Not very professional, but we're people, aren't we, not machines? And if I can't be upset when I lose a dear friend, then there's something wrong with the world.'

'No need to apologize,' said Gabe kindly, who I happened to know had cried every night for two months when Mimi died. And had said something similar about Mimi's blue eyes.

'Strictly speaking, wills don't have to be read formally any more,' said Percy. 'But as there are two of you, it might be easier. Shall I just get on with it?'

Gabe reached for my hand.

My heart was thumping so loudly that I was sure even Percy would be able to hear it. 'Yes please.'

'I, Gloria Ramsbottom, being of sound mind . . .'

'You OK?' Gabe asked.

We were standing on the pavement outside the antiques shop. Our meeting was over but my pulse was still racing.

345

I took deep breaths to soothe my lungs, staring blindly at a Royal Albert dinner service displayed in the window.

Percy had summarized Gloria's wishes. In a nutshell (his words), Noah was to inherit Gloria's cottage and various investments; Gabe and I had been left equal shares in the cookery school. He and I had stared incredulously at each other at this. There were one or two other bequests, such as a lump sum for Mags and various charity donations, but the main beneficiaries were Gabe, Noah and me.

Percy then solemnly gave us a letter she had written to both of us. And as I'd read it, I'd heard her voice in my head as clearly as if she'd been in the room with us. It got more and more difficult to see the words as my eyes moved down the page.

'Verity?' Gabe's worried voice jolted me back to the moment.

'I'm . . . No, I'm not.' I stared up at him but my vision was still blurred with unshed tears and I couldn't see his features. 'I'm overwhelmed with loss. I miss her and I still miss Mimi and everything has happened so fast. And this inheritance . . . it's . . .' I choked back a sob. 'I don't deserve it.'

'Now that's not true.' Gabe wrapped his arms round me and we stood, as we'd done so many times in the last two years, with his cheek resting on the top of my head. United in our loss. 'No one deserves it more. I think the fact that she's left us in charge of her beloved cookery school must mean she didn't hold any grudge against us, what do you think?'

'I hope so. And she left Noah her cottage,' I conceded. 'That means a lot.'

Gabe nodded. 'He was her grandson. Mimi's son. That was all that mattered to Gloria.'

I exhaled a shaky breath that I felt I'd been holding since that afternoon in the hospital.

She knew about us.

My head felt swimmy and my legs were doing their best to keep me upright.

'The relief, Gabe.' My voice caught in my throat and I swallowed a sob. 'Keeping my promise to Mimi has been so difficult at times, and to think Gloria knew all along. I wish I could have spoken to her about it.'

'I know.' He sighed and raked a hand through his hair. 'You've been brilliant, just as Mimi knew you would be. We couldn't have wished for a better person to have on Team Baby Green. And I . . .' His voice faltered. 'I couldn't have managed without Mimi without you. If that makes any sense at all.'

After a long moment, I brushed the tears off my face and eased back to give him a watery smile. 'You know what? I will be OK. I just need some time to take it all in. Are you all right?'

Gabe nodded. 'Shocked, to be honest.' His face broke into an impish smile. 'I mean, you've got to see the funny side, Bloomers. Me, a man who can burn water, co-owner of a cookery school.'

I let out a most unbecoming snort. 'Gloria and Mimi will be having a right old giggle at that.'

'At my expense,' he said.

'What do you think you'll do?' I held my breath as a clutch of differing emotions crossed Gabe's face.

Finally, he spoke. 'Noah's growing up; maybe it's time to give up life on *The Neptune* and settle somewhere ready for him to go to school. But whether that's in Plumberry—' He broke off, looking unsure of himself and then gazed at me with a look that I couldn't quite decipher. 'Well, that sort of depends on you.'

'Me?' I raised an eyebrow.

'Actually . . . Look, forget I said anything.' He looked flustered all of a sudden. 'Gloria's will is a lot to take in; let's talk about it another time when we've had a chance to digest it. We're partners now.'

'Oh, gosh. So we are,' I gasped.

My head span suddenly. How did I even get to this point? Me, Verity Bloom, inheriting a business with Gabe Green. It was as if fate was determined to throw the two of us together. I shuddered as the familiar wave of guilt surged over me. Once again I appeared to have stepped into a situation that should have been Mimi's. Why was life so unfair to some and bountiful to others?

Gabe pressed the key fob to unlock the car and the lights flashed. 'Come on, let's get back to see whether that son of mine has caught any fish.'

I shook my head; I wasn't ready to go back. Not yet.

'I think I'll go for a walk, clear my head. If you don't mind?'

'Course not.'

He pressed a swift kiss to my cheek and with a cheery wave, drove back to Plumberry.

The river running through the centre of Thickleton, dividing the village in two, must be the same river that ran behind the cookery school. We were simply further downriver in Plumberry.

I called into a little sweet shop, bought myself a bottle of water and a Bounty bar and looked round for somewhere to perch. Further along the road, where the river crossed the village, was a grassy bank overlooking the water. A wrought-iron bench caught my eye and I wandered over and sat down.

I tore open the wrapper and began to nibble the milk chocolate away from one of the edges. It was the start of lunchtime and there were a few people milling about, coming in and out of the bank and the sweet shop I'd been into; there was a queue outside the post office and a young couple were staring at the antiques shop window display.

But I barely took them in; one bite of my chocolate bar and I was instantly transported back to the end of April when Gloria had called me. It had been the day I'd been made redundant and she'd asked me to come to Plumberry to help. I remembered thinking how appalled she'd be if she knew what I was eating for lunch.

How things had changed in only six weeks. Since then, we'd successfully opened a wonderful cookery school which had become the heart of the community, I'd fallen in love with cooking again and almost . . . My stomach churned as I got to the part about Tom. I'd almost lost my heart to him. But *almost* was a long way from *actually*. Maybe Gabe was right and it would be a good thing if Tom left Plumberry; I had enough to contend with, without my heart pinging every time Tom MacDonald walked into the room.

I blew out a sharp breath and dropped the chocolate bar into its wrapper. Stick to the point, Verity, I told myself firmly. The point was that Gloria had started something very special that she now couldn't be part of. She wanted Gabe and me to take over. Gabe and I were to be joint owners. And if I was right, reading between the lines of her letter, she was hoping that we would be more than simply business partners. Stepping into Gloria's shoes and running the cookery school was one thing. Stepping into Mimi's shoes was quite another.

A twig caught my eye as it swirled past, carried along by the river. I knew how it felt; right now confusion and guilt inside me were flowing so strongly that I was in danger of being washed away on a tide of tears.

I slipped the letter out of my bag, took a fortifying breath and read it again.

Dear darling Gabe and Verity,
Percy has all the details of what I want doing with my assets, house, business and whatnot. But the really important thing is what happens to the people I love after I've gone.
My true legacy isn't an accumulation of objects or money, but the wonderful unconventional family that I leave behind. You

two aren't my flesh and blood, and yet you are as much like my own as Mimi ever was and I love you just the same. And little Noah, the brightest star in our family's sky . . . When Mimi's test revealed her infertility, I never thought she'd be a mother or that I'd be a grandmother. He is our little miracle and although I have often been far away from him, I love him with every beat of my heart.

I know that you care for one another and that what binds you is your love for Mimi and Noah. My greatest wish is that this love grows deeper and that the two of you will guard my legacy with every breath. To be a family is to be part of something very special, and you, Verity, Gabe and Noah, are my legacy, my future and the most special part of my life.

Be happy my darlings,
Love always
Gloria

A shiver ran down my spine as an image of Mimi on her wedding day popped into my head. Her eyes shining up at Gabe as they turned in slow circles on the dance floor, Lou Reed belting out 'Perfect Day' in his leathery voice. There might have been no one else there; they were totally and utterly absorbed by their love for each other.

If Gabe had read the same message into Gloria's words as I had, he didn't mention it. But why would he? I was just Bloomers, Mimi's mate, Noah's godmother, wasn't I . . . ?

A familiar figure strode along on the other side of the river and I felt my mouth curve upwards at the corners. It was Dave, dressed in outdoor gear: lightweight stone-coloured trousers, hiking boots and one of those T-shirts that is supposed to wick away moisture before you could say 'damp patches'. He was holding a brown paper bag by its top corner.

Dave's calming presence was exactly what I needed right now. I drew in a mighty breath to yell his name at the precise second that he spotted me with my mouth open and eyes wide. He gave me a startled look and raised his hand in a tentative wave. I quickly closed my mouth and waved back.

He crossed the stone bridge over the river and walked towards me.

'Greetings.' He looked down at the melted chocolate bar. 'Lunch?'

I grinned sheepishly. Didn't look great, did it, the new owner of the Plumberry School of Comfort Food scoffing junk food for her lunch?

'Not the healthiest, but I'm afraid I seem to have reverted to comfort eating.'

'If it's not an intrusion, I'll share mine.' He held up the paper bag and raised an eyebrow questioningly. 'This is healthy-ish and definitely comforting.'

I shuffled up the bench in response and Dave sat down.

He opened the bag and a mouth-watering aroma of spices and steam escaped. Inside were about a dozen golden balls, deep fried and still hot.

'Have a Gujarati kachori,' he said, holding the bag under my nose. 'The humble cousin of the samosa, but no less delicious.'

'Where did you get these from?' I scanned the row of village shops for a likely outlet but couldn't see anything. I took a kachori, blew on it and inhaled its glorious smell.

'My friend, Neeta – actually, she's my yoga teacher – lives in Thickleton. She sends me a text when she's made a fresh batch and I walk over to collect them.' He bit into one. 'Mmm. Worth a special trip for.'

'Yum,' I said, biting into the centre. Inside the crispy outer layer was a bright green pea filling and the flavours of India burst into life in my mouth: ginger, chilli and mustard seeds. My tastebuds gave a silent cheer at the arrival of real food.

'Neeta says that every meal is worthy of celebration,' said

351

Dave with a reproving look at my mauled Bounty. 'Have another.'

'Neeta knows what she's talking about. And boy, can she cook. *And* she teaches yoga? I'm surprised you haven't snapped her up.' I smiled teasingly at him. 'She sounds just your cup of tea.'

He smiled softly. 'We were close for a while. But Neeta floats through life without rippling the pond. She's a delight but . . .' He shrugged.

My eyebrows lifted a notch. 'But?'

'She's not got enough oomph for me.' He glanced sideways at me.

I understood; it was all about yin and yang. Neeta was perhaps too similar in personality to Dave. 'Mags has got oomph.'

'Bags of it.' Dave grinned.

I studied his face, so open and honest. He was obviously smitten with Mags and my heart twisted with happiness for him. For a second. And then my face fell.

'I'm sorry,' said Dave instantly. 'Very insensitive of me, smiling like a Cheshire cat when you've lost a loved one. Not that I wasn't fond of Gloria, I was, of course, but . . .' He shuffled on his seat awkwardly and shoved the bag at me. 'Have another.'

I did and the two of us ate in companionable silence for a minute or two. I took a drink from my bottle of water and then offered it to him.

'I'm not great company today, I'm afraid, Dave. My emotions are all over the place.'

He took a sip and set the bottle on the bench between us.

'Life may seem like a hill too steep to climb just now,' he said, patting my hand, 'but take your time and you'll get there.'

I stared at him, really wanting to unburden myself. I doubted he'd truly understand that I felt guilty at profiting from such sadness but I knew he'd be a good listener. He was such a wise man and I couldn't think of anyone better to talk to.

'Have you ever felt really guilty about something even though it wasn't your fault?' I asked.

Dave's brow creased with concern. 'Verity, if there's something troubling you, you know I'll help if I can.'

I chewed my lip for a second.

'OK. Well . . .' I took a deep breath and haltingly told him how when Mimi died and I'd survived the initial shock of her tragic death, my overriding emotion had been one of guilt. Guilt that I was still alive, guilt that I was turning thirty-one, then thirty-two, and still living my life. I felt guilty for seeing Noah take his first steps, for helping him blow the candles out on his third birthday cake and guilty for hugging her husband tightly when he sobbed into my hair that he couldn't do it without her. Sometimes I'd even felt guilty for breathing.

'Because if Mimi can't do any of these simple things, then it isn't fair that I should either,' I said, brushing the tears from my face.

Dave sat so still that for a moment I thought he'd dropped off to sleep but when I looked at him his eyes were moist. He nodded encouragingly and took my hand in his.

'And now Gloria has left the cookery school to me and Gabe,' I said in a wobbly voice. 'Which is a wonderful, generous thing to do. And yet . . . if things had been different, it would have been him and Mimi. And even though the logical part of my brain is telling me that Mimi isn't here, I feel as if I'm stepping into what would have been Mimi's life instead of striking out on my own. And I am not sure if I can do it.'

Dave fumbled in his pocket and handed me a clean napkin.

'Well, I absolutely know that you can do it. And more than that, I'm one hundred per cent sure that Mimi will be cheering you on every step of the way.'

I shook my head. 'That's just it. What if she's not? How do you know?'

He exhaled a long, heartfelt breath. 'Because I've been through the same thing and I know exactly how you feel.'

I dabbed at my tears. 'Do you?' I said doubtfully.

'I was a twin, you know,' he said with a faraway smile. 'I had a brother, Michael. He was disabled, spent his life in a wheelchair. He died when we were twenty-two. The doctors had said he wouldn't live that long, so every birthday that we celebrated together was a gift.'

'Oh Dave, what a thing to live with.'

He nodded. 'My twenty-third birthday felt very odd, I can tell you, with no one to share it with. So there's not a lot you can teach me about guilt.'

'Sorry.' I winced, ironically feeling a teensy bit guiltier now. 'I have been a bit self-absorbed.'

He chuckled. 'No need for that. Anyway, when we were kids, there were none of these fancy wheelchairs with motors. My brother had arms like Popeye from pushing himself around. When it came to arm-wrestling, no one stood a chance against Michael.'

His eyes softened and he gazed out at the river, lost in his memories.

'All the lads used to play football on the street in front of our house. "Coming out for a game, Dave?" they'd say. And my skin would crawl with guilt that Michael couldn't join us. I'd be outside playing and Michael would be stuck inside watching from the window. Sometimes I felt so bad about it that I'd pretend I didn't want to play.'

'That must have been hard for you,' I said softly.

He nodded. 'Michael wasn't having any of it. "Get out there and play. And play twice as well, have twice as much fun," he'd say. "You're playing for me too, remember." I never forgot that.'

He scooted closer along the bench and took my hand.

'Just because Michael couldn't enjoy something, he had

no wish for me to lose out. Do you see? It's the same for you and Mimi.'

I swallowed. 'Really?'

'Yes! It is incredibly sad to lose someone so young; it's sad to lose anyone we love. But I'm sure neither Gloria nor Mimi would want you to miss out on life just because they're not here. Why waste your life feeling guilty? Live for Mimi too, remember, and have twice as much fun.'

I nodded slowly, letting his message sink in. The more I thought about it, the more I realized that Mimi would have loved that idea. A glow of happiness began to build and build inside me until my face broke into a wide smile. She had always been like a ray of sunshine in my life; somehow I had let that light go out, too scared to let it shine. But Dave was right: Mimi's life might have been cut short, just like Michael's, but she would be cheering me on to see me achieve my dreams.

'I never thought of it like that. You are so right. Thank you.' Impulsively I threw my arms round his neck and kissed his cheek. 'For the food and for the words of wisdom. And for making Mags so happy and for putting things in perspective so wonderfully.'

'You're welcome,' he said with a gentle smile.

'You know, your philosophy on life reminds me a little bit of Mags's principle of pleasure. No wonder the two of you get on.'

He chuckled. 'I've worshipped her from afar ever since I became Gloria's accountant. I thought she was out of my league. Still do, if I'm honest.'

'Well, I think you're a match made in heaven.'

He went pink and I reached to hug him again before standing to leave.

'Namaste.' I bowed. 'The spirit in me adores the spirit in you.'

Dave's eyes twinkled. 'Namaste, Verity.'

*

355

I hopped on the Plumberry bus feeling happier than I'd done in ages and with my thoughts in some semblance of order. Mimi would always be a part of who I was; she'd been there when I was growing up, she'd shared some of my best moments and I would never have another best friend like her as long as I lived. And Gloria . . . well, Gloria had told me, only a couple of weeks ago, that life was short. Gosh, how prophetic that had turned out to be.

Promise me you won't waste a single chance to be happy, she had said.

As the bus bounced along the country lanes away from Thickleton, I sent up a silent promise to Gloria. I was very much still alive and I planned to make the most of every moment.

Chapter 33

The bus dropped me outside the Plumberry cheesemonger's. I waved to Harriet, who was lifting a wheel of stilton out of the chiller in the window and she immediately plopped the cheese down and scampered outside.

'Sorry,' she said, wrinkling her nose as she released me from a cheesy hug. I was hugged a lot now, as Gloria's friends and acquaintances seemed to do it to express their sorrow. She wiped her palms on her apron. 'You'll probably smell of stilton for the rest of the day now.'

'That's OK.' I grinned. I liked Harriet; she'd been one of the few contenders at the Plumberry Bake Off to remain unruffled despite the fact that her twice-baked soufflé had sunk almost without trace. 'Thanks for coming to the funeral, by the way.'

'Wouldn't have missed it for the world. Such a shame; she was a feisty old bird,' said Harriet with a lopsided smile. She looped her long fair hair behind her ears and studied me. 'I'm glad I caught you. I've had a couple of customers ask about cheese-making courses and I think you should run one.'

'Oh, right, well,' I hesitated, 'I'll look into it.'

We had all the equipment to make cheese. Gloria had thought of everything. But I needed to get my head around the running of the business before we started anything new. I'd have to arrange a meeting with Dave straight away,

I realized. And Gabe, of course. And sit Mags and Pixie down and let them know what was happening. Gosh, now that I thought about it, I had heaps to do . . .

A small sigh escaped from my mouth and Harriet's face fell.

'I hope you don't think I'm tactless talking about work so soon after Gloria's death,' she said, 'but . . . Well, I can't help noticing that you're still closed and the trouble is, people soon find somewhere else to spend their money. And Gloria wouldn't have wanted that, I'm sure.'

'You're right, she wouldn't.' I smiled. 'Actually, that's just the sort of advice I need to hear.'

She squeezed my arm. 'Phew. I've been running this shop for ten years; feel free to pick my brains any time you need to.'

My eyebrows lifted. Ten years? She didn't look old enough.

'Family business,' she said, in answer to my expression. 'Took over from my dad. Were you and Gloria related?'

I thought back to Gloria's letter: *You are as much like my own as Mimi ever was and I love you just the same.*

'Sort of.' I laughed softly. 'We're family, anyway. Albeit an unconventional one.'

Harriet nodded and then we both stepped aside as a man came out of the shop clutching a paper bag.

'Bye, thank you,' Harriet called after him.

I had a sudden flashback to the moment I'd bumped into Tom in this exact spot when Comfrey and Sage had done a runner.

'Hey, have you got any Yorkshire Blue?' I asked impulsively.

I bought a hefty wedge of the local soft blue cheese from Harriet and some plump tomatoes from Pete, the greengrocer, who insisted on giving me his mother's chutney recipe and a jar of it to try. Then Jack the butcher flagged me down to suggest the idea of running a butchery course. Nobody knows how to even joint a chicken these days, he'd grumbled, tucking two large marrowbones for the dogs into a bag.

Gabe's car – or rather, Gloria's – was in the car park when I turned into the side street towards the cookery school. I was pretty weighed down with all my bags, but my heart was light; the people in Plumberry genuinely wanted the cookery school to succeed and with that sort of support behind me right now I felt I could conquer anything.

The cookery school was just ahead and to me it had never looked so beautiful. The sun bounced off its welcoming stone walls and glinted off its acres of sparkling glass. The waterwheel, which was my absolute favourite bit of the building, had ripples of light running across it from the sun's reflection in the river and my spirits soared.

I lifted my eyes to the blue sky and the cottony clouds.

Thank you, Gloria, for trusting me with your business. I will make you proud.

There was so much I could do – we could do – with the cookery school. So far we'd barely scratched the surface. We could run joint courses with some of the other neighbouring businesses, I thought, raising a hand to Judy, who owned the candle shop at the far side of the car park. And then there was the brewery next door; perhaps we could run a beer and food matching event . . .

A sudden thought hit me. Would Gabe want all this? To leave his simple life on *The Neptune* behind, where he only worked as much as he needed to get by? It would be another massive change for him and Noah. But he must be considering it because . . . what had he said earlier . . . ? Something about it depending on me? And if he didn't move to Plumberry, what then? Would he want to sell his half? My stomach lurched. I didn't want that, although I didn't see how I could afford to buy him out . . .

Breathe, Verity.

I forced myself to calm down and stop second-guessing Gabe's thoughts. I'd ask him, simple as that, and then I'd know. Right, panic over.

I pushed open the doors and went into the cookery school to find him.

There was an almighty racket coming from the Aga kitchen. The sort of noise that could only be generated by a three-year-old boy.

Sure enough, Noah and Pixie were marching across the room towards the deck; he was crashing two saucepan lids together whilst she was banging the bottom of a pan with a wooden spoon.

'What's cooking?' I said, laughing as I set my bags down.

'Not *cooking*,' said Noah, bouncing up and down on the spot. 'I'm starting a band.'

'I see.' My heart squeezed at his total gorgeousness. His green eyes danced with delight and his floppy hair, just like his dad's, fell over one eye. He was practically edible.

In the very dim and distant past, Mimi and I had done the very same thing, raiding kitchen cupboards for things that made the most noise. The cheese grater and a metal spoon had been a particular favourite, I remembered. Although we'd quickly grown tired of hitting the pans (as had our mothers) and had started cooking with them instead. Hopefully, Noah would go the same way.

'We're setting up outside on the deck, where we won't disturb anyone quite so much.' Pixie ruffled Noah's hair and smiled at me. 'I said I'd keep an eye on him, while Mags gives Gabe the proper tour. He's told us the news. About you and him being the new owners. I'm happy for you, if that doesn't seem too weird in the circumstances?'

'I know what you mean.' I nodded. 'It hasn't quite sunk in yet.'

Gabe and I needed to have a proper talk, I had no idea how he felt about co-owning a business in Yorkshire. But asking for a tour sounded promising. Unless he was checking out the assets for a quick sale, of course . . .

I brushed the thought away and held my arms out to Noah instead. 'Do I get a hug?'

'OK.' Noah sighed dramatically and lolloped over to me, not overly enthusiastically, I had to say.

I caught Pixie's eye and we shared a smile but inside I felt a tiny stab of disappointment. How long until he outright refused? Surely I'd have a few more years of burying my face in the soft hollow between neck and shoulder, inhaling his toasty smell, before he held himself at arm's length?

'Do shout if you want help, Pixie, won't you?' I said, releasing Noah, who instantly ran outside and commenced banging again.

Although we had cancelled all the cookery courses for this week, the blogger day for Fresh from the Sea was still going ahead as planned tomorrow. It didn't require much input from us, Tom had reasoned, all we had to do was get the workstations ready for the bloggers and have refreshments laid out for them in the morning when they arrived. They were providing everything else themselves: from the food to the staff to the goody bags. But because we'd had Gloria's wake here on Friday, this room needed some reorganizing.

'I can manage.' She shrugged. 'I'm going to give all the surfaces an extra polish, I think. I want everything to shine.'

'Is this still to impress Tom? Because I'm not sure he'll be able to organize an internship for you at Salinger's if he's sold his share.'

The thought of Tom made my insides quiver. He was due in later this afternoon and I was hoping to have a private word with him, set a few things straight. Even if I had totally blown my chances with him, I wanted him to know the truth about Gabe and me.

Pixie scuffed her toe against the wooden floor and shook her head.

'Not really. This blogger day could be good for us. I want the bloggers to go away and write about how amazing we are.' She paused to look at me. 'And then you won't shut the cookery school down.'

'Oh, Pixie.' I opened my arms and she stepped forward for a hug far more readily than Noah. 'We won't be closing the cookery school if I've got anything to do with it. But I appreciate your efforts.'

'Good. Because I love this job,' she said tremulously. 'I love it here. And as my granddad always says, if you want something badly enough you have to fight for it.'

'Well said, Granddad,' I chuckled.

'Didn't do him any good when he got caught taking snuff at the day care centre, mind you,' she said philosophically. 'Got banned for a month for punching the staff.'

We snorted with laughter until Noah started waving his arms.

'Kingfisher!' he yelled from the deck. 'Look!'

Pixie and I exchanged amused looks and I left her to investigate the appearance of the kingfisher. My mind full of images of a snuff-pinching, staff-punching geriatric, I popped my food purchases in the fridge and went off in search of Gabe and Mags.

Upstairs in the office, Gabe was sitting in Gloria's chair and Mags was standing behind him, boobs almost resting on his shoulder. They were engrossed in the computer and didn't hear me come in.

'So if we want to add a quick note, like "course fully booked" or something, we can just type it in here and the website is instantly updated,' Mags explained, pointing at the screen.

Gabe pushed his chair back and looked up at Mags. 'The last time I worked in an office, I was a solicitor and my desk was covered with stacks of files and more paperwork than I could read in a year. I'm impressed; you seem to be almost paper-free.'

'Hello, you two,' I said, coming forward. 'But not quite paper-free. This is Gloria we're talking about, remember? She had scraps of paper coming out of her ears. Try the drawers.'

Gabe tugged at the top one. It was so crammed full of paper that he struggled to open it.

'I see what you mean,' he grunted.

'Ooh, Gloria's recipe bible,' Mags exclaimed, lifting the large folder from the top of the heap. 'These are all the recipes she collected throughout her career.'

Several pages fluttered out of the folder and I stooped to pick them up.

'This was the starting point for the cookery school, you know.' Her eyes glittered with tears as she looked down at the pages. 'She wanted to share her passion with people. And she never got to do that.'

Gabe and I exchanged glances and I slipped my arm round Mags's shoulder.

'The Plumberry School of Comfort Food is here, though, Mags,' I comforted her. 'She poured her heart and soul into it, even if she never got to teach a course.'

'And hopefully it'll be here for a long time to come,' Gabe added.

I looked at him and my heart jolted; I hoped so too.

'She was a wonderful woman. And friend. I miss her so much,' said Mags, adding with a wan smile, 'and her lovely food. But I'm so glad she had you two to pass the school on to. We're in safe hands, I'm sure.'

I nodded and squeezed her tightly. But a lot still depended on Gabe and the sooner he and I could get our heads together, the better.

After a moment of silence, she slipped the folder back into the drawer.

'All this paperwork will have to be sorted out, I suppose,'

she said, sighing heavily. Her chin began to wobble.

'Plenty of time for all that,' I said softly. 'We'll do it between us when we're ready.'

Mags pressed her lips together and nodded bravely. 'If you've seen everything you need to see, Gabe, I'll go and put the kettle on and see if I can find Tom's secret stash of biscuits.'

Gabe confirmed that he'd seen enough for now and Mags set off downstairs.

'By the way, Noah's starting a band,' I called after her. 'You might need ear plugs down there.'

She laughed and shook her head.

'Great.' Gabe grinned.

'Noah *is* great,' I agreed, perching on the edge of Gloria's desk. I was going to have to stop calling it that . . . 'It's impossible to feel low when he's around. I could munch him up. He's—'

'Verity . . .' Gabe's urgent tone stopped me in my tracks and sent a shiver down my spine. 'That note that the physio handed me in the hospital . . .'

I stared at him. 'From Gloria? Yes?'

I'd asked to see it when Tom had done his disappearing act, but Gabe had glanced at Noah and Rosie meaningfully and shoved it in his pocket, muttering that it could wait.

Now he took a deep breath and placed his palms on the desk as if bracing himself.

'She said that she had always had her suspicions about Noah and when she saw the photos of his sports day it all fell into place. But the important thing is, she gave us her blessing, she knew how important you are to Noah. To me.' He gazed at me so intensely that I could almost feel his eyes on me. 'Verity, she left us both the cookery school so that we could run it as a *family* business.'

I nodded. 'I thought that too. But it would be tricky for you, wouldn't it? I mean, I'd already accepted a permanent job here. Not that I've had a chance to talk to Rosie about it properly yet, what with the funeral . . .' I paused, conscious of beginning a nervous waffle. 'Sorry.'

He scooted his chair along the desk until he was sitting directly in front of me and took my hands.

'I think Gloria was giving us her blessing.'

I swallowed, not entirely comfortable with the direction this conversation was taking or the new way Gabe was looking at me, touching me . . .

'Do you have the note?' I blurted out.

He shook his head. 'I was all over the place that day: losing Gloria, and trying to shield Noah from what was going on. And seeing you upset about Tom . . . I put it in my pocket but by the time I got back to the cottage, it had gone. Dropped out probably.'

I sighed. 'What Tom heard did such a lot of damage to our relationship, I really—'

'Noah needs a mum,' Gabe cut in. 'And who better than you? We can be a proper family: you, me and Noah. Verity, I've loved you for years.'

My heart pounded; he was right. There was no one better than me. But *me and Gabe*?

'As a friend,' I said, half-laughing. 'You've loved me as a friend, that's all.'

'Verity,' he stared at me with his soft grey eyes, willing me to listen, 'nobody knows me better than you. Nobody understands me like you do. Even when I jacked in my career, you didn't try to change my mind, you simply accepted it and helped me through it. I couldn't have survived these last couple of years without you by my side.'

My mouth had gone bone dry. Where was Mags with that tea?

'Thanks, Gabe, but we're mates, that's what mates do. And Noah . . . Well, after all the flippin' effort we went through to bring him into the world, I'm not going to abandon him now he's here, am I?' I laughed, trying to diffuse some of the electricity in the room.

I much preferred it when he punched my arm and called me Bloomers.

Mimi, I'm mortified. Please know that this isn't going to happen. He's lonely and clutching at straws, that's all.

'Oh, Verity. We're much more than just mates. You know that.'

And then everything seemed to stand still, the room slipped out of focus as Gabe cupped my face in his hands and kissed me gently. We'd kissed before millions of times but this kiss was different. This kiss crossed a boundary. One I wasn't sure we'd ever be able to uncross. My skin pricked with goosebumps and my heart crashed wildly against my ribs.

'Gabe!' I gasped, pulling away from him. 'Wow. Um, I don't know what to say.'

His shoulders sagged as his eyes scanned mine anxiously.

'Look,' I said, deliberately keeping my tone light, 'I love you too . . .'

But only as a friend, I was going to say, but the words died on my lips as a flash of movement caught my eye.

Tom had appeared in the doorway.

'Tom. Hi!' A wave of nausea ricocheted through me. I leapt to my feet, adding unnecessarily, 'You've arrived.'

He was already backing away.

'Whoops, I'm sorry,' he winced, holding his hands up. 'Didn't mean to intrude. Ignore me, I'll come back later.'

'No, no, don't go, you're not interrupting . . .' I spluttered.

'Verity?' Gabe cleared his throat in a tone that implied that yes, Tom was very much interrupting.

Poor Tom. His eyes locked on to mine for a second. He rubbed a hand across his forehead and then stared down at the floor. My heart went out to him and it was all I could do not to run over and pull him into my arms.

This was such a mess.

Think, Verity. I took a deep breath. OK. First I needed to make my feelings clear to Gabe and then explain absolutely everything to Tom.

But before I had the chance to do anything, raised voices wafted up from downstairs.

The three of us stared at each other for a split second before we heard a scream followed by a shout from Mags.

'Oh my God! Noah! Gabe, Verity? Quick, Noah's missing!'

Chapter 34

'Shit.' Gabe shot out of his chair and bolted for the door.

I propelled myself forward, almost falling over my feet in my haste to follow him. My heart seemed to double in size and all I could hear was a deafening heartbeat.

Tom and I raced down the stairs behind Gabe.

Pixie had tears streaming down her face and was waving her arms round, her words getting scrambled as she tried to explain what was going on.

Mags was trying to pacify her. 'Calmly, Pixie, tell us what happened.'

'He was there,' Pixie sobbed, pointing through the open doors to the Aga kitchen. Her cheeks were streaked with black mascara. 'Just there. On the deck banging his saucepans and shouting at the top of his voice. I went to the loo and when I came back. Nothing. Silence. I ran out to the deck and it was empty. I even looked over the railings and he wasn't there. I'm so sorry, Gabe.'

'Hey, it's not your fault.' Gabe was frowning, both hands in his hair as his eyes roamed reception. 'I'm sure he can't be far. He might even be hiding.'

I have no idea how his voice could remain so calm, I didn't even think I could speak right then. My knees were trembling and my mind had gone into overdrive. Had he been snatched? Had he simply taken the hand of a stranger and been led away? Did he know about stranger danger? And would he even recognize a situation as being potentially dangerous? Possibly not. Lovely innocent little Noah would go anywhere if the lure of chocolate or the chance to see puppies had been dangled in front of him.

'Mags, could he have come past you?' Tom asked.

'I don't know. Possibly,' she said, wringing her hands together. 'I popped in the prep room to put the kettle on for a few seconds.'

We all glanced at the glass doors. They were very heavy. I doubted he'd be able to open them by himself. And the railings on the deck were high; he couldn't have climbed over them, could he?

My heart heaved with pain. If anyone – *anyone* – had touched a hair on his beautiful little head, I'd kill them, I was sure of it. Although right at that second I couldn't even move. I was petrified. Literally rooted to the spot. I didn't know what to do with myself.

Oh God.

A knife twisted in the pit of my stomach and I clutched at the desk to stop myself from fainting with fear. Tom grabbed my arm and hauled me up. I leaned into him, grateful of his solid presence.

'NOAH!' Gabe yelled. 'Come on, dude, where are you?'

He darted into the men's toilets and came back seconds later shaking his head.

'Mags, call the police.' Tom spoke with calm authority. He glanced at Gabe. 'Just to be on the safe side. If he has wandered off, we don't want to waste any time.'

Gabe nodded grimly and Mags ran to the phone on her desk.

Police.

The word galvanized me into action. I shook free of Tom's hand on my arm and ran through the Aga kitchen, my eyes scanning under the tables, behind the huge cream Aga that stood at the front of the room; I looked behind every door, opened every cupboard. There was no sign of him.

'Noah, are you in here?' I cried.

No reply. The room was empty. I stumbled outside and the sight of the pile of saucepans, metal lids and wooden spoons – the makings of his little band – abandoned on the wooden deck nearly undid me. Fear stabbed at my lungs so sharply that I thought I'd never breathe again. This was every parent's nightmare. To lose a child. To not know where he is even for five minutes was torture. I couldn't bear it. I couldn't bear to lose him.

I leaned over the edge of the balustrade and searched the rocks below. There was no sign of life. Just the urgent chirp of some bird or other and I couldn't even see that. Where was he? A wail rose in my throat.

'Noah!' I hurled my voice out at the river. 'Where are you, baby boy?'

There was no reply. I sank to my knees, my hands sliding down the wooden balustrade as silent, heaving sobs racked my body.

'Let's split up,' I heard Tom say. 'Pixie, try every nook and cranny in the cookery school. Gabe let's go outside, we'll take one side of the car park each.'

Tom. Thank goodness he was here. While all of us were flapping, he was taking charge.

I heard the entrance doors open and close again as the two men ran outside, shouting Noah's name. I heard Mags on the phone giving the details to the police and I heard Pixie opening doors and calling to him too.

Meanwhile I stood up, blood whooshing through my veins and my head pounding. My body was shaking so violently that I thought I might actually keel over. I gripped the wooden railings tighter and sucked in big panicky breaths.

Had he climbed over here, perhaps? Was he unconscious on the rocks below? A sob hiccupped in my throat and I let my head droop and the tears course down my face and drop on to the rocks.

So this was terror. This was what it felt like to have your heart ripped out.

'NOAH!' I yelled again.

A glimpse of white fabric caught my eye. Not fabric, but leather, I realized, as my eyes focused on the object wedged between two rocks. My heart pounded. It was one of Noah's trainers.

'His shoe!' I screamed.

I thought back to Gloria's letter to Gabe and me: *Guard my legacy with every breath.*

A fine job we'd done of that so far.

Without stopping to consider the wisdom of my actions, I kicked off my high heels and climbed over the wooden railings. I lowered myself gingerly down the other side. My shoulder muscles burned instantly from holding my own body weight and I could feel my fingers already beginning to slip. I didn't dare look down, I guessed it would probably only be a couple of feet to the rocks, but even so, I realized, I could potentially break an ankle as I fell. I waggled my toes around but I could only feel empty air.

What had possessed me to try this without help? I could have kicked myself, what a stupid thing to do; now not only was Noah lost, but I was in trouble too. I was about to shout for help when my fingers suddenly lost their grip and I landed with a thud, crying out in pain as I stubbed the toes of my left foot on a sharp rock.

I squatted down on to my bottom to relieve the pressure on my ankle. I had landed on a rocky ledge that jutted over the water, thankfully just high enough to stay out of the spray from the river. If the rocks had been wet, I'd probably have slipped and fallen in. It was deep and fast-flowing, the water a dark green murky colour. I eased myself forward and dipped my sore foot in the cold water. The strength of the current and the icy temperature took my breath away.

The river was narrow here and I could probably cross it in one long stride. But Noah wouldn't be able to. I shuddered; if he'd fallen in . . . I shook my head, not wanting to contemplate that possibility.

In the distance I could hear Gabe shouting for his son. He must be somewhere at the side of the building by the waterwheel. My heart sank; that meant Noah was still missing.

Noah, where the hell are you?

The mud bank on the other side of the river was covered in trees with ferns growing beneath them down to the water's edge. I scanned left and right, but there was no sign of a small boy.

I pulled my foot out of the water and stretched out an arm to pick up Noah's trainer. The lace was still done up in a tight double bow and my heart thundered as my mind raced: how could it possibly have come off? A struggle? Another wave of nausea hit me and I groaned.

'Noah!' I yelled again and turned over on to all fours to begin a search along the rocks.

'Oh!' I gasped.

There was a gap of maybe a metre between the underside of the deck and the rocks and there was Noah, sitting with his legs stretched out, completely hidden from view from up above.

My little angel. Our little miracle. His bright eyes wide with delight as he pressed a finger to his lips.

I burst into tears again and crawled towards him, easing myself under the deck, shaking with relief and pent-up fear.

'Oh thank goodness, you're all right!' I sobbed.

'Shush!' He pointed excitedly at something he was shielding with his other hand on his lap. 'Look! Baby bird, Aunty Verity.'

'Noah Green!' My voice came out as a squeak. 'We were so worried about you.'

He removed his hand as I got closer to reveal a tiny

bird. Its beak was almost as long as its entire body and it opened its mouth hopefully as I moved to stroke it. The little thing was covered in dull blue feathers on his back with two white flashes at the neck and an orange tummy. A baby kingfisher.

'It fell out of the nest and its mummy has been looking for it. She has been making a lot of noise. Shouting PEEP, PEEP, PEEP really loud. I think she was scared,' he whispered solemnly. 'So I'm keeping it safe.'

Oh, the irony.

I scooped him and the baby bird on to my lap. I have never hugged another person so tightly in my life. I kissed his face over and over again, until he protested at being soaked by my tears.

I had loved the bones of this boy since he entered the world. He was only an hour old when I first saw him, first experienced that rush of love that had grown and grown with time. The last ten minutes had been the worst of my life; I'd never forget them for as long as I lived. But they were over, he was safe, and I doubted whether I'd ever be able to let him out of my sight again.

My stomach was still fluttering with love and nerves and the after-effects of sheer panic and I inhaled two or three times before speaking again.

'Didn't you hear us calling you?' I said breathlessly.

He nodded. 'But this is a baby,' he explained, looking down at the little kingfisher in his lap. 'At nursery we're not allowed to shout near the babies.'

'Oh, I see,' I said, my face breaking into a smile. 'Well remembered.'

'And all babies are special, aren't they?'

'Yes.' My voice was muffled from burying my face into his neck. 'Especially you.'

He stuck his bottom lip out, protesting that he wasn't a baby and I laughed and cried at the same time, feeling deliriously, hysterically happy.

'Now I've got to shout. Just once,' I added as Noah opened his mouth to complain. 'Because everyone is looking for you.'

He tutted and cupped his hands to protect the bird's head.

'I've found him!' I yelled as loudly as I could, my voice still wobbly with emotion. 'I've found Noah; we're on the rocks under the deck.'

And then after I'd fitted Noah's trainer back on to his foot (it had got trapped between the rocks so he'd pulled his foot free, he explained), we crawled out from underneath the wooden boards and I picked up my godson and held him close, breathing in his little-boy smell.

Gabe came thundering around the corner, slipping and stumbling on the rocks. He threw his arms round both of us.

'Oh, mate.' He brushed Noah's wavy hair from his face and kissed him. 'Don't do that to me.'

'Careful, Daddy!' Noah gurgled, holding up the kingfisher fledgling. 'You'll crush the baby. I'm looking after it.'

Gabe looked at the bird and then at me. Our eyes softened with shared relief.

'Well done for finding him,' he murmured. His lips came close to mine and I turned my face so that his kiss landed on my cheek.

I cleared my throat. 'I've never been so scared in my life, Gabe.'

Gabe tightened his grip. 'That's because you love him just as much as I do. Think about it, we're family. That's what he needs. That's what I need.'

I didn't know how to answer that. I swallowed, tears burning my eyes and took a deep breath.

On our annual bluebell walk back in April to celebrate Mimi's life, Gabe had hinted that he might be ready to move on, start another relationship. And although I'd been shocked at the time, he was a young man with a young son and he'd been on his own for two years; it was only natural that he would want a woman in his life again. But never in a million years had I expected that woman to be me.

I'd said I loved Gabe. And I did. And today I'd realized just how fiercely I loved Noah too.

Gabe was waiting for some sort of response. His soft grey eyes burned into mine with such intensity that my insides trembled.

'I can see that,' I said finally. 'But right now this baby bird needs his mum.'

A shadow of disappointment passed across Gabe's face and his eyes fell away from mine.

'That must be the burrow,' he murmured, pointing to a small hole in the mud bank opposite. He took the baby bird from Noah's little hands and carefully straddled the river, popping the little kingfisher back inside.

'There,' I beamed, blinking away the tears. I brushed my lips against Noah's face. 'Safe and sound. Just like you.'

'Hello down there,' Pixie called from the deck, waving her arms to catch our attention. 'Mags is calling the police back with the good news. Hey, little dude, what was with the Spider-Man act?'

'Sorry,' said Noah. He pressed his face to mine. 'But I'm a good climber, aren't I?'

He grinned cheekily and we rubbed noses.

'The best,' I agreed.

'You've got him?' Tom appeared from the same direction as Gabe had come from. His dark hair was standing on end and he was out of breath. He pressed a hand to his chest and exhaled. 'Thank heavens for that.'

'Yeah, thanks, mate,' said Gabe, stepping forward with his hand outstretched.

Tom shook Gabe's hand distractedly. He was staring at me. And at Noah. And then at me. His eyes narrowed.

'You two look so . . . so similar,' he said, shaking his head incredulously. 'The green eyes, the curve of your cheek bones, the line of your eyebrows, even your earlobes. It's uncanny.'

A shiver ran up my spine and I felt a flush to my cheeks.

Noah wriggled to be let down and I lowered him to the rocks, reluctant to ever let him go again. It was true, I thought, looking at Noah's eyebrows. I'd inherited my dad's straight eyebrows, always envying Matt for getting Mum's lovely arched ones. And I had weird earlobes like Noah, as in hardly any lobe at all. Noah had got his dad's unruly hair but not his pale grey eyes. His eyes were as green as mine.

My eyes flitted to Gabe. His mouth twisted and he raised his eyebrows. *It's up to you now,* he seemed to be saying.

I looked back at Tom and my heart thumped for him. There were a thousand different things I liked about him, his dark good looks – obviously – but more than that. He had a loving heart, he was kind and thoughtful and he made my own heart rise like the perfect Victoria sponge. I cared about him and I wanted him to care about me again, the way he had before Gloria died, before he'd suspected me of having an affair with Gabe.

And all of a sudden I'd had enough of keeping Mimi's secret. Wouldn't honesty be the best policy anyway? For all concerned? Gloria had already guessed and for all I knew she'd told Mags and one day, probably soon, we'd have to start feeding titbits of information to Noah. Surely it would be better all round to come clean . . .

I took a deep breath. I took a step forward and reached for Tom's hand.

He frowned and his eyes flicked to Gabe.

'It's complicated,' I began, tightening my grip on his warm strong fingers.

Mags chose that moment to come barrelling on to the deck. 'Come on back up, my lovelies, the kettle's boiled and I've got Noah's favourite.'

'Chocolate cake?' Noah bounced on his toes.

'Got it in one, chuck,' she laughed.

'Chocolate? Bagsy the biggest slice.' Tom grinned. He withdrew his hand from mine and leaned in close.

'It's OK, Verity, you don't have to explain yourself to me, it's fine,' he said stoically. 'Come on, Noah,' he said, holding out his hand to the little boy. 'You can tell me all about your boat. What's it called again?'

'*The Neptune*,' Noah answered, merrily falling into step with Tom. 'I've got a bed under the window and twelve dinosaurs.'

Gabe slipped an arm round my shoulders and my stomach lurched as I watched Tom walk away hand in hand with our boy.

'Coming in for cake?' he murmured.

I pressed my lips together and shook my head. 'I need to get home and let the dogs out. I'll see you later.'

He caught my fingers as I moved away. 'I do love you, you know.'

I gave him a watery smile. 'I know,' I whispered.

But falling in love with me had never been part of the deal.

Chapter 35

I left the others enjoying thick wedges of a delicious-looking chocolate torte that Tom had brought back from Salinger's and walked out of the Plumberry School of Comfort Food with my bags of goodies from my earlier shop.

Simon from the micro-brewery pulled into the car park just as I was leaving. We waved to each other, but I wasn't in the mood to stop and chat. I wanted to be alone for a few minutes, just me and my whirring thoughts . . .

I rounded the corner on to Plumberry high street, my heart lifting as usual at the striped awnings over the shop-fronts, the lovely creamy-yellow stone of the buildings and the huge planters filled with riotous summer flowers. I smiled at Annabel in the wine merchants and bent to inhale the fat bunches of sweet-smelling stocks outside the florist.

What a day it had been! My lips curved into a smile. The Green men had always been a source of excitement in my life; well, so had Mimi, I supposed.

I left the high street behind and lost myself in my memories as I headed back to Hillside Lane.

Mimi had been devastated when she found out at the age of twenty-seven that she was infertile. She'd gone through the menopause early. It was called Premature Ovarian Failure, she'd told me.

'My ovaries are a failure, I'm a failure and Gabe will probably want a divorce.'

What could I say to make matters any better? Nothing. So I simply held her and soothed her, handing her tissues and topping up her glass when she attempted to drown her sorrows in White Zinfandel.

Despite Gabe's assurances that he'd be happy to adopt if she wanted to or even not have children at all if that's what she'd prefer, Mimi couldn't get over the fact that she couldn't have the baby she longed for to make her family complete.

It had been an awful couple of months and for the first time in their relationship I began to wonder whether the two of them would make it through.

'All I've ever wanted is to be a mum,' she'd sobbed over a bottle of rosé and a takeaway pizza one night, after Chris, my fiancé, had tactfully made himself scarce for the evening. She'd cradled her hoody in her arms. 'To hold my own baby like this, tuck him or her into bed at night.'

It had torn me apart to see her so defeated. Out of all our friends at school, she'd been the first to get married, the first to buy a proper house and now the first to encounter a real, desperately sad, grown-up problem.

At the time, Chris and I were storming ahead with our careers. We were engaged, had the house in Heron Drive, and had tentatively talked about a wedding abroad the following year. But a family? No, that was way, way, way off our radar. Something for the future, definitely, but I wasn't even thirty; I had plenty of time to have a baby.

'And you still can be a mum,' I'd said gently. 'It just might be a bit more complicated.'

She'd shaken her head, a hollow expression in her blue eyes. 'Adoption is not for me. And IVF using my own eggs isn't an option. My only hope is going on the waiting list for a donor egg.'

'There you go,' I'd said brightly. 'Where there's hope, there's life. Anne Frank said that, so it must be true.'

Her face had crumpled, lines of tears making tracks

down her pale cheeks. 'That could take years. I could be forty before I reach the top of the list.'

'If it's eggs you want,' I'd said straight away, 'you can have some of mine. Then you won't have to wait.'

She'd blinked the tears from her eyes and stared at me. 'You'd do that for me, for me and Gabe?'

'Absolutely,' I'd said simply.

'But promise me it will be our secret,' she'd whispered, squeezing my hands until I thought they might drop off completely. 'Just mine, yours and Gabe's? Then everyone will think it's really my baby.'

I'd thought about that for a moment, watching as she pressed a hand to her flat stomach, a smile spreading across her face as she imagined the baby that could grow inside her.

'I promise, but Chris needs to know. And my parents,' I'd countered. 'Just in case anything goes wrong.'

'OK,' she'd conceded. 'But I'm not telling anyone, not even Mum. I want my baby to be mine from the very first second I get pregnant.'

'And it will be.'

'Verity, I love you so much. Never forget that.'

Her eyes had sparkled for the first time in weeks and my heart sang with joy that it had been me that made her smile again.

'And don't forget: mum's the word,' she'd added, wagging her finger playfully.

After that the human dynamo that was Mimi Green sprang into action. She talked Gabe round. That was the easy part – Gabe Green had been wrapped around Mimi Ramsbottom's little finger since he was sixteen. The rest took some time, effort and lots of money.

The three of us formed Team Baby Green and together we attended various counselling sessions: 'You're going to be reminded of this baby's existence every time you see him or her,' the counsellor had warned me. 'It's more complicated than being an anonymous donor.'

But it was only my egg, I reasoned, when I broke the news to Chris. This was about Mimi and Gabe and giving them the raw materials they needed to make a family.

My fiancé had been against it from the outset. He had been worried for me and for us.

'What about the risks?' he'd argued. 'The fertility drugs you'll need to take. Not to mention the procedure when they harvest your eggs. What if you can never have your own kids after that? What about us?'

'I'm young and healthy,' I'd countered. 'The risks are so minimal they're hardly worth bothering with. There'll be plenty of time for us, I promise.'

I'd have my own shot at motherhood further down the line, I'd explained to my mum. But this was something I wanted to do. It would cost me nothing and would mean the world to Mimi and Gabe.

'You make it sound so clinical,' Mum had mithered. 'What if you fall in love with the baby? I don't want to see you hurt. And I'm telling you now, you're in danger of losing Chris over this. Think of him. Verity, be careful, I really think you might regret this.'

She'd been right about Chris. He was adamant that I shouldn't go ahead and gave me an ultimatum: him or Mimi. I'd been devastated. I was hurt that he was making me choose and upset that he wouldn't support me in doing what I felt wholeheartedly was the right thing to do. It had broken my heart to call off our engagement. But what could I do? By this time Mimi was knee-deep in baby names and Gabe had had to ban her from any more online baby shopping. I couldn't have let her down. It had been unthinkable.

My decision didn't go down well with my family. Mum had urged me to reconsider and save my relationship with Chris. Dad had been less vocal, but I knew he'd been upset by the whole business too. It had pained me to lose their support and when my brother announced that he and Celia were expecting a baby and my parents made the decision to emigrate to be near their family, my sadness was compounded. The inference wasn't lost on me and for the first time I almost wavered. But Mum had been wrong about having regrets. Because only a year and a half later, after a course of fertility drugs for both of us and countless ultrasound scans and blood tests, Noah Gabriel Green came bawling into the world weighing a whopping nine pounds and ten ounces.

Our baby had been born. And I hadn't regretted a single thing. Although keeping that first promise had been a bit of a tall order.

I slipped my key into the front door at number eight Hillside Lane and lowered my bags to the floor as two little dogs came scampering towards me.

'Wait until you see what Jack the butcher has sent for you,' I laughed, pressing kisses into their whiskery faces.

Comfrey and Sage tucked straight into their marrowbones on the patio while I settled myself with a pot of tea and my phone in the garden.

After the dramas of the day: meeting the solicitor, hearing Gloria's will and losing and finding Noah, there was only one person's voice I was longing to hear.

It was mid-morning in Canada and I held my breath as the international dialling tone began to ring, hoping that she was at home.

'The Bloom family residence,' Mum answered gaily.

My chest heaved with emotion and it took me a moment to muster up the power of speech.

'Oh, Mum.'

'Darling, what is it?' I could almost see her furrowed brow.

'Today has been one of the most traumatic days of my life,' I said in a wobbly voice. 'I could really do with a hug.'

And breaking off only to sip my tea and dab my tears, I poured my heart out to my mum. I told her about inheriting the cookery school with Gabe and that although it was an amazing opportunity, I'd felt guilty about Gloria's generous bequest. I told her about Dave and his philosophy on life and how he'd made me realize that I needed to make the most of life and that Gloria had even said something similar a couple of weeks ago. I described how it felt as if Gloria was trying to encourage Gabe and me to get together and how weird that was, especially as Gabe seemed to be thinking along those lines too. And that now he had kissed me and was waiting for an answer. We could be a family, he'd said . . .

Finally, I took her through the harrowing ten minutes during which Noah had been missing. My little boy. My not-quite-but-almost son.

'The sheer horror of it, Mum, I can't begin to explain,' I said tearfully, shuddering at the memory. 'That little face, his pudgy arms, the little curls at the nape of his neck . . . Every inch of him is so precious to me. And if I lost him . . .'

'Oh, darling. What a time you're having,' she gasped. 'And you didn't lose him, thank goodness. But what an ordeal for you all.'

'Say it if you like,' I said in a small voice. 'Say, I told you so. *It's only an egg*, I said when I told you my plans. I thought I was just supplying the magic ingredient that Mimi and Gabe were missing. But it was more than that, wasn't it?'

I could hear the hesitation down the line. 'For what it's worth, looking back, I think what you did for Mimi was an incredibly selfless thing. Brave and caring. I couldn't have done it. I was bitterly disappointed for you and Chris, of course. I'd been so looking forward to seeing you get married. And I felt cheated, too, that I had a grandchild that I couldn't openly acknowledge. I knew that would

383

be too hard to bear, which was one of the reasons that your father and I decided to move to Canada, to remove ourselves from the situation.'

'Mum,' I gasped, 'I had no idea you felt so deeply about it.'

'Which was exactly how I wanted it, Verity,' she said softly. 'You had enough on your plate without worrying about silly old me. Anyway, I worried enough for the both of us. My big concern in this was that you would get hurt somewhere along the line, that you would have regrets and want the baby back. And my levels of worry quadrupled once Mimi died and there was a mummy-shaped hole in his little life.'

'It has been really hard to keep my distance since then,' I admitted. 'But I had to; I'd promised Mimi that she would always be his mummy.'

'And legally she will be, won't she?' Mum pointed out. 'But that doesn't mean that you can't love him too, listen to all his stories, be there when he needs you. You can still do that, can't you?'

'I've always loved him, Mum. And even if I have children of my own, you know, with a man and everything—' We both giggled at that. 'I'll still love Noah, but today felt different somehow, like I'd uncovered a new depth to my love for him.'

Mum sighed such a heartfelt sigh that I felt her concern all the way from Canada. 'You know what that is, don't you?'

'Panic? Fear?'

'It's more than that, darling,' she said softly. 'It's maternal love.'

I nodded even though she couldn't see me. She was right. Mothers were fiercely protective creatures, I'd discovered; I'd have given my own life today for Noah if I'd had to.

'I wish I could put my arms round you, Verity. I miss you so much. Not just now, but I miss the relationship we had before all this. I should have been more supportive, I realize that now. I was selfish and I regret that.' She paused and then murmured so softly that I had to strain to hear her. 'I miss the little things we used to do together.'

Tears pricked at the back of my eyes. I'd pushed Mum away when I began my fertility treatment because she didn't agree with my life choices. I hadn't wanted to listen, thought she was trying to interfere, talk me out of it. Now I saw that she was motivated by a special love that I'd only just begun to appreciate for myself, a bond so strong that we would fight like tigers to protect those that we cared for – the love of a mother.

'Me too,' I said huskily.

'Oh, darling.' Just hearing the smile in her voice made me feel warm inside. 'Whenever you were sad, do you remember what we'd make together to cheer you up?'

'Er . . .' I racked my brains to pinpoint a memory of the two of us in the kitchen. 'Oh, chocolate bites!' I said with a grin.

'That was about my limit in the baking department.' She chuckled. 'Good job you came across Gloria when you did.'

'Mum,' I pressed a hand to my throat, 'I'm sorry for how things have been between us.'

'Me too,' said Mum, with a crack in her voice. 'I miss having my girl around. Celia's nice enough but,' she whispered close to the phone, 'very strict where sweets are concerned. Cake is a big no-no in her house.'

We shared a chuckle and I felt Mum's love, as sweet and comforting as the simple chocolate fridge cake I'd forgotten about, wrap itself around me across the miles.

'Have I helped at all, love?' she said finally after we'd finished laughing.

'More than you'll ever know, Mum.' I smiled. 'I love you.'

*

After I'd hung up, I swallowed the last of my tea and, checking that the dogs were still happily chomping on their bones, I went inside.

I set a bowl above a pan of simmering water, broke a bar of chocolate into it and added butter and golden syrup.

I must have been about five when Mum and I had first made this recipe together. I'd been out in the car with Dad and he'd accidentally shut my thumb in the car door. We'd driven home, both of us ashen-faced – he was mortified and I was in shock. He'd managed to drive one-handed, his other hand wrapped around mine with his white handkerchief soaking up the blood from my throbbing thumbnail.

Mum had made Dad a cup of sweet tea and sent him to watch telly, put a plaster on my thumb and sat me at a high stool at the kitchen worktop. Together we had broken up cubes of chocolate and smashed digestive biscuits with her rolling pin. She didn't tell me off when I'd turned the biscuits into a pile of crumbs instead of the large pieces she'd wanted and I'd been allowed to lick the spoon after measuring out the golden syrup and scrape the bowl after we'd melted the chocolate in it. She'd kissed my poorly thumb over and over again and told me that I was her precious girl.

Happy, happy times.

Now I opened the cupboard, took out Gloria's red silicone baking tray and pressed the gooey chocolatey mixture down firmly before popping it into the fridge.

The next time I make this, I thought, as I licked the spoon, I shall make it with Noah and I shall tell him just how precious he is to me.

Chapter 36

Later that night, Dave joined Mags and me for dinner. I did feel a bit of a gooseberry at times, but it was nice to have company. Dave left after a pudding of strawberries and cream, to go and help his mum get ready for bed. She'd moved in with him after having a stroke a couple of years ago, he'd told me, and he'd become her chief carer. At which point Mags had gone all gooey-eyed and I left them to it and cleared up.

After he'd gone, Mags and I made a start on tidying away some of Gloria's things. Just toiletries from the bathroom; we weren't ready to tackle her bedroom yet. It had been sad, but we'd felt better for making at least a little progress and had rewarded ourselves with a glass of rosé or three in the garden, swapping stories about Gloria.

Mags told me about the time Gloria made Scotch eggs for a picnic feature on a TV show. She had been in such a panic to get them ready for the start of filming that she forgot to peel the eggs. She realized just as the programme went live on air and sat cringing out of shot. She thought she'd got away with it until right at the end, when the presenter finished the feature by saying '*Bon appetit*' and taking a big crunchy bite of Scotch egg, shell and all, before adding in a strangled voice, 'Mmm, delicious.'

'She's never touched one since,' Mags recalled with a laugh.

'Gloria was so patient with us,' I said with a chuckle, 'despite us creating havoc in her beloved kitchen at home.'

I passed Mags one of my chocolate bites. She bit into it and we laughed as a shower of biscuit crumbs disappeared down her cleavage.

'I'll never forget the day Mimi and I tried to melt chocolate on Gloria's hob. It was the first time I ever made these without Mum's help. And I almost got it right,' I remembered, twinkling my eyes at Mags. 'I set the bowl over the pan and turned the heat up high.'

She nodded. 'Sounds right to me.'

'Then Gloria came in sniffing the air. "Something's burning," she announced. Mimi rolled her eyes at her mother as only teenagers can do just as a plume of grey smoke appeared from under the chocolate bowl. We'd forgotten to put water in the pan and we burned a hole in the bottom!'

We said goodnight not long afterwards and despite half-expecting to have nightmares about losing Noah again, I slept very well. Quite possibly thanks to the bottle of wine Mags and I had downed between us.

The next morning dawned bright and clear with just a hint of haze over the grassy lawn as the dew began to evaporate in the warm sunshine.

The Fresh from the Sea crew were arriving before nine to get set up and I wanted to be in early to talk to them about joint marketing opportunities before the bloggers arrived for their morning pastries at ten. Len, Mags's elderly neighbour on the other side, had already collected Comfrey and Sage and was treating them to a long walk by the river followed by a lazy morning in his garden. Which meant that I could be out nice and early too.

We miss you, Gloria, I murmured to myself as I passed the box of her make-up and body lotions that we'd parcelled up last night in the hallway. *Your things might be disappearing from sight, but you'll be forever in our hearts.*

Tom was upstairs in the teaching kitchen sharpening his knives on a steel when I arrived. I hovered indecisively, wanting to break the ice before going into the office. He looked up briefly and nodded, before concentrating on the blade again. Fair enough; one slip and he could lose a finger but even so . . .

How had we come to this, I thought with a pang of disappointment. Only two weeks ago, we were shooting each other secret smiles across the room when no one was looking. Now he could hardly bear to look at me.

I'd had my doubts about going ahead with the blogger day today, but now I was glad, if only to see Tom in his chef whites, I thought with a flutter. It would be wonderful to see the cookery school buzzing with life again and as we hadn't had to organize this session ourselves, it was a nice way to ease back into business. Running the cookery school had been such fun in the beginning; the atmosphere between us all had been great. It would take some time to get back to that, I realized, after losing Gloria. But aside from that, would Tom and I ever get back to the easy banter we'd shared? Maybe today, having strangers around us would help ease the tension?

OK, thirty seconds in and neither of us had spoken. *Come on, Verity, say something.*

'Morning, Tom.'

'Morning.'

I cleared my throat and stopped next to him to watch while I waited for conversational inspiration to strike. It was mesmerizing. Back and forward went the blade of his knife in smooth strokes, over and under the steel so fast that the long blade became a blur of glinting metal.

He stopped and grinned and my heart literally went boom. He held the knife and the steel out to me.

'Fancy a go?'

I swallowed and nodded. 'Will you show me?'

'Sure,' he said in that lilting Irish voice that made my heart sing.

He moved to stand behind me. I was completely conscious of the mere centimetres between us and it was all I could do not to cave in and wrap my arms around his neck.

But I didn't. Firstly, because things between us were all stilted and wrong. Something I planned to sort out today. Now, in fact, if I got a chance. And secondly, he was holding a very sharp knife very close to my bare arm.

He was so close I could smell him: a faint perfume of clean linen, lemons and something inexplicably Tom. I could pick him out in a blindfold test just by his smell, I thought randomly. He was entirely nerve-tinglingly delicious.

It was that scene from *Ghost* again. Just like when he showed me how to knead bread, before he thought that Gabe and I were a thing. And, I remembered with sudden clarity, before he'd rung the newspaper and claimed the new Supper Club as his idea . . . Something else to sort out today. My stomach lurched at the prospect.

'Now,' Tom murmured softly in my ear, 'are you paying attention?'

His voice sent shivers down my spine.

'I am,' I said, glad he couldn't see my face, which had gone pink.

'OK.' He placed the knife in my right hand and the steel in the other. 'Keep your fingers away from the butt.'

'Yeah, that goes for you too,' I laughed.

There was a pregnant pause when Tom appeared to process my innuendo. Just long enough for me to really regret it.

I cleared my throat. 'Sorry.'

'This is the butt,' he said, rubbing his thumb over the metal guard that separated the handle of the steel from the shaft.

'Long strokes. Connect the bottom of the steel with the bottom of the blade and stroke it up.'

He paused, as if expecting me to make another joke. I didn't dare; I focused on the knife instead and tried to think pure thoughts.

His strong hands guided mine as the knife glided across the steel at a forty-five-degree angle.

'Sharpen the whole of the blade. Over and under, over and under,' he said softly, his breath tickling my ear.

'Got it,' I said. Then instantly regretted it as he released my hands and let me work alone.

'Concentrate and relax.'

Concentrate *and* relax? Easier said than done. My arms had already turned to jelly now they were doing it by themselves. And with him watching me like a hawk, I was all fingers and thumbs.

I decided to do a few more strokes to show willing until I couldn't take the silence any more.

'About yesterday,' I began, laying the knife and steel on the counter in front of us.

Tom folded his arms and smiled softly. 'Ah yes. How is Noah? None the worse for his adventure, I hope?'

'He's fine,' I said, unable to stop my lips curling into a smile. 'Although Gabe said he sat on deck glued to his binoculars last night on the lookout for any more baby birds that might need rescuing.'

He chuckled and shook his head. 'He's a lovely lad,' he said, his dark eyes piercing mine. 'You must be proud.'

This was my opening. 'Yes, I am.' I wet my lips and searched for the right words. 'Tom. Gabe and me—'

Tom held his hands up. 'There's no need to explain, Verity.'

I met his gaze.

'Yes, there is,' I replied defiantly.

Tom gave an exasperated sigh, glanced up at the ceiling and ran a hand through his hair.

'Look, if you don't mind,' he said in a low voice, 'let's stick to business. The sale of Salinger's is going through quicker than I thought and I need to consider my options. I don't mean to be insensitive so soon after Gloria's death, but what are your plans for the cookery school?'

I chewed the inside of my mouth, wondering what to say. Gabe had plans, but they revolved around the two of us taking our relationship to a place that I'd never contemplated. Would he still want to run the cookery school as a 'family business', as he'd put it yesterday, when I turned him down?

'Honestly? I don't know.' I sighed. 'Gabe did mention something about moving here. Settling down so Noah will be ready to go to school in Plumberry next year.'

'Figures,' Tom muttered.

'Well, Noah does own Gloria's cottage.' I shrugged, refusing to be drawn. 'So it kind of makes sense.'

Tom gave a hollow laugh, which made my skin prickle with goosebumps. So much for clearing the air. 'It makes perfect sense.'

One more time, Verity, give it another go.

I took a deep breath and stepped towards him, conscious of my racing pulse.

'Tom, I can see how things must look to you. But I made a promise to Mimi not to talk about . . . stuff and—'

'Mimi?' He shook his head in confusion. 'What about me? What I don't understand is why you didn't come clean about you and him?'

'There isn't a me and him,' I retorted.

'So that kiss yesterday was a figment of my imagination? You said I love you to Gabe, or did I mishear that?' He stared at me challengingly.

'No, but—'

He frowned and folded his arms even tighter until his shoulders were almost at ear-level. 'I thought for a while back there that you and me . . . That we had a chance to start afresh. Especially after what our respective partners had done to us. You know how I felt when Rebecca cheated on me and all the time you had this secret thing going on with Gabe.'

My temper flared suddenly. He was being so infuriating; refusing to let me explain and now accusing me of this.

'I could say the same of you,' I said, cursing my high-pitched tone.

'I beg your pardon?' Tom's eyes narrowed.

'Going to the newspaper, telling them about the new Supper Club.' I folded my arms to mirror his body language. '"I won't steal your ideas like Liam did," you said. You *promised* me. Yet only hours later I caught you red-handed when that journalist phoned. I even had to supply the date for the first one for the article!'

My voice had gone a bit shouty and I cleared my throat.

'Oh, that's out today.' Tom frowned absentmindedly as if he'd just remembered.

As if. I bet he'd ordered a copy. I bet he had a folder of press clippings marking all his cheffy achievements.

'Great,' I said sulkily.

Tom's face softened. With guilt probably.

'Look, I'm sorry if you're not happy about the article. It was Gloria's idea, she asked me to arrange it as a surprise.'

I pursed my lips. 'Wow. Now that *is* low. Blaming it on Gloria.'

He shook his head. 'I'm not blaming anyone.'

'Oh, really?'

'Let me explain.' He held his hands up in a calming gesture but I'd heard enough.

'Why should I? You won't listen to me and I've tried to explain dozens of times.'

The two of us stared at each other angrily. I was breathless with indignation and he looked utterly cheesed off. But neither of us spoke; there was someone stomping up the staircase and once again the chance to resolve our differences had vanished into thin air.

Pixie bounded up to us, completely oblivious to the bad vibes, and looked from Tom to me and back again.

'Er, let me guess,' she grinned, pressing both hands to her temples, 'it was the chef in the kitchen with the carving knife. That was a Cluedo reference, in case you didn't get it.'

'I got it,' I said stoutly, feigning a smile.

'And what do you think to my T-shirt?'

She stretched the sides out so we could see the whole slogan. It read 'plenty more fish in the sea'.

'Like it?' She elbowed me in the ribs. 'See what I did there?'

'Very good,' Tom muttered.

'Because we've got Fresh from the Sea coming in, yeah?' Pixie explained unnecessarily.

'We got it the first time,' said Tom through gritted teeth.

'Oh, for God's sake.' Pixie rolled her eyes dramatically. 'Anyone would think someone had died.'

I closed my eyes and took a deep breath.

She squealed and clapped both hands over her mouth. 'Sorry. I'm such a numpty.'

I sighed and rubbed her arm. 'No harm done.'

'Pixie, did you come up here for a reason?' Tom asked, still looking stern.

She nodded. 'The seafood people are here. Mags is showing them round.'

'Thanks,' said Tom curtly.

Pixie bit her lip and looked about to say something else but evidently changed her mind and ran off downstairs. Tom picked up his knife and the sharpening steel and slid them both back into his canvas knife roll.

'Look, Tom,' I exhaled a sharp breath, 'Gloria would hate to see us at loggerheads like this. Let's just put our differences aside for today and give these bloggers a day to remember.'

'You can rely on me to be professional,' he said, and with a brief nod strode off down the stairs to greet our guests.

Tears pricked at my eyes as I watched him disappear from view. I just hoped I could rely on myself to be the same.

Chapter 37

When I joined them all on the deck, Pixie was leaning over the railings pointing out the wildlife below to a portly man with rimless glasses and a white coat. Tom and Mags were chatting to a girl wearing a cream and blue smock-style dress that reminded me of Cornish blue crockery. Her shoulder-length brown hair was tucked behind her ears, which stuck out just a bit more than the norm.

'I'm sooo grateful to you for hosting us today,' she was saying. She moved a lot when she talked, jiggling from foot to foot. Her arms were all over the place too. Mags flinched as the girl's coffee slopped out of her mug and splashed Mags's arm.

'Our place was totally flooded out and our test kitchen has had to be ripped out and rebuilt. Total nightmare,' she continued, shaking her head in despair. 'You were lucky not to be affected, being on the river.'

'Rachel, can I introduce Verity, our marketing director,' said Tom. He placed a hand in the small of Rachel's back and gestured towards me as I approached them.

Rachel turned, one hand resting on Tom's arm. Her cheeks were rosy and her skin glowed with youth and health. She was standing far too close to Tom for my liking.

'Hi.' I smiled, which made me realize that I'd been clenching my jaw. I extended a hand, forcing her to remove hers from Tom. 'Good to meet you.'

'We've spoken on the phone,' Rachel and I said in unison and then both laughed.

Rachel dragged her colleague from the railings of the deck to meet me. He was Leon, the company's recipe developer and former fishmonger. What he didn't know about fish wasn't worth knowing, she announced proudly.

Leon and Tom fell into conversation about pin boners and filleting knives, and Rachel took Mags and me through her itinerary for the day.

'The bloggers should be here any minute,' she said, checking an enormous rose-gold watch.

'Well, we're all ready upstairs for them,' I said. 'There are fifteen, aren't there?'

'We've had two cancel at the last minute, so thirteen are coming.' She pulled a face. 'Hope that isn't going to be unlucky for some. I need this event to go swimmingly; the last one I organized was a disaster. You heard about the food poisoning at our launch, I presume?'

Mags and I nodded.

Rachel lowered her voice to a whisper. 'Thought I was going to get the sack. Especially when I heard your Tom was ill too. A Michelin-starred chef. The shame! I felt so guilty.'

Your Tom. My heart performed a somersault. If only. I liked her a lot more for saying it, though.

'And a food journalist was poisoned too, wasn't he?' Mags put in.

Poor Rachel shuddered. 'Don't remind me.'

'But it wasn't your fault,' I soothed, giving her arm a pat. 'You shouldn't feel guilty about it.'

Listen to me, doling out advice about shrugging off guilt. I felt quite proud of myself.

'You're too kind,' Rachel beamed. 'In fact, you're all lovely.'

She cast a lingering look Tom's way.

'Come on, I'll show you upstairs,' I said swiftly, taking

her arm. 'We can talk about joint promotional opportunities while we're at it.'

By eleven o'clock the thirteen bloggers (eleven women, including one heavily pregnant one, and two men) had arrived and were tying up their Fresh from the Sea aprons in the teaching kitchen. I'd assumed that they'd all write food blogs, but that wasn't the case.

'We're reaching out to all corners of the blogging community,' Rachel explained, in between shepherding her guests into two rows for a group photo. 'Mummy bloggers and lifestyle bloggers as well as the foodie ones.'

I raised my eyebrows, impressed. 'And what is your goal for today?'

'We want to show that preparing and cooking fish from scratch can be fun, quick and easy. Just as good for a simple family supper as for an elegant dinner. We aim to be the number-one fish brand in the UK within five years.'

'Very ambitious.' I thought briefly of my box of Birds Eye fish fingers languishing at the back of my freezer back in Nottingham. My ultimate comfort food, as it had been since I was knee high to a prawn. I didn't fancy Rachel's chances of success, but I liked her optimism.

Leon was laying out a whole side of salmon at the teaching station. He coughed, stood up straight and laid his palms flat either side of his chopping board.

'Ooh, excuse me.' Rachel widened her eyes. 'Looks like Leon's ready. Wish me luck!'

'Good luck!' I said, holding up crossed fingers.

I moved to the back of the room to get out of the way and Pixie came to join me while Rachel beckoned everyone to the waiting chairs set out around the teaching station.

'I've got all the recipes in this pack for you,' she said, holding up a pile of plastic wallets with her company logo on them. 'And Leon is going to start by demonstrating how to slice a whole side of smoked salmon.'

'You'll each have one of these at your workstation,' said Leon in a gruff Scottish accent. He held up a long thin knife with a rounded end. He waggled his eyebrows. 'Ingeniously known as a salmon slicing knife.'

'Once he's done that, you can all have a go at slicing your own salmon,' Rachel chimed in.

'And I'll come round to assist those that need it,' said Leon.

Tom raised a hand. 'I'll be hanging around to give anyone a helping hand too. I've sharpened my knives especially.'

His eyes sought mine across the seated crowd and my heart gave a little squeeze. He dropped his gaze instantly to the floor and my spirits dived with it. He looked as sad as I felt. What a crazy situation to be in. I could kick myself for letting this misunderstanding continue between us, but there never seemed to be enough time to clear the air. I'd do it this evening, I resolved. I'd wait until the Fresh from the Sea party had left and then nab him when he was on his own . . .

'Tom and I have met several times,' said Rachel as an aside. 'And it's always a pleasure to work with such a talented man.'

'What's that got to do with the price of fish,' I muttered to Pixie, folding my arms.

She polished her glasses on her T-shirt and snorted. 'Very good.'

'I think she's got a soft spot for Tom. Do you think it's mutual?' I whispered, as the two of them enjoyed a bit of banter for the amusement of the bloggers.

'Nah.' She wrinkled her nose, popping her glasses back on. 'I think there's only a place in his heart for one woman. Plaice.' She nudged me in the ribs. 'Do you get it?'

I grinned at her and nodded. 'Very good,' I said, mirroring her comment.

'And I think you're the woman,' she added. 'You've tamed him; he's loads nicer since he fell for you. Long may it continue.'

I felt my face heat up. 'Enough already. I wasn't fishing for compliments.'

'Oh, you are good,' she giggled.

Rachel was in luck; the morning session went swimmingly. No one sliced themselves on the extremely sharp knives, or felt ill after lunch, or choked on a fish bone, and at three o'clock she felt confident enough to leave the group in Leon's care and join me in the office for a chat.

'I don't want to count my chickens,' she said, crossing her fingers and beaming at me, 'but today is going very well. And I'm so excited about working on future events together.'

She took a seat next to me at my desk and wriggled to pull her dress down over her thighs.

'Glad to hear it.'

I grinned at her. Despite her crush on Tom I couldn't help but like her; she was brimming with enthusiasm and she was a breath of fresh air after the grotty couple of weeks we'd all had. And listening to her talk about the aims of Fresh from the Sea had highlighted how lacking in direction we were here at the cookery school. The whole business had been a little spontaneous ever since we opened. Take the Plumberry Bake Off, for example, and the *Challenge Chester* filming and the Plumberry Signature Dish competition. What were we actually trying to achieve here?

I supposed our scattergun approach was partly down to Gloria's unfortunate accident and since she died . . . Tears sprang to my eyes, an occupational hazard at the moment.

Rachel leaned over and touched my leg. 'Oops! Are you OK? I didn't mean . . . What did I say?'

I brushed away the tears and smiled.

'You've said exactly the right thing; I'm excited for the future too.' I patted her hand. 'I've been bumping along worrying about whether we should re-open for business and how I can run the cookery school without Gloria and whether—' I broke off, not wanting to explain about my sudden inheritance and about Gabe being a co-owner and all the baggage that went with it.

I took a deep breath. 'And you've made me realize that I need to dive right into it and start making plans.'

She blinked at me earnestly. 'Well, if it's plans you need, how about this . . . ?'

An hour later our diaries had several exciting ideas pencilled in, including a fish course exclusively for Fresh from the Sea newsletter subscribers, a fish-themed Supper Club night in the autumn and a 'money off a cookery course' voucher when customers spent over fifty pounds on the Fresh from the Sea website.

I beamed at Rachel. 'Thanks, I feel better already.'

It was early days, only a matter of days since Gloria's funeral – even profit-and-loss-focused Dave would forgive me for not being completely on the ball, business-wise – but I couldn't mooch around Plumberry endlessly waiting for something to happen, I had to make it happen. And now at least I felt like I'd made a start.

It felt weird to be organizing stuff for the months ahead, especially as I was now the new co-owner, and I didn't yet know whether either Tom or Gabe were planning on being part of the new team. But at the same time it felt cathartic, too. Maybe Tom would leave – my stomach flipped at the thought – and perhaps Gabe would decide to move up here permanently – there were definite advantages to that, namely one small tousle-haired boy — although I still had to have a chat with Gabe about his proposal yesterday.

And yes, my personal life was in total chaos; everything might change in the next month or so. But at least if we had plans for the cookery school, I would have something to anchor myself to. That had to be better than floating rudderless towards the future, didn't it?

'They'll be breaking for afternoon tea soon, shall we go and mingle?' Rachel suggested.

At that moment Tom and one of the male bloggers shared a raucous laugh about something and Rachel and I looked across at him.

A small sigh escaped before I had a chance to curtail it and Rachel glanced at me slyly.

'Tom is a quite a catch, isn't he?'

I cleared my throat. 'Absolutely. He's so talented and such an inspiration in the kitchen and—'

'And hot,' she said with a smirk.

'Oh, it's strictly professional between us,' I said, shaking my head.

Rachel's eyes danced with amusement. 'Oh yeah?'

My gaze was drawn back to Tom and I watched as he twirled the little leather strap round his wrist.

If I ever took it off a fairy would lose her wings.

I heaved a sigh. Oh sod it. 'He's adorable,' I admitted.

Rachel made a moue with her lips. 'Pity.' She got to her feet. 'I was going to invite him to dinner.' She caught my expression and held her hands up in defence. 'Hey, don't worry. I'll invite you both as a thank-you for today instead.'

I smiled and she gestured towards the door. 'Come on, let's charm those bloggers into writing us glowing reviews.'

Rachel skipped off to charm people, while I wandered round the room chatting to those I hadn't yet had a chance to meet.

The pregnant woman was sitting on a chair at the workstation near the windows. She'd pinned her hair up and had opened the window, but she still looked a bit warm and frazzled.

'Can you eat prawns when you're pregnant?' I asked, looking at the layered dish that she was constructing from avocadoes, tomatoes and prawns.

'I can if it's free.' She grinned at me, her mischievous eyes crinkling at the corners. 'I haven't seen so much luxury since I won a Fortnum and Mason hamper at my works do. I mean, a tian of prawns, how posh is that?'

'Very,' I agreed, never having even heard of one before.

'Until today, I used to think I was la-di-da if I had a prawn salad sandwich,' she confided with a wink, wiping what looked like a streak of mayonnaise from her hot cheek. 'I tell you, lunchtimes in the office will never be the same again. I'm Kylie, by the way.'

'Verity,' I said. 'But you are OK to eat all this?' I asked again nervously. I could see the headlines: pregnant mum in Plumberry prawn poisoning . . .

'Oh yeah.' Kylie wrinkled her nose. 'The current advice is no pâté and stuff. Seafood is fine if cooked. So no raw oysters for me. What a shame. Not.'

We pulled a face at each other and laughed.

'Do you know what you're having?' I asked, looking at her quite considerable baby bump.

'Yeah, twins,' she laughed. 'Want to swap places in about . . . ooh, seven weeks?'

'Let me think about that.' I pretended to ponder the prospect. 'That'll be a no. So I'm guessing you're writing a baby and pregnancy blog?'

Kylie wiped her hands on a cloth and began to rub the base of her spine. 'Actually, no. I write a blog about my experiences as a kid growing up in care.'

'That's different,' I said, surprised.

'Growing up in a children's home was tough,' she said, taking a sip of water. 'But I came through it. In fact, I think I'm stronger for it. I went to uni, got a good job and now I'm married and expecting twins.'

'Wow.' I nodded. 'Good for you.'

'You're surprised,' she said bluntly but with a hint of a smile. 'And the reason for that is that I've beaten the odds. So I thought I'd write a blog about my life to inspire young people in the position I was in, educate others who make snap judgements about kids in care—'

403

I couldn't help but go pink at this.

'And now I'm going to be a mother myself, I thought it might help me to be a better mother if I connected with the blogging community to find out how it's done.'

'I'm sure you'll be a great mum,' I said, meaning it. Kylie was such a warm and open character with bags of personality.

'But will I know how?' She shrugged. 'A mum is someone who tucks you in at night with a kiss and a cuddle and tells you how special you are to her. That never happened to me so I don't know how it feels. She shows you how to do all the little things. The important things that they don't teach you in school. Never had that either.'

She sighed, picked up a prawn and began picking the shell off.

'Tying your shoelaces, learning to ride a bike, to swim . . .' She gave me a sad smile. 'Even how to cook . . . I had to teach myself all those things. Except the cooking part. That's still ongoing.'

I thought of Noah suddenly, growing up without a mother. He had Gabe, of course, and no one could wish for a more devoted dad. And he did have me.

'I know this is crazy, because I just met you,' I began.

'If you say, "but here's my number", I shall cram prawn shells down the neck of your dress,' she said, chuckling.

'I honestly believe that you'll do great.' I squeezed her arm. 'Mums come in all shapes and sizes. There's no job specification. There's no checklist on how to be a perfect mother. But I can tell what a good heart you've got, and what a huge capacity for love you've got too. The fact that your blog is there to inspire other kids says it all. All your babies need is someone who loves them unconditionally.'

Kylie pressed both hands to her stomach. Her eyes glistened as she grinned at me. 'I already do love them with all my heart. Thanks for the pep talk. I needed to hear that.'

I hugged her impulsively and laughed. 'Funnily enough, so did I.'

By five o'clock, the teaching kitchen was clean and sparkling again and the only hint that Fresh from the Sea and their bloggers had paid us a visit was the faint aroma of fish in the air.

Mags, Pixie and I went out to the car park to wave off Rachel and Leon in their van. Tom had a quick job to do, he'd said, so had shaken hands with them both in reception.

'It was great to see the place buzzing again,' Mags said as we turned to go back inside.

'Wasn't it just?' I agreed.

'So are we opening up soon?' Pixie asked, twisting the bottom of her T-shirt into a knot. 'Only I don't mean to be pushy, but I'll have to find another job if not.'

I stopped and took their hands. 'I know it hasn't been easy on any of us, these last couple of weeks. But I've started to make plans and I'm feeling really confident about the cookery school's future.'

'That's brilliant news!' exclaimed Mags, pressing a noisy kiss to my cheek.

'But before I rush into anything,' I said, feeling my stomach churn, 'I need to talk to Gabe. There are a few things I need to deal with.'

Like *his* plan for the three of us to be a proper family and all that it entailed.

The conversation was halted by Tom's rapid footsteps as he ran down the stairs. 'See you all . . . er, soon,' he called over his shoulder as he left the building.

'Where's the fire?' muttered Pixie, raising her eyebrows.

'Tell him,' Mags urged, elbowing me sharply. 'Tell him what you told us, that we're opening up again. He needs to know where he stands.'

'Really?' I hovered indecisively, watching him leave.

'Yes,' they both agreed, shoving me in Tom's direction.

Hmm, I thought, running after him. They don't know the half of it . . .

'Tom!' I panted, catching up with him as he unlocked his car.

He turned and smiled a smile that didn't reach his eyes. 'Hi.'

'I was hoping to have a word with you tonight,' I said.

He shifted uncomfortably. 'Sorry. Got to dash.'

'Look.' I reached a hand out to touch his arm. He had taken off his chef whites and was wearing a crumpled linen shirt and soft worn jeans. The temptation to step closer until I was in his arms was overpowering but after the row we'd had earlier, I kept my distance.

'That silly argument this morning . . . Can we put that behind us and be friends again?' I attempted a cheeky smile.

He glanced at the cookery school and then down at the floor. 'That's just the problem, I'm not sure I can.'

'Oh.' I swallowed. My pulse was throbbing anxiously in my neck. 'But what about working together?'

'Verity, I—' Tom held my gaze as a flurry of emotions crossed his face and then he sighed helplessly. 'I've left you a note on your desk. I should go.'

My heart sank. 'OK,' I said, removing my hand from his arm.

He opened the car door, began to climb in and looked over his shoulder at me one last time. 'You're a great girl, you know that?'

A note? My stomach clenched as he shut the door.

I turned and ran back inside with his words ringing in my ears. *I'm not sure I can* . . .

'Is everything all right?' Mags enquired from behind her desk.

'I don't know,' I replied, frowning as I ran up the stairs to the office.

Sitting on my desk, propped up against my laptop, was an envelope with my name on it.

I dropped into my chair and picked it up. My heart was pounding and my chest felt tight.

Please say this isn't what I think it is.

Chapter 38

My hands trembled as I tore open the envelope and read Tom's message.

> *Dear Verity,*
> *It is with sadness and regret that I tender my resignation with immediate effect. We have been through quite a lot together in the last few weeks, which perhaps explains why my feelings for you run as deep as they do.*
>
> *But I've come to the conclusion that it's in no one's best interests if I stay.*
>
> *I am happy to pass on details of a couple of chefs who might be able to help you out when you re-open the cookery school. For now, I wish you and Gabe every success for the future.*
> *Love*
> *Tom*

A huge lump formed in my throat. *Resign?* How could that possibly be the best thing to do? Everything about Tom's letter was wrong except that last bit about love. That was unbearably sweet. This was crazy. How had I let our relationship get into this state? What an idiot.

And now I'd probably lost him for good and what's more, the cookery school had lost an incredibly talented chef.

Oh God, Gloria, I'm sorry. I only inherited your baby yesterday and I've already messed it up.

I chewed my lip. He'd said 'with immediate effect'. Perhaps he'd already found another job, or a venue for a new restaurant? Maybe he was using this as an excuse to leave for a better offer. Deep down I'd always known that the cookery school wasn't enough of a challenge for him, but I guess I'd hoped that he'd stay at least until we found our feet again.

I lowered my head in my hands and closed my eyes.

I just wanted to rewind time, go back to this morning when he'd stood close to me, guiding my hands as he showed me how to sharpen the knife.

I forced my eyes open and stood up.

Don't give up so easily, Verity, I thought, pacing the room. All was not yet lost. It wasn't as if he'd left the country or anything. He'd probably just gone back to the flat in Pudston. He wouldn't be far.

Right. OK.

I took a calming breath. This situation was easy enough to sort out. I'd simply tell him how much he meant to me, how I felt about him, explain the thing with Gabe and Noah, everything . . . I had made a promise to Mimi, but the circumstances had changed. She wouldn't want me to be unhappy or lose out on the love of someone who really cared for me because of her.

And I was sure Gabe wouldn't mind if I told Tom the truth. My stomach lurched suddenly, remembering that right at this moment Gabe was waiting for my answer, hoping that the two of us could start a relationship. The thought of that – lovely as he was – was enough to bring me out in a rash.

Oh God, what a mess. I'd have to tell Gabe exactly how I felt too, just as soon as I'd told Tom.

I brushed the tears off my face, picked up my mobile and called Tom's number.

I could have wept with frustration when the call diverted to voicemail. I was about to hang up, but summoned up all my courage and left a message instead.

'Tom, this is Verity. I got your note,' I said, trying to keep my voice bright and breezy. 'But I'm afraid I don't accept your resignation. So there. Please call me back at your earliest convenience. Goodbye.'

I ended the call with a groan. *Earliest convenience?* That sounded like an urgent summons from the library to return an overdue book. Hardly the most romantic message he'd ever received, I was sure.

I looked at the phone in my hand, willing it to ring. It sat there taunting me with its unlit screen and lifeless body and after the longest ten seconds in history I stuck it in my pocket with a sigh.

It was quite likely he was still driving, of course. Even though the last couple of minutes had seemed like a life sentence, it probably was actually only, well, a couple of minutes. If he really cared, he'd call me back, I was sure of it, librarian voice or not. I'd tell him everything – better still I'd arrange to meet him, *then* tell him everything. That way we could make up. Making-up kisses with Tom would be delicious . . .

I let out a shaky breath, checked my phone wasn't on silent or divert and began tidying my desk ready to go home.

As I moved round the office, clearing away the day's activities, putting rubbish in the bin, filing loose papers and collecting dirty cups, my mind began to construct plans and ideas for the cookery school and my future.

I wasn't completely out of the woods; I still had to let Gabe down gently, somehow explain that even though I loved both him and Noah, I could never fill Mimi's shoes. And neither did I want to. Gabe would always be Mimi's husband to me and the sooner he got back to punching me in the arm and calling me Bloomers, the better.

I also had to persuade Tom that there was a place for him at the cookery school *and* in my heart. The corners of

410

my mouth lifted as I remembered Pixie's plaice pun. I was a great believer in fate and good intentions. Things had gone awry between us, but if it was meant to be, it would all be salvageable. I just had to have faith.

And the business, too, would come right, I was sure of it. Closing it so soon after it had opened was a setback but it had been the right thing to do under difficult circumstances.

My phone beeped and I grabbed it quickly, holding my breath. But it wasn't from Tom, it was from Rosie:

> Hope you're OK? How's everyone? What's going on with Tom? I'm here when you're ready to talk R xxx

My heart swelled with affection for her. She had been entirely baffled by what had happened between Tom and me at the hospital and by Gabe's comments. But she hadn't pushed me for answers, for which I was massively grateful. Once all this mess was cleared up I would ring her and tell her everything. I owed her that much.My thumbs flew over the screen as I sent her a quick reply.

> Mad busy but OK. I now own half a cookery school! Speak soon with ALL the details V xxx

I wandered out of the office and through the teaching kitchen, trailing my fingers across the gleaming granite worktops, admiring the run of stainless-steel ovens and the shine on the creamy wooden kitchen cabinets. I paused now and then to rearrange the coloured utensils in their pots, humming softly to myself. It truly was a special place.

And the sooner we could have it bustling with people and full of mouth-watering aromas again the better.

Gabe and I (and hopefully Tom) would have our work cut out to kick-start the business that Gloria had set her heart on running. Put some oomph back into our advertising, contact all those who'd enquired about courses only to be told we were closed temporarily. Whip up a storm of publicity to bring in new bookings. Busy, busy, busy.

It would be a challenge, but it was possible. Anything is possible if you set your mind to it. What had Pixie's grand-dad said? If you want something badly enough you have to fight for it . . .

And I would fight for it. Because the Plumberry School of Comfort Food had given me back my zest for life and now I had it, I never wanted to let it go again.

My chest heaved with determination and resolve and I headed back to the office to collect my handbag, ready to go home. The sun was still shining and it would be a warm evening. I'd perhaps have a glass of wine in the garden and jot down a few marketing ideas on paper unless Tom called and then who knows what the night would bring . . .

As I walked back into the office, the corner of a folder sticking out of a drawer under Gloria's desk caught my eye. I pulled open the drawer to push it in properly and noticed that it was Gloria's recipe bible that was protruding.

I pulled it out for a look and smiled at the sight of her handwriting on the front. She had quite spiky writing, as if she was always in a rush to get her words down. I opened the folder and flicked through the first few pages.

Her writing might be difficult to read, but her note-taking was meticulous. She had recorded exactly when she'd made each dish, which TV show it had been for and the description of the feature. She'd made a Greek mezze platter for a romantic sharing platter for a Valentine's Day spot, a chestnut and cranberry pithivier for a vegetarian Christmas menu and a fatless sponge cake for a cake-lover's diet feature. Such a talented cook, I thought with a sigh, and such a shame that these recipes were languishing in a drawer. No wonder Mags missed her; the two of them had cooked up a storm together every evening for the past year.

I closed the folder and was about to replace it in the drawer when I hesitated. Maybe the recipes could have a new lease of life, maybe I should do something with them . . .

A flash of inspiration made me leap into action and I turned Gloria's computer on. Five minutes later my brain was fizzing with a new idea. And this one, though I'd said this many times before, did take the absolute biscuit. It might not meet with Dave's approval, because I doubted it would be a huge money-spinner, but not everything had to be about money, did it? Some things are worth doing simply because of the joy they would bring to the people around us. And I knew someone with a principle of pleasure who would not be able to resist this idea.

I grinned to myself, debating whether to shout down to Mags and tell her straight away. But maybe I should do a bit more digging first, see if I could source a photographer. I decided to tell her in the morning and as I started to replace the folder, the edge of a DVD case caught my eye amongst the confusion of papers.

I tugged it out, thinking that perhaps it was a compilation of clips from the TV programmes that had featured her food. But when I prised open the plastic case, a folded note fell out, dated two years ago.

I might as well read it, I mused, no one else was going to and we'd have to clear this desk out sooner or later anyway.

Hi Gloria,

After our conversation I managed to salvage these videos from various cameras and computers. I know Verity deleted their YouTube channel but I kept these so that I could show them to Noah one day: films of the two most important women in his life cooking together. If nothing else, he'll get a lesson in how to cook something halfway edible if my skills haven't improved by then!

Anyway, thought you might like them. They made quite a pair, didn't they!

   Love
   Gabe

My heart thumped wildly; Gabe must have compiled some of mine and Mimi's cooking videos. Videos I hadn't had the courage to watch since she'd died. Precious memories of the two of us doing what we loved best: having fun in the kitchen. I scrapped the idea of wine in the garden; I knew exactly what I'd be doing as soon as I got in . . .

'Wakey, wakey!' Mags laughed, bustling into the office.

'Mags,' I yelped, dropping the note. 'You frightened the life out of me.'

'Sorry,' she trilled, not in the least apologetically. 'You were gazing into the distance dreamily. Anyway, I just came to tell you I'm off. Dave's picking me up early tonight.'

'Going anywhere nice?' I asked, suppressing a sigh.

Much as I was pleased for them, I'd miss not having someone to eat with. Although they'd happily oblige, Comfrey and Sage were somewhat lacking in the conversation department.

'We're taking his mum to the cinema.' She grinned mischievously, patting her bun. 'So no snogging in the back row tonight.'

I laughed; it was good to see her smiling again.

'There's a first time for everything, Mags.'

She nodded and cast her eye around the room.

'I'm glad you're planning on making a go of the cookery school,' she said in a more serious tone. 'It doesn't seem five minutes since it was Gloria sitting in that chair, telling me her hopes and dreams for the place. It would be such a pity if all that went to waste.'

I glanced down at Gloria's recipe bible still lying on the desk and made a snap decision to tell Mags. Research was overrated anyway.

'It definitely won't go to waste,' I beamed, wrapping my arm round her shoulder. 'We are going to make this cookery school the hub of Plumberry, a place for foodies to share their passion, just as Gloria wanted. We're going to pass on her love of comfort food and more importantly we're going to share her recipes.'

I picked up the folder with both hands.

'The bible,' Mags breathed reverently.

'Or rather, *you're* going to share them.' I twinkled my eyes at her.

She blinked at me. 'Me, how?'

'Remember how you suggested that we produced a recipe book for the cookery school? Well, I thought you could produce a book from all Gloria's recipes instead. The ones she'd planned to teach to her students.'

'Do you think?' She pressed a hand to her bosom. I held my breath as she stared at the folder for a long moment and gradually began to nod. 'I'd love to do that. What a fabulous idea! Mind you, it must be fifteen years since I published a book, I'm sure things will have changed.'

'Possibly.' I shrugged. 'But I've no doubt you've still got the skills.'

Her eyes glittered and I could see the idea both excited and delighted her.

'The idea has only just come to me,' I said. 'I've barely had a chance to think it through. There'll be lots to do but I bet the printer will help us and we'd need to find a good photographer.'

'Oh, don't worry about that,' she said, waving a hand. 'I can look up some of my old contacts. Hey, I know exactly what we can call the book too: *Food, Gloria's Food.*'

'That was the name for the cookery school you came up with.' I grinned. 'You do know how brilliant you are, don't you?'

'It has been said.' She waggled her eyebrows, took the folder from my hands and reverently turned the pages. 'Me,

Mags Honeyford, back in publishing. Who'd have thought.' She chuckled.

'I remembered you saying that you sort of regretted leaving the job years ago, so this is your chance to have a last hurrah.'

'It is, isn't it?' she said, her eyes sparkling with excitement. 'I can't think why it didn't occur to me myself. Ooh, look at that, salmon en croute, that was her favourite, that'll have to go in. And this one . . .'

We spent a nostalgic – if a little tearful – ten minutes flicking through Gloria's recipes.

'And Mags,' I said, waiting until she looked me in the eye, 'this would be more than just recipes; this is you paying the ultimate compliment to your friend. And in a way it would be a legacy for you both.'

Mags's eyes misted over. 'Gloria was right about you,' she said, squeezing my hand. 'You've been a ray of sunshine in our lives since you arrived in Plumberry.'

I smiled, wondering if Tom felt the same way. I was pretty sure Gabe would disagree once I'd let him down, but for now I simply nodded and kissed Mags's cheek.

'So what are you planning to do tonight?' she said, tucking the folder under her arm and making for the door.

'Um . . .' I slipped my phone out of my pocket to check for new messages. Nothing. I picked the DVD off the desk instead and waved it at Mags.

'Looks like I'm staying in with a cup of tea and a DVD,' I said wryly. 'Unless I get a better offer.'

Chapter 39

Back at Gloria's cottage – or Noah's as it was now, I supposed – I let myself in, scampered around the garden with the dogs and a ball for a few minutes to let off steam and then made myself a cup of tea. A very strong cup of tea with sugar.

My pulse, already racing from my jaunt outside, picked up pace as I plucked the DVD case from my bag and strode purposefully into the living room.

I paused in front of the mirror and set down my mug, taking in the slightly hot and pink face, dishevelled hair and wide anxious eyes staring back at me.

I looked at the DVD. It held remnants of mine and Mimi's happy times. A reminder of the fun we'd shared and the silly things we used to laugh over. I'd shied away from these memories for too long; it was time to let them back in.

'This probably doesn't look very much to you, boys,' I said, stooping to scratch behind their ears. Sage slipped into the gap between Comfrey and my leg to get an extra portion of fuss. 'But this is a big deal. A proper turning-point.'

As I knelt down on the floor in front of the TV and tried to work out which remote went with which device, I remembered a leaflet that someone had thrust in my hand about bereavement when Mimi died.

There were five stages of grief, apparently, and I recalled being able to identify with all of them at once at the time. And while it had been useful to know that what I was feeling was perfectly normal, it hadn't helped me prepare for what was supposed to come next, i.e. building a life for myself without Mimi in it. OK, I'd thought crossly at the time, I've had the denial and anger stuff, when does the moving-on kick in?

But maybe that was something you simply had to arrive at by yourself. Let your inner grief-o-meter be your guide. I switched the TV on at the wall and waited for the blue light to come on.

I hadn't watched any videos from the old days for ages. Two and a bit years, to be precise. As soon as Mimi's funeral was over, just as Gabe had written in that note to Gloria, I'd closed down our YouTube channel and ignored the emails that came though from confused subscribers wondering what had happened to the links they'd shared and what we'd be baking next. I felt awful about that now. I should have explained really, I supposed. Told people that Mimi had gone to some hi-tech, designer kitchen in the sky and was probably delighting all the angels with daily batches of buttery shortbread.

But the time had come.

Heart thudding, I slotted the disc into Gloria's DVD player and sank on to the sofa, waiting for Comfrey and Sage to finish their habitual circle-turning to get themselves comfortable in the crook of my knee before pressing play.

You know how when you buy a DVD you have to sit through a million ads for films you're completely not interested in and then endure a warning on the perils of piracy? And even though you'd really rather slip straight to the film, you don't mind too much because it gives you chance to adjust cushions, slip your shoes off and put your tea exactly where you want it. Well, you don't get that with a home DVD compilation. Oh no. Two seconds after pressing the play button Mimi's face filled the screen and I gasped so loudly that I startled the dogs.

Tears sprang instantly to my eyes. I brushed them away before offering a comforting pat to the boys.

'Welcome to the kitchen of Mimi and Verity's delights.' Mimi beamed and waved at the camera.

I was instantly whisked back in time to the nineties and the winter's evening we'd decided to make nachos. (They were quite the in thing at the time.) Judging by our outfits, we must have been about sixteen.

'Hello, my lovely friend,' I cried at the TV screen, laughing at the scrunchy in her unruly golden hair. 'Oh my God, Mimi, it's so nice to see you again.'

This was pre-YouTube, when we'd been teenagers simply filming ourselves for the hell of it, pretending to be TV chefs. We'd had a great big chunky camera then and editing the videos had taken longer than the actual cooking. Gabe had helped quite a bit, I remembered. In fact, it had been round about this time when he'd become a more permanent fixture in Mimi's life.

'Nachos make a great snack for watching TV,' said a super-cool me in hideous coral lipstick. 'And you can mix it up with jalapenos, sour cream and guacamole—'

'Aka vomitus gloop,' Mimi cut in, thrusting her head between the camera and me. 'I just stick to grated cheese.'

I settled back on the sofa and lost myself in the memories, laughing and crying as the two of us as teenagers giggled our way through a host of calamitous cooking capers.

Gabe had managed to compile the DVD in chronological order and after an hour, during which time I'd got through a stack of tissues, I came to a more recent clip.

'Welcome to our recipe for the best mac and cheese ever!' I announced.

'Mac and cheese is the ultimate "I love you" food,' an older Mimi said with a twinkle in her eye.

This video had been on YouTube. I sat up straighter in my chair. This was more like the Mimi I remembered. Effortlessly radiant, hair smoothed with serum and her teenage chubby cheeks slimmed down to reveal cheekbones that Kate Moss would kill for. We must have been about twenty-five in this clip.

'Feed this to the one you love and you're guaranteed to put a smile on their face,' she purred.

'Or if you're still single like me . . .' I pulled a cross-eyed expression.

Mimi snorted. 'Can't think why that is.'

'. . . it's also perfect comfort food,' I continued, 'for nights alone in front of the TV.'

I pretended to cry and Mimi patted my arm.

'Now we all have our own way of doing it,' she went on, waving a hand over the assembled ingredients.

'Hmm,' I said, pulling a face. 'For example, Mimi adds a dollop of Dijon mustard to her cheese sauce.'

She put a hand to the side of her mouth. 'Shush! Don't tell Gabe, he claims to hate the stuff.'

'And I like to add crispy bacon to mine.'

I chuckled as I watched Mimi trying to prove just how much she loved mustard by licking it off the spoon only to burn the back of her nose.

'Too strong,' she winced, swiping a hand at me as I bent over double in the background, breathless with laughter.

Suddenly the dogs jumped up and began yapping, jolting me back to the present moment in Gloria's living room. A second later the doorbell chimed. I pressed a hand to my beating heart, paused the DVD and went out into the hall.

'RAR!' yelled Noah, waving a sword about in the air as I opened the door. 'I'm a Viking, RAR!'

Gabe was standing behind him looking shattered. He rolled his eyes indulgently at his son.

'Hello, you two!' I smiled.

Noah rammed a plastic helmet on his head, pushed past

me and ran along the hall, straight through the kitchen and out into the garden, roaring jubilantly. The dogs pattered along behind, pleased to have someone to play with.

Gabe raked a hand through his hair and grinned self-consciously. 'Hope we aren't disturbing you? We've been to the Jorvik Viking Centre in York and Noah was adamant that you'd want to see his new sword and helmet.'

I nodded. 'He's right. I've never seen such a fierce Viking.'

I felt unsure and awkward; Gabe and I had always hugged, always kissed our hellos. But the last time I saw him he'd kissed me full on the lips and I didn't know what to do or how to be any more.

'Come in,' I said, standing aside to let him into the hall.

He dropped a rucksack on the floor and stepped towards me, his arms dangling at his side. Poor Gabe; he looked as uneasy as I felt. I was on the verge of diving on him for a hug to break the tension when he cleared his throat.

'Verity, about the other day.' He folded his arms and looked at his feet. 'I . . . I . . . probably shouldn't have kissed you.'

My heart melted for him.

'I probably agree,' I answered.

He grinned at me and my heart gave a whoop of relief.

I looped my arm through his and led him into the living room. 'Funny you should have turned up now; look what I'm watching.'

I nodded towards the TV where Mimi's lovely face filled the screen.

Gabe's eyes widened and he sank on to the sofa.

'Oh, look at her. Look at my golden girl,' he breathed. 'Press play!'

I did as I was told and sat down next to him and the two of us watched as the recipe for the best mac and cheese ever unfolded on screen.

'Now,' said Mimi, spooning a generous portion of pasta

on to a plate, 'Let's put my theory to the test: Is this the ultimate "I love you" food or not.'

'I remember this,' Gabe whispered, shooting a sideways glance at me. His eyes looked suspiciously moist. As were mine.

We edged nearer to one another as Mimi cupped her hands to her mouth and yelled, 'Gabe? Come and taste this.'

'Wow!' I said as a young suited Gabe with short neat hair appeared in the kitchen and slipped his arms around his wife's waist. He must have come straight from his solicitor's office.

'Jeez,' muttered the real-life Gabe, swiping at a stray tear. I reached out and grabbed his hand.

Mimi loaded a fork with piping-hot macaroni. 'Blow,' she ordered.

Gabe blew on it and then she popped the forkful in his mouth.

'Mmm, I love it.' Gabe kissed Mimi tenderly. 'And I love you too.'

She winked at her audience. 'Kisses guaranteed.'

The video finished, Mimi's laughing face disappeared and the screen went black. The seconds ticked by as neither Gabe nor I could find the words to speak.

Finally, I turned to face him and squeezing his hand tightly, I drew in a shaky breath.

'Gabe, I love you and Noah and I loved Mimi with all my heart. We were closer than any sisters ever could have been. Donating my eggs, particularly the one super-duper egg that made Noah, was my gift to you both to make your happiness complete.'

'Becoming parents was the icing on the cake for us, especially her,' murmured Gabe. 'I hope you don't regret what you did, under the circumstances?'

I shook my head fervently. 'It was a gift I was privileged to give. None of us could have foreseen what would happen to Mimi.'

I hugged him then and told him that I didn't have a single regret about what we'd done. We'd got Noah as a result. He would always hold a special place in my heart and even though they had only been a family for a short while, they had been a very happy family and that was more than some people ever had.

Gabe nodded slowly and fixed his pale grey eyes on me. 'I want that again, Verity. I want to walk along the street with a woman, swinging Noah between us. I want to cuddle up at night under a blanket on the deck of *The Neptune* and stare at the stars. I want someone to share special moments with us, like his first day at school, his sports days, his school plays. Is that too much to ask?'

'Of course not,' I said gently, 'but I hope you understand that that woman can't be me.'

He lowered his gaze to his knees. 'You seemed like the perfect choice to me.'

My heart squeezed for him. 'And I'm honoured. Truly. But one day, Gabe Green, you'll meet a girl who makes your heart skip. And she won't be a better or a worse match for you than Mimi, she won't be a replacement, she'll simply be the person who takes the next step on life's journey with you. The person whose very smile sends your spirits soaring. Now be honest, is that me?'

He looked sideways at me and we grinned at each other.

'You are cute, though. And,' he shrugged sheepishly, 'I thought it could work seeing as we know each other so well. I thought you'd be easy to get on with, like a pair of comfy slippers.'

'Gabe!' I hit him with a cushion. 'You are seriously going to have to work on your lines if you're ever going to get another girlfriend. Slippers!' I tutted, shaking my head.

'Sorry,' Gabe laughed. 'Beautiful slippers.'

'Enough already,' I said, holding up a hand. 'You're not helping yourself.'

We smiled at each other then and I leaned towards him, bumping him with my shoulder.

'Now that he's a bit older, perhaps Noah can start coming to stay with me for the weekend now and then? I'd love to spoil him like a proper Fairy Godmother and teach him to cook. I think Mimi would like that, don't you?'

He wrapped an arm round my shoulders and kissed the side of my head. 'Yes to all of the above.'

We talked then about the future of the cookery school and how we thought it might work, us co-owning it. Gabe admitted that he'd probably be better going back to Nottingham where his parents were on hand to help with Noah. And we agreed that I would stay in Gloria's cottage and run the school on a day-to-day basis and refer to him for big decisions for the first twelve months and see how it turned out.

I breathed a contented sigh. 'I'm so relieved that all that's out in the open. About the cookery school and, you know, you and me.'

Gabe chuckled.

'And what about you? Have you met someone who does that heart-skipping business for you?' He cocked an eyebrow rather knowingly. 'Hmm? Are Verity Bloom's spirits getting any soaring action?'

I took a deep breath. 'Well—'

'Daddy!' came a panicky yell from the garden. 'Daaddy!'

The two of us leapt to our feet and ran outside. Noah had managed to climb up on to the fence separating our garden from Mags's. He was stuck on the top and had just got to the red-faced about-to-cry stage. Gabe lifted him down and after he'd finished wincing at the pain in his privates, the two of them ran round and round the garden roaring like Vikings.

And as the sun started to set in an orangey pink sky, kissing the tops of the trees with golden light, I watched happily, feeling blessed to be part of such a loving, unconventional family. Noah would always know that I loved him, I vowed. And when he was old enough to understand how babies are made, Gabe and I would explain everything so that he would know just how special he is. And why he had green eyes just like mine when his mum's were the colour of bluebells.

Noah soon ran out of puff and Gabe declared it was time to head back to *The Neptune*.

'Are you sure you won't stay for supper?' I said, walking them to the door.

Gabe shook his head. 'We had fish and chips in York. At least Noah did. He tripped me up with his sword, my cod went flying and he laughed so hard he needed a wee, so I had to abandon mine and find a loo.'

'You're a brilliant dad,' I said quietly, slipping my hand into his. 'Mimi would be very proud. As am I.'

We stared at each other for a long moment until Noah poked his dad with his sword. 'Daddy, come on.'

'OK, dude. Oh, I almost forgot.'

Gabe fumbled in his rucksack and pulled out a newspaper.

'Picked this up for you. Page thirty-something. Business section.'

Of course; I'd almost forgotten about this. The Supper Club write-up was in today's *York Mail*. I flicked through the pages, expecting to see a typical cheffy photograph of Tom: his white tunic, arms folded, perhaps against a backdrop of stainless steel.

Oh. Gosh. The breath caught in my throat. I'd made a terrible mistake; it wasn't about Tom at all. It was about me. My eyes scanned the headline: *Plumberry School of Comfort Food Appoints New Marketing Director and She Has Had Her Best Idea Yet!*

And there across two whole pages was a picture of me. Pixie must have taken it on the day of the *Challenge Chester* filming. I was standing alone amongst a bustling crowd with my hands on my hips, mouth upturned in a secret smile, gazing at some faraway sight. Behind me was the beautiful plum and cream cookery school logo and just visible at the edge of the frame was the old mill's lovely waterwheel. It was quite a flattering photograph; it almost looked like it must have been posed. But I hadn't even been aware it was being taken.

Tears pricked at my eyes as realization dawned: Tom had promised me that he'd never steal my ideas and he hadn't. I felt awful for doubting him. I should have known he was a better man than that.

I quickly skimmed the article while Gabe walked Noah to the car and strapped him into his car seat. It talked about how successful the launch of the cookery school had been and the various marketing ideas I'd come up with. And how since we'd been open we'd grown our bookings to almost maximum capacity, helped in no small way by our TV appearance on *Challenge Chester.*

And now, thanks to Verity Bloom's constantly creative approach to marketing, the cookery school is venturing into monthly Supper Clubs, filling a much-needed gap in the Plumberry food offering. The cookery school aims to reproduce a restaurant-standard dining experience in a relaxed and entertaining environment, sharing their passion for food, the ethos handed down by cookery school founder, Gloria Ramsbottom.

'Verity is fond of saying that she has had her best idea yet,' commented top chef and the cookery school's tutor, Tom MacDonald, 'and this time I'd have to agree with her. I think Verity Bloom is the Plumberry School of Comfort Food's magic ingredient.'

That was possibly the nicest, most generous thing anyone had ever said about me.

'It's nice, isn't it?' said Gabe softly.

'It is.' I nodded, lowering the newspaper and looking up at him.

'Is your heart skipping?'

'Practically doing the double Dutch,' I said with a laugh that came out a bit gulpy and weird. 'Unfortunately he handed his notice in this afternoon. I was going to tell you, you being the co-owner . . .' My voice drifted off. I felt tearful all of a sudden; I really, really needed to see Tom.

Gabe grabbed hold of my shoulders and pressed a firm kiss to my forehead. And then he punched my arm. I grinned with relief. Equilibrium had been restored.

'Then go and sort it out, Bloomers. Go and tell him what he means to you.'

'I will,' I promised.

I kissed them both goodbye and waved them off. I closed the front door and leaned against it for a second before charging towards the kitchen.

I would go and sort it out. And I knew just how because a brilliant idea had just occurred to me.

I plunged two cups of pasta into boiling water and then added a third for good measure. I took out a pan, contemplated making a roux for about one second before deciding that Tom would be none the wiser and bunged a jug of milk in the microwave instead, thickening it with cornflour mixed with a drop of water.

Next, the cheese. The most important ingredient in mac and cheese, or perhaps I should say the *magic* ingredient.

I giggled headily to myself and opened the fridge to find the cheddar. Mimi had been all for combining cheeses: cheddar for tanginess, mozzarella for gooiness and parmesan for no good reason at all that I could fathom. I, on the other hand, had always been a purist: mature cheddar all the way – in the sauce and on top for a glorious brown crust. But there on the shelf was the thick wedge of creamy blue cheese I'd bought from the Plumberry cheesemonger's. Tom loved Yorkshire Blue.

I unwrapped it and popped a piece in my mouth. The sourness of the blue vein was there but at the same time it was mild and sweet and buttery. My face split into a huge smile; this would be perfect.

There was just one thing left to do. My heart hammered anxiously as I took my phone out of my pocket and began to type a message.

Tom, I know you are ignoring my calls, but this is very, very important . . .

Chapter 40

I'd drained the pasta into a pretty ovenproof dish, stirred in the sauce and slammed it in the oven to brown by the time he sent me a reply.

> It's not that I'm ignoring your calls, I just know that you'll try and persuade me to stay and I can't do that. I'm packing a bag and heading off into the Yorkshire Dales for a couple of days to clear my head. I'll call when I get back. Take care, Tom x

Crikey, there wasn't much time. If I didn't make it to his flat in Pudston before he left, who knew how long it would be until I got another chance to talk? And I'd cooked for him – *food made with love* – and he needed to know that before it was too late.

I whacked the oven up to max, dashed upstairs, dragged a brush through my hair, spritzed on a bit of perfume and ran back down.

'Keys, purse, lipstick, bag,' I muttered to myself, racing round locking doors and finally removing the dish from the oven. A bit singed on one side but it would do.

'Right, boys,' I called, looking round for the dogs as I opened the treats tin. 'In your basket.'

No response.

I found them sitting neatly at the front door, bristling

with excitement at the prospect of an outing. And the expressions on their bright little faces were so hopeful that I couldn't refuse.

It wasn't easy transporting a scorching-hot oven dish along with two dogs with a penchant for cheese. But by looping the dogs' leads around the seatbelt and laying the dish on a towel in the foot well, I cracked it.

So far so good.

My face had gone red from cooking and rushing and I opened the window. Now all I had to do, I thought, breathing in lungfuls of cool air, was show Tom exactly what he meant to me. I glanced down at the food, which was already starting to steam up the windscreen.

Would Mimi's theory work on Tom? I pondered. Would it be the perfect 'I love you' food? Or would I be coming back, tail between my legs, eating supper alone and consoling myself with mac and cheese as comfort food.

I exhaled a calming breath and started the car.

Time to find out whether the way to a man's heart truly was through his stomach . . .

Juggling leads and a still piping-hot dish cradled in a towel, I ran up the steps to Tom's flat with Comfrey and Sage scampering beside me, squeaking with joy. As I raised my hand to knock on the door it opened. I jumped, startled by the sudden movement, and the dogs' leads slipped through my fingers. Two triumphant sausage dogs took instant advantage of the slackness in the lead and made a dash through the gap, as a tall red-headed man with a wonky bruised nose and a black eye appeared, carrying a large sports bag.

'Sorry about the invasion.' I grimaced, peering past him for the dogs. And Tom.

He laughed. 'No worries. Verity, I presume?'

I nodded and tried not to stare at his nose. It looked very sore.

'I'm off to cricket practice.' He grinned, lifting his bag. Adding with a gesture towards his face, 'God knows I need it.'

'Right.' I really wanted to go in but Tom's flatmate showed no sign of moving. 'Well, be careful then.'

'So you'll be alone,' he said with a wink. And then hoicked his bag over his shoulder and sauntered off.

Thank goodness.

'Hello?' I edged into the hall, looking for somewhere to put the dish down as soon as possible. The heat had seeped through the towel and was getting too much for my fingers.

The tiny console table piled high with letters and tucked behind the door would do. I deposited the dish and blew on my fingers. The smell of cooking wafted out from the kitchen but there were no dogs or humans to be seen.

'Tom?'

There was a clatter from the kitchen and then Tom poked his head out, a tea towel thrown over his shoulder. His eyes, as dark as espresso, looked bemused. He glanced over his shoulder shiftily, blocking my view of the kitchen. Comfrey and Sage appeared immediately afterwards, licking their lips triumphantly, and flopped at his feet.

'What are you doing here?' he asked. But in a nice, amused sort of way. 'Not that I don't enjoy your visits.'

We both blushed. I was remembering the last time I was here and how we'd kissed on his sofa, ignoring our Eggs Benedict and forgetting to watch *Challenge Chester*, which had been the whole reason for my visit in the first place. I hoped he was too.

I swallowed. 'I'm glad I caught you. I really needed to see you before you left.'

'I meant what I said,' he said, folding his arms and looking down at his feet. They were bare. Like last time. Only today he didn't look like he was going to play footsie with me any time soon. He looked defensive and determined. 'I need to get away. And I think perhaps you and Gabe need space.'

This was going to be harder than I thought. My stomach was churning like mad and I felt sick. Only I wouldn't be able to be sick because my throat was so constricted and tight. What happens then, I wondered, if sick can't escape? I shuddered. And what was going on with my armpits? I swear I never normally perspired; today it felt like someone had turned the hot tap on under there.

'I don't need space,' I argued. '*We* don't. Because there isn't a *we*.'

Tom frowned and threaded his fingers through his hair roughly. 'You and I have both had a tough time over the last few weeks: losing Gloria, me splitting up with Rebecca, selling the business and then, Gabe turning up . . .' His voice tailed off and he looked down at his feet.

He had to be the most stubborn man on the planet. I'd said there was no 'we' but it was as if he couldn't hear me. I decided to change tack, talk his language.

'And I've cooked for you,' I blurted out, feeling the heat rise to my face. I pointed towards the table.

His face cleared then and he stared at me for a long moment, a tentative smile playing at his lips. 'Nobody ever cooks just for me.'

'Well, I have because . . .' I blinked at him. 'Because . . .' Mimi's words rang in my head: *it's the perfect 'I love you' food*. I didn't dare say that.

'Because mac and cheese,' I said, my voice barely a whisper, 'is the ultimate comfort food.'

His lips twitched. 'But I have it on very good authority that a fish finger sandwich is the ultimate comfort food.'

'Well, so is mac and cheese.' I smiled at him, feeling my body relax. He hadn't thrown me out yet and he was almost smiling. He hadn't smiled at me like that for ages. That had to mean something, didn't it? 'And I couldn't very well bring a sandwich to Plumberry's answer to Michel Roux, could I?'

'There'd be no need anyway.'

He took a step backwards, his eyes still on mine and a cheeky grin on his face. And reaching into the kitchen, he brought out a fish finger sandwich on a plate.

'*You* made that?' I exclaimed, laughing. 'I thought you were a skate-in-black-butter sort of man.'

'I needed cheering up.' He shrugged bashfully. 'I'm a fish finger sandwich virgin, how have I done?'

How adorable was that? And sad at the same time. Tom needed comfort food presumably because of me. Well, not any more, because I was here in person and I had every intention of cheering him up.

'Let's have a look,' I grinned, taking the plate from him, 'seeing as I *am* the authority on these things.'

The bread was soft and fluffy and the fish fingers had been grilled to have just the right amount of crispiness on the outside and flakiness on the inside. He'd even invested in a bottle of Heinz tomato sauce.

'Hmm, just one small thing,' I concluded.

'No way!' he said, pretending to be outraged.

'The ketchup should go on the fish, not the bread, in my opinion. But not bad for a first attempt.'

I handed him the plate. 'And now for my attempt.'

I carried the ovenproof dish into the kitchen, brushing his arm as I passed him, and made a space on the worktop. Even that small touch was enough to send my stomach into a fit of fluttering. The dogs, sensing that I was about to serve up, started squeaking with delight so I fetched a chew stick each from my handbag and dropped them in the hall to keep them quiet and rejoined Tom in the tiny kitchen.

He was leaning against the worktop, arms folded, his chest rising and falling and a tiny tuft of hair was just visible at the neck of his T-shirt. His smile had slipped again.

'Verity,' he said softly, 'you know why I resigned?'

I nodded. 'I think so. But you've got it all wrong; it's all been a big misunderstanding. But I couldn't explain because I made a promise.'

He raised his eyebrows, intrigued.

'But I do owe you an explanation, I realize that now.' I swallowed. 'So here I am.'

'OK.' He lifted a shoulder. 'I'm listening.'

'Well, the thing is,' I floundered, wrapping the towel I'd brought with me round and round my hand like a tourniquet. Discussing the merits of a fish finger sandwich was a whole lot easier.

'Would you like a glass of wine?' he asked, taking pity on me.

'God. Yes,' I groaned.

He pulled a cork out of an already open bottle of red wine and poured us both a glass.

I gulped at it and tried again. 'Right, here goes . . .'

So many things had happened over the past few years, so many times I'd done things to make other people happy, that I'd sort of forgotten that what I wanted mattered too. Not that I had any regrets about Noah, or continually bailing Liam out at work. And I certainly had no regrets about moving to Plumberry when Gloria needed help opening the cookery school.

But now it was time to do something purely for myself, to reach for what I wanted. And what I wanted was standing right in front of me: passionate, thoughtful, massively talented and frankly the most gorgeous man on the planet . . .

Tom was watching me pensively but at least he wasn't interrupting so I ploughed on.

'There never was a "me and Gabe". Well, there was one physical occasion, I suppose, when our planets collided. But it happened in a test tube or a petri dish or whatever they use,' I laughed. 'I never was any good at science.'

'Oh, Verity,' said Tom, rubbing his neck.

I blathered on, undaunted by his discomfort. Correction: I *was* daunted; my knees were trembling terribly. My dress was probably quivering like a magnetic field. I reached out and took his hand as I explained that once my donated egg had been fertilized and implanted into Mimi's womb, from that moment on that tiny spark of life was Noah, Gabe and Mimi's son. We shared DNA and a bond that was incredibly precious to me, but my part in his creation was over, never to be revealed according to Mimi's wishes. And I'd done my best; keeping my secret from everyone, even Rosie, even during the depths of my grief when I really needed to talk. But that had meant misleading the very person who had grown to be more and more important to me over the last couple of months. And I couldn't do it any more.

Tom's forehead furrowed and he nodded, taking it all in. 'But that kiss . . .'

'What you saw in the office on Monday was just a silly mistake. Gabe is lonely; he wants a woman in his life again and someone to mother Noah. He'd confused the love we have for each other as friends as something else. It's all sorted now. So,' I worried a piece of skin on my lip and looked down to where my hand was holding his strong one, 'what have you got to say to that?'

'I think he's a great kid and a very lucky one to have you in his life.' Tom's eyes glistened as he set his glass down and brought my hand to his lips, kissing my fingers lightly. 'You are an amazingly gorgeous and generous woman. Selfless and kind-hearted and—'

'Don't say nice.' I shot him a warning glance.

He laughed and touched my cheek, filling my entire body with a warm glow. 'I was going to say that I've been blown away by your spirit since I met you. I should never have doubted you. And I'm touched that you cooked for me. I meant what I said: people are always scared to cook for chefs. I think I can count on one hand the things Rebecca made for me.'

I glanced at the slightly odd-coloured mac and cheese. The melted blue cheese had given the whole thing a greyish tinge. Perhaps Mimi had been right to do a combination of cheeses. The Yorkshire Blue for flavour and then a sprinkling of cheddar on the top for colour . . .

Tom cleared his throat, jolting me back to the moment.

'I made the sauce with Yorkshire Blue,' I began falteringly. 'It reminds me of the day we met. And I made it not only because it's comforting but because my best friend once said that it was also the perfect "I love you" food.'

'Is that right?' He quirked an eyebrow.

'Yep. Guaranteed to put a smile on your loved one's face,' I said boldly. 'So, I thought I'd test out the theory.'

'And I'm to be your guinea pig?' he said, twisting his mouth into a smile.

'Well, as I've been banging on about ever since I met you, to cook for someone is to show how much you . . . care.' I eyed him nervously, chickening out of the 'L' word at the last second.

He was gazing back at me with a curious expression, which was doing incredible things somewhere down in the pit of my stomach.

'And I haven't been very good at making you aware of that recently. In fact, I'd go as far as to say that my actions seem to have made you think that I don't care. But for the record, I do.' I swallowed.

Tom's mouth twitched into a smile. 'So what now?'

'You pass me a spoon.'

He opened a drawer and rummaged around, muttering to himself that it was really about time that he moved out and into somewhere with a decent kitchen and eventually pulled out a spoon. I waited anxiously, licking my lips like the contestants do on *MasterChef* when awaiting the judges' verdict.

He dug into the centre and lifted a spoonful out and a clump of pasta tubes fell off, splashing the floor with blue sauce. My heart sank; the sauce was too runny. The spillage was quickly hoovered up by the dogs who squeaked at the temperature of it.

Comfrey and Sage, seemingly none the worse for burning their tongues, stretched up on their hind legs to reach the dish for more.

'Get down,' I scolded, sneakily pleased they liked it.

'They've got good taste.' Tom grinned. 'Like their owner.'

We shared a sad smile then, remembering the first time we met when he'd assumed I had been their owner and now, of course, unbelievably, I was.

'Well, try it then,' I said, blinking back a tear.

He put the spoon in his mouth and chewed. He narrowed his eyes consideringly and widened them again, nodded and made appreciative noises.

'It's good.'

'Really?' I didn't believe him; I took the spoon from him and took a mouthful.

It was dire. The pasta was undercooked, the sauce tasted of raw flour and the burnt bits were acrid.

'It's the best mac and cheese I've ever had,' he said stoutly.

'Is it?' I said with a dubious smile.

'Yes, because you made it. For me.' He reached across to smooth my hair from my face. 'I've cooked all my life, trying harder and harder to perfect my craft. Experimenting with techniques and flavours and pushing myself to be a better chef. But until I met you I never really understood what food could do for the soul. For the heart.'

He took a step towards me. He didn't need to say any more, his eyes told me everything I needed to know and my heart soared.

'I'm so glad you came tonight,' he murmured.

'I know; you couldn't have possibly gone another moment without tasting my mac and cheese, could you?' I giggled.

His dark eyes were mere inches from mine. 'No. Or you.'

And then he kissed me, softly and then deeply, once, twice and then I stopped counting.

Mimi was right, I thought happily a few minutes later as we came up for air: kisses guaranteed with that recipe.

'Tom?'

'Mmm.' He looked up briefly from kissing my neck.

'Does this mean you're not resigning? Because I'll understand if you'd rather open your own restaurant.'

'You didn't accept my resignation, remember? Besides, opening a restaurant can wait,' he said stroking my cheek. 'I want to enjoy being near you for a while.'

I sighed happily.

'Seriously.' He stared intently at me. 'You don't know how hard it has been for me, letting you go.'

'Hmm,' I tutted playfully. 'Thinking about it, you hardly put up much of a fight for me.'

'I couldn't, not when there was a child involved. Not that I understood exactly how Noah was involved. To be honest, I didn't know what was going on.'

I nodded. 'I know what it must have looked like. But I'd made a promise to Mimi and at that point I still wasn't sure about breaking it. But now I think she'd be happy for all of us to move on in the way that feels right for each of us.'

He traced a line so tenderly and slowly along my face with his fingertip that my stomach fizzed.

'I was pretty confused,' he admitted. 'Especially when I saw the likeness between you and Noah . . .' He shook his head.

'You truly thought I could have a son and not acknowledge him?'

He raked a hand through his hair. 'Look, you're talking to a man who completely missed that his girlfriend was having an affair with his sous chef; my instincts have let me down big time this year. I thought I was doing the right thing, standing back, not staking my manly claim.'

'I quite fancy you staking your manly claim.' I flashed my eyes at him daringly. 'And what are your instincts telling you now?'

'Well,' he cupped my face in his hands and my pulse quickened in anticipation, 'if I'm reading this right, they're telling me to do this.'

And he kissed me softly on the lips.

'I think your instincts are pretty spot on,' I said breathlessly.

His arms circled me and he pulled me close, so close that I could feel the beat of his heart through his shirt, the warmth of his breath on my face.

'That's a relief.'

And as he leaned in for another kiss, something in my heart clicked. Like a recipe when you finally get the flavours just right after discovering the missing ingredient. Or *magic* ingredient, in this case.

'Hey, I nearly forgot,' I gasped, 'I owe you an apology. I saw that article in the newspaper, you didn't steal my ideas at all. You said some lovely things about me, like me being the magic ingredient.'

He nodded sheepishly. 'I wasn't really talking about the cookery school.'

'Oh?' I pulled back to stare at him.

'I was talking about the recipe for making me happy. You're my magic ingredient. When I'm with you my heart explodes like popping candy.'

What a lovely thing to say. My heart flickered in response.

He traced a line with his finger from my chin to my collarbone and then kept going.

'You are adorable, Tom MacDonald,' I said, shivering with pleasure.

'And you are the cutest, sexiest woman in Plumberry.'

'Only Plumberry?' I said in mock horror.

He chuckled. 'OK, England, Britain, Europe—'

'Tom,' I said, pressing a finger to his lips, 'stop talking and kiss me again.'

'That,' he said, lowering his mouth to mine, 'is your best idea yet.'

Epilogue

Extract from *York Mail*, November 2016:

New Restaurant Opens in Plumberry, Food Capital of Yorkshire

Tom MacDonald, who recently sold his share in Manchester's Michelin-starred Salinger's, unveiled his new venture in Plumberry last night to great acclaim from his peers who travelled from all over the UK to show their support to the talented Irish chef.

Tom, pictured with his arm around girlfriend Verity Bloom, credits her with the idea.

'It started with Verity's idea of running a Supper Club at the Plumberry School of Comfort Food,' MacDonald explains. 'The first one took place in June and we have been inundated with bookings ever since. The demand for fine dining in Plumberry has blown us away. When the brewery offered the pub on Plumberry high street for sale it was an opportunity for me to start a new venture. Whilst I'll remain as head tutor at the cookery school, opening Dinner at Tom's is something I've dreamed about all my life.'

Located in the village pub, which closed down two years ago, Dinner at Tom's claims to offer the best in British cuisine made traditionally, always seasonal with precision and flair. And if the hordes of foodie fans who queued up to be amongst the first diners last night are anything to go by, MacDonald looks to have a winning formula on his hands.

'Tom and I are very privileged to live and work in Plumberry. It's a food lover's paradise here,' says Bloom, who co-owns the cookery school with silent partner Gabe Green. 'For us, food should be about flavour and fun, sharing good times with loved ones. Both the cookery school and the new restaurant allow us to indulge in our passion for food and we couldn't be happier.'

MacDonald will be assisted in the restaurant by a hand-picked team of talented staff, including Aaron Collins, who won the Plumberry Signature Dish competition at the cookery school earlier this year, a contest that they aim to run every year to promote new talent.

So have Plumberry's culinary couple got any more plans for next year?

'Verity's always full of ideas,' says MacDonald, pausing to gaze dotingly at his girlfriend. 'But for now we're focusing on moving in together and making Plumberry our permanent home.'

And judging by the packed cookery course schedule and the three-week waiting list for a table at Dinner at Tom's, that is just as well.

The Thank Yous

This book is another team effort; I'm sure my thank-you pages get longer each time!

Thank you to the extremely clever team at Transworld; you're doing a Plumberry job (yes, it's a word) with my books. With special thanks to Christina Ellicott, Sophie Murray, Laura Swainbank, Sarah Harwood, Sarah Whittaker and Alison Tulett.

Thank you to my lovely, lovely editor, Harriet Bourton, who never so much as turned a hair when the manuscript arrived bearing no resemblance to the agreed synopsis. Thank you to Francesca Best who arrived late to the Plumberry party, but nonetheless donned her pinny and got stuck in.

Thank you to the people who helped me get the details right: Lynn Gibbins and Elaine Fearnley for coming up with village names, Rachel Woolley and Dan the Boat Man for knowing EXACTLY how long it takes to get to York. A special thank you to Marie Ward for your expert knowledge of falls and Dr Gina McLachlan for your in-depth knowledge of drugs. Any errors are entirely mine!

A huge thank you to my lovely friend Lucy Nicholson, owner of the wonderful Lucy Cooks cookery school without whom I wouldn't have had the idea for this book at all. Thank you for inspiring me on all sorts of levels. Thanks too to the marvellous Linda Lawler who introduced me to a 'pan of scouse' and who kindly shared her recipe with me for this book.

To my agent and friend, Hannah Ferguson, thank you for all the extra love and support this year. On that note, there are three authors, each with their own busy schedules who have checked in with me regularly this year to make sure all is well. Thank you Rachael Lucas, Sam Tonge and Sue Watson; you ladies are the best.

Thank you to my amazing daughters, Phoebe and Isabel, who contribute to my books in all sorts of ways, from character names, locations and plot ideas and who rearrange my books prominently in shops.

Love and heartfelt thanks as always to my wonderful husband, Mr B, who is my cheerful cheerleader. You're the bee's knees.

Finally, to my best friends, Lisa and Alison, to whom I've dedicated this book. Thank you for always being there for us. xxx

Cathy Bramley's sparkling new story of friendship
and dreams come true is:

White Lies and Wishes

What happens when what you wish for is only half the story . . . ?

Flirtatious, straight-talking **Jo Gold** says she's got no
time for love; she's determined to save her family's failing
footwear business.

New mother **Sarah Hudson** has cut short her maternity
leave to return to work. She says she'll do whatever it takes
to make partner at the accountancy firm.

Bored, over-eating housewife **Carrie Radley** says she just
wants to shift the pounds – she'd love to finally wear a
bikini in public.

The unlikely trio meet by chance one winter's day, and in a
moment of 'Carpe Diem' madness, embark on a mission to
make their wishes come true by September.

Easy. At least it would be, if they hadn't been just the
teensiest bit stingy with the truth . . .

With hidden issues, hidden talents, and hidden demons to
overcome, new friends Jo, Carrie and Sarah must admit
to what they really, really want, if they are ever to get their
happy endings.

Coming in January 2017 in paperback and ebook

Read on for an early extract!

Chapter 1

It was the last Monday in January. 'Blue Monday' according to the newspapers. The most miserable day of the year. The sky was miserable too; charcoal clouds scudded angrily across the horizon and a mean wind rattled at window frames and snapped weak branches from trees.

How apt, thought Jo rubbing her hands together for warmth.

Frédéric Lafleur's funeral had already cast a shadow over the day but now, at three o'clock, the thin light was fading from the afternoon and the little village of Woodby in rural Nottinghamshire was descending into gloom. Jo shuddered, dragged her gaze away from the steamed-up window of the village hall and blinked away tears that had been gathering since before the service.

Coffee. She needed coffee. It would warm her up and give her something to do. She pushed her way through the crowd towards the refreshments and was vaguely aware of a petite young woman with a cloud of pretty red curls attempting to hang a brightly coloured coat on a peg which was too high for her to reach.

The room was muggy and Jo felt hot and restricted in her tight black skirt suit. She undid the button of her jacket and grimaced at the noise around her. The conversation, at first a respectful whisper, had risen to a more sociable hum as the mourners, with pinched faces and frozen fingers thawed over tea and sandwiches.

A searing flash of fury gripped her and she had a sudden urge to scream.

For God's sake, it's not a bloody tea party.

She took a deep breath and reminded herself that this was how people dealt with death in England; a nice cup of tea and a muted chuckle over shared memories. The hall was packed; tons of people had come to see him off, there was bound to be noise. Besides, Fréd had been a noisy bugger; he'd have hated a quiet wake.

She braced herself as Abi stumbled blindly into her arms.

'Hello, you,' said Jo, returning the hug. Abi had lost so much weight this past year; Jo could feel every knot in her spine.

If anyone were to ask her how she was, Jo would probably smile through gritted teeth and reply that she was fine. She wasn't though. Jo was angry. So furious in fact that she wanted to punch something or someone really hard. God, probably.

This was all wrong. Funerals were for old people. Abi and Frédéric were still young, she told herself for the umpteenth time. Or *was*, in Fréd's case. They should be popping out more babies left, right and centre, enjoying life, planning for their future. Fréd should be here, arm draped round his beautiful wife, knocking back the red wine and making jokes about English food.

Jo could feel her breath rattling against her ribcage, her throat burning with the effort of keeping her own emotions in check. Jo kissed Abi's hair and released her, dabbing the tears from her friend's face with a tissue that had seen better days. What do you say to your thirty-four-year-old friend who has just lost her husband to cancer?

'Thanks for doing the reading in French, Jo,' murmured Abi.

'Yeah, cheers for that,' said Jo, twisting her mouth into a

smile. 'As if I wasn't stressed enough, you make me wheel out my rusty old French.'

At least now the service was over she could start to breathe normally again.

'It was brilliant; you still sound fluent.'

Jo shook her head slightly. Abi was amazing, even now she managed to see beyond her own pain. 'Old Maman Lafleur didn't think so, she was giving me daggers.'

Abi winced. 'Sorry about my mother-in-law, she still blames you for introducing us at Uni. If it's any consolation, she looks at me like that all the time.'

'Poor you.' Jo smiled in sympathy. Her eyes roamed the room until she located Frédéric's parents queuing at the buffet table. 'Fréd's dad, Henri, is lovely though. Obviously where Fréd got his looks from.'

Abi's face crumpled.

Shit, wrong thing to say. Jo pulled her friend close again, cursing her own stupidity as Abi sobbed hot tears into her neck. The French relatives were examining a pork pie as if it were a suspicious parcel; curiosity and distrust on their faces. Henri picked up a slice, sniffed it then nibbled the edge. Showing every bit of his Gallic origins, he shrugged and pulled the corners of his mouth down. The others shook their heads and moved along.

Abi pulled away and gave Jo a wan smile. 'Anyway, it meant a lot to me. You read at our wedding and Fréd would have liked the poem.'

Jo nodded. A sudden longing for the day to end, to leave all this sadness behind, sent guilty shivers through her body. She ran a hand through her short, wavy blonde hair distractedly. At times like these it was so much easier being single, no ties, none of this heartache.

Abi looked round the hall. 'I suppose I'd better go and mingle.'

Jo gripped her arms. 'Bollocks to them. You do exactly as you like. People don't expect you to make polite conversation. Get yourself a coffee and let them come to you. And make sure you eat something.'

'What about you?'

Jo wrinkled her nose and pulled a single, slightly bent cigarette out of her bag. 'Not hungry. I'm going out for a fag.'

'Thought you'd given up?'

Jo shook her head, gave Abi a swift kiss and wiped away a smear of red lipstick on her cheek with her thumb. 'Not today.'

Carrie set down the heavy teapot, shook out her arm and wiped the sheen of perspiration from her brow. It was going well so far. If that was the right thing to say.

She bit her lip, flushing in case people could hear her thoughts. What she meant was that everyone had had a hot drink, and no one had asked for something she didn't have. In theory, they could help themselves from now on. She supposed she would have to come out from behind the table at some point, go and offer her condolences to the family. But not yet. She felt safer behind the table.

Goodness, her mouth was watering! She'd only had one sausage roll all afternoon and she was starving. Her eyes scanned the trestle tables. There had been plenty of food in the end; she needn't have worried. Not very French though, unless you counted vol-au-vents. And quiche, maybe. That sounded French. Doing the catering on her own had been hard work, but it had been the least she could do for poor Abi, plus, if she was honest with herself, she had enjoyed being busy, feeling useful for once. Was that really self-centred?

A blonde middle-aged woman in a long navy coat touched Carrie's arm. 'Lovely spread, Carrie. Did you do the altar flowers too?'

Carrie blushed, batted the compliment away with her hand and glanced at her chest. How did those crumbs get there? 'Oh gosh! Thanks, Linda. Tesco's finest!'

'Oh?' Linda pulled the corners of her mouth down in surprise.

Damn! Linda believed her. Carrie could have kicked herself. Why did she always make a joke of things? Of course she had done the flowers. She had been to the wholesalers at five this morning to collect those flowers. Long-stemmed roses, masses of them: white for youth, red for courage and pink for love. Not chrysanthemums. She shuddered. She hated them: the symbol of death.

Linda leaned forward and lowered her voice to a whisper. 'I think you've got jam on your chin.'

'Oh? Thanks.'

How did that get there?

Carrie was still scrubbing at her face with a napkin as Frédéric's mother approached the table and handed Carrie her paper plate.

'Thank you,' said the elegant Frenchwoman, ashen-faced and stooped under the weight of her grief. Carrie's heart sank as she took in the abandoned, barely-touched food. Fréd's mum had hated it. She should have listened to Alex, perhaps she should never have offered to do this at all; her cooking wasn't up to catering standard.

'I'm so sorry. For your loss. And for the food,' she stammered.

Madame Lafleur didn't smile, but inclined her head and swept away off to re-join her husband.

Carrie regarded the remains of the buffet with dismay. It struck her as rather macabre now; chicken drumsticks, sandwiches, cake . . . like some sort of sick joke. It looked like birthday party food, or a wedding anniversary.

Strange how you had a wedding breakfast but a funeral tea. Or was it? If your whole life were to be crammed into one day, you'd want your wedding in the morning, save the funeral for the end of the day.

But some people didn't make it to the end of the day, did

they? And some had their lives taken before they had even begun.

A massive lump threatened to block Carrie's throat. She shook her head to get rid of her maudlin thoughts, selected the largest slice of quiche and took a bite.

Oh my Lord! She had died and woken up in savoury pie heaven.

She took a second bite. The salty bacon, crumbly pastry and creamy custard disappeared in seconds.

She closed her eyes and then snapped them open, automatically checking to see where her husband was. He was easy to spot; Alex was one of the tallest men here. And the most handsome. As she brushed more crumbs from her bosom, he looked over and caught her eye. Damn. Heat rose to her face; she felt guilty enough for eating without him catching her raiding the buffet. She couldn't stick to her diet today. Today she was too het up.

Patches of sweat prickled under her arms and her face felt hot, it would be as red as a beetroot. Her dark hair would be a mess too; the steam from the hot water urn would have turned it to frizz. Fresh air was called for. She grabbed a couple of chicken drumsticks and made for the door.

After eventually managing to hang her coat up on a peg that was ridiculously high, Sarah had stayed in the corner of the village hall waiting for her blushing face to return to a more normal colour. She pressed a hand to her cheek – still warm – and groaned inwardly. That was possibly one of her worst foot-in-mouth fiascos ever: 'I'd kill my husband if he did that,' Sarah had said, trying to make conversation with two women who were moaning about their other halves. Only to find Abi standing right beside her. Everyone had glared at her, Abi had burst into tears and run off and now Sarah felt like a social outcast, like a rabbit with MixyMcwhatsit.

She glanced at her nails for something to do and noticed that she had burst a button on her emerald green blouse.

Great. That would just about top it off if she flashed her boobs at a funeral. She was never going to make any friends in this village at this rate.

Had anyone seen? She whipped her head round to check. No, thank goodness. Shame Dave wasn't here to appreciate a peek at her bra. Not that it was a racy number; feeding bras, she had learned, were built for smooth operations, not to make the wearer feel the least bit alluring.

It was nerves; that was what she put her blabby mouth down to. She was normally quite comfortable in other people's company, but today she felt awkward and isolated and conscious that she really needed to be in two places at once. Sarah sighed.

Story of my life these days.

Supporting Abi and showing respect for Frédéric was the 'good neighbour' thing to do, she told herself firmly, pushing aside the fact that she had inadvertently made Abi cry. But Sarah couldn't help remembering her boss Eleanor's sucked-in cheeks when she had asked for the time off so soon after coming back to work at the accountancy firm after her maternity leave. It was a massive day for the company; Sarah understood that, a big meeting with a new client. She sighed, twirled a lock of red hair round her finger and looked round for any familiar faces.

The funeral was just such bad timing.

NO! No, no! She didn't mean it! That made her sound like a monster! She almost gasped aloud with shame, took a deep breath and rearranged her thoughts. But try as she might she couldn't stop thinking about work.

Finch and Partners' new golden boy, Ben, would probably be given that client to manage now, even though Sarah had done all the preliminary work. And she needed a biggie like that if she was going to make partner. At this rate Ben would be promoted before her even though he had only been there five minutes and wasn't even thirty. But instead of furthering her career, she was standing in a village hall like a lemon, in a shirt which was still far too tight, with no one to talk to.

But she was doing the right thing. Definitely. Very neighbourly.

Food. That would give her something to do. Sarah approached the buffet table and picked up a paper plate. Her hand hovered over the egg and cress sandwiches as an idea occurred to her. She chewed on her lip and mulled it over. What if she jumped into the car now? She could make it back to the office before the new client left, and at least say hello. Stake her claim before Ben got in there first.

But what about Zac? Her stomach flipped. She had promised to get home early to feed him and when was the last time she had done that on a Monday? Time with her six-month old baby was so precious, early finishes so rare. Her heart swelled with love for her darling little boy.

Sod the office. She'd stay here. She plonked the sandwich on her plate. Decision made.

There were about a hundred people here she reckoned. Black, black, black. Why did everyone insist on wearing black at a funeral? Sarah didn't even own anything black. She liked happy colours. Her boss had once said that she would look more at home in the circus than in the boardroom. She'd thought it was a compliment at first until she had noticed two of the junior accountants sniggering.

She might as well try and meet people while she was here, assuming she could avoid any more social gaffs. She and Dave were still new to Woodby and with one thing and another: short winter days and dark nights, Zac arriving early and a new house needing a lot of attention, she hadn't made any friends yet. Except Abi.

Sarah felt the heat rise to her cheeks. How selfish to be worrying about her own trivial work issues with everything that poor Abi was going through!

There was no one manning the tea pot so Sarah helped herself. She would drink this and then go and apologise to Abi for her faux pas earlier. She scanned the room but couldn't see where she was. She'd spotted her a few minutes ago hugging the elegant platinum blonde woman who had done the French reading in church. Sarah recalled the woman's immaculate suit, endless slim legs and flat stomach and ran a hand through her own corkscrew curls and got a finger stuck. It could do with a wash really. God, she was a scruff bag, there never seemed to be enough time to see to her own appearance these days.

Sarah noticed a group of women her own age gathered at the stage end of the hall. One of them had even brought her baby, for heaven's sake! How awful for the poor little mite to be at a funeral in the midst of such misery! He could be scarred for life. A few of the faces were familiar from the mother and baby group and her heart sank. She had only managed to go a couple of times and although they'd been friendly at first, they had all stared at her like she had two heads when she announced that she was going back to work full-time. Still, no harm in trying again. She attempted her best friendly smile and began to cross the hall.

At that moment, the baby started to wail. Oh no! Sarah cringed and pressed an arm to her chest.

It was as if she had pulled the toggle on an emergency life vest. She only had to hear a baby cry, even if it wasn't Zac, and her boobs inflated, ready to leap into action. She felt warmth flood her bra and hardly dared glance down. The sensation was ten times worse than needing a wee. She normally expressed milk at lunchtime if she wasn't with Zac, but with the service starting at one o'clock, somehow she had got out of sync.

Sarah abandoned her plate and hurried towards the ladies' toilets, praying that her painful personal problem wasn't visible.

She barged through the door feeling like she had two live hand grenades stuffed down her bra, but the only cubicle was taken and just as she contemplated expressing over the basin, an elderly lady entered. Sarah dashed from the toilets feeling all panicky. The front of her blouse was definitely wet and the desire to relieve the pressure unbearable. With burning cheeks, Sarah ran from the hall and into the car park. Heavy clouds dulled the sky and the wind took her breath away. She shivered but there was no time to go back for her coat; if she didn't do something about this in about five seconds, she was going to explode.

She dived round the corner of the building, out of sight, to a narrow sheltered pathway bordered with shrubs. She yanked her blouse up, ripping off a button in the process and then in a practised manoeuvre, unhooked the bra cups and squeezed both breasts.

'Ahhh!' Thank God! She let her head fall back, closed her eyes and exhaled deeply. Relief as two jets of warm milk squirted over the pyracantha.

It took Sarah a few seconds to detect the smell of cigarette smoke. A prickle of mortification crept across her scalp and down her back. She opened her eyes and looked over her right shoulder. Two women were staring at her open-mouthed.

Sarah swallowed a groan. This had to be a new personal best of total loss of dignity. They didn't tell you about this in the baby manuals. The look on their faces! She didn't know whether to laugh or cry, but she certainly couldn't stop yet.

'Bloody hell,' said Abi's blonde friend, taking a long pull on her cigarette.

'Should I call an ambulance?' said the other, wiping her mouth with the back of her hand.

'No, I'm fine, nearly there.'

That short burst had eased the pressure. It would do until she got home. Sarah swiftly tucked herself back in and turned to face her audience.

*

Jo stretched out an arm and flicked ash into the shrubbery. She should probably look away but she was transfixed. She had never really given much thought to the practicalities of motherhood. Does everyone have to do that . . . that squuezing thing? A moment's peace to get herself together with a crafty ciggie, that was all she had needed and she had already been joined by the plump woman with a handful of chicken drumsticks who Jo recognized from the refreshments table. And now this – the tiny human milking machine. She wondered where the baby was. Her thoughts flashed briefly to Abi having to bring little Tom up alone. Poor love. For the second time, Jo's commitment-free philosophy looked quite appealing.

The woman tugged the lapels of her green velvet jacket across her chest, folded her arms and stared. She reminded Jo of a curly-haired Kylie Minogue, only with bigger boobs. For someone who had just performed a full frontal flash at strangers at a wake, she seemed terribly calm.

'Any other party tricks?' said Jo with a grin, blowing smoke sharply out of the side of her mouth.

The woman shrugged. 'There's this thing I do with ping pong balls, but not usually at funerals.'

Jo snorted with laughter at the unexpected humour. She dropped her cigarette to the floor, ground it out with the pointy toe of her shoe and picked up the butt. She scouted round for a bin.

'Here.' The chicken muncher stepped forward and held out her napkin. Jo dropped the butt on top of a pile of greasy bones.

'Thanks. I'm Jo, by the way.'

'Carrie. Pleased to meet you.'

'Sarah Hudson. Look I'm really sorry about that; I thought I was on my own.'

'We all did,' said Carrie.

Even in this light Jo could see how embarrassed Carrie was. She wouldn't even meet their eyes.

'Sarah, you're shivering,' added Carrie, 'let's go in and have a hot drink.'

Sarah nodded. 'Good plan.'

'No milk for me,' said Jo.

There were a few funny looks, Jo noticed, as the three women re-entered the hall together. Probably surprised at the sound of their laughter. The other two didn't seem aware of the attention: Sarah was occupied with preventing her cleavage from making another appearance and Carrie was busy foisting tea and cake on anyone who moved. According to Carrie, Jo needed fattening up a bit, and as Sarah was breast-feeding, she had to keep her strength up. Carrie wasn't the greatest advertisement for more cake, thought Jo, shaking her head to decline the offer of a slice of Battenberg.

Was Abi OK? Jo's gaze did a quick once over of the room and spotted her friend deep in conversation with a group of women. She seemed fine, considering. Jo accepted a cup of tea from Carrie and smirked at her blushing face as the rather delicious vicar joined their group.

'Are you friends of the family?' the vicar asked, smiling round at them.

Jo watched with amusement as Carrie took his empty cup and, with a shaky hand, poured a fresh one. Jo had heard about this new vicar from Abi. He held most of the village in thrall. He could only be in his thirties, he drove a Lotus and had brought a whole new congregation into church – predominantly female. He also had the most amazing eyelashes. What was the dating protocol with vicars, she wondered.

'Yeah, we're bosom buddies,' said Jo.

Sarah giggled softly and momentarily released the front of her blouse to cover her mouth. Jo noticed the vicar clap an eyeful of bra before looking Sarah in the eye. 'I've seen you in the village, but we haven't been introduced,' he said.

'Vicar, you naughty boy, she's married,' said Jo huskily.

Carrie's eyes widened. Jo wasn't bothered. A good looking man was a good looking man, reverend or not.

The vicar choked on his tea and Carrie handed him a napkin.

'I'm Sarah Hudson,' replied Sarah, struggling to keep a straight face.

'You've got a baby haven't you, planning on having him or her christened?'

'Um, we haven't really discussed it yet.'

'My favourite thing, christenings – more fun than weddings even. Are you, er, married?' he asked Jo.

'Good God, no!' Jo leaned in towards him with a wink. 'I prefer dirty weekends to dirty socks. Much more fun.'

The vicar opened his mouth to speak and then closed it again. Carrie made a faint high-pitched squeak and tried to refill his cup a second time. 'More tea?'

He shook his head and with darting eyes managed to make eye contact with someone across the room. 'I should, er . . . circulate. By the way, Mrs Radley, nice food.'

He smiled again bravely and moved away. The women watched him and shared a look of appreciation.

'Nice *bum*,' muttered Jo, whistling under her breath.

Sarah cleared her throat. 'Did you do all this, then?' she said, pointing at the buffet table.

Carrie nodded. 'It was the least I could do. Poor Abi.'

'Are you a caterer?' asked Jo, dragging her eyes away from the vicar's rear.

Carrie blushed. 'Goodness, no! I'm just – just a housewife. And it's only a few sandwiches.'

Wow! If Jo had been in charge of the food, it would have been a job lot from Marks and Spencer. This amount of homemade stuff must have taken hours! Jo opened her mouth to object, but Carrie jumped back in.

'What do you both do?' she asked.

'Apart from being wife to Dave and mummy to Zac,

459

I'm an accountant,' said Sarah, 'I work in the city centre, corporate mostly. Don't say it, I know – boring.'

Jo raised a perfectly arched eyebrow. 'After that floor show outside? I don't think so.'

'Not full-time though, surely?' said Carrie.

'Yes.' Sarah thrust her chest out. 'Some of us don't have any choice. Do you have children?'

Carrie's face flushed. 'No, I–'

'And I run a small family business,' said Jo, changing the subject rapidly as Carrie shrank under the force of Sarah's stare. 'Badly, most of the time. And I'm married to it, "til death do us part.' Oops, poor taste.' She clenched her jaw, cross with herself. 'How do you both know Abi and Fréd?' she asked.

'We live in Woodby, I didn't know Fréd that well, but I thought I should come,' said Sarah.

'My husband is the General Manager at Cavendish Hall, where Frédéric worked as head chef,' said Carrie.

'And *you* obviously have some French connection,' said Sarah. 'That reading you did was amazing.'

Jo shrugged and swallowed her tea. 'I did French as part of my degree. I spent a year out there, got to know Fréd. Abi came out to stay with me for a holiday and met him. *Un coup de foudre* as they say.'

Carrie shook her head slowly, her eyes looking moist. 'Such a lovely couple. So unfair. To have your life cut short like that. And that beautiful little boy.'

Jo's heart grew heavy again and she felt guilty for enjoying the last half hour. 'I don't know how Abi's going to cope once the funeral's over. I think she's been focussing on that to get her through so far. I'll come over when I can, but I'm based in Northampton.'

'I know it's a cliché,' said Sarah, with a sigh, 'but you've got to make each day count. Cherish every moment.'

'Carpe diem,' said Carrie, quietly.

Jo looked round at the hall; some of the mourners had

gone now. Someone had brought Abi's son Tom along and he was sitting on his granddad's knee bouncing up and down giggling. With his dark wavy hair, he was the image of his father. Jo wondered what was going through Henri's mind. Probably looking at Tom and remembering Frédéric as a boy. It must be heart-breaking to lose a child, at any age, even if he was a grown man. Another good reason not to have kids. If she told herself this often enough, she might even start to believe it. She shuddered and tuned back into the conversation.

'A bucket list. You know, like in that film with Jack Nicholson and Morgan Freeman? *The Bucket List*.' Carrie was saying to Sarah.

'I've seen that one,' said Jo. 'They're both terminally ill and decide to do a load of mad things before they die.'

'Exactly. Perhaps everyone should have a bucket list? So when you die, you'll at least have done *some* of the things you always wanted to do,' said Carrie glumly.

Jo tried to read Carrie's expression; there was something behind that shy smile, as if she had a whole list of regrets. Mind you, that probably applied to everyone.

She picked a piece of fluff off her black wool jacket. 'Fréd's dream was to open his own restaurant. He was waiting for the right moment. And now . . .' She swallowed a lump in her throat.

'We could . . . Why don't we . . . ? Oh, nothing,' said Carrie, stirring her tea again for no apparent reason.

'Go on,' said Jo.

Carrie swallowed and gave her a shaky smile. 'I thought we could perhaps start doing the things we want to. Make a list together. We can all add stuff to the list and tick them off when we've done them!'

Sarah rolled her eyes. 'I've got a new baby, I can't start sky diving or jetting off to Timbuktu,' she tutted.

'It's probably a stupid idea.' Carrie blushed and Jo felt sorry for her.

'I might think this is crazy by tomorrow,' said Jo. 'But I am a workaholic. I've got to take something from losing Fréd so young. This could be the push I need to live a little.' She thought about it for a second. What the heck. She winked at Carrie. 'I'm in.'

Carrie beamed but Sarah frowned. 'Don't you think it's a bit morbid? Thinking about your own death?'

'What about a wish list then?' Carrie suggested. 'If a genie granted you three wishes, what would you wish for? I don't mean an endless pot of gold, or anything like that. Real things, attainable goals.'

'Oh God, that's easy,' laughed Sarah, 'eight hours' continuous sleep, the ironing pile to have magically disappeared . . .' She tugged at her skirt. 'And my clothes to fit me again.'

'Perhaps instead of a genie,' said Jo, wondering what she was getting herself into, 'we have to make our wishes come true by ourselves.'

'With help from each other,' added Carrie.

Sarah chuckled and shook her head, making her curls bounce. 'I think you're both barmy, but go on then.' She caught sight of the village hall clock and gasped. 'Blimey, it's Zac's tea time. I need to get home.'

'Oh,' said Carrie, her face falling, 'we haven't chosen our wishes yet.'

'I need to get back too,' said Jo, checking her watch. 'Let's exchange email addresses and we can arrange to meet up again soon.'

Carrie blushed. 'I haven't got email.'

Sarah and Jo stared at her.

'How do you shop?'

'Or communicate with anyone?'

'Or do anything?'

Carrie shrugged and gave a small smile. 'Something for my wish list, I guess.'

Jo opened her slim black clutch bag. Nestled between her keys, iPhone and lipstick was a silver business card holder.

'Here's my card with my email and mobile number on it. Let's organize a date over the phone.'

Sarah tipped out the contents of her Mary Poppins style handbag to reveal baby wipes, nappy sacks, two large cotton wool circles and a packet of baby breadsticks. She finally handed over a couple of rather dog-eared cards. 'Sorry, I'm normally really organized.'

Jo took in the gaping blouse, crusty white stain on her jacket and the patch of matted hair at the back of Sarah's head and said nothing.

'I don't have a card or even a pen,' said Carrie, 'so I'll phone you both. And thank you.' She lowered her voice, 'I hate social occasions like this, and meeting you two has made it infinitely more bearable.'

An awkward moment followed as Sarah tried to shake hands and Carrie leant forward to hug her.

'Sorry,' stammered Carrie, pumping Sarah's hand.

Jo strode over to say her goodbyes to Abi wondering just what she had let herself in for.

Or the delightful

Wickham Hall

Holly Swift has just landed the job of her dreams: events co-ordinator at Wickham Hall, the beautiful manor home that sits proudly at the heart of the village where she grew up. Not only does she get to organize for a living and work in stunning surroundings, but it will also put a bit of distance between Holly and her problems at home.

As Holly falls in love with the busy world of Wickham Hall – from family weddings to summer festivals, firework displays and Christmas grottos – she also finds a place in her heart for her friendly (if unusual) colleagues.

But life isn't as easily organized as an event at Wickham Hall (and even those have their complications . . .). Can Holly learn to let go and live in the moment?

After all, that's when the magic happens . . .

Available now

Or the irresistibly charming

Freya Moorcroft has wild red hair, mischievous green eyes, a warm smile and a heart of gold. She's been happy working at the café round the corner from Ivy Lane allotments and her romance with her new boyfriend is going well, she thinks, but a part of her still misses the beautiful rolling hills of her Cumbrian childhood home: Appleby Farm.

Then a phone call out of the blue and a desperate plea for help change everything . . .

The farm is in financial trouble, and it's taking its toll on the aunt and uncle who raised Freya. Heading home to lend a hand, Freya quickly learns that things are worse than she first thought. As she summons up all her creativity and determination to turn things around, Freya is surprised as her own dreams for the future begin to take shape.

Love makes the world go round, according to Freya. Not money. But will saving Appleby Farm and following her heart come at a price?

Available now

Irresistible recipes inspired by
The Plumberry School of Comfort Food

Salmon en croute

My friend Alison is one of those people, who despite having an extremely busy job can manage to whip up a buffet for twenty without turning a hair. This salmon en croute recipe is one of her stalwarts . . .

You will need . . .

One packet of ready-made puff pastry (defrosted and ready to roll)

One piece of salmon fillet, boneless and skinless about 600–700g

A packet of watercress

A small tub of crème fraiche

Beaten egg (optional)

Pre-heat the oven to 180°C (fan 160°C), gas mark 4 and lightly grease a baking sheet.

Roll out the pastry on a floured surface into a rectangle twice the length of the salmon. Lay the salmon towards one end of the pastry, leaving a margin of an inch and cover with the crème fraiche and finally the watercress. Brush the pastry edges with water and fold the pastry over the salmon, pressing the edges together firmly. Brush with beaten egg if desired. Cook for 40 minutes until golden brown.

Linda's Pan of Scouse

My friend, Linda told me years ago that when she was growing up, there was always a pan of scouse on the go. If anyone was ill, or needed a bit of a helping hand, Linda's mum would always pop round with a pan of scouse. So when Mags appeared in this story, I just knew that it was a recipe that she would love, so it became her signature dish. Linda has very kindly let me reproduce her mum's scouse recipe to share with you.

You will need . . .

> 500g good quality stewing steak, chopped
>
> 2 tbsp flour
>
> 4 medium sized potatoes (I use king Edwards as they mush down better)
>
> 1 large onion
>
> 2/3 carrots
>
> 3 sticks of celery
>
> Some chopped swede or turnip
>
> 2 pints of beef stock
>
> Salt and pepper
>
> A few mixed herbs
>
> Oil for frying
>
> To serve: pickled red cabbage, pickled beetroot and crusty bread

Toss the chopped meat in flour and seal in a large saucepan. Add all the chopped and sliced vegetables, (potatoes in cubes of approximately 2cm). Add the stock, salt, pepper and herbs. Bring to the boil. Give it a good stir then simmer gently for about ninety minutes until all is cooked and the potatoes are falling apart. Taste to check seasoning, if you like it with a beefier flavour then add an Oxo, works every time! Some people like it served with red cabbage or beetroot, I like it just with crusty bread.

Lucy's Saucy Lemon Pudding

Now this is probably the most important recipe in the book because my friend, Lucy owns a cookery school *and* she is the inspiration behind the story! She also runs a restaurant in Ambleside, Lucy's On A Plate, which does the most amazing puddings. So of course I had to ask her for a summery dessert! Lucy says: 'Saucy Lemon Pudding is almost like a "soufflé" but baked to create a denser, squidgy dessert where the "pond" of citrus sauce lurks beneath. Use a mix of lemon and lime if you prefer.

You will need . . .

60g unsalted butter, softened

250g caster sugar

4 eggs, separated

2tsp finely grated lemon zest

50g self-raising flour

350ml milk

80ml lemon juice

Icing sugar, to serve

Heat the oven to 180°C (fan 160°C) gas mark 4. Grease a deep 1½-litre soufflé dish. With an electric mixer, beat the butter, half of the sugar, the egg yolks and the lemon zest until the mixture is light and fluffy. Alternately fold in the flour and mix through the milk to make a smooth batter. Stir in the lemon juice. The batter may look like it has separated at this stage, but this is as it should be. In a separate, clean bowl, whisk the egg whites until frothy, then continue to whisk while adding the remaining sugar, a little at a time, until it's all incorporated and is firm and glossy. Gently fold the egg-white mixture into the batter. Pour the batter into the prepared dish. Place the dish in a large baking tin and fill the tin with enough lukewarm water to come a third of the way up the side of the dish. Gently transfer it to the oven and bake for 50-55 minutes, or until the top is golden and risen. Dust with icing sugar and serve with cream.

Mozzarella In Carozza

My editor, Francesca is half-Italian and so to pay homage to Verity's house-mate, Rosie, I asked her for her favourite Italian savoury treat and this is what she came up with:

I like the fact that the literal translation is 'mozzarella in a carriage'. It's basically a fried cheese toastie, so not the healthiest of snacks, but with its lightly crunchy exterior and gooey, creamy contents that stretch into strings as you tear into it, these are oh-so deliciously moreish . . . The perfect comfort food!

Mozzarella in carrozza makes me think of my mum (who is Italian), who'd cook these little goodies on a camping stove in our back garden (in London) as a summery treat for a picnic lunch outdoors. You can of course make them in your kitchen! I like them with the saltiness of an anchovy fillet tucked in the middle, but you can leave those out if you and anchovies don't get along.

To make 3 sandwiches,

You will need . . .

6 slices of white bread, crusts cut off

A ball of mozzarella, cut into thickish slices

Anchovy fillets (optional)

125ml milk

3 heaped tbsp plain flour

1 egg, beaten

Salt and pepper

Oil for shallow frying – eg. Sunflower or vegetable oil. It should fill your saucepan an inch deep.

Pour the milk into one shallow bowl, the flour into another, and the beaten egg with the salt and pepper into a third. Now make your sandwiches – put pieces of mozzarella on a slice of white bread, leaving about a centimetre of bread about the edges uncovered. Add an anchovy fillet if you're using them, and then place the second slice of bread on top, squashing the edges of the bread together so you've made a little sealed parcel.

Heat your oil in a saucepan and when it's nice and hot, you're ready to start frying. Obviously be careful, don't leave the oil heating unattended.

Dip a sandwich quickly (you don't want it to get too soggy and start to come unstuck at the edges) into the milk, then into the flour, and then finally a quick dip into the egg mixture. Now fry it until crispy and lightly golden on the outside – turn it over in the oil to make sure it cooks evenly.

Remove the sandwich to a plate covered in kitchen towel to absorb any excess oil. Repeat until you've cooked them all. Eat as quickly as you can without burning your tongue or fingers. They're best when still piping hot and gooey on the inside . . . Enjoy!

Easy Chicken and Chorizo Paella

I'm a big fan of one-pot dinners, especially when I have
people coming over, because I tend to get carried away
chatting over a glass of wine and forget my timings! So
something like this lovely paella is perfect. I can prepare it
in advance and pop it in the oven as soon as they arrive and
simply relax! This recipe serves six.

You will need . . .

2 tbsp sunflower oil

300g cooking chorizo cut into chunks

12 chicken thighs (bone in, skin on)

3 shallots, sliced finely

4 fat cloves of garlic, crushed

1 green and 2 red peppers, sliced finely

1.75 litres of chicken stock

450g paella rice (or any risotto rice will do)

2 tsp smoked paprika

Fry the chicken pieces and chorizo chunks in the oil until
the chicken skin is brown and all the lovely orangey oils
are released from the chorizo. Remove the meat and set
aside. Add the onion, peppers and garlic and fry gently
until soft and then sprinkle the paprika over and mix in.
Pour in the stock, put the chicken back in and simmer
for 25 minutes. Heat the oven to 180°C (fan 160°C) gas
mark 4. Add the rice and chorizo, stir well and put a lid on
the pan before transferring it to the oven. (My paella pan
doesn't have a lid, so I make a tight-fitting foil one instead.)
Cook in the oven for around 30 minutes and then test to
see if the rice is soft and the chicken is cooked all the way
through. Check seasoning, adding a little salt and a good
twist of black pepper before serving with green salad,
crusty bread and a nice glass of red wine!

Gin and Tonic Cake

I asked followers of my Facebook page to suggest recipes to be included in this book and Louise Bourne suggested this delicious cake. Several other followers expressed quite an interest in the recipe, so here it is!

You will need . . .

For the cake:

3 eggs

170g softened butter

170g caster sugar

170g sieved self-raising flour

Juice and zest of an unwaxed lemon

50ml gin

For the drizzle:

80ml gin

110g granulated sugar

A splash of tonic water

Juice and zest of an unwaxed lemon

Pre-heat the oven to 180°C (fan 160°C) gas mark 4. Grease a 1kg loaf tin and line with baking parchment. Cream the butter and sugar together until pale and fluffy. Beat in the eggs one at a time, adding a spoonful of flour if the mixture starts to curdle. Fold in the flour. Once mixed, add the lemon zest, juice and gin. Pour the batter into the tin and bake for 30–40 minutes or until a skewer comes out clean. Leave in the tin for five minutes and then transfer to a cooling rack.

Place a baking tray under the cooling rack.

Mix the ingredients for the drizzle together. Prick the cake with a skewer while it is still warm. Any drizzle that collects in the baking tray, collect and spoon over the cake again.

Dig in as soon as it is cool enough to slice!

Kale and Stilton Gnocchi

I asked Transworld's super-healthy Digital Publishing Manager, Helen Jenner, if she had any delicious recipes using kale. Something that she thought my daughters might like. She suggested this and it has been a big hit. It's also extremely quick and easy!

You will need . . .

  200g kale washed (tough stalks removed)

  500g pack of gnocchi

  100g stilton

  100ml crème fraiche

  Parmesan, or any other hard cheese you have in your fridge, just enough to sprinkle over the finished dish

Put the kale into a colander and pour boiling water over it. Once the leaves have wilted a little, shake off the excess water and leave to one side. Drop the gnocchi into a pan of boiling water for 2-3 minutes. When the gnocchi is cooked, it will cleverly pop up to the surface of the water to let you know. Drain it and put it into an ovenproof dish, add the stilton, crumbled into small pieces and the kale, covering it all with the crème fraiche. Season and sprinkle over the grated parmesan.

Grill until the cheese is bubbling and the top is golden.

Rhubarbs' Fruit and Ale Cake

I am very lucky to have Rhubarbs Café and Tea Room, in the lovely village of Burton Joyce so close to where I live. I'm even luckier that the boss, Lauren has let me have the recipe for her delicious fruit and ale cake, which she got from her granddad!

You will need . . .

170 ml ale, something like Old Peculier would work well

1kg mixed dried fruit and peel

125g glacé cherries

50g cranberries

255g softened butter

255g caster sugar

3 beaten eggs

255g plain flour

125g chopped walnuts

Some walnut halves to decorate top (optional)

Soak dried fruit and peel in the ale overnight if possible or for at least several hours. Cream the butter with the sugar until light and pale. Mix a spoonful of the flour into creamed mixture to prevent curdling, and gradually beat the eggs into the mixture. Stir in rest of the flour and finally add chopped walnuts and fruit and ale. Stir well together before putting into a greased and lined 8inch (20cm) square cake tin. Smooth over the top and place the walnut halves in a pattern over the surface if using. Bake in a pre-heated oven at gas mark 3, 170°C (150°C fan oven), for 3 hours, or until a skewer inserted in the centre comes out clean. Delicious with a cup of tea!

Cheese Cod Casserole

This recipe was one of the first things I used to cook for the family in my Mum's little brown casserole dish when I was a teenager. I mention it in the book served with new potatoes and sugar snap peas; it also goes very well with baked potatoes. I haven't given a method for cheese sauce because either you can already make it or you use a packet mix! This recipe serves four.

You will need . . .

  1 onion thinly sliced

  Butter for frying

  1 pint of cheese sauce

  600g white fish

  A handful of extra cheese to sprinkle on the top.

Pre heat the oven to 180°C (160°C fan oven) gas mark 4. Fry the onion until soft in the butter, but don't let it go brown. Cut the fish into large chunks and add to the casserole dish with the onion. Pour the cheese sauce over. Sprinkle the top with cheese and bake in the oven for 20 minutes.

Fish Finger Sandwich

I couldn't not include Verity's favourite comfort food, could I? I *know* you know how to make a fish finger sandwich; that isn't why I've included the recipe. I've included it to remind you how deliciously satisfying it is, particularly if there is just you to cater for, to sit down with a melt-in-the-mouth fish finger sandwich and love every joyful mouthful.

You will need...

Two slices of bread

Some frozen fish fingers (no one's counting)

Ketchup

OR...

You could go really sophisticated and add some tartare sauce and a few round lettuce leaves

Grill the fish fingers evenly on both sides until they are golden, taking care not to let them burn. Distribute them fairly on your bread, smother in ketchup (or posh tartare sauce) and slice in two. Enjoy!

Macaroni Cheese

It seems to be called Mac and Cheese now, but I always feel a bit silly when I call it that, as if I'm trying to sound American. So I've gone old-school with this recipe. Whatever you call it, it is definitely comfort food! This dish serves four and goes well with a nice green salad.

You will need...

A quantity of cheese sauce* using 500ml milk and 250g mature Cheddar

I tsp English mustard

350g pasta

50g bread, whizzed into breadcrumbs

50g Parmesan cheese

*I use an easy method to make cheese sauce, simply adding cornflour to milk and bringing it to the boil. Some people like to make a roux, others use a packet mix. Do whichever you prefer.

Preheat the oven to 200°C (fan 180°C) gas 6. Cook the pasta in a large pan of boiling water with a pinch of salt for two minutes less than the packet suggests. Make the cheese sauce and stir in the mustard. Drain the pasta and tip it into a large ovenproof dish with the sauce. Mix and top with the breadcrumbs and Parmesan cheese. Place in the oven for twenty minutes until the top is deliciously golden and crisp.

Easy Smoked Salmon Pâté

This is fresh and tasty and (most importantly) looks like you've gone to a lot of trouble! I serve it as a starter or with crusty bread and salad for a summery lunch with friends.

You will need . . .
   250g smoked salmon
   115g cream cheese
   Juice of half a lime
   1 heaped tbsp chopped coriander (plus extra for garnish)
   Pinch of sugar
   Black pepper to taste

Place all the ingredients in a food blender except the sugar and pepper. Blitz until it reaches your preferred consistency. I like mine really smooth. Taste. Add sugar if required and pepper to taste. Transfer to a bowl, cover in clingfilm and chill until needed. Garnish with remaining coriander just before serving.

Cathy Bramley is the author of the best-selling romantic comedies *Ivy Lane*, *Appleby Farm* and *Wickham Hall* (all four-part serialized novels), and *Conditional Love*. She lives in a Nottinghamshire village with her husband, two daughters and a dog.

Her recent career as a full-time writer of light-hearted, romantic fiction has come as somewhat of a lovely surprise after spending the last eighteen years running her own marketing agency. However, she has always been an avid reader, hiding her book under the duvet and reading by torchlight. Luckily her husband has now bought her a Kindle with a light, so that's the end of that palaver.

Cathy loves to hear from her readers. You can get in touch via her website: www.CathyBramleyAuthor.com,

Facebook page: Facebook.com/CathyBramleyAuthor or on

Twitter: twitter.com/CathyBramley

Do you love talking about your favourite books?

From big tearjerkers to unforgettable love stories, to family dramas and feel-good chick lit, to something clever and thought-provoking, discover the very best **new fiction** around – and find your **next favourite read**.

See **new covers** before anyone else, and read **exclusive extracts** from the books everybody's talking about.

With plenty of **chat, gossip and news** about **the authors and stories you love**, you'll never be stuck for what to read next.

And with our **weekly giveaways**, you can **win** the latest laugh-out-loud romantic comedy or heart-breaking book club read before they hit the shops.

Curl up with another good book today.

Join the conversation at
www.facebook.com/ThePageTurners
And sign up to our free newsletter on
www.transworldbooks.co.uk